Hold for Hiker Trash

Hold for Hiker Trash

K.A. Hrycik

Creators Publishing
Hermosa Beach, CA

Hold for Hiker Trash
Copyright © 2017 K.A. Hrycik

Cover art by Peter Kaminski

CREATORS PUBLISHING
737 3rd St
Hermosa Beach, CA 90254
310-337-7003

This is a work of fiction. Names, characters, businesses, places, events and incidents are either the products of the author's imagination or used in a fictitious manner. Any resemblance to actual persons, living or dead, or actual events is purely coincidental.

Library of Congress Control Number: 2016961773
ISBN (print): 9781945630415
ISBN (ebook): 9781945630132

First Edition
Printed in the United States of America
1 3 5 7 9 10 8 6 4 2

Contents

CHAPTER 1

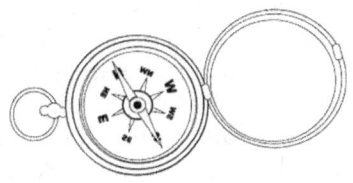

VIKA SAT BY THE SIDE OF THE ROAD and watched the car burn. She had never seen a car fire before, and she didn't much appreciate that it was *her* car on fire.

A bead of sweat slid behind her ear and down her neck.

She sighed.

Then there was a loud pop as the gas tank exploded, and she jumped. The car rocked on its frame, disappeared into a ball of flames for a moment, and Vika choked on the gas-fueled wave of heat that rolled off.

She sighed again and continued to watch pieces of her precious blue Volkswagen flake off and float skyward, partly because she was mesmerized by the dancing flames and partly because she didn't know what else to do. Not a single car had driven by, and it was *hot*. She always thought that Washington was cold and wet, but that was not the case. It had to be pushing 90 degrees without a cloud in the sky. She leaned against her suitcase and took a tiny sip from her water bottle. There was maybe one swallow left, but she didn't dare drink it. She didn't really know what she was saving it for, but the sound of water sloshing around gave her an element—even if minor and slightly delusional—of comfort.

She wracked her brain, trying to think of the last house she had seen, but it was miles back. She could sit there and wait for someone to drive by, though that could take hours. Vika looked back at the fire.

"Well, there goes *that* plan," she mumbled to herself, as she thought of the image she'd taped to her dashboard of deep, blue waters at the base of snow-dusted mountains. "Can't find the North Cascades through a melted windshield."

She would have to walk. She reached down and brushed some dirt off her shoe then pushed herself up to her feet. First she looked left, and then she looked right, but unfortunately, they looked the same. Six of one or half dozen of the other. Vika took a deep breath and slid the handle out on her suitcase and set off down the road—her luggage bouncing on its wheels behind her. She let herself have one last aching glance towards the car, which sizzled and crackled behind her.

The road stretched out in a long gray band, the heat and stillness of the air oppressive on her North Dakotan skin. It didn't help that even among the pasty people of the upper Midwest she was considered pale. She pulled up her long auburn hair into a bun. She could feel strands stuck to her neck from sweat, and that horrible sensation of her epidermal cells frying one by one with nothing she could do about it. She didn't tan. Not even a little. She turned different shades of red, but never tan.

A wheel of the simple black suitcase rolled up and over a large rock and it tipped over on its side. She grunted and yanked the handle to bring it back upright.

The road was going nowhere, or so it seemed. The backs of her shoes rubbed against her heels and Vika hoped they wouldn't blister.

SHE KICKED A ROCK. It had been an hour and the road looked pretty much the same. No houses, no cars, no civilization. It was just her: Vika Carmichael, who had too recently become carless, jobless, and lost on the side of a road in Washington with sweat stains under her boobs.

Thousands—if not millions—of insects kept a chorus around her, though she preferred not to think too much about that. She tried not to think about the bigger animals in the woods waiting for the perfect moment to pounce either. And she tried not to think about every horror story or ghost story she had ever read. She tried not to think about the impending darkness—not soon, but eventually, and *then* what would she do? She tried not to think about--

A rumble sounded behind her and interrupted her daydream. At first she looked towards the sky for a plane, and then for a thundercloud, but soon a dark shape drove over the bluff half a mile behind her. Vika squinted, but the heat radiating off the ground blurred its form and she couldn't quite see what it was. It was big, though, probably a tractor-trailer.

She felt her heart pump faster as her mind raced through different scenarios, most of which left her dead or almost dead in a ditch somewhere. It drove closer and closer and she knew even if she decided to run, no doubt they'd spotted her already.

As it approached, Vika realized it wasn't a tractor-trailer after all. It was a bus. A dark-green school bus. The front was flat, and her eyes followed a line up from the bumper, over the grill, and through the window to the driver. Massive sunglasses swallowed much of the driver's face—at least the part that reached over the steering wheel—and white curls sat atop her head. Arthritic hands clutched the wheel at eleven and one. The engine slowed and snorted, hiccupped and coughed as the bus went by Vika and bumbled off the road. It came to rest on the shoulder in a swirl of dust and exhaust, the rear emergency door covered with dirt and grime, preventing her from seeing inside. Curiously, it also came with a smell of fried chicken. And maybe French fries.

Vika, heart racing, cautiously walked up along the bus and read 'ORANGEVILLE MARCHING BAND' written on the side in white. As Vika walked, she could see enough into the vehicle to know there weren't seats and she doubted there were any components of a marching band.

Vika's knees shook and she wanted to run again, but then she thought about her lack of food, water, and energy, and she wanted to climb onto the bus, no questions asked. Her feet compromised by remaining planted right where they were.

With a *whoosh* the doors flung open and the face of a woman about the age of Vika's grandmother appeared.

"Hi, deary!" she called, as Vika stood in the cloud of exhaust. "Was that your car back there? Do you need a ride?"

The old woman looked harmless enough, but God knows what she had in that bus. An array of guns, an anklet of human bones, the possibilities were endless. The lady gingerly stepped down from the bus and made her way to where Vika was standing. The sunglasses covered her face, below perfectly permed white hair and above apple-red lips. She was dressed in a floral shirt and coral-colored capris with little white shoes on her feet. A string of pearls circled her neck. The woman was a few inches shorter than Vika, and Vika herself stood just over five feet tall.

"Come on, honey, you look like you could use a ride," she said and gently patted Vika on the shoulder.

"Yeah, that was my car back there," she answered, stalling and nervously shifting from foot to foot.

"Well, come on," the lady said, already walking back to the bus, "I know a tow truck driver in town."

Vika looked around and saw no other options. She followed the old lady towards the bus and waited as the woman climbed the stairs.

"Call me Grandma Peach." The old woman settled into the driver's seat, the springs bouncing her gently as she shifted to find her seatbelt. "You can sit on the couch."

"I'm Vika," she offered hesitantly as she climbed the stairs and took in her surroundings. She felt the cool breeze of the air conditioner on her face.

The bus had been turned into a house on wheels. Other than the couch on the left side, there was a wood stove behind the driver's seat and a kitchenette on the dividing wall between the "living room" and the back of the bus, which she assumed was the "bedroom." Overflowing bookshelves lined the walls under the windows, most strapped in with a complex system of bungee cords, an occasional spider plant falling over the top. A braided rug lay on the floor in front of the couch, and colorful mugs hung from hooks over the sink.

"This is great," Vika said, still half-looking for a body pushed behind the bookshelves as she slowly made her way to the couch to sit on the worn blue cushion.

"Thank you, dear," Grandma Peach responded, fastening her seatbelt. "My son takes it to lectures. Now hang tight. We have to get going." She stomped down on the clutch and threw the bus into first. It lurched forward and gained speed, lurching again as she shifted into second.

Vika held on to the arm of the couch as they careened around the curves, watching the foliage pass by out the window.

"Vika," Grandma Peach yelled over the sounds of the bus, "that's an unusual name."

Yes, it was. It was the only evidence that her parents had a hint of creativity in their bodies. She didn't mind, though, she liked the fact that it was so unique. Well, unique in the states anyway. Probably not so much in Eastern Europe, but she had never been there to confirm.

"My parents were on vacation in St. Petersburg while my mom was pregnant with me and my brother," Vika called back. "My full name is Victoria, but they always intended to shorten it to the Russian nickname of Vika."

"Oh, how fun! Do your parents travel a lot?"

"Not really," Vika answered. Not at all, actually. They went to Hilton Head the third week in July every year until Vika and her brother started college four years before, and then they changed their vacation time to the third week in September. The weather was much better for golfing, her father explained, and since she and her brother were in school and expected to do internships or co-ops during the summer, their schedules were no longer taken into account.

"They won the trip through my dad's work." She looked out the window as they wound around the road, seeing trees, ferns, wildflowers, guardrails, the occasional car, but no houses.

"This area is beautiful. Have you lived here long?" she asked Grandma Peach, after taking a beat to enjoy the scenery.

"No, no," she answered. "I live in Maine for most of the year. I used to be a teacher. I was so used to having summers off and traveling, it stuck once I retired."

"Oh, that must be nice," Vika said. "And your son is here?"

"Yes, well, he lived in Spokane until last September. He bought a house in Stacklen." Vika didn't recognize the name, but then again, she wouldn't be able to name many of the towns around the area.

"It's a beautiful house," Grandma Peach continued, "an old Victorian. It needs a little work, but really, it's breathtaking. Oh, how he loves the mountains. He has a daughter, about your age, dear, in Seattle, so he's closer to her being farther west." Vika nodded, intrigued about the house. She had a soft spot for things of old, hence her newly acquired art history degree from Brown. She relaxed into the cushion of the couch, the first time she felt her muscles ease since her car made the journey to its afterlife.

"So what, dear, are you doing in Stacklen?" Grandma Peach looked at her in the massive mirror.

"I, um," Vika started, "I'm on...vacation."

"Vacation, hmm? That's nice. Where are you staying?"

"I, uh, nowhere." Vika sat, with her mouth half-open, as she wrangled her thoughts as coherently as possible. "I'm on my way to Lake Chelan," she continued, "I was just driving through."

Shortly after she arrived home from her failed interview in Boston with a Renaissance scholar—a trip she aptly named the Trail of Deception—to Jessup, North Dakota, she went on her computer and typed in, "heaven on earth," because, well, that seemed like a nice place to visit and figure out her life. After sorting through some religious paraphernalia, a picture of mountains and a gorgeous blue lake popped up.

"Ah, Lake Chelan," Grandma Peach replied knowingly, "you like the wild."

Vika nodded enthusiastically, fearful words would give away her lie. Well, not so much a lie as...OK, a lie. She never had liked wilderness of any kind. It looked nice on postcards and screensavers, but truth be told, everything about it intimidated her. She liked roads and screened-in porches, coffee shops, and online shopping. The list could go on and on, but when the picture of the lake filled her screen, she thought instantly: That is where I want to be.

She sat staring at the pictures on her computer and instead of imagining bears and cougars tearing a visitor to pieces, as she normally did, she saw mountains where she might find clarity, a purpose, a place that would give direction in her life. Plus she hadn't fared so well on the East Coast; she might as well try the West. Vika never realized she had a case of wanderlust. Wanderlust, temporary insanity—she was having a hard time distinguishing the difference between the two.

It was a trait that did not run in the family—that was for sure. When Vika announced she would be going on a road trip west, her mother yelled at Vika out the door, down the driveway, and halfway around the block. If she didn't have lasagna in the oven, Vika had no doubt she would have followed her to the first red light and proceeded to yank the car battery out with her bare hands.

"How long are you staying there?" Grandma Peach asked.

"Oh, a week," Vika answered. "Maybe two."

"You don't know?" Grandma Peach asked gently.

"Well, I'm really just winging it," Vika shrugged. "Or *was* anyway. Until, you know, that mishap with my car."

"Lovely," Grandma Peach said and Vika blinked. She had thought of a couple words to describe her situation, but "lovely" wasn't one of them. "You'll fit right in."

CHAPTER 2

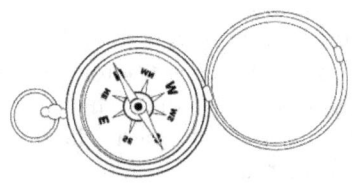

AT LAST, GRANDMA PEACH grabbed the wheel and swung the bus into a short, dirt driveway. Images of Thomas Kincaid paintings faded away and were replaced by thoughts of haunted houses. The old Victorian stood two-stories high, long and narrow, with an extra floor in the tower. The roof and walls were jagged, sharp, eerie, and, even against the blue sky, the tall windows dirty and foreboding. Much of the light blue paint had weathered off and the dark blue trim was fading dramatically.

The only element of the entire house that looked as though it was both in good shape and was new was the porch. The wall on the house that the porch backed against was completely stripped of paint, as were the boards on the floor and support beams. Unpainted and, Vika imagined, freshly sanded. There was a bench on one side and a porch swing on the other, a small table in between. It was an odd sight, to have a decrepit house with a newly constructed porch. A hole gaped off the porch in the shape of a door, but there was no door to be seen.

The door wasn't the only thing missing, though. Shutters hung off the house—the ones that were left—and one had fallen and leaned against the house; an old pile of leaves blown up against it. They drove slowly by, and Vika caught glimpses of hallways and corners of rooms through the dirt-smudged glass.

As they reached the end of the driveway, a large barn stole the landscape. Though the paint had chipped and faded with time like the house, the barn appeared better taken care of. Or perhaps the idea of barns as rustic validated its rundown façade more readily than a Victorian house, designed to be grand, detailed, ornate, Vika thought, chewing her lip. Even though the door stood open, Vika couldn't make out anything inside.

Grandma Peach slowed the bus as they drove closer to the barn and turned off the ignition. "Home, sweet home!" she said.

Grandma Peach opened the doors as Vika made her way to the front of the bus, the hot and humid air making her stride slow. She stood for a moment at the top of the stairs knowing the moment she moved her feet forward, she was willingly stepping into the unknown. Her heartbeat, nearly normal for much of the bus ride, picked up its tempo to Full Anxiety with a touch of nausea in her stomach. The heavy air filled her lungs as she took a deep breath and swung her leg forward to hover over the first step. Even her suitcase dragged in apprehension.

The yard wasn't in much better shape than the house. The grass—if you could call it that—looked as though a tractor had mowed it down. Thick, harsh ends stuck up around Vika's feet as she stepped down from the bus, and the smell of French fries wafted around them, the same smell that had greeted her on the side of the road.

Trees lined the property amounting to at least two acres, Vika guessed, enclosing what looked like it would have been a little paradise about fifty years before. A small shed they must have passed driving in that went unnoticed by Vika, sat quietly on the far side of the driveway, one of the two bay doors latched open with wood chips spilling out the opening.

The sound of a weed whacker powered down in the distance, and only moments later an imposing figure came around the side of the house. His face was round and red, his thin chin-length brown hair flattened to the side of his head by the strap of the '30s-style aviator goggles that rested on his forehead.

He had a full beard flecked with grey, and blue eyes that looked solidly at Vika, unnerving her slightly. A torn, purple Led Zeppelin T-shirt stretched over a well-nourished belly and bits of plant sprinkled old jeans and sneakers.

"Bringing home hitchhikers again, Mom?" The man said amused, his voice a deep rumble that sat soundly in Vika's stomach, his eyes fixed on her. Hitchhiker? Who was he calling—?

"She blew up her car, Dane," Grandma Peach said.

"Um," Vika started. That wasn't exactly true. She was the only one present and maybe she should have done more upkeep—like checking the oil or whatever people did to keep from accidentally incinerating their cars—but she didn't blow it up. It did that all by itself.

Before Vika could voice her thoughts, Grandma Peach continued, "We should probably talk with Ted about that. Get the mess cleaned up and off the road. What are you wearing, dear? I tried to throw that shirt away about six times." She patted Dane on the shoulder as she walked by, across the yard.

Two chickens flew out from behind the corner of the house as Grandma Peach passed by, feathers flying off, squawking in an incessant manner. They were still in a panic when a tiny thing tore around the side of the house and beelined for Vika. Its eyes were wide, ears plastered to its head, and tongue hanging out the side of its mouth in the goofy grin only a dog can master, one that screams, "friend!"

It didn't look like a dog, though. Vika had never seen a dog as ugly as that in her life. It was the size of a cat, with coarse, wiry, blonde hair that made it look like it had mange, and skinny little legs. A small curl of hair stuck straight up from the top of its head, with another little curl off the tip of its tail.

It bounded around at her feet but Vika didn't bend over, she instead eyed it cautiously.

"He's hideous to look at, but friendly. We call him Quasimodo. Found him trotting along the side of the road, no tags or anything. Skinny as a thru-hiker, that one. Thought he'd drop dead within a day."

Grandma Peach yelled from the other side of the yard as she snatched clothes off the line, "Quasi's had all his shots!"

Vika gave a tight smile and bent over to pat the dog on the head.

"You smell like French fries," Vika told the dog.

"That's the bus," Dane said. "It runs on vegetable oil. Even shit food like that can be good for something."

"So your car blew up, huh?"

"Vegetable oil. Huh." She let her voice trail off. "So, my car, I...I don't know what happened," she managed.

"Shame. Well, we have plenty of places to sleep. Would you prefer the house or the camper?"

Vika eyed the house, the cracked gingerbread trim, crumbling foundation, and thought of the hole where the front door should be. It looked like a tetanus trap.

She shrugged and said against her better judgment, "Wherever is more convenient for you. I don't mean to impose."

"I'm just kidding," Dane said. "We don't let people sleep in that asbestos cloud."

Grandma Peach had slowly made their way back, arms full of laundry. "Don't be silly," she assured Vika, "you aren't imposing. You'll sleep with me in the camper. Come on, I'll show you."

Vika, relieved to be back with Grandma Peach, picked up her suitcase and followed.

"Whose pack is that?" Vika asked, gesturing to a dirty backpack leaning against a tree near the front porch as they walked past.

"New Pants'." Grandma Peach's little white shoes disappeared into the straw-like grass with each step.

"What? No, whose pack is that?" Vika asked again. She never hiked before but it always intrigued her.

"New Pants'," Grandma Peach repeated.

"New—" Vika looked again but didn't see any pants anywhere. She pulled at the handle on her suitcase, forcing it to bounce along, an assault on luggage with wheels. She grunted.

"You need help with that? And the pack belongs to New Pants," Grandma Peach said. "I think he's only staying tonight. He might be at the store right now."

Of course she came upon a house occupied by a person named New Pants. Next, she'll be meeting Shiny Shoes and Granny Panties. That saying, "when life hands you a lemon" never applied to her before. It was always like, "when life hands you a lemon, look out, because thirty other grapefruit-sized 'lemons' are about to come flying out of nowhere."

"I'm good, thanks," said Vika. "So, there's someone here named New Pants?" Past experience informed her the best tactic was to ride it out.

"Yes," Grandma Peach said, as she pulled open the door to the camper. "Here we are!" she said brightly. "You can take the bed on the left."

Vika walked in and put the suitcase down next to wardrobe.

"I'll let you unpack. There is hot water on the stove if you would like any tea. There's some green tea and some cranberry, blueberry, pineapple something or other—Dane picks up the strangest concoctions when he does the shopping. My favorite is gingerbread spice; you should try it. Anyway, they're all in the cupboard so help yourself."

"Thank you," she answered, looking at her suitcase wondering where to begin. "I mean, this is very nice of you, but maybe I should just stay packed. I don't think I'll be staying long."

Grandma Peach was pouring water into a mug. "Don't be silly," she said again. "You blew up your only mode of transportation."

"I didn't—"

"I think you'll be here for a few days—at least—and we love company. So unpack and stay awhile! Plus that thing," Grandma Peach gestured to the suitcase, "is large. I don't want either of us to trip over it. I'm not getting any younger, you know."

"Right," Vika agreed. She opened up the suitcase and tossed a blanket and her little airplane pillow on the bed and opened the door to the wardrobe.

She picked around the dirty clothes in her suitcase and found that her procrastination of doing laundry was catching up to her, though she did manage to scrounge up a clean T-shirt and some jean shorts. Her feet were begging to be free of her sneakers and she pulled them off without untying her laces to wiggle her toes in the fresh air. She put on a pair of flip-flops and closed up her suitcase. Out of habit, she looked for her wallet—didn't she just have it? She flipped back the blanket and swept her hands over the bed, despite a little voice in the depths of her mind telling her she had left it in the car. But Vika, convinced it would reappear, opened her suitcase and looked through her clothes again. And again. It was gone. She groaned. Two hundred dollars in cash and her debit card just...POOF. *Shit.*

VIKA FINALLY STEPPED DOWN from the camper to find Grandma Peach had moved outside to pour water into the pots of a half dozen hanging plants. The air was even hotter and more humid than before.

"Thank you for letting me stay," Vika said, her clean clothes giving her a touch more comfort about her current situation.

"Of course, dear," Grandma Peach answered, maintaining her attention on the flowers. "Have you called home?"

Vika fidgeted. "I think it might be better until I figure a little bit more out. I don't want my parents to panic." Panic, call the National Guard, whatever.

Grandma Peach nodded slightly.

The chickens pecked at the ground and scuttled behind Vika as she walked by.

"Shoo, Henrietta," Grandma Peach said, waving her hands at the wandering fowl. Quasi followed happily behind Grandma Peach, nipping at this chicken and that but upon spotting Vika, took a U-turn to follow her, no doubt to see if his new visitor passed inspection. He sniffed her ankles and wound between her legs.

Vika climbed the porch to peek into the house and Quasi followed. Cracks zigzagged through the plaster, the floors were worn and scratched, and it smelled of moldy dust, if that were possible. She backed up with the memory of Dane's asbestos joke and moved to the swing to check her cellphone. Quasi stood on his hind legs and rested his front paws on Vika's knees, looking up at her. She patted his head briefly, and shifted her attention back to the screen. Not surprisingly, she had one bar and it flickered. She read the three texts from her mother from just that morning, telling her to get her stubborn little rear home RIGHT. NOW. She sighed and looked at the curious dog watching her.

"We're a long way from Kansas, Toto," she said to him and thought for a second—in the right light—he didn't look diseased. In fact, he almost looked cute.

Her thumb hovered over the call button. What would she tell her? Maybe she should call her father. He was probably still at work, and her mother wouldn't be able to steal away the phone. She scrolled through the contacts and found "Dad", but her thumb hovered again. Maybe she should just call her brother, Alex, or —

The putter of a motorcycle broke the quietude and Vika looked up to see a skinny man with a giant beard easing the bike up next to the barn. She shoved her phone in her pocket, deciding she'd call them later.

The rider's button-up shirt, a light tan, was dirty and stained. His shorts were loose and came down over thin, tanned legs and knobby knees. The running shoes on his feet must have been years old and nearly shredded by wear. He unclipped a grocery bag he had strapped to the back of the seat and pulled off his helmet to hang it on one of the handlebars.

Vika felt her heart rate quicken and her back stiffen as he grabbed his grocery bag and moved to exactly where she was sitting. He walked easily, lightly, and tall over the grass, and then hopped onto the porch with no more than the effort of a blink. He sat on the chair next to the swing and stuck out his hand to her.

"New Pants," he said, his hand steady, eyes blue, and teeth white, an odd juxtaposition to his tattered clothing and tanned face. She expected him to be old and tired, likened to his clothing, but when he smiled, the corners of his eyes were smooth. At least smooth enough for her to guess he was in his mid-20s.

"Vika," she said, taking his hand hesitantly. His clothes were dirty but he smelled like soap, another oddity with the visitor.

"Nice to meet you," he said. He opened the bag at his feet and pulled out a sports drink and a cheeseburger wrapped in tin foil.

"So how'd you land here?" he asked over the crinkle of the foil.

"Car fire," she said sullenly. "My car. You?"

"Ouch," he answered, taking a swig of his drink, capping it and placing it at his feet. "I walked."

"Where from?" Vika asked, watching him unwrap his burger and taking a healthy bite. "I saw your pack."

"Mexico," he answered, chewing.

She laughed out loud. "Mexico? No really, where'd you walk from?"

He looked at her with those clear blue eyes and raised one brown eyebrow. Vika realized he was serious and a feeling of unease crept up her back again. Maybe he wasn't old, maybe he smelled like soap, maybe his eyes were clear, alert, and even intelligent, but he was serious and this story was likely to be his ticket to Crazy Town. She felt her smile start to slide and she tried desperately to pull it back up before he noticed.

His beard twitched with the effort of trying to hide a grin, apparently noticing her discomfort. "Have you ever heard of the PCT? The Pacific Crest Trail?"

Vika answered slowly, "No."

New Pants nodded and began explaining, "It's a hiking trail that goes from Mexico to Canada. Or Canada to Mexico if you want to hike it that way—but not a lot of people do. It's about 2,660 miles through the desert, the Sierras, Trinity Alps and Shasta in Northern California, and then through Oregon and Washington. It goes through Three Sisters, Mt. Jefferson, Mt. Hood, and then Mt. Adams in Washington, Goat Rocks— that was so great—and it'll go by Glacier Peak, through the North Cascades and end at the Canadian border." He took a bite of his cheeseburger. "A couple hundred people attempt it every year. I'm not the only crazy one," he added for good measure.

By the time he had finished, Vika's mouth was open and both eyebrows were raised. Subtlety was never her forte. She closed her mouth, sat up straighter and tucked a piece of auburn hair behind her ear. "You're kidding."

"You ended up at one of the hotspots on the trail!" he chuckled. "I bet you'll be seeing a lot of hikers this summer."

"Oh, I'm not staying—"

"Word travels on the trail and even though you guys are new, people will hear about you. Though, probably not for another month or so. I think the pack is still in Northern California."

"The pack?" she asked, confused as to where the conversation had gone.

"Yeah, the pack is the majority of the hikers," New Pants told Vika as he moved from the cheeseburger to an apple and a package of mini donuts.

Dane walked by carrying an axe towards the barn. "Still in California, did you say?" A chicken pecked his heels, and then spotted the donuts and brazenly hopped onto the porch to inspect.

New Pants swatted it away and replied, "Yeah. I know three guys are a few days, maybe a week behind me, but most of them are still in Northern California."

Dane grabbed the chicken and gently tossed it on the ground saying, "Don't bother the hikers, Henrietta." Turning back to New Pants, he nodded, "That's good that you are all spread out. I'm sure they'll string in for months."

"Have you hiked the trail before?" New Pants asked.

"No," Dane answered, "I did a couple hundred miles of the Appalachian Trail, oh, about twenty-five years ago. Some of the best times of my life. I met my wife on the trail. And that turned into some of the worst times of my life." He paused to shake his head at the memory. "Like Elliot Ness and Al Capone, we were. Anyway, I lived in Maine for about fifteen years and had a little barn I let hikers stay in sometimes."

"Really?" New Pants said, interested, straightening his posture slightly. "I hiked it two years ago. Where were you?"

"We were just before the Hundred Miles Wilderness, but that was five years ago. I moved out to Spokane to teach and then bought this house last fall."

He straightened his back and gestured to the doorless doorway. "Have you guys checked out the house yet?" His eyes lit up, though his smile—if there was one—was hidden under his beard.

Vika shoved her phone into her pocket and stood up, determining that it was probably safer to get a tour from Dane than wander in on her own and fall through a rotten floor or something. "No, not yet. I'd love to see it, though."

New Pants brushed the powder from his donuts off his shorts, grabbed his drink and stood up. "Me, too," he said.

"Well, follow me," Dane said, his hulking figure squeezing past them on the porch. "Obviously, we need to do a little deconstruction before we can do any reconstruction; we have to gut it down to the studs first. The house was built in 1880 by a couple who owned the mill in town. Their name was, hmm, what was their name...?" He waved off the thought and walked into the house. "Anyway, here is the foyer. Victorians were known for high ceilings, large windows, French doors, extravagant furniture..."

DANE CONTINUED TALKING while New Pants and Vika looked around. She had a fleeting thought that Grandma Peach was right—this house was magnificent, glorious even, and a chill went down her spine as she imagined the house in its former glory. Then she looked to another room and all she saw was crumbling plaster, a sag in the ceiling from a leaky roof, and warped hardwood floors from water damage.

Dane flung open a door off of the living room to reveal old furniture stacked on top of other old furniture, piled higher than Vika stood tall and threatened to explode the room. Some of it looked to be in good condition, some was dusty and torn, and some fell on the spectrum in between.

"This is the good stuff I got out of the house. I already cleared out an entire dumpster of useless knockoff shit," Dane explained. Vika squinted at the pile of "good stuff," as Dane called it, springs sticking out here and there, missing handles on dressers and faded or ripped material. She bet at least six different families of mice lived in the furniture of that room and wondered briefly what the "bad stuff" looked like.

Vika only barely listened to Dane's assessment of the importance of proper re-upholstery. Instead, she watched a curious chicken peek around the side of the front door frame and hop into the foyer. It jerked its head as it walked, pecking at this and hopping there, until it made its way to where they were standing and yanked on the skirt of a ratty couch with its beak. Dane clapped his hands at the bird, which squawked and headed towards the dining room.

They moved on into the kitchen, where dusty dishes still filled old cabinets—the actual coloring Vika was unsure of—and cans of food, so old the labels had fallen off, piled the sides of an antediluvian sink seemingly held together by spiderwebs.

"Aren't the cabinets superb?" Dane asked, waving his hand as though showing diamonds in jewelry store. "They're original black cherry. Quality work. The countertop is shit though."

Vika watched a spider scuttle across the counter and into a crack in the yellow tile countertop. She shuddered.

Dane was already moving on. "I'm going to knock this wall down," he was saying, "to extend the kitchen here, maybe have a breakfast nook. That'd be nice, wouldn't it?" He gestured to the far corner. "I would need another window I think, don't you? But that will just face the chicken coop and there's nothing less appetizing than watching your food before it becomes your food, am I right? Well, actually, I can think of a lot of things that are less appetizing, but we won't—" Dane abandoned his monologue midsentence with a wave of his hand and turned to point in another area of the room. "Then I would put the table here, sink there, island there," he gestured as though he were cuing an orchestra. "And in the middle," he had both hands up to cue the grand finale, "my fridge of beer."

"Oh, and there's the bathroom," he waved his hand to address it. "Tile, maybe a claw-foot tub, I haven't decided. Here, look at this shit job of plumbing, though." New Pants followed Dane into the bathroom, but Vika caught one whiff, gagged, and stopped in the doorway.

She choked out, "It smells like something died in there."

Dane shrugged. "Wouldn't doubt it," he said. "This place had been empty for a while when I picked it up. Squirrels don't live forever, you know."

Vika backed up and waited in the kitchen as Dane pointed to pipes that she didn't know the purpose of.

Eventually, Dane and New Pants emerged and together the three of them walked to the last room on the first floor. Dane squeezed through a narrow doorway to stand in the center of a room that looked like it might be a den, hands on his hips and scowl on his face. "This has to go. It's unnecessary and the dumbasses who built it did a shitty job on everything. The wiring is a mess, there's no plumbing, there's a leak where it joins to the original house, and it smells like cat piss. The soffits extend too far over the side of the house. I don't know if they were blind or just stupid, but it doesn't match the original architecture of the house."

To Vika, it looked like another room. There was bare insulation on one of the walls that didn't have drywall and it smelled a little odd—not nearly as bad as the bathroom—but compared to the rest of the house, nothing seemed amiss.

"Maybe I'll just bulldoze it and build another porch. You can't have too many porches, right?"

"How many porches do you have?" New Pants asked.

"Just the one," Dane answered.

"Why did you build it first?" Vika asked.

"What?"

"The porch," Vika repeated. "You have so much work to do inside, and that seems like something…that would come later."

"Later?" Dane asked, disgusted. "Why would I wait? It's the best part."

"Well, I just—"

"The porch is the most fundamental architectural structure of human sanity. If you don't need a porch, you're either not sane or not human," Dane said.

"It is a place designed to mentally remove oneself from the ho-hum of life. To daydream! Oh, I love myself a good daydream. A porch is a black hole for the human fascination of the movement of time so one can exist in the past, present and future simultaneously!"

Vika stared at Dane, and realized her mouth had parted slightly again, and she stole a glance at New Pants, whose expression looked similar.

Dane spread his hands wide. "Trained well enough, a daydreamer can breathe life into something as intangible as an idea. They live in a parallel reality to the non-daydreamers, who like to call the life of a daydreamer 'lucky.' Though we all know luck is an excuse, don't we?

"So, show me someone who doesn't need a porch and I'll show you a lazy person with fickle morals. That is why here, at the Dancy house, we have a porch."

He turned on his heel and marched off to continue the tour, New Pants wandering after him.

"That's what I would have guessed," she said to no one but herself, and lengthened her stride to catch up with the two men as they disappeared to climb a twisting staircase to the second floor.

She reached out to touch the wall and let her finger trace a jagged crack in the plaster as she followed them. Her hand bounced up and down as it followed the fissure, but suddenly stopped when her finger hit a hole. Vika paused and hooked her fingernail under the plaster and pulled. A chunk the size of her fist popped out, arched through the air and exploded into dust on the stairs.

"Whoa," she said.

"Easy there, Hulk Hogan," Dane called out from above her. "There are easier ways than ripping down the walls with your bare hands."

"Sorry," Vika answered as she jogged up the last couple steps to Dane and New Pants.

Dane walked quickly to the end of a short corridor and turned. His white teeth shone through his beard and the corners of his eyes crinkled with the smile.

He rubbed his hands together. "Look at these two bedrooms! Big windows, good lighting, large rooms, and—" he stopped himself and pointed to where Vika could see between the wooden floor boards into the room below. "Watch where you're walking. Water damage. The boards are really thin. Don't step on them or you might find yourself in the living room. And the chaise lounge isn't there yet so it'll hurt."

Then he looked around the room again as if taking it in for the first time. "God," he breathed, "look at those moldings. They're perfect."

Vika stepped forward until she was no more than a foot away from the wall. They were wide, at least six inches around the windows and eight or ten inches on the moldings that ran along the floor. Square blocks with small designs adorned the corners where the moldings met, and her artist's eye noticed a tiny difference in the circles, likely alluding to handcrafted moldings.

"All right, come on," Dane said, leading the way to the other bedroom across the hall. Vika remained in the room for a moment to further inspect it on her own. The windows were enormous, the floors were in good condition, though they sloped horribly toward the back of the house, and she had a view of the driveway and far line of trees. She walked around a cast-iron radiator, closer to the windows and discovered they were almost exactly her height. If she leaned forward, the bottom of the molding would come to about her hairline, and the window extended all the way down to her shins. The pit of her stomach dropped to her toes, as she felt completely exposed to an unfortunate tumble. Logically, she knew she wouldn't fall, but some primordial instinct kept her away from unsecured heights. She closed her eyes to center herself and turned back to the room. Vika could picture a bed in the middle, maybe a chest with a quilt laying on top at the foot of the bed, a dresser, just there, a mirror hanging over it—

"The best place in the house is in the back," Dane's voice boomed through her imagination as he passed by in the hall. "To the back bedroom!"

He led the way to a dark room, where the walls were naked two-by-fours, and the only window in the room was on the far wall: tiny, covered in dirt, and off-center. The roof sloped down nearly to the floor, disappearing into dark corners that Vika would rather not look too hard at, for fear of what she might see scurrying through the shadows.

"This is the back bedroom?" Vika asked skeptically. "It seems a little…rustic."

They walked farther into the room and dirt, leaves, and God knows what else crunched beneath their feet on the plywood slabs. Wind pushed through gaps where the roof met the vertical wall and dragged little finger marks of dirt and dust across the floor.

"Yes, it is!" Dane declared. "Just imagine what I could do with this space: bookshelves, a pool table, an art studio, a microbrewery, an observatory...hell, there's enough room to have a Civil War reenactment up here." He paused. "That's not historically appropriate though. I wonder if they do Prohibition reenactments. Of course, we'd have to do it in secret, keep it real."

Vika cocked her head at him.

Dane shrugged. "The possibilities are endless."

A tap-tap-tap sounded above Vika. "Is it raining?" she asked absentmindedly, trying to look past Dane out the smudged window.

"No, just bats."

"Bats?" Vika choked on the word.

Then, as if on cue, a series of little squeaks and clicking sounded above them in the rafters, and Vika saw tiny bits of debris fall from the ceiling where the noise came from. She quickly backed out of the room.

"I'm going to wait outside," she said, as her feet propelled her down the hall, past the bedrooms and down the stairs.

They landed her in the foyer and she paused for a moment, trying to slow her breathing. She took another walk-through of the first floor to try and retrieve the first fleeting vision of the house in its day, but she couldn't. All she saw were warped floors, broken walls, and dirty windows.

It didn't make sense to her. This house seemed more work than it was worth. She knew it was impressive back in the day, but now...now it was a lost cause. She didn't know if Dane *could* save it, and she understood even less why he would *want* to.

She walked out the front and stood on the porch looking out into the lawn.

Dane's voice became louder, as did New Pants', as they descended the stairs and exited the house.

"Vika, do you want to see the coop where the hikers will stay?" Dane asked. "We can't let people stay in the house while we're working on it. There's too much shit in the air."

"Sure," she shrugged.

They continued across the lawn, past the barn with a sizable garden behind it, and into the bigger of the two coops. New Pants and Vika followed Dane across the threshold of the building and into a large living area with old couches and armchairs arranged in a half moon. A wood stove, which looked remarkably like the stove in the bus—maybe Dane got a two-for-one deal—occupied the corner opposite the doors and old dressers of various colors and sizes occupied the wall next to the wood stove.

On the wall closest to them, an old electric kitchen stove rested unevenly on the slightly sloped floor. It looked like it hadn't been used yet that century.

Past the couches and the kitchen, bunk bed after bunk bed occupied two aisles of sleeping quarters. Some were plain wood, some were pink with little flowers, or blue with trucks traveling the boards, and there was one that was in the shape of a giraffe. Some looked old and worn, some looked mildly used, all Vika bet Dane had found either on the side of the road or at garage sales. Either way, there was a pillow on each of the beds with fresh sheets and a blanket carefully folded at the foot of each mattress.

"Wow," New Pants said, letting his pack slide down his arm and gently into the cushion of the closest couch.

"The Wi-Fi password is on the fridge, and there are two laptops hikers can use in that shelf over there," Dane gestured. "The wiring in this place is a little temperamental, but it shouldn't be a problem. Let me know if it is."

New Pants nodded, "Yeah, thanks, I'm sure it'll be fine."

"You have TV there, if you want it," Dane said shifting uncomfortably as though he was...nervous?...about the hiker's reaction. "If you want to watch a movie or something.

"There's wood for the stove there," Dane pointed to the wall to the right, in case New Pants somehow missed it. "There are replacement clothes in the dressers there, but we don't have a washer and dryer here yet. There's a laundromat in town, but if I see a good one I'll pick it up." He turned to go and stopped abruptly and turned back, adding, "There's a compost bathroom right out the door on the far side of the beds. Toss some sawdust in there after you go. One handful for number one, and two for number two."

New Pants nodded again, "Got it."

DANE AND VIKA LEFT New Pants to settle in, and he came out to meet Vika on the porch half an hour later while Dane was busy on chores in the back.

New Pants pushed the swing back and forth. "Dane," he said, "he's quite a character."

"To put it mildly," Vika acknowledged. "I can hardly keep up with him when he's talking."

"He is hard to follow sometimes."

"So, New Pants," Vika went on, "does that trail that you were talking about go through this property?"

He shook his head, "No, it goes through the mountains about twenty miles from here."

"Twenty miles?" she asked. "How did you get here?"

"I hitched," he told her.

"Hitched? As in hitchhiked? By yourself?" Vika thought about the movies she'd seen, the articles she'd read, and the rumors she'd heard. People were killed all the time hitchhiking, weren't they? That's what homeless people and murderers and drug addicts did.

"Yes," New Pants said confused. "Didn't you hitchhike here?"

"I did not!" Vika shifted, remembering Dane said something similar earlier. "My car was on fire! I was *walking* into town and—"

"You got picked up?"

"Well, I—"

"You didn't have a ride, someone drove by, and offered to let you in her vehicle. That's pretty much the definition."

He said it as fact, a simple observation, but Vika couldn't help but be offended. Had she forgotten her priorities that quickly? A little sun, a little heat, and she hitchhikes in buses that run on vegetable oil?

She could feel her face flush and oh, she hated that. With her fair skin she looked like a goddamn Matisse painting.

Unaware of her discomfort, New Pants poured himself a cup of tea. "I have fun hitching. It kind of restores my faith in humanity. People aren't overanalyzing the situation. Someone needs a ride, and someone gives him a ride. Problem and solution. Simple as that."

"It still can be dangerous," Vika retorted, taking her own sip of tea.

"Sure it can," New Pants replied, "but everything has risk."

"Can I ask you," Vika cleared her throat, "how…how you got your name?"

New Pants laughed. "It's a trail name," he began, "I started with a pair of pants but around Big Bear, they blew into my stove and got a hole in the leg so I ordered a new pair on the trail. When I picked them up in Kennedy Meadows, they were three sizes too small. They came down to about there," he said, leaning over and making a gesture with his hand about mid-shin. "Kennedy Meadows didn't have an outfitter, so I had to wear them a couple hundred miles to Mammoth. It was awful. Anyway, that's how I got my name."

"So it's like a nickname?" Vika suggested.

"Yeah, I guess. Well," he gave a little snort of disapproval, "that makes it sound so childish. I don't know. It's more tradition. Another element of the hiking life that separates a hiker from the outside world."

"Ah," Vika said, "so everyone has a trail name?"

"Most people do. Some don't. The trick is to get your name before you do anything really stupid." He took a sip of tea.

"Do most hikers hike alone?" Vika asked.

New Pants shook his head. "Nah," he said, "but you have to hike your own hike. Mine didn't match anyone else's," he shrugged.

"Hike your own hike? That's deep," she teased.

He laughed. "It's a hiker mantra. It's hard enough to do in ideal conditions, even harder if you're hiking for someone else's ideal conditions. A lot of people have similar ideas of how to do a thru, plus the bonus of socializing allows a lot of people to hike their own hike with another person."

"Makes sense," Vika said and chewed on her cheek. "Do you carry a gun?"

New Pants gave her a blank look. "For what?"

"For what?" Vika echoed. "Aren't there...bears and things? What do you do for protection?"

"Not carry a gun." Vika waited and New Pants added, "A gun would weigh too much."

"What if you were attacked by a bear?" Vika asked, the setting sun egging her on about things that go bump in the night.

"Well, let's hope that doesn't happen" he smiled. "Bears are pretty skittish, though."

"Oh," Vika said, not convinced. Her mind was bursting with questions. No plans? Just hoping for the best? She changed the subject. "What do you eat?"

"Well," New Pants started, "lots of dried stuff. Oatmeal, granola bars, trail mix, peanut butter, banana chips."

Vika sat and thought. "And you just walk?"

New Pants nodded, "And walk and walk."

"For how long?"

"My hike will be just about 90 days—"

"90 days! That's such a long time!"

"Most people do it in 130."

Vika stared at him unabashedly. "Don't you get bored?"

New Pants laughed again. "Sometimes," he conceded, "it doesn't last very long, though."

"What do you do for..." Vika grappled with her words, "entertainment? Do you bring books or what?"

New Pants raised a shoulder and let it drop. "I don't read on the trail."

"Weighs too much?" Vika guessed.

"No, I don't have time," he said after a moment. "I have a small music player I charge in towns."

"Huh," Vika pondered as she leaned back into the seat. "How did you hear about this hike?"

"I read a book about the Appalachian Trail in high school and heard about the PCT when I was hiking the AT."

"And you thought, 'hey, hiking from one end of the country to another sounds like fun'?"

"Pretty much. Have you hiked?" New Pants asked.

"Me? No. I mean, it sounds interesting, but...I don't know much about it. I haven't really had the opportunity. Or haven't looked for it, I guess."
"You should. You don't have to hike thousands of miles, but you should give it a try. You're in one of the best places in the country to do it."

Vika smiled. "Yeah, maybe."

A breeze swept across the porch and sent a ripple of goose bumps up Vika's arm. As the sun was getting low, the temperature was dropping quickly.

"I think I'm going to run and get a sweatshirt," she said, slowly standing. She realized then how tired her body had become. Her limbs felt heavy and her muscles seemed to have already gone to sleep.

New Pants gave a nod and said, "I'm going to turn in for the night. Dane offered to take me to the trailhead early tomorrow."

"Already?"

He gave Vika a crooked smile. "Nine o'clock to you is a hiker's midnight." He put out his hand, "Nice meeting you, Vika."

"You too, New Pants."

She walked slowly over the harsh grass, past the decrepit house, between the barn and the chicken coop, rubbing the cool air off her arms as she went. She felt as though she had made a friend and lost a friend, all within the space of a couple hours.

Grandma Peach sat on the loveseat reading a book and sipping tea when Vika climbed the stairs to the camper.

"Hello, dear," Grandma Peach said, with hardly a glance up from the pages that demanded her attention, "I brought out some blankets and sheets for your bed."

"Thank you," she said, squeezing by the sink and table.

She stretched the sheets over the thin mattress, threw the blanket over, and climbed in. She eased her sore muscles onto the bedding and practically heard her lower back sigh with relief as she did so. A moment later, she reached up and clicked off the light by her head. She realized just how dark the darkness was.

Vika was tired, but sleep would not come. The nocturnal insects sang at the top of their lungs and Vika's mind tried to process both the familiar and foreign sounds that occupied the wilderness surrounding her. They did not have this harmony in Jessup. She would have only heard some crickets, maybe a frog in a garden pond, all through the hum of an air conditioner, broken up by the occasional car driving through. The thoughts from earlier in the day on her long walk along the dusty dirty road returned with vigor. The small animals, the big animals, the serial killers, corpse roads, meth houses, and all the Acts of God in between. If anything happened, no one would be around to hear her scream. She couldn't block these thoughts easily, and spent most of the night tossing and turning, her limbs fatigued but restless.

CHAPTER 3

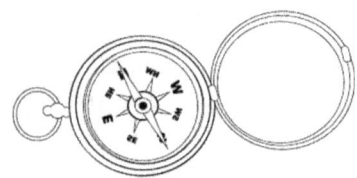

NEW PANTS WAS ON THE TRAIL before the sun had come up and, needless to say, long before Vika rolled out of bed. Ted drove out in a tow truck and had a cup of coffee with Dane and Grandma Peach while Vika busied herself by collecting old, rotten shingles that had fallen off of the roof. Some had been annihilated by the lawnmower and lay sprinkled far and wide throughout the yard.

Grandma Peach walked up to her after Ted and Dane climbed into the truck and drove away. "Ted said one of his cashiers is about to have a baby and he would appreciate a little help in the store. If you're looking for a job, that is."

The proposition took her off guard, but she realized that her wallet was missing and she didn't have enough money for another car. Or a plane ticket. Or a bus ticket. She was stranded. The only way to get home, or wherever she was going, was to get some cash in her pocket.

"What would I have to do?" she asked.

Grandma Peach patted Quasi, who had run up to her. "I expect you'll be counting money. You can ask Ted when he comes back to drop off Dane." She turned back to the dog and asked him, "Right, Quasi? Do you want to go work at the store, too?" The dog looked so blissful just to be alive, eyes wide, tail wagging hard enough to rock his whole body, and tongue hanging out; hell, Vika imagined the ugly dog would agree with anything.

Ted came around on the way back into town, Vika's Volkswagen in tow. It was a sad sight. The windows had blown out, the cushions were nearly gone, and springs stuck out at odd angles.

Vika swallowed the lump in her throat and walked up to the driver's side window as Dane climbed out the other side. Everything was covered in black. Black steering wheel, black dash, and black radio knobs. Glad she was wearing dark colors, she walked around to the passenger's side and opened the glove compartment. Her maps were ash, the registration card—not that it mattered—probably was past a state of ash and completely gone. She pulled out a small metal ring and wiped off the soot. Though faded and grimy, she could still read *Glacier Park* written across the fob with a tiny image of a grizzly bear. She had bought the keychain for her father when she passed through the park almost a week before.

He had a fascination with grizzlies, ever since his college days when he went camping with a couple buddies in Glacier Park and a grizzly tipped over their car to get the cooler inside. All the while, all three of them were hiding in the cabin watching, which her mother would mention after he told that story a time too many for her. Regardless, her father still talked about it as though he'd won a gladiator fight.

Vika suspected that incident was the reason he moved the family to the suburbs and never took them camping. Even so, she shoved the filthy souvenir into her pocket to wash later.

Vika tried the door and it creaked open. She leaned carefully over the exposed wires and picked up some of the coins in the cup holder. She pocketed the little black circles with the intention of cleaning them later. The two hundred dollars she had in the glove compartment had burned up and her debit card was a deformed rectangle of melted plastic, stuck to the inside of the door. She groaned.

Vika quickly looked through the center console, under the seats, and in the trunk, but found nothing else worth saving. She shut the door and patted the roof as though patting an old pet before walking through the weed-grass to the front of the tow truck to meet the two men.

"Excuse me, Ted?"

"Yeah?" He turned toward her and waited for her to continue. He was a very thin man, thin enough that it was hard to imagine him in any type of work that required physical labor. Moppy brown hair with blonde streaks fell to his eyebrows, over an evenly tanned face. His teeth were crooked, and a shade close enough to yellow to age him, but not close enough to seriously question his hygiene.

Vika continued, "I'm Vika. Grandma Peach was just telling me you are looking for someone to help you in the store. I'd really like to help out. I can swing by to pick up an application if you—"

Ted interrupted, "We don't have none of those. You timely?"

"Yes, sir."

"You a thief?"

"No, sir."

"Good. You're hired. Come by the store tomorrow, say nine, and we'll get you trained."

"Really? Oh, thank you. I'll be there."

"Wear sneakers and tie your hair up."

"Will do."

He climbed into the cab of the truck and Vika watched as he swung around in the yard, her pathetic car bouncing along behind. She felt like there should be a ceremony, a speech, a tribute to the memories they shared, something. Instead, she just stood there in the spiky lawn under the pounding sun and listened to the hum of the tow truck as it picked up speed on the road.

No sooner had the sound of the engine faded, than another—turning faster and quieter—approached from the opposite direction. Vika watched as a delivery truck slowed and stopped at the mailbox. The silhouette in the cab leaned forward, as though peering into the lawn where she stood. She looked over her shoulder, but Grandma Peach and Dane were looking from the porch towards the barn where Dane was gesturing. Vika turned back to the truck. The driver had backed up and had begun to pull down the driveway.

"Hey!" the driver yelled, "is this the Dancy's?"

Vika stepped over the unruly lawn. "Yep," she said, "who do you need? Dane's just—" But his torso had disappeared into the back and he reappeared with two large boxes. One had bright blue duct tape wrapped like a luggage strap around the width.

He shoved the boxes at her then stuck out a flat screen. "Sign here."

"Wha—" She looked down at the boxes, and sure enough they had 'Dancy' written across the address line. The man waited impatiently, arm outstretched. She put the boxes on the ground and quickly scribbled her signature onto the board.

"Thanks," he said, and stashed it in the side pocket of his seat. He leaned back into his seat, jammed the truck into reverse, and backed out without another word.

Vika redirected her gaze to the labels. She found "HOLD FOR HIKER TRASH. ETA 8/8" written in at least six different places. The second was similar, but with a different date scrawled on the sides.

She scooped them up and carried them over to the porch. "Um," she said, and Grandma Peach and Dane turned away from the barn. "What do I do with these?"

Dane's eyes lit up. "Our first hiker trash boxes!" He picked one up and hefted it. "Light," he said after a moment, and then switched to the other box to do the same. "Ultra light," he declared to a clueless audience.

"So," Vika inquired as he stacked them on the corner of the porch next to the steps, "what is a hiker...uh, trash...box?"

"Food."

"Oh," Vika nodded.

"Sometimes gear. Can't go almost 3,000 miles on a single pair of shoes."

"Oh. So food for, like, people with special diets?"

"No. Some people don't want to rely on the supermarkets. This way they know exactly what they'll be eating until the next town. Some places on the trail don't have a store but they'll take packages."

"Oh," Vika said. "Why is it called trash?"

"The people are called trash," Dane responded simply.

"You call them trash?" Vika asked, her mouth open in horrified astonishment. "Isn't that insulting?"

"You have to meet more hikers."

Vika shrugged. "If you say so." She turned to Grandma Peach. "Well, I talked to Ted about the job at his store. He said for me to come in tomorrow morning and get trained." She couldn't help but smile, even though she knew next to nothing about her job description.

"Oh, that's wonderful, deary!" Grandma Peach said, patting Quasi, who had curled up on her lap.

"Well, now that you have a job, you need a way to get there," Dane said excitedly, a bright smile barely discernable under his massive beard, but his eyes lit up like her car did the day before. "Can you drive a motorcycle?"

Vika fidgeted. "Uh, no."

"A bus?"

"No."

"A camper?"

"No."

"A tractor."

Vika hoped she wouldn't have to drive a tractor to work. "No."

"A boat?"

Vika hadn't seen anything substantial enough to drive a boat on in three days, so she was pretty sure he was kidding but it was hard to tell because his face didn't change. She twisted her hands. "No. No, but I can drive a car."

"Well, you toasted the last one you drove. Let's start you out with a motorcycle—that's easy enough. You've had experience with a stick?"

"Uh, no. Mine was an automatic."

Dane squinted his eyes and put his hands on his hips. "Jesus Christ, girl. Do you let computers take over every part of your brain, or just the part for driving?"

"You mean, by driving a car from this decade?"

"Makes people lazy." He flicked a hand in the direction of the camper. "You go get real shoes on your feet, and I'll go get the bike."

Vika's face flushed and she turned to find sneakers.

She was stepping down from the camper as he was returning from the far side of the barn, pushing the silent motorcycle across the lawn and waving at her to join him.

"Hop on," he said. Like the house—and the bus and tractor and lawnmower, for that matter—the bike was aged. Duct tape held the seat together and there were rust spots popping up along the handlebars. *Honda* was written along the black gas tank.

She bit her lip, contemplating the bike, and eventually swung her leg over the to straddle the seat and hold on to the hand grips.

Dane started pointing to different parts on the bike. "Here's your clutch, your handbrake, your throttle, your kickstart, shifter, and footbrake. Then here is the ignition and choke. All right, you ready to go?"

Vika looked at him like he was speaking German. "Uh, Dane," she frowned, "I don't know what any of that means."

"Which part?" he asked.

Vika cringed. "All of it."

Dane stared at her with piercing blue eyes, and then explained, "The clutch connects the engine to the transmission. It's spring loaded with disks inside. I have no idea how many—probably three or four; it's a multiple disk mechanism. A car clutch is different.

"So this pack of disks, they have linings and are spring loaded so it compresses when you let out the clutch. The friction of the disks drives the transmission, and the transmission is connected to a sprocket. The transmission drives the output to the chain sprocket—"

"Dane," Vika said loudly to end the rambling.

"What?" he asked. "You understand now?"

"Understand? No...a chain sprocket? What the...is this how you explain everything?" she asked. She thought her conception of car mechanics was zero to none, but she was mistaken, it was actually in the negative numbers.

Dane didn't respond, instead looked at her deadpan and waited.

After a moment, she decided that if she asked again, it would be the same kind of gibberish so she said, "Never mind. Yes, I understand. Let's get started."

Dane paused to point to the bike and said, "A lot of motorcycles today have a two-stroke engine, but this one has four. Intake, compression, combustion or power, and exhaust."

But by the time he got to number four, she couldn't remember the first three. Her muscles became twitchy at how ignorant she was in this conversation; she was a smart girl, and rarely felt completely lost. It was frustrating and she shifted her weight.

Dane kept talking, "It's a good thing I fixed it up last week. Before then it wouldn't idle. Had to have an open throttle the entire time it was on. Have you ever driven though the town on a motorcycle that can't idle? Parking lots were a riot. Every dipshit and his brother tried to back out in front of me. Gave me a couple gray hairs, that's for sure."

She managed a laugh, succeeding in perpetuating the idea that Dane was talking to her and not *at* her; she still didn't have a clue what was coming out of his mouth.

"Well," he said, gesturing to the bike, "let's go."

"Okey doke," she said.

Her foot slipped off the kickstart the first bunch of times, but on the sixth try it roared to life with a vengeance. Dane leaned over and eased her hand on the throttle and it immediately quieted some.

"OK, Peter Fonda," he said, taking a step back, "hold in your clutch." Vika pulled it in as far as it would go. "Good. Kick it into first." Her foot rested on the ground, and she brought it so she could push the shifter down with her toe. "Good. Now give it some gas and let go of the clutch."

"Got it." Vika gave it some gas and let go of the clutch. The bike lurched forward five feet and stalled—enough time still for her to give a little squeal, her feet dragging on the ground, and enough g-forces to rock her head back as she barely held on to the handlebars. She sat in the thick, exhaust-filled silence as embarrassment crept up her neck.

"Not all at once! Not all at once!" Dane said, coming up beside her. "You looked like a 3-year-old walking a Rottweiler. A *little* gas, just enough to keep it from stalling and *ease* out the clutch. We'll get to wheelies later."

Vika nodded.

Dane stood with his hands on his hips. "Well, try it again."

She shoved stray strands of her hair back into the sides of her helmet and wiped her sweaty hands on her jeans. Her hands shook and her throat tightened.

It only took her three times to get the engine fired up. It lurched twice and made it about fifteen feet before it stalled.

"Progress!" Vika called out.

Dane didn't answer right away. "Sure," he eventually said.

She tried several more times with similar results, and then finally, she lurched and lurched again, and the motorcycle was still going! She held onto the handlebars with white knuckles, as it seemed to weave across the yard on its own accord. Her feet dragged along the ground, but bounced off unhurt. She steered around a wheelbarrow and overcompensated when she tried to bring it back on course. The bike leaned, the tire pointed toward the shed, and her foot planted solidly on the ground. She pushed up, but lost her balance and her other foot went down on the other side as she rocked. Vika finally centered her weight again and looked up to see the edge of the lawn lined with blackberry bushes at thirty feet and counting.

Just like that, she forgot how to brake.

"Dane!" she yelled as the distance closed between the dirt bike and the pricker patch. "Dane!"

She heard him yelling something about her foot but it wasn't processing. She vaguely remembered there was a brake she could use, but her brain would not pick her foot up off the ground. She felt her heart quicken and she sucked in air as the front tire went into the pricker patch. She felt thorns nipping at her pants as though they were caught in a huge spiderweb, until the bike lost all speed and began to tip over in slow motion. Vika tried to get her foot underneath to catch the bike, but the blackberry thorns kept her legs caught up and she and the motorcycle fell sideways together. She could feel the bushes had enclosed her completely.

Vika had brought an arm up to protect her face and didn't see Dane approach. He reached under the bike and killed the engine. She could feel him move her leg to the side and pull the bike off of her. With more maneuverability, she was able to get her feet underneath her and fight through the bushes to a standing position, grunting and groaning, tossing in the shaky curse word. She heard and felt the prickers tear through her clothing as she waded through the shrubbery to where Dane was standing with the motorcycle.

"Dane, I'm so sorry!" Vika said, shaking out her arms and some nerves. "I don't know what happened, I just…forgot."

"If that happens again, make sure to turn the engine off immediately," he said calmly, looking for over the bike for damage, "and don't be afraid to use the brakes."

She was inspecting her arms and legs, taking stock of the tears in her clothing Grandma Peach trotted as fast as an eighty-year-old woman could trot around the corner of the house, her eyes wide and her hands clutching her chest. "Are you OK, dear?" she asked, walking up to the girl. She grabbed Vika's chin and turned her face from side to side, inspecting for injury. "Oh, my," she fretted, "you're bleeding. Let's get you cleaned up and get some of that ointment on you. We don't want that to scar." Grandma Peach pulled Vika by the arm towards the camper.

"It just happened so fast," Vika said.

Grandma Peach patted her arm and gave a sympathetic smile, "Well, it didn't happen all that fast, but I'm sure it gave you a start." Vika felt her ears heat up and a blush spread across her cheeks. "At least you didn't hit my garden. I'd really like to have lots of tomatoes this year. Lord knows I've had trouble with them in the past and tread marks probably wouldn't help the matter." She shook her head. "Milly gave me this excellent recipe for canning them, sweet and spicy.

"Come on, Quasi!" Grandma Peach called suddenly, towards the porch where he lapped up some water out of a bowl. "Let's go get Vika cleaned up!"

The mangy dog looked up, water dripping from its mouth, and in an instant tore across the lawn, scattering chickens along the way. Every time she saw that dog run, Vika wondered how such tiny little legs moved so fast. Every time.

LATER THAT AFTERNOON, Vika paced in the lawn, twirling the phone in her hands. Overdue, she scrolled through her contacts and dialed up her mom.

"Vika?" The voice was her mother's, but it sounded so far away. "Vika, is that you?"

She swallowed. "Hi, Mom."

She heard her mother gasp, "Vika. Where the hell have you been? My God, I almost put your face on a milk carton."

Vika had no doubt she was telling the truth and refrained from making a sarcastic comment. "I'm in Stacklen, Washington," she said. "And I'm just calling to say hi. I'm living with—"

"You'll come home right now, Vika Carmichael." Her voice was a hiss.

"I will...soon, but really, I'm doing OK."

"You will come home, now." Her voice was climbing rapidly. "We have been worried sick. We don't know where you are—"

"You make it sound like I was kidnapped. I texted you—"

"Anyone could have sent those texts from you. Why didn't you call?!"

"You're right." Vika looked skyward and felt her hand tighten on the phone. "I should've called sooner."

"You could've been hurt, in God knows what kind of trouble, and you just leave us in the dark."

"I'm sorry," Vika told her. "I'm fine, I had a little car trouble. I'll be on my way home soon."

"What happened with your car? Can't you rent one?"

"I don't think there are many car rentals around here."

"Vika," her mother said her name like a drawn out question. "Where are you? Seattle? Portland? We'll get you a plane ticket home, and then we'll talk about your car situation."

"Stacklen, and thanks," Vika said, "but I can buy the ticket on my own."

"With what money? You refused to get a job after Boston and then drove off to who knows where!"

"Mom, I don't need you to buy me a ticket."

"I told you not to go. Now you can't even afford to make your way home! Do you know I ran in to Joann at the post office the other day? Guess where Lauren is working now. She—"

"Mom? Stop." This time, Vika pulled the phone away from her ear, and counted to three as she inhaled through her nose. She brought the phone back and said, "I just wanted to let you and Dad know I'm OK, but I have to go."

"Vika—" but Vika hung up before her mother could finish. It felt like they were running in circles after each other and it would only end with one or both of them in tears. Even so, she felt awful.

"Hungry, dear?" Grandma Peach greeted her as the smell of lemon-pepper chicken wafted down the steps as Vika pulled open the door of the camper.

"Starved," she answered, glad to have a distraction from hanging up on her mother. She kicked off her boots and walked up the stairs past Quasi lying guard at the foot of the sofa to wash her hands in the sink. "Need any help?"

"I haven't cut the bread yet," Grandma Peach looked up from the lettuce she was chopping. *Chop, chop.* "Milly makes this incredible honey quinoa nut bread when her kids come into town. She always makes me an extra loaf. The knives are in there," she gestured to a drawer as Vika pulled out a cutting board from a cabinet.

Grandma Peach picked up the entire pile of lettuce and placed it in a wooden bowl. She bent to open the small refrigerator. "Do you like radishes in your salad?" she asked.

"I do," Vika answered. *Slice.*

"Radishes?" Dane's voice boomed through the screen door a moment before it opened and his hulking frame stomped up the stairs. *Chop, chop, slice.* "I love radishes."

Vika and Grandma Peach finished their prep work and placed the knives in the sink.

They all took their plates and filled them at the counter before sitting at the bench-seating table.

Red wine splashed into glasses and reached up the opposite side, tempting to slosh up and over, but only leaving a thick, curved, pink stain.

Dane raised his glass. "To the Pacific Crest Trail," he said and took a sip, both the others following suit with a taste.

"Steph called today," Grandma Peach said, taking a bite of the chicken.

"Like Nancy Kerrigan and Tonya Harding."

"What was that?" Grandma Peach asked.

"Except without the physical abusiveness nature of their relationship. Maybe more like Copernicus and the pope."

"Dane, what are you talking about? Oh, never mind." She waved off the question. "She said Cassie's done with an internship and she's getting a little restless. She thinks a little fresh mountain air might help her out a little."

"A little fresh mountain air, huh? What does she think is going on around here? We meditate and commune with nature all day? This is a construction project. Not exactly Cassie's cup of tea."

"Dane," Grandma Peach said, exasperated as she set down her fork on the side of her plate. "If not for Steph, do it for Cassie. You haven't see her since Easter."

"Of course I want to see my daughter!" Dane said, leaning forward. "She doesn't want to see me."

"Oh, pfft," Grandma Peach scolded, rolling her eyes.

"If she did, she wouldn't have brought that asshole in skinny jeans to my door at Easter dinner. Good Lord, he was a body shield—a fuckin' poor excuse for one—but that's why she brought him, so she would have someone to hide behind and not talk to me."

Vika looked down, content with focusing on the number and shape of the pepper flakes on the piece of meat before she pulled off a tiny piece with her fork, and very quietly, very thoroughly, chewed the chicken.

Grandma Peach rolled her eyes again. "You are exaggerating, Dane. He was a nice boy."

"You could shoot an arrow through those goddamn holes in his ears."

"Does that make him less nice?"

"It makes him have too much to prove. Cassie is smart! Confident! And there he is, full of hot air. He had no skills and no intention of gaining any. That didn't keep him from talking, though, on and on about carbon footprints and saving the whales."

"Those aren't important?" Vika asked, an eyebrow raised.

"He bought a case of bottled water the first day he got here! All that blabbering is worthless bullshit if he doesn't do anything about it. All talk, no walk."

Grandma Peach frowned. "Do you hear yourself?"

Dane sat back and took a deep breath. "OK, OK." He put his hands up in a minor show of surrender. "Maybe I'm being too hard on him. He *did* get an Ivy education. I'm sure he sits around campfires and commiserates over corruption and civil liberties with his buddies." He let that sit with them for a moment before he brought his chin up and leaned forward again. "Only problem is," Dane burst out, "I bet that commiserating is accompanied by smoking some weed hot off the Juarez Cartel mules. Damn fuckin' hypocrite. Nothing says 'keeper' like helping to drive a genocide."

"You don't know that," Vika said.

"I know he's cheap as hell, so the odds are good."

"What'd he do to make you hate him so much?" Vika asked, barely loud enough to be heard. Dane's eyes flashed for a second, but Grandma Peach cut in.

"Oh, Dane," Grandma Peach said, letting her glass clank against her plate. "Now you're being ridiculous."

Dane had his arms spread wide as he continued, but wasn't looking at either of them. "What a waste of time. Cassie's better than that. I know it; she knows it. The only reason she brought him was to piss me off."

"It worked."

Dane dropped his hands to the table and shot Grandma Peach a glare that Vika thanked the heavens she was not on the receiving end of. Grandma Peach glared back.

"If you were really that upset, you could have just talked to her instead of insulting her," Grandma Peach said.

"I did talk to her."

"Oh, Dane," Grandma Peach sighed, "you didn't talk to her, you gave her conditions."

"Reasonable conditions."

"And you ended it, if I remember correctly, 'to put that hippie—'"

"Hipster," Dane said, "entirely different species."

"'—slimeball back on a bus back to Comma Con or wherever he came from.'"

"Comic-Con," Dane corrected, "though, an organization for the correct usage of punctuation would do our society well."

Vika swallowed a laugh.

"And if he wasn't a fucking pantywaist he could've taken it," Dane finished.

"Dane, please," Grandma Peach huffed her interruption. "Watch your mouth at the dinner table."

Vika ate another tiny piece of chicken and avoided eye contact with all parties involved.

"So are you or are you not going to ask your daughter to visit you?"

"I'll ask her, but that irrational poser is not invited."

"Honestly, Dane," Grandma Peach said, shaking her head, "I don't know where you come up with these things. No one knows what you are talking about half the time."

CHAPTER 4

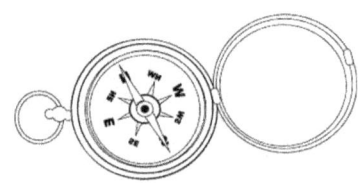

GRANDMA PEACH CHEERFULLY tooted the horn of the bus the next morning while Vika was in the camper bathroom tucking a stray piece of red-brown hair behind her ear. She leaned toward the mirror and slid a little mascara across her lashes. Just a hint of femininity. Vika stared at her reflection for a couple seconds, her bright blue eyes seemed a little less cynical than in the days following the Trail of Deception, her skin as pale as ever, with a pink tinge across her cheeks and over her nose. Her hair, for the moment, stayed where she put it. It was long and thick, though, so she knew her bun would be sagging within the hour.

Finally, Vika pulled on her sneakers and rushed out the door. As she climbed into the bus, Quasi rushed passed her and bounced into Grandma Peach's lap.

"All righty," Grandma Peach said as she grabbed the giant handle that swung the door shut. "Let's hit the road. Are you ready for your first day of work, dear?"

"I guess so."

Grandma Peach put the bus into first and Vika held on to the arm of the couch.

The ride seemed to last longer than she remembered and at the same time, not long enough. Soon enough, the shops, houses, and at last, Ted's store, passed the windows of the bus.

"All right," Vika said as she stood up and Grandma Peach slowed to a stop. "Here I go. See you in a bit."

"Good luck, sweetie," Grandma Peach called after her.

Ted stood behind the counter reading the newspaper when Vika walked in.

He gave her a once over, gave an approving nod of her attire and waved her over to the counter.

"Good morning!" she said brightly, hoping to ease some of the tension that was building up inside her with the beginning of a job she knew nothing about.

He grunted in response and pointed to where the counter split. "Come on through," he said. He touched a computer screen that was clearly the cash register and the drawer popped open. "The first thing you'll do when you walk in is count your drawer. You'll start out with two hundred, when you get up to five, you'll have to drop some."

"Drop it where?"

He ignored her and went on for the first hour explaining this, that, and the other thing. "It's really not that difficult," he said. "We'll give you a couple days to settle."

"Sure," she said.

After the lunchtime rush, Ted told Vika to take a break. "I gotta fill out some paperwork," he said. "Just punch out and be back in half an hour."

"Sounds good," Vika said as she turned and found Ted had already disappeared around the door.

The other cashier, whose name Vika still could not remember, leaned over and said, "Don't take it personally. He's silent to everyone."

"I got that impression when I met him yesterday." Vika raised a shoulder and let it drop. "Who else works here?"

"Smith," the other cashier answered. "He works three days. He's great though. Kind of a downer, but nice for the most part. Unless you throw out his pasta before it's expired. Don't do that. Jill works the other four."

"Good to know," Vika nodded, and wanted to ask more questions, but she was looking forward to a little break, too. She asked the other cashier for help punching out and headed for the door.

The rest of the day went pretty well, but somehow she was off sixty-two cents when she counted down her drawer.

Ted gave a low whistle. "Well, not the worst by far," he said after a beat. "Come back on Wednesday."

It was three o'clock in the afternoon, but it felt like bedtime. She dragged her feet out the door and looked around for Grandma Peach. She heard a little toot behind her, and turned to see Grandma Peach, her trademark sunglasses peeking over the steering wheel. She waved to her from the driver's seat of the bus, while Quasi paced along the dash.

She smiled and walked over to them. Quasi sprinted down the steps when Grandma Peach opened the door and tore towards Vika to sniff her shins. She patted him once, after which he rocketed across the pavement towards the bus and launched himself up the three steps in one bound. He lay down next to Grandma Peach, crossed his front paws and rested his head on them, panting.

Unconcerned for Quasimodo's consistently bizarre behavior, Grandma Peach asked, "So, dear, how was your first day?"

Vika climbed the steps and sat back into the couch and practically heard her body sigh with relief. "It was good," she heard herself say, and struggled to keep her mind from zoning out. "Ted's nice. Quiet, but he's OK."

Grandma Peach nodded. "So tell me what you did today. They have fantastic sandwiches. Did you make sandwiches?"

Vika smiled. "No, I worked at the cash register mostly, and got ice."

"Oh, ice. Lovely."

Vika smiled at her earnestness. "It was fine. Ted asked me to come back on Wednesday, so I guess he thought I did OK, too."

"Oh, good!" Grandma Peach said loudly and Quasi gave a noise between a bark and a squawk of approval.

"How was your day?" Vika asked, as they rolled over the curb and out into the street, the smell of French fries in their wake as they cruised out of town.

"Oh, it was wonderful, dear," Grandma Peach answered. "I went to Jo's house this morning and we played some 'Phantom of the Opera.'"

"Huh," Vika said, "that sounds...fun."

"I needed something edgy today," Grandma Peach responded firmly. "Do you ever have those days? If only I could have hit all the chords. Jo's been helping me, but these old hands can't stretch like they used to."

"Who is Jo?" Vika asked.

"Jo?" Grandma Peach paused as they bounced through a pothole. "She's my piano teacher. Not from the beginning, though, I had a lovely young man named Richard when I lived in Maine."

"Your piano—" Vika looked at her incredulously. "You take piano lessons?"

"Well, yes," she shrugged. "I started them about...oh, seven years ago. I started to lose my memory and thought, we can't have that now can we? So I took up piano lessons. It exercises my brain. Oh, dear!"

Grandma Peach yanked the bus to the side of the road and Vika gasped as she grabbed on to the arm of the couch. She felt the tires on the right side bounce off the pavement and crunch on the stones that lined the road.

"Grandma Peach!" Vika called out, as Grandma Peach was already unbuckled and walking down the stairs, Quasi racing behind her. Vika stood up to follow. "Grandma Peach! What—"

Vika stopped abruptly at the top of the stairs when a man in his mid-forties blocked her exit. He wore a pack, a bandana around his head, and dirty clothing. His face was leathery tan, his legs were pure muscle, and he stank. The man looked up at Vika and gave her a warm smile. Quasi wound through his legs and up to Vika, wiggling in happiness.

The idea of him in the bus with them made the bottom of her stomach fall out. "Who are you?" she shot at him. "Where's Grandma Peach?" The man's smile faltered and his eyes shifted with confusion. Vika saw Grandma Peach's arm pat his on the arm and he took a cautious step up into the bus.

"What are you—?"

But Grandma Peach kept shoving him up the stairs and past Vika.

"Meet Macho Nacho!" Grandma Peach said cheerily.

"Hi," Macho Nacho nodded to Vika and hesitantly put out a hand to fist bump.

Of course, he was a hiker. Vika rocked back on her heels, still on edge, wondering why hikers had to look so grungy. She fist bumped the man and stepped to the side, gesturing to the couch. Vika opted to sit on the engine cover next to Grandma Peach and stared at the visitor. Quasi lay down next to her feet.

"Thank you for picking me up," Macho Nacho said, fidgeting as Vika stared him down. She had come to like New Pants, but she also was never locked in a bus with him.

"You're welcome, dear," Grandma Peach called over her shoulder. "I couldn't just leave you on the side of the road. We have a coop set up for hikers. Lots of beds, a shower, just make yourself at home."

Vika stiffly nodded. Macho Nacho returned a tight smile and turned his attention to the window to watch leaves pass by the window.

They turned into the driveway and parked next to the coop. Vika stood up and walked quickly through the heat to the camper while Grandma Peach and Quasi took the new hiker on a tour of the property. Vika pulled the store T-shirt up and over her head and shrugged into a loose fitting shirt she had found on her way through Idaho. After she pulled on a pair of workout shorts, she could feel her muscles relax into the slow hum of late afternoon. She sauntered back into the kitchen and grabbed some cheese and crackers, and quickly inventoried the refrigerator while she was at it. With paychecks coming in, she'd be able to help buy the groceries, too.

Vika twisted off the cap to her iced tea and took a glug. The cool, sweet liquid chilled her mouth and all the way down her esophagus until it spread out in her stomach. She felt more awake and alert almost immediately.

She stepped down into the stuffy heat that existed outside the air-conditioned camper and nearly turned around to curl up on her bed.

Instead, she walked toward the house where she heard the clanging of tools.

"Where's Macho Nacho?" Vika asked, taking a sip of her tea while she watched Grandma Peach heft a hammer in the foyer.

"Putting together his resupply," Grandma Peach explained. "He wants to be back on the trail tonight."

"Ah," Vika said, and then turned her eyes back to the box of tools. "What are we doing today?"

Grandma Peach's eyes twinkled. "Demo."

"Deconstruction!" hollered Dane from somewhere inside the house.

Grandma Peach shrugged, "If there's a hammer in my hand, I assure you it will be demolition."

Vika stepped over scattered pieces of wood and leaned over to grab one of the many hammers in a bucket at the foot of the stairs. "What's the difference?"

A couple loud footsteps sounded behind her. "The difference?" Dane echoed in a loud, full voice. She jumped at his voice, sure he couldn't do anything quietly. "The difference is that demolition uses a crane that swings a ball into a building and eliminates all originality!" He threw up his arms to emphasize his point and continued, "Now, deconstruction is the conscious effort to remove old, worn, crumbling pieces while maintaining authenticity. You have to deconstruct with purpose! With vision! Otherwise you end up with a skeleton and nowhere to go, because a crumbling house is still a house, but a gutted house with no future is just a bunch of two-by-fours. It can't hold heat, can't block the rain, there is no definition. Nothing to tell you where the kitchen is, or the living room. A person could get lost in a house like that. Even a smart person, like you, Vika." He backed into the foyer and waved her to follow him.

She put the hammer back in its place and hurried to catch up. "What are you doing with this house when you're done?"

"With this house?" He was standing in the room he called a dining room, staring at the wall. She walked up to stand next to him, and without looking her way, he passed her a pair of safety goggles. She didn't have to ask; she put them on.

"It's going to be a hiker hostel."

"A hostel?"

"That's what I said, didn't I? Now, back up," he said.

She did.

He swung a hammer out of his tool belt, cocked the hammer back and pounded it into the wall.

She jumped at the noise and her hands came up towards her ears on instinct. She quickly put them back down at her sides as Dane turned to her with a raised eyebrow.

"So we're just—"

BAM! He interrupted her with another hammer blow and she flinched again. Little spider cracks radiated from the point of impact. BAM! He hit the wall a third time and a triangle chunk of plaster popped from the wall and shattered on the floor. Vika slid her shirt over her nose to block some of the particle dust. She could see narrow slats of wood underneath the hole where the plaster fell off.

"OK then," she said.

"This house," Dane explained, "was constructed to last for a hundred and fifty years." He paused and looked pointedly at Vika. "Not the shoddy work people accept now-a-days, houses that last fifty years," he scoffed.

"The floor sags some in the middle of the house, but the walls of the house kept it standing out of grit, will, or spite. That's the only way things should be built, if you ask me." He took a breath, "There are tons of pounds of plaster and lath that hold it up and we are going to take it out and put new in. There are three walls in the entire house that are still in good shape, but it's not worth the work to try to go around them. All of the plaster and lath is coming down. I'm keeping the moldings up, so don't hit them."

"Uh, sure," Vika said. "Where do I put it?"

"You can make separate piles on the floor for now. Jim's dropping off a dumpster tomorrow morning for the plaster, and the lath we might just burn." He turned to walk back towards the foyer. "Hammers are in a bucket near the stairs and masks are in a box on the radiator."

She followed him back and found Grandma Peach pinching the nose of her mask to her face.

"This'll be fun!" came her muted voice.

Vika gave her a smile and then asked Dane, "Are you going to stay here, too?"

"What?" Dane half turned to her. "When?"

Vika jogged three steps to catch up to Dane as he walked back to where he had made the first hole, hammers and masks in their hands. "You know," she started, "when you make this a hostel. Are you going to live here?"

"Don't know."

"Oh," Vika brought the elastic band of the facemask over her ponytail. "Do you get enough hikers through for it to be feasible?"

Dane shrugged, "Doesn't matter."

"It doesn't matter? You won't last very long if you don't get enough revenue."

"Not doing it for revenue."

Vika was confused. "Then why are you doing it?"

"The hikers. Now let's go, or we won't have a house for this to matter anyway."

Vika hesitated, looking at him but the only thing he offered was an impatient wave for her to begin. She stepped up to the wall and was aware of Dane watching with his hands on his hips as she brought the hammer back. *Thud.*

"What was that? This is going to take until the next ice age. We're not tapping in lawn ornaments here."

Vika sighed. She brought back the hammer again and swung it to the plaster a little harder. *Thud.*

"What are you afraid of? Making a hole in the wall?"

"Yeah, come on," Grandma Peach said, "give it a little *oomph*, girl." She held hers like a baseball bat and little bits of plaster exploded outward when she connected.

"Wow," Vika said, impressed, and then shifted her attention to Dane and finished, "maybe you could give me a few hints, instead of just heckling."

"You're right," Dane responded deadpan. "Here, take this hammer, and hit that wall."

Vika glared at him.

"Oh, Dane," Grandma Peach said as she moved closer. "Move your hand down to the bottom. Let the weight of the hammer do the work for you."

Vika cocked the hammer back and swung. *BAM!* A tiny chunk of plaster popped out and hit her dead center in the middle of her forehead. She blinked and leaned forward to inspect the hole and the spider cracks around it. She smiled.

"Good!" Dane said. "Now you only have to do that three thousand more times. Today. Then again tomorrow." Dane turned and walked out.

Vika shook her head and hit the wall again. Grandma Peach started swinging at the wall next to her and soon, bits of the wall zinged around them—tiny bullets in the square room. She turned the hammer around and used the claw to rip out more sections. The wall came down faster and piled around her feet, and she realized it felt really good. So she kept at it, hitting, pounding, yanking, wrenching, twisting, detaching. She felt her heart rate climb slightly and her arm muscles warm.

Vika wondered why Dane was building a house without any concern about his ability to maintain it. He didn't seem like the type to be able to afford it, what with the duct tape that accessorized nearly everything on the property. The camper she and Grandma Peach slept in was decent, though he didn't mention about Grandma Peach staying around to work on a hostel once it was finished.

There wasn't much in the town—definitely not a tourist destination—which left the hikers on a trail twenty miles away as their only source of income. The idea, like so many things about Dane, didn't quite make sense.

Her mind drifted for a couple moments and when it focused again, she thought about her car. She thought about her home. She thought about her future. And her heart rate climbed a little more as she swung faster and faster. She thought back to a week before and the hotel she stayed in, where she received an email from one of her best friends who told her he had gotten accepted into med school. Another friend was doing an internship in the Bahamas and starting a Ph.D. program in the fall counting sea turtles or something. Her arm swung. BAM. BAM.

She was happy for them, and truth be told, a little jealous. She was on that track, too, until she stepped onto the Trail of Deception. BAM. Just weeks earlier, she had left her little hamlet in North Dakota for Boston to get a Big Girl Job at the art museum downtown. She could see herself in a career like that. She could lose herself in the archives for weeks at a time studying the paintings of long dead geniuses, deciphering every brushstroke, every line of perspective, every X-ray of subjects painted and repainted or painted and removed. Every painting was a map to history. To context, to society influence, to patron wealth.

Her résumé was spotless, highlighted by the internship she did at the Met the summer before with an acclaimed Italian Renaissance scholar and, of course, her grades were good. To top it off, a friend of one of her references was the head curator at the museum in Boston, a lovely woman from the emails she and Vika exchanged. During Vika's spring break senior year, she was given a tour of the museum—an exclusive tour—and she thought this made the job a lock. She flew east to what she thought was her future.

Apparently, the economic downturn could sabotage even the best-dealt hand.

The wall was crumbling in front of her.

"Thank you for applying for the position. Unfortunately, we've offered it to another individual with more experience in this particular field. It was a pleasure to meet you and we wish you the best in the future." The secretary left the voicemail exactly one hour and twelve minutes after the end of her interview. The first three times she listened to the voicemail, she listened to the name. It was apparent to her that the message was rejection, but to another individual mistakenly listed with her phone number. The next two times, she concentrated hard to identify the voice that was surely playing a joke on her. The sixth time, she buried her face in her pillow and cried. The life she had envisioned for herself: the apartment, job, status, security, and intellectually stimulating work, would never be more than a "what if."

It was not to happen. Not there, not then. Vika had left her phone on the small bedside table at the hotel so she wouldn't be reminded of the recent destruction of her pride and she walked across the street to the nearest convenience store. She bought a six-pack of her favorite raspberry wheat beer, a pint of her favorite ice cream, and her second-favorite romantic comedy.

It took her exactly an hour and thirteen minutes to realize that was the worst combination of stereotypical vices that could possibly exist. Vika yelled shamelessly at the screen when the female protagonist walked away from "true love" two-thirds of the way into the movie, though she yelled just as loudly when the couple got back together, remembering—though fuzzy—that the words, "Bullshit! Happy endings aren't real!" came out of her mouth. She took an extra large scoop of chocolate cookie dough ice cream to drive the point home.

She went to bed that night feeling depressed, fat, and a little drunk.

The next morning, Vika woke up feeling tired and vengeful. Though instead of writing hate emails or depressing social media updates as a good little 21st-century individual might do, Vika canceled her flight home and called a taxi to take her to the train station. Before she left the parking lot, she turned off her phone and zipped it away in her suitcase.
She needed time to think.

It turned out, an eighteen-hour train ride was not enough time and she rolled out of the taxi in front of her house looking like she had been dragged by her ankles through the Badlands. Her cinnamon-colored hair was knotted and greasy, she hadn't taken off her makeup for two days, and her shoulders drooped with the weight of her career—or lack thereof.

She shuffled wearily up the sidewalk, luggage in tow, through the front door, and towards her bedroom. She heard her mother gasp as she walked by the kitchen and her twin brother, who was using his computer programming degree to manage a local video store in their hometown, said, "Join the club."

Vika passed his shiny Princeton diploma on the wall of the staircase as she climbed towards a shower. Her luggage bounced and flipped as she made her way numbly down the hall to her room. God, she hated that room. It was still a pale pink she had chosen in sixth grade. She was sick of it by high school, but knew she would be leaving for college and was never motivated enough to paint over it. Of course, she never thought she'd be moving back.

No wonder she wasn't getting laid, she thought, as she pulled her suitcase up next to the white dresser on the far wall. Not that she had been looking too hard, though; she was too busy trying to get a job.

The hammer seemed to swing on its own and steadily demolished the wall in front of her. She hit it over and over and over again.

Now she didn't know what she wanted. Maybe she didn't know what she wanted because she couldn't get what she thought she really wanted: a job. A job in which she could use her art history degree. Where she could be in the constant presence of Michelangelos and Albertis and Da Vincis. Oh, what she wouldn't give to work on a Da Vinci. She spent the next three weeks within the four pink walls of her bedroom, searching and applying for any and every job that listed the word "art". She'd make a pot of coffee at six at night and move her workstation to the garage to paint landscapes—they were always the most soothing for her—on any medium she could find. The legs of an old desk that had been on its way to the trash turned into a forest. A watering can transformed into the ocean, and leftover wood from their deck remodeling became an in depth examination of creek beds.

She liked to paint for self-prescribed therapy. She wasn't very good at it, but it was methodical stress relief. In the evenings, the sky would darken, the air would cool, the crickets would come out and she would paint. Hunched over her tubes of color, she mixed and mixed, painted and repainted for hours. Then she would go to bed, wake up, send out another couple handfuls of resumes and paint again.

She had done everything she was told, everything *right*, to make employment happen, and yet, no one was hiring. Or at least, they weren't hiring *her*. God, that voicemail...

No, she wasn't going to think about that right now. She let her head fall back at the same time she closed her eyes and took a deep breath. When she brought her eyes to the wall again, her fingers gripped the hammer with renewed energy.

She hit the wall over and over, this time trying to center her chi until her hands were covered in plaster dust, and the pieces of wall had built up too high on the floor for her to move easily from one spot to another. She looked up and out the window, and saw it was already dusk. She looked around, taking notice that Grandma Peach was nowhere to be seen. Hell, she could have left right after they started and Vika probably wouldn't have noticed.

She looked at the mess around her and the dust plumes that were taking their time to settle. She set the hammer in the corner of the room and moved to the foyer to see what she could find. Her eyes settled on an old snow shovel. She grabbed it and took it back to the room to plow everything into a couple large piles.

Finally satisfied she made an acceptable dent in the mess—and it was getting too dark to see—she put the shovel back and left the house. She moved her aching body slowly, step by step across the grass. Vika rolled her head to the side and back. At last, she reached the door of the camper and pulled it open.

As her foot landed on the bottom step, Grandma Peach cried, "Stop!" Vika looked up, startled. She sat in the armchair reading a paperback, her robe wrapped around her and a cup of tea steaming on an end table next to her. Quasimodo bounced off Grandma Peach's lap and stood at the top of the stairs, looking at Vika with a cocked head.

"Oh, my," Grandma Peach said, using both arms to push herself up. "I'm sorry, but you'll have to get undressed outside. Maybe you could shake out your hair a little, too."

"What? OK, I—"

"Let me get you a towel," Grandma Peach said, as she moved down the hall to the closet.

While Vika waited, she turned toward the glass door that had been fastened opened and stared. A solid layer of white plaster covered her forehead, caked her eyebrows and hair, absent only where the mask had covered her face. Her clothes were no better. She looked down at her feet and could already see she would leave behind two white powder outlines of footprints on the step.

Grandma Peach returned with a towel and held it out. "So much dust," she said, "I just would prefer it stay out of my house. You'll jump in the shower?"

Vika nodded as she took the towel. "Yes," she answered. "Yes, of course, I didn't realize."

She shook out like a dog before she stripped and wrapped herself in a towel. She hung her clothes on the line, not even bothering to bring them in the camper. She'd just put them back on the next morning, might as well be efficient.

Vika entered the camper again, carefully stepped through the kitchen, and finally closed the door to the tiny bathroom behind her before she hung up the towel. At last, her feet met the cool linoleum floor of the shower. She slid the glass door closed and turned the faucet. The warm water tired her, and by the time she finished washing all the plaster dust off, she felt as though someone pushed the gravity button to turbo-charge. Her eyelids drooped in her effort to fight it; her knuckles almost dragged on the floor as she battled it; lifting her foot up and out of the lip of the shower floor was like picking up a boulder. Even her insides felt heavy and her chest wouldn't move to accommodate a deep breath. She pushed and pulled her body, baby step by baby step, until she grabbed her towel, trudged to her suitcase for clean pajamas, and was at last climbing into bed.

"Good night, dear!" she heard Grandma Peach call from her seat in the chair. Vika opened her mouth to say good night back, but she was asleep before she got the chance.

CHAPTER 5

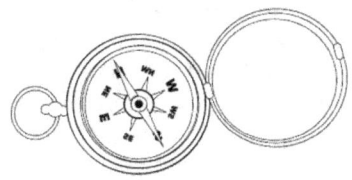

VIKA WOKE THE NEXT morning to muscles that still felt like lead, and a headache pulsed dull in the center of her head. She wiped the drool from her mouth and rolled over with a groan. She could hear and smell bacon sizzling in the kitchen, only about seven feet away, and her stomach grumbled. She decided hunger would indeed win out against lethargy.

But maybe in another two minutes.

Pans clanked and the coffee maker churned and shook while Vika knew it spit out the nectar of the gods.

She took a deep breath and rolled out of her bunk and her feet hit the floor with a DA-DUM. Slowly, carefully, she willed her aching body into the kitchen area.

"For such a small girl," Grandma Peach said with a smile, "you sure do make a lot of noise in the morning." She stirred a skillet of scrambled eggs with just about every available vegetable scrambled in, and Quasi lifted his head slightly from his position at Grandma Peach's feet when Vika entered.

Vika half chuckled, but stopped short as the effort made her head hurt worse. She cringed and reached for the coffee pot.

"Just some soreness," she answered, pulling a mug out of the cupboard with the other hand.

"Ah, ah," Grandma Peach said, guiding Vika's hand with the coffee pot back to its place on the burner. "Do you have a headache? You need water. Hydration. I have some Gatorade mix over there, too."

Vika sighed and knew she was right and the coffee would have to wait. "Yes," she said, long and drawn out. "Where's the Gatorade?"

She mixed it in the mug she got for coffee and guzzled one full mug before mixing another for her meal.

They ate quietly, slowly. The night had not cooled much and Vika's shirt stuck to her skin from the humidity.

"Maybe it's good," Grandma Peach said, breaking the silence and Vika paused to look up.

"What's good?"

"Your headache, dear. The way you're so sore. Maybe it's good."

"You lost me, Grandma Peach," Vika said. "Why would that be good?"

"Well," she suggested, "maybe you're finally letting some tension out since you've been here. And you've had a lot. Stress relief—" She shrugged. "—that's what it feels like."

"Oh," Vika looked down at her food. As a matter of fact, she did feel as though she was on the edge of a marathon for the several days—maybe weeks, she couldn't remember anymore—not sleeping soundly, not quite feeling comfortable.

Until last night.

She poked at her eggs. "Yeah, maybe."

She finished her bacon and poured herself a cup of coffee, ignoring the raised eyebrow of Grandma Peach. "I never said I had strong willpower," she told her.

They finished up and went into the house to continue stripping the walls. The dust had settled on the piles of plaster Vika created the night before, the lath exposed up to about six feet, the height limit of her hammer swing.

Dane was already busy atop a stepladder, pounding away at the plaster that was left on the wall as well as the plaster on the ceiling. He stopped as they entered.

"Jim came by this morning," he explained. "Dumpster's behind the house. Plaster goes in there. Lath goes behind the barn a little. I already have a pile of old wood from the porch. We'll burn it later."

"You got it, boss." Vika grabbed a pair of gloves and a bucket to throw the plaster into. After she tossed some in, she hefted it up and shuffled out the door-hole in the front of the house, down the stairs of the porch and around the back.

A ladder leaned against the side of the dumpster, and she climbed to grab a hold on the top with one hand and boost the bucket up with the other. The plaster pieces tumbled out and a silent plume of dust rose up from where it landed.

She did this over and over—into the house, out to the dumpster, into the house, out to the dumpster—until Dane had moved on to another room and she had cleared the dining room.

Vika used the claw on the hammer and started pulling at the lath. The nails held fast and squeaked in protest as she pulled them from the wall support after more than one hundred years. Some boards broke, some pulled off and left the nail behind, and some popped off easily. By lunchtime, the three of them had the living room and the dining room down to the two-by-fours. The day was long and hot, Grandma Peach escaped to the air-conditioned camper for much of the afternoon, but Dane and Vika continued to work hard.

DANE MET VIKA OUTSIDE standing next to the motorcycle the next morning. "You're going to take it to work, right?"

"Dane," Vika stuttered, "I don't know if I'm ready to—"

"You'll be fine," Dane said. "There's no traffic around here. You go slow enough anyway that even if you drive off into the jingleweeds again you probably won't get hurt."

"Oh, that's comforting," Vika said.

"Right," Dane nodded. "Well, practice makes…good enough. Hop on."

Vika was frozen for a moment, though, picturing herself crashing one hundred and eight different ways. Then she thought back to her practice session. It *was* mostly flat, she reasoned, and there *wasn't* much traffic on the road.

"What?" Dane said. "I can lend you the bus instead."

She was puttering down the driveway on the motorcycle two and a half minutes later, engulfed in a leather jacket from Dane and the massive helmet. She turned on the road and the rear tire jumped on the pavement. She opened the throttle a little and the engine roared underneath her. She looked at the shifter near her foot, and eased her toe up to it and underneath. A truck flew by her going the same direction and she white-knuckled the handlebars as dust and little stones flew up, hearing one bounce off her helmet. Her foot was already back on its peg, safely away from the shifter as she bounced down the road at a steady ten miles per hour. Later. She would work on shifting out of first later.

It felt like an eternity, but at last she pulled into the parking lot, and eased up to a spot in the back of the lot. Right into the curb at the end of it. She bounced off, cursing the footbrake that did not work as firmly as she thought it would, and looked around to make sure no one had seen. It didn't look like it, but she'd find out soon enough. She pocketed the key— just in case, she'd never hear the end of it if someone stole that piece of crap on her watch—pulled off the helmet and patted down her hair as best she could.

The bell tinkled with her entrance, a cashier she hadn't met yet reading a magazine at one of the registers.

"Hi, I'm Vika," she said.

The cashier looked up from her reading material. "Jordan."

"Is Ted here?" Vika asked, walking behind the counter.

Jordan shrugged. "I think he went to the post office or somewhere. He said you'll be on my register today."

"Great," Vika answered and stuffed the leather jacket Dane had lent her into a shelf under the counter.

She stood behind the counter looking out into the empty store. She rolled her shoulders forward, and then she rolled them backward. They were tight and sore and didn't loosen up even the slightest, despite all her efforts. She was sure she wouldn't have this problem if she weren't susceptible to existentialist tendencies that had her driving around in the mountains aimlessly, ripping out walls in a Victorian house.

The door from the kitchen swung open and instead of Jill, an older man who looked to be in his sixties, walked into the storefront carrying a stack of pasta salads. His head was nearly bald, and thick glasses sat on a large nose. He had some extra pounds on him, but he carried it well. He was tall, possibly as tall as Dane, maybe an inch or two shorter. His buttoned-down shirt was tucked neatly into black pressed pants, with wingtips to finish the look.

"Hey, Smith," Jordan said, "How's it going?"

He gave a nod, "I'm back for another day, aren't I?" His gaze shifted to Vika. "New girl?"

"I'm Vika," she said, giving her best first-impression smile.

"Nice to meet you, Vika," he said, without a smile. He quietly went over to the cooler and swapped out old salads for new before going back to the kitchen.

"And that's Smith," Jordan said, as the kitchen door shut behind him.

"Ah. He's a talker."

"Sure is."

The day was uneventful and Vika was assigned some cleaning busywork, but she didn't really mind. Her shift seemed to go by quickly, and before she knew it, she was punching out.

IT WAS JORDAN she worked with the next two days and Jordan's shift she covered on Saturday morning. Smith worked each shift with her.

Vika was behind the counter when Smith chose that moment to walk out of the kitchen waving a five-dollar bill. "All right, kid," he said to Vika, "give me a winner."

She walked over to the scratch-offs.

"How'd you get stuck with Saturday?" she asked him as she tore off two two-dollar tickets and handed him a single back.

"I'm just a nice guy," he answered. Then he shrugged and said, "Jill had to go to a dance recital or something for her goddaughter."

"Oh," Vika said, and then gestured to the tickets, "good luck with those."

"Pfft," he responded, "you say that to everyone."

"Only to you."

He looked at his two tickets, one in each hand, and then waved them like they had wet ink on them.

Like he did every morning.

Then he grabbed a penny from the penny dish and went to work on the tickets.

Like he did every morning.

"Smith," Vika started.

He grunted in response, his focus concentrated on the tickets.

"Do you take in hikers?" she asked.

He raised an eyebrow at her and went back to scratching his tickets. "No. Why?"

She bit her lip. "Dane and Grandma Peach take them in all the time. They pick up a lot of hitchhikers, too."

"Oh, good for them," he remarked. He was standing up straight, looking down through his bifocals at the numbers. "Ten bucks, would you look at that."

He handed her the ticket, which she scanned and handed him his winnings. "Do a lot of people take them in?"

Smith thought for a moment, and then said, "No. Five or six years ago there was a couple who let them camp in their yard, but they moved to Arizona to be with their kids and grandkids."

"Is it…dangerous?"

"Dangerous? No, not dangerous," he said as he shoved the ten bucks into his pocket. "The trail is like a family, Vika. Not a family that you're used to, but a family. Sometimes it's the only reminder that we have that strangers still help each other. Blindly. Like Dane and Grandma Peach. I don't even know if they understand why people would want to hike for thousands of miles or whatever the hikers do. They support them anyway. They don't care the reason, they just want to help."

He bent to grab a box of markers he used to mark his pasta with and again straightened. "After all," he said plainly, "they took you in, didn't they?"

Vika bit her lip. They did. They asked no questions, just opened the door to her without any questions or conditions. She was just one of the wanderers without a bed. She felt embarrassed for asking the question to Smith, the question she realized now was based in extreme hypocrisy.

Smith had disappeared into the kitchen. Luckily, the bell tinkled with the entrance of two customers.

She straightened her back, put on a smile, and pushed the discussion to the back of her mind. At least she would not be left alone to wallow.

"Good morning. How can I help you?" she asked flawlessly.

CHAPTER 6

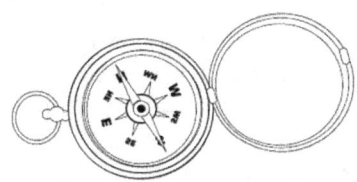

IT WAS DAYS BEFORE Vika worked in the garden at the Dancys'. Most of the planting had been done long before she got there and other than weeding, there wasn't much to do. Vika was in need of fresh air, though, so weeding it was.

"I hope we have lots of tomatoes this year," Grandma Peach said, "and zucchini. I love to make zucchini bread."

"That sounds delicious," Vika agreed as she was on her knees, pulling up the resistant invading flora. "What else do you have growing in here?"

"Oh," Grandma Peach sighed as she straightened her back and thought about it. "Carrots," she said. "Radishes." They started to come to her faster. "Beans, squash, tomatoes, pumpkins, about six different kinds of potatoes, corn, and we have blueberries and blackberries on the edge over there," she gestured to the edge of the lawn, "of course, you already know where those are. And there are a few apple trees behind the coop. I've been trying to get them under control, but no one's lived here for six years. It's difficult. Though, I got a box full of good applesauce out of them last fall."

"Wow," Vika said, "sounds like you have a lot going on."

"Oh, yes," Grandma Peach answered fervently. "It all goes well with the chicken."

They worked in comfortable quietude for much of the morning, breaking once for the sweet tea Grandma Peach had in the camper.

When a car pulled up in the early afternoon, Grandma Peach put down her trowel and gardening gloves, called Quasi to come visit with Judy, and walked over to the driveway. Vika put her trowel down as well and went to meet the new group of hikers who hitched the ride into town.

Sasquatch stood at least a foot taller than Vika, with legs bigger than her waist, hair down to his shoulders and a beard that could hide an entire family of birds. Candle Maker was the second one to grab his pack out of the trunk and walk over to Vika and Grandma Peach. His dark skin glistened with sweat and he smiled wide.

"Man," he said, "that house is great. How long you guys had it?"

By this time, the third hiker, Jason—or rather, No Trail Name Jason, as Candle Maker called him—and Dane had joined the group. Vika, slowly getting used to unkempt strangers in desperate need of a bath showing up on their property, smiled at the lot of them.

"Last September," Dane explained to Candle Maker, "but we couldn't really do much. We just boarded up and waited for warmer weather. We have a ways to go, but she's a gem, isn't she?"

Judy chuckled, "If it were up to me, I would have knocked it down and started over."

Dane glared at her. "Knocked it down?"

Vika felt bad for the woman, she was at least seventy years old and stood there staring at Dane, her mouth open, eyes wide, clearly wondering what she said wrong.

"Knock it—why would anyone—how could I—No!" he exclaimed. "I didn't knock it down because it wasn't a lost cause! Its problem was that everyone who owned it added to it, but no one cared enough to re-construct along the way. Just add, add, add. Then what do we get? We get a house that is so weighed down by everyone's shit and problems they dumped in here, no one wanted to clean it up. No one wanted to get their hands dirty because it was easier to cover up a crack in the plaster by a goddamn knockoff Monet."

"Oh, my," quietly escaped Judy as she brought her hand up to her throat.

"That's all it was, too much extraneous bullshit. There's still a house here," he declared. "There's still potential, there's still a reason to re-construct. What will we have when we're done? We'll have a house that can breathe again. We'll have a house based in old, timeless ideologies, filled with modern ideas. We'll have a house people can come to and enjoy, and it won't have anything to do with money or connections or bloodlines or politics or lifestyles, because I don't give a fuck about that." Judy flinched at the word and Grandma Peach glared at her son.

Of course, Dane seemed unfazed. In fact, he seemed energized by her wide eyes. "Not. One. Single. Fuck," he said. "If you know this house exists, you are more than welcome to enter through the hole where other people would put a door."

Judy looked as though she was on the verge of a stroke, heart attack, ulcer, or all of the above.

"She sure is a gem," Candle Maker re-directed the conversation gracefully. "What are you putting on the roof? Slate?"

Dane let his gaze slide away from the old woman and smiled with all of his teeth. "Sure am! I was in Buffalo a couple months ago and met up with a slate contractor there. Young kid, maybe a little older than you. Knows his stuff, though. I have an order of semi-weathering sea green with ten percent variegated purple coming at the end of the month."

"Why not just use shingles?" Vika asked, not having a damn clue what he just rambled off. Most of the buildings on her college campus had slate and it looked regal, but to put on a house in the mountains? It didn't seem practical.

"Only those who hate nature use shingles!" Dane boomed, still feeding off his anger generated by Judy's remark about knocking down the house.

She shook her head at his catchall opinion. "That's not true at all. It's affordable."

Dane responded without so much as a blink, "So is cardboard, but you don't see people making houses out of that, do you? Shingles are not heat efficient, they have to be replaced all the time, and the production of them releases carbon dioxide and other shit into the air. You want to save a polar bear? Get a slate roof. Save a polar bear and support the arts, all in one move."

Dane marched off towards the house, and Sasquatch, Candle Maker, and No Trail Name Jason weren't far behind. The hikers left their packs under the closest tree and Dane led them up the stairs of the porch, chatting the entire way. Sasquatch looked intrigued, Jason just looked tired, and Candle Maker was all smiles, asking questions, pointing to this and that, which of course just fueled the fire for Dane. She imagined they might be digging up clay to make their own kitchen tiles by the end of the night.

Vika turned her focus back to the women. "Good group of guys," said Judy hesitantly, as she watched them walk across the yard, and Dane was far enough away to offer any other commentary. "They said they're doing the trail in three and a half months. I can't imagine! To be young again." She turned her attention to Vika and smiled. "You must be Vika."

"Hi," she said and put out her hand.

"Oh, where are my manners!" Grandma Peach exclaimed. "Yes, this is Vika. Vika this is Judy. We're in Bible Club together."

"My, you are a pretty young thing, just like Grandma Peach said." For the second time, Judy muttered, "To be young again."

The women chatted more, and Vika excused herself and went back into the house to locate her hammer. She could hear Dane and the group of hikers upstairs, toward the back of the house.

Vika didn't notice Candle Maker walk up behind her until he said, "Want some help?"

She turned with a start and after a beat or two she answered, "Sure. Um, we're just taking down the plaster and lath now. There are some hammers and masks in the foyer."

Candle Maker nodded excitedly and turned to find supplies. He returned a moment later. "All right. Tell me what to do!"

"Basically," Vika said, "you just hit the wall with a hammer. Be careful around the moldings and obviously the radiators."

"Cool," he answered, giving the room a once over. "Sounds easy enough."

"So, Candle Maker," Vika inquired, "what has been your favorite part of the trail so far?"

"I've never built a house before," he chuckled. "Haven't torn one down I guess I should say," he corrected. "This is really cool what you all are doing."

Vika felt a little pang of unease in the pit of her stomach. She didn't consider herself one of the "all" that lived here. She happened on this house by...good luck? Bad luck? Either way, it wasn't *her* house, but she didn't tell him that.

Instead, she said, "Yeah, Dane is really unique like that. So other than this house, what are you going to remember when you go home?"

Candle Maker exhaled loudly as he thought, a bucket of plaster in his hand and his eyebrows scrunched together. "I hope I remember it all. I really do. The good, the bad, everything. We were caught in a snowstorm in the Sierra and had to go out Kearsarge Pass for more food. ... I saw my first bear on the trail—and second, and third. ... We saw a forest fire start in Northern California. ... Yeah, I'll remember that one for a while," Candle Maker said, thinking.

They turned back to the wall and yanked at it with the claws of their hammers. "So, what's the best story you've heard from the hiker trash that comes through?"

"Well," Vika said, "there was only New Pants." She pounded at the wall a couple times. "He came in the same day I did."

"Sure, sure," Candle Maker said. "We never met him. He must have passed us while we were sleeping because he just showed up in the registries in Northern California." He shrugged and looked back to her. "Well, this is only the beginning. You're going to hear a lot of crazy stuff this summer."

"Why do you call each other 'hiker trash'?" Vika asked.

Candle Maker shrugged. "Because we're pretty trashy." He chuckled. "Dirty, smelly, expert moochers, and we're awesome at gear repair with...well, trash. All in good fun."

Vika laughed, "I guess that makes sense."

She shifted and stepped up to the bottom stair. "So what do you do when you're not hiking?" Vika asked.

"Kind of figuring that out," Candle Maker answered. "I'm just out."

"Just graduated?" Vika asked as she swung at the plaster.

"Military," he said. "I went to college. Well, quit my junior year to enlist."

"What branch?"

"Navy."

Vika nodded, "Not a lot of places hiring?"

He raised a shoulder and let it drop. "To be honest," he said, "I haven't really looked. I planned this before I my contract was up. What about you? I take it you're not normally in construction?"

"I, uh," Vika stumbled, looking for the words, "same as you, I guess, trying to figure it out. I went to school for art history."

"What do you want to do with it?"

"I, well, I want to work at the Met. Eventually. I mean, I've applied lots of places for something, anything really. But so far, nothing." Something about that sentence didn't taste exactly...right. Her voiced trailed off at the end of it and she cleared her throat to cover up her fumble.

Dane walked into the room. "Dinner's in about fifteen. Grill's warm, I'm going to throw on the burgers and dogs now."

He twirled the hammer into his belt and walked out the hole for the door whistling.

CHAPTER 7

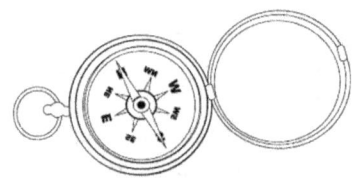

THE NEXT SUNDAY CAME and Grandma Peach left early to drop the three hikers off in the mountains, and then take the bus into town to attend a service.

Dane woke up late and had a cup of coffee on the porch. Vika, bored of the camper, went to join him. Neither spoke. Vika because she didn't know what to say to Dane, and Dane because he reveled in silence. Or other people's discomfort of silence. Vika was unsure which. So they sipped their coffee and watched the harsh grass grow.

Grandma Peach returned two hours later, pearls around her neck and chatting about the church gossip. She asked Dane to bring her a chicken for dinner, and when he did, Vika almost wretched all over the porch. Grandma Peach took the headless chicken and hung it up in the sink of the coop, putting a bowl underneath the neck, its cream-colored wings falling open. Vika was about to ask what the bowl was for, when the first drop of blood fell into it. Grandma Peach was oblivious—or unconcerned—for the trauma Vika was going through and moved to put a pot of water on the stove.

"And then Myrtle," she continued, "now, Myrtle is getting older and she's having trouble with her eyes. Well, she was on the way to see her grandbabies and got pulled over by the cops. For driving too slow! Isn't that something?"

She continued to chatter about at least half of the congregation, and Vika found that she didn't mind listening; Grandma Peach was a great storyteller, even though the stories were not ones to remember. When she finished one about the Millers' new baby who was almost eleven pounds, she went up on her tiptoes and lifted the lid of the pot.

"Dear, can you go get me that chicken?" Grandma Peach asked over the erupting bubbles.

Vika swallowed hard, "Yeah. Yeah, sure." She walked slowly over to the sink and stared at the body. She closed her eyes, took a deep breath and counted to ten, and tried not to pass out. She wanted nothing to do with handling a freshly executed chicken. Vika didn't feel the ground smack her in the face, so she opened up her eyes. She opened and shut her clammy palms, shook out her hands, and moved to the hooks around the chicken's feet. The scaly legs felt cold and bony against her hands and she bit back a shriek. It took everything she had to resist dropping the headless chicken on the floor. *Plop.* Shit, she thought. Red blood on the cream-colored tile was not exactly feng shui. *Plop.* Shit! She swung around. The bowl! The bowl, where was the goddamn bowl? *Plop.* She snagged it off the counter and held it under the neck. Once she was certain she could maintain an effective carrying method, she walked quickly across the coop to the stove, swallowing down bile.

"Thank you, dear," Grandma Peach said pleasantly, and grabbed the chicken by the feet from Vika's hands. She plunked it down into the water. "Whoa, now. You're a fat one, ain'tchya? Almost made the water spill! But it'll loosen your feathers right up," she soothed the dead chicken.

"It's nice," Grandma Peach said, watching the chicken as the bubbles quieted, "to create a meal, dear. To know how it came and how it went. It's a lovely feeling to have just a fraction more control of day-to-day operations.

"The first time I plucked a chicken, I was eight. My grandparents used to have a coop, and I'd have to go in and collect the eggs.

"I eventually went to college and away from the farm. Then I married, had kids, and little Dane brought an egg home for an experiment. We never ate that chicken, but I remembered my grandparents' coop and I talked my husband into building a shed. I wanted our family to be more sustainable, and what better place to have it than in our own backyard?" Grandma Peach smiled. "It was wonderful. We put in the work, saw the result, and we were able to survive a bit more independently off of the effort. It's the same reasoning with our garden. To be able to support yourself, to report only to yourself, is empowering." Grandma Peach spoke with ease as she continued to putter around the kitchen, grabbing necessities for the meal.

"Some people test themselves to live by only the things they can carry on their back. It is just as empowering. That is why people—some of them at least—hike thousands of miles. That is why we support them, dear. That sense of dignity is so important. Whether it's hiking 2,600 miles, starting a garden, or moving to a new home. For us to be able to support that feeling and give them clean sheets and clothes for a night, well, I wouldn't want to do anything else." Grandma Peach ended her speech with a content sigh while Vika looked down at her feet, thinking about her last conversation with Smith. How could she think that the Dancys were reckless for taking in hikers? Her self-pity spiral was interrupted by Grandma Peach. "Now, Vika, can you grab me a garbage bag from under the sink?"

The chicken morphed into a succulent dish over the course of the day, carefully decorated with potatoes, greens, red peppers, butter, and seasonings. Once they were all seated around the table in the camper, Grandma Peach stood at the head and put a knife to the breast of the meal. She placed a juicy piece of meat on each of their plates.

Dane took his wine glass, lifted it in a toast and said, "Here's to the Pacific Crest Trail."

Vika took a small sip of wine to the trail worthy of a toast, and she remembered he said the same toast a week earlier over the lemon-peppered chicken—the chicken! Oh, the thought had not even passed through her mind at the time...

Though, she couldn't deny the chicken was delicious. More than delicious, really. The potatoes were delicious. The beans were delicious. Everything she had on her plate filled her mouth with flavor each time she chewed. The table was quiet for a long while as the three of them enjoyed the feast, until Dane finally spoke.

"There's a small college outside of Seattle that called and asked if I wanted to teach a six-week course. Won't be until October." He took a bite of the potatoes.

"Oh, that's wonderful!" Grandma Peach said, excited. "Are you going to take it? You'll be so close to Cassie!"

"Yes," he said, "the hikers will be gone by then, most of the house will be done."

"What do you teach?" Vika asked and carefully placed a measured piece of chicken in her mouth. Big enough that she got sustenance, not too big that would give her trouble, and if conversation would require, she would be able to swallow the piece and answer a question in relative swiftness. She had her mother to thank for that one. Praise the heavens for debutante classes.

"Studio art," Dane declared.

Vika swallowed the chicken, and despite its calculated size, it almost shot down the wrong pipe. Welding, carpentry, mechanics of any kind, OK. But studio art? That was unexpected. "Oh, that must be interesting," Vika said neutrally. "I got my degree in art history."

"Sure, sure," Dane nodded, "I always have a history lecture or two somewhere in my course."

"Where is it you teach?" she put another not too big, not too small piece of chicken in her mouth.

"Here and there."

Grandma Peach let out the most lady-like snort Vika had ever heard in her life. It topped her mother's.

Dane ignored the extra input, whether words or otherwise, and said, "I've done seminars and workshops open to the public, and there was Northwestern, Vassar, Chestertown University, Bos—"

"Tell her why you left Chestertown University," Grandma Peach edged in, looking at her son.

"What a bunch of close-minded—"

"Just tell her why you left."

"Fuckin' politics. Everyone's so goddamn concerned about--"

"He was asked to do a lecture of Christianity—art based—for a religious studies class and named his lecture: Cryptozoology 101," Grandma Peach put in, lacking patience to wait for Dane to finish with his derogatory remarks. Vika rolled her lips in and tried her hardest not to laugh.

"It was a little humor to break the tension," Dane finally said.

"Humor?" Grandma Peach nearly roared. "Humor? You equated the Lord with Bigfoot!" She jabbed a fork in his direction and looked at Vika. "In the Bible Belt, too. He insulted most of the lecture hall within three seconds of his first presentation." Grandma Peach looked at Vika with an exasperated smirk. "It was also a required freshman course at this school."

"That doesn't mean they have to be mentally constipated," Dane said as he leaned back, defensiveness prickling at the back of his neck. "That's why I don't bother with intro classes anymore. Anything with 'general' and 'studies' in the same breath is a joke. Haven't they been studying generally for the first eighteen years of their lives? Normally I teach upper levels so I don't have to deal with that closed-minded bullshit."

"Oh, is that really necessary?" Grandma Peach looked irritated.

"Well," Vika shrugged, "it sounds like you should have gotten a warning maybe, but fired?"

"The daughter of the president of the University was in the class," Grandma Peach said, daintily scooping green beans on her fork. "A devout Christian, I might add—"

"Oh, please!" Dane exclaimed. "That girl would spread her legs faster than you could say Mary Magdalene."

"Dane, watch your mouth at the dinner table!"

He clapped his hands on the table. "That girl screwed more people than Bernie Madoff! She—"

"Dane Joseph Dancy! I said watch your mouth at the dinner table! And, that's...just...that's..." She sputtered, a slight pink glow in her cheeks.

"I'm not judging growing up. But there's growing up," Dane told Grandma Peach, "and then there's syphilis with a side of herpes." The pink glow in Grandma Peach's cheeks turned a dark red. Dane turned to Vika. "Frankly," he said. "I didn't want to know this. I wish students would keep more shit to themselves than they do, but word gets around."

Vika nodded in agreement, hoping her own cheeks weren't as inflamed as Grandma Peach's. Most times, she just ignored gossip. Really, it was complicated enough to figure out her own relationships, let alone bother with other people's. Her mother never concerned herself with giving advice about matters of the heart, so she had to figure it out on her own. The only thing she ever said to Vika about sex was as she left Vika's dorm room the day Vika moved in freshman year.

"Don't give it away if you can't define it," she'd said. Come to think of it, Vika didn't even know if she meant it to be about sex, or love, or toothpaste.

Either way, Vika applied to that tidbit of advice to her past relationships—whatever the meaning of it was—and knew what she had given to whom and what she kept to herself.

Grandma Peach held her glare at her son and Vika could see Dane quietly surrender.

Eventually, the silence became unbearable.

"So," Vika said, trying to keep the amusement from her voice, "it'll be nice to be so close to Cassie."

Dane nodded.

"Have you called her to come out, yet?" Grandma Peach said.

Dane shook his head. "Not yet. I'm trying to figure out the best time for her to visit." He scooped the last scrap of food from his plate and exchanged his fork for his glass of wine and leaned back.

"Does she like hiking?" Vika asked.

Dane shrugged. "Sure," he answered and sipped. "She's outdoorsy. She's not going to hike the PCT, but she's outdoorsy."

"Oh," Vika chewed her last piece of potato. "She might like it when more of the pack comes through. You know, to hear the stories and stuff."

"Oh, yes!" Grandma Peach said enthusiastically, "She would love the hikers! They'll be coming in what? Another month?"

"Should be," Dane answered. "By then, we should have most of the debris cleared out of the house and we could have some more living areas, too."

"Sounds perfect," Grandma Peach said. "Ask her."

GRANDMA PEACH HAD A PIANO LESSON early the next morning, and Vika lounged in the empty camper for a while before putting on her work clothes. Vika and Dane found themselves in the same room of the house, prying off boards of the house. They worked without conversation for nearly an hour.

Dane was the first to speak.

"Which era is your favorite?" he asked.

"Era? Of art?" she clarified.

"That's what you said you went to school for, right?" Dane stood there, holding a hammer cocked back. He was half turned, as though he expected this discussion to last only a couple seconds.

"The Renaissance," she answered without having to think about it. "Italian, mostly."

"The Age of Enlightenment!" Dane's voice echoed through the house. "A worthy subject for scrutiny. Why is it your favorite?" His blue eyes focused on her.

"I, um," she bit her lip—he caught her off guard. "The, um, discoveries of earth, art, nature, were so extensive?"

"Are you asking me?" Dane said, swinging the hammer back and forth like a pendulum at his side. Vika mentally kicked herself for her response. She *loved* the Renaissance; it was her future, right? Oh, god, she was asking herself *that*? Of course it was! She mentally kicked herself again and—

"The combination of art and nature is my favorite part. I mean, it was really the first time—and the only time since—they were one and the same," she felt her argument come to the forefront of her mind. She charged on, "They were beautiful and so realistic. Well, I suppose they were idealistic based in a realistic anatomy study."

She paused for Dane to respond, but Dane was Dane, and he stood there, again holding the hammer cocked back. Still half turned.

"I mean," Vika continued, "they understood their subjects. Not just intellectually, but physically. They knew the muscles of the body, which ones would be flexed in certain positions and how that would twist and turn and, well, affect the body in other ways."

Dane let the hammer fall to his side and he turned to face her. His blue eyes remained fixed on hers, focused, unblinking. There was no judgment, no move for argument or discussion, simply...intrigue.

"Faces, body language. There is one, Raphael did it, I think. With the Virgin Mary, Jesus, and John the Baptist. Jesus is probably two, maybe three, and the way he leans against his mother is...so *exact* for a two-year-old."

"I know the one," he said.

"Their art was not a model in a studio. It was a study of the human body. A complete observation. It was like they visualized the body—structure, function, all of it, from the inside out. From the layers of the muscles to the marrow of the bones." Vika had taken anatomy and physiology for this purpose—to understand the paintings further, to try and comprehend how and why these artists chose specific postures, shadows, etc. It was a false study, she thought, to examine only the surface.

She had taken a biology class in horticulture that coincided with an art history class in Renaissance gardens. She learned about xylems and phloems and photosystems…she could go on and on. It was for art, she had told herself, even though she loved the classes. Why would a flower would be placed here, or here, or next to this type of tree, pruned, trimmed, and grafted in this manner? She liked the mechanics of paintings. The color mixtures to create a specific hue. Brushstrokes to define land and sky, the perfect placement of a subtle shadow to give a form life, depth.

The mechanical manipulation of the structures interested her more than the genetics manipulations people were capable of in the current century. She liked mechanical. It was easier to shape.

It was easier to fix.

"That type of art doesn't exist today," Vika continued, "because the people that are focusing that much on the human body are physicians, physical therapists, exercise consultants."

Dane answered with, "If Michelangelo lived today, he would be a doctor."

Vika looked hard at him. "A doctor!"

"What? You just said so yourself."

"No, I didn't. He was one of the most brilliant artists ever to have lived."

"Well, yes he was, because he had such brilliant engineering skills and understanding of the human body. Just like you said. Da Vinci, too."

Vika raised her eyebrows. "Come on. If anyone is more well-known for his art than Michelangelo, it's Da Vinci."

"Even the great tend to drift towards a reliable source of income. Doesn't make it any less true he was a master of his craft. Have you ever seen Da Vinci's levers and models of planes, parachutes, saw mills?"

"No, I…" Vika scrunched her eyebrows, "I've heard of them but we focused on his art in art history. What do you mean about income?"

"The Renaissance was in the thirteen, fourteen hundreds right?"

"Yes."

"Who held power?"

Vika frowned. "The kings, royalty, the—"

"The Church, Vika."

"Well, yes, but—"

"The Church held power."

"OK, but—"

"And the Medicis—kind of one and the same. Death held power, too. People are afraid of death. Always have been, always will be. Waste of time if you ask me." Dane rattled on, quickly, as he was prone to do, his eyes losing contact with Vika's and the conversation becoming a monologue of thoughts. He continued, "Sounds like too much effort to worry about something that will inevitably happen. I mean, what are they researching these days? Cryogenics? Well, I guess they've been on that kick for a while now. That and gene therapy. They put so much money into curing every disease under the sun." He shrugged. "I can understand that, I suppose, you don't want to see people suffer. But they're still going to die. Everyone's going to die and it's probably not going to be very pretty, whether it's at fifty or eighty. The point is, you can't get around death, you can just make it more of a tragedy."

"What does that have to do with the Church?" Vika interrupted.

Dane looked at her, confused, as she watched him mentally retrace the steps of their conversation to pick up where they left off. "Well," he said at last, "the cryogenics of the Renaissance was prayer. Prayer would get them to Heaven so they could live forever. Or they'd have themselves painted into pictures with Mary and Jesus so they could get to Heaven. People paid big money to stay out of Hell. And who is going to back that campaign? I'll give you a hint. It wasn't the blacksmith on the corner of the street. Hospitals would have murals upon murals of Heaven and Hell for the dying to make any last-minute decisions if they happened to be on the wrong side of God's word."

Vika was silent. Of course she knew political motivations of the paintings, but in comparison to…cryogenics? He was insane, that's all. He liked to blast through these far-fetched ideas by the handful, not waiting for the listener to catch up. By the time she had wrapped her head around one, Dane had moved through about six other ideas and Vika was left standing there with a stupid look on her face. God, it was frustrating.

"They had to have someone to paint those, Vika," he said. "A bishop wouldn't be hiring someone to paint the Sistine Chapel if they painted flat eyes and hands that looked like dead fish. The only guys out there with the talent were the ones able to put those features on a grid, make proportions. Skills an engineer would have. A mathematician, a doctor, a scientist. These were the Da Vincis, Michelangelos, Raphaels, hell, all the Ninja Turtles. Donatello, too. He was my favorite."

"Dürers," Vika interjected quietly.

"Oh, yes, fantastic watercolors," murmured Dane. "Anyway, people go where the money is, and money is where the hope of immortality lives. Then it was art, now it is science and technology," he finished, his eyes bright and his cheeks taunt with a smile Vika knew hid under his beard. He turned back to the wall and started to pry loose the wood panel.

"Well," Vika stumbled over her words, "but if they could…they may have still chosen to be artists."

"Yeah," Dane said over the sound of a few pieces of lath hitting the floor, "and maybe Dr. Schweble would have, too, if he trained that hand of his to paint landscapes, instead of spending his money on med school so he could shove a camera up my ass."

Vika rolled her eyes. "God, you are so offensive," she muttered.

"Vika," he said exasperated, "a child can go down a number of paths. That path may split to a number of other paths, and on and on, each getting more specific and further from being a blank canvas, a blastula, a seed, a whatever. How would you backtrack and go down a different path? How do you pick a path to begin with? How do you choose?" He pursed his lips as he jammed the claw of the hammer under a nail and yanked. "A lot of it," he continued, "can fall into the same reason people murder: love, money, and revenge."

Vika's hands flew up. "Dane!" she said. "That makes no sense. You're comparing choosing careers to murder?"

"I'm just saying that similar things motivate people in different situations. Like I said before, money is where the hope of immortality lives. Everyone wants to be immortal, right?" He cocked his head to the side and looked at the ceiling. "Though, I suppose with choosing careers you could swap out revenge for nepotism." He nodded after a moment of thought. "Yes, that makes sense. People choose jobs based on love, money, or nepotism. I had a friend in high school who became CEO of a toothpick factory. That had to be a hoot. Full of excitement, I'm sure."

"Dane."

"Raphael was an orphan by the time he was eleven," he rambled on, "you can count nepotism out for that one. Da Vinci, too. He was born out of wedlock. So that leaves love and money." He yanked at a piece of lath.

"Well, following your insane logic, love's still in the running. They couldn't paint like they did without a love for it," said Vika.

"Don't Gatsby the Ninja Turtles. My bet's money. Maybe a little love and a lot of money." Dane shrugged, still facing away from her and at the wall.

"Haven't you ever done anything for love?"

"Sure," he answered and yanked out more of the wall. "When I was young and stupid. It got me a couple years of indentured servitude and ended with half my shit in Seattle."

Vika put her hands on her hips. "You also got a *daughter*."

"Sure. And I would do anything for her. But that's a different kind of love. One you can't even begin to fathom, so don't pretend like you do," Dane said without turning around.

"Well, what are you working on the house for?" Vika continued to prod. "You told me it's not for money, so it's not that. Revenge? Are you building this house out of revenge?"

Vika saw his shoulders rise and lower as he let out a sigh. "No, I'm not building this house out of revenge."

"So is it nepotism?"

This time, Dane turned to squint his eyes at her.

She leaned forward and said, "Because I think it's love."

"You do, huh?"

"I do."

"Look, you can be a romantic all you want, but it's not going to get you very far."

"In what?"

"In anything."

Vika raised her eyebrows. "In anything? Are you kidding me?"

"No, I'm not kidding you. You're just going to be unhappy and jaded when you find out for yourself that no one else is as 'pure of heart' as you're hoping to be. Either take a hint from the Renaissance artists and make some cash, or consider yourself warned and buy a box of tissues."

"Well, you're just full of inspiration."

But Dane offered nothing further.

She may have started this discussion, but Dane ended it. He probably wouldn't have minded if she continued to argue, but they both knew he wasn't going to budge if she did. Vika didn't know what to say anyway. The old masters were like gods to her. They existed as the epitome of artistic greatness, and yet they were only interested in making a buck? The thought was blasphemous. But...damn Dane and his absurd half-assed speculations!

Yes, that's all they were. Speculations. Nothing more than an opinion of one man. She stared at the wall, her eyebrows scrunched so tightly together she could pinch a nickel between them. And what the hell did Gatsbying the Ninja Turtles mean?

"The lath isn't going to pull itself out," Dane said, and she turned to look at him with her eyebrows still pulled together.

THE BELL TINKLED AS SHE PUSHED through the door to the store at the crack of dawn the next day. She said hello to Ted and got the usual grunt in response. She counted her drawer, took down her closed sign at the register, and cashed out three customers as if on autopilot.

"Hey, kid," she heard Smith's voice and looked up to see her friend. "You don't look so good. What's stewing? If it's lady business, I don't want to hear about it."

Vika shook her head. "No," she said, sullenly. "It's not lady business." She hated going to bed angry because it lingered the next day. Case in point, Smith's most recent observation. Though she did manage to decipher Dane's ramblings. "I Gatsbied the Ninja Turtles," she said.

"You what?"

"I Gastbied the Ninja Turtles. Da Vinci, Donatello, Michelangelo, and Raphael. All of them. They were just in it for the money." Vika picked at the duct tape holding part of her cash drawer together. There sure was a lot of duct tape around this town.

Smith sighed, "I'm going to need coffee for this, aren't I?"

"Probably," she grumbled.

While he was getting his caffeine, Vika priced some leftover chicken wings.

"Well, I'm probably going to hate myself for asking," Smith said, "but what the hell does Gasbying the Ninja Turtles mean?"

"Have you ever read the book 'The Great Gatsby'?"

Smith raised his eyebrows. "Yes, I've read it. Who hasn't?" Vika silently conceded that truth. The book was one of her Top-Ten Read Before Going to College books. Along with the likes of "Jane Eyre," "Of Mice and Men," and "The Scarlet Letter."

"Well, you know how Gatsby thought about Daisy for years and years and idolized her past anything mortal?" Smith nodded, waiting for more.

"Well, Dane," Vika continued, "uses it as a verb."

"Oh, I see. And the Ninja Turtles come into this how?"

"Well, not the *ninja* Ninja Turtles." Smith raised his eyebrows and took a sip of coffee. "The actual Renaissance artists, Donatello, Da Vinci, Raphael, and Michelangelo."

"Ah," Smith nodded, "Donatello's my favorite."

"We were talking about them last night and Dane said that they only did art because they were paid well to do it since they were so good at it."

Smith looked at her blankly. "So?"

"He said that if they lived today they would be scientists, doctors, or engineers because that's where the money is and people always go towards the money."

"Vika—"

"They were supposed to be geniuses! Not like everyone else. They were supposed to have painted out of pure brilliance and love for art!"

"Just because they wanted food on their table doesn't make them any less of a genius."

"And I Gatsbied them," Vika continued feverishly. "Now I don't know what to do."

Smith laughed.

"It's not funny!" Vika was agitated. "I invested my entire college career in them because I thought they transcended mankind!"

"Well, I think you might be going a little overboard there—"

"Now they're just like any Joe Shmoe trying to climb a social ladder?"

"Vika!" Smith said firmly, watching her eyes darting back and forth as she became confused in her own thought process. "Most of what you've learned is probably true. Still. It's still true. You just got other information that you'll have to also consider and that is might change your perspective. That's called life. These turtles still can be geniuses if you let them. How many people do you know were hired by the pope? In that way, they *did* transcend mankind."

Vika chewed the inside of her cheek. "Yeah, I guess," she said finally.

"Vika," Smith said, looking at her strangely, "you're smart, you know. You can come up with your own conclusions."

"I know, I just—what if he's right?"

Smith shrugged. "So what if he is?"

"Smith!"

"So what if he is?" he repeated. "What's right for him might not be right for you."

Vika nodded, her gaze in a far corner of the store.

"All I'm saying is allow yourself to be open to new interpretations, you don't have to believe them."

"I know."

"Do you?"

Vika looked down at the register and picked at the duct tape again.

"Smith?"

"What?"

"Where did you work before you started here?"

Smith looked at her for a beat, and then said, "I owned my own bakery."

"What happened?"

"What happened to this conversation? I thought we were talking about you," he chuckled, but it was forced. Then he sighed and went on, "The economy. People had to tighten their belts and cakes were some of the first things they cut out."

"Oh," Vika said sympathetically, "I'm so sorry."

Smith shrugged, "Don't be. At least I got my chance." He puffed out his chest and clapped his hands together. "Now enough talking. It's getting depressing. What with the Ninja Turtles conspiring with the Catholic Church to convince the upper-middle class of fifteenth century Italy to squander their money on gold and ultramarine paint and all that business."

Vika looked in awe at her co-worker. "Where'd that come from?"

"I've been to Florence six times. That's where my parents are from."

"Six times!" Vika said, "I'm jealous."

"Well, give me some winning tickets and we'll blow this taco stand so you can see the Orsanmichele for yourself."

Vika laughed and ripped off two scratch-offs but alas, winnings of two dollars were not enough to start over.

"Next time," Vika said.

"Next time," Smith echoed.

CHAPTER 8

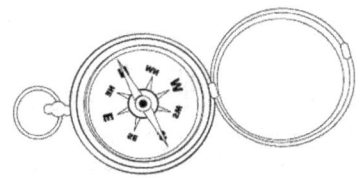

FORREST CAME TO THE HOUSE after Vika had returned back from her shift at the store and he quietly set up his tent in the lawn. He actually *had* a tent, unusual for fast hikers. Most opted to roll out their sleeping bags under the stars, and might throw up a tarp if clouds rolled in, but few were fully enclosed while they slept. He spoke with Dane briefly and gave a polite nod to Vika on the porch. He was in his mid-fifties, the oldest of the thru-hikers they'd seen on the trail and one of the larger hikers. He wasn't fat—they hadn't met a single hiker who was—but his gut seemed a little more stubborn than the rest. He resisted the thru-hiker beard, and kept a well-groomed goatee, grey overtaking brown facial hair, even though his head was still a deep brown. He wore a simple trucker hat, a T-shirt tucked into his old jeans, and a wedding ring. His pack was old, the kind Vika had only seen in books and magazines, with a metal frame that sat high on his hips and extended up past the back of his head, with his blue, egg carton-modeled sleeping pad rolled up and fastened to the bottom.

She watched him from the porch, over the top of her book. Not that she was making much progress with the book anyway, since her mind was focusing more on the Ninja Turtles and not on who killed whom in her novel. Thrillers were her favorites and normally, she ate them up like chocolate-covered popcorn. But this time, she had to read the same page at least twice, if not more, because too many questions were interrupting the storyline. What else had she 'Gatsbied'? What if Smith were right? Worse, what if Dane were right? Of course she had to make a living. She'd never questioned that, but didn't that follow passion? Isn't that what people had been telling her for years?

She could feel doubt dig its heels in and start to morph into certainty that she would never work on a Da Vinci, Raphael, or Michelangelo. Italy might as well exist on another planet, it was reserved for the elite anyway, and what was she? Amateur with a capital "A." Her inability to land an art job had made that perfectly clear.

She grunted and watched Forrest. Unlike most hikers who came into town and gorged on store food, Forrest pulled out a stove and pot and cooked himself up a modest portion of some rice concoction that Vika could smell from half an acre away. Hikers would say they ate around 4,000 calories a day, and that little pot didn't seem to accommodate very much.

As Vika watched, her mind drifted again. Speculations of five-hundred-year-old motives tried to elbow their way back into her thoughts. She shook her head against the doubt. Besides, she couldn't imagine herself doing anything not related to the history of art, and she sure wasn't about to reserve her place in some aimless line of work just to count pennies, regardless of what Dane tried to tell her.

She wondered if the old masters had doubts whispering in their ears, too.

Vika watched Forrest move his hands with such precise muscle memory that Vika supposed that if she blindfolded him, he would still be able to cook his meal without spilling a single grain of rice on the ground. She felt for the first time that she had caught a glimpse of the trail. Her breathing slowed, her muscles stilled, as though she was afraid of scaring the moment away. She could picture him on the trail now, in the trees, on a ridge, or near a lake. It was a very soft, quiet, sturdy kind of profoundness. She had imagined hikers in camp, a picturesque campfire next to a cozy tent, and a six-course meal.

But there was Forrest, diligently stirring and tasting, stirring and tasting, and evidently, that was enough.

A chicken, equally as intrigued at the scene, strutted out from the coop and paced about five feet from the new arrival, looking for scraps. A second chicken arrived but Forrest remained unfazed.

She turned back to her book, catching glimpses over the top of the pages, watching as he turned out the fire and let it set. Watching as he pulled out a small notepad and scratched a couple words, watching as he blew on his dinner before taking the first spoonful.

Vika poured herself another cup of tea. She imagined what he wrote, where he came from, who worried about him on the trail. He had talked about his wife, but Vika wondered if he had kids, too. They'd probably be about her age, she thought, maybe a little younger; she was always bad at telling age.

When she finally headed toward the camper an hour later as the mosquitoes emerged from wherever it was they hid during the day and started gnawing on her bare feet, Forrest remained near his tent, his hat pulled down over his eyebrows.

"Good night, Forrest," she called to the hiker, again writing on his notepad. He looked up and dipped his head towards her.

SHE THOUGHT HE WOULD QUIETLY move on and she would not see him again, but his tent was still there the next morning. His tent was there, but he was not, and neither was the motorcycle. Odd, she thought, because she hadn't heard it earlier.

"He pushed it down the driveway before he started it up," Grandma Peach spoke as Vika looked over the sink into the empty lawn, answering Vika's thought.

"I saw him when I was up letting out Quasimodo," Grandma Peach explained as she carefully sipped her hot tea. "I guess he didn't want to wake us all up. What a gentleman," she said and turned towards the refrigerator.

After a moment, Vika turned away from the window and went to join Grandma Peach for breakfast.

Twenty minutes later, when they walked through the front doorway devoid of an actual door, they moved on into the kitchen to pound on the plaster around the cupboards and the wooden panels that ran waist high around the entire room.

"Where's Dane?" Vika asked as she staked out her wall for destruction.

"Oh," Grandma Peach said, "I don't know. I heard his music earlier. My bet is, he's painting. Best not to bother him."

"Why?"

Grandma Peach smiled at her. "Because he's not the most agreeable when he's in a...mood."

Vika nodded. "Right," she said.

Forrest walked in shortly after they had begun.

"Good morning!" Grandma Peach said brightly, welcoming the guest.

He nodded, hands deep in his pockets and elbows locked straight. "Ma'am," he replied. "Mind if I join y'all?"

Grandma Peach smiled warmly. "The more the merrier! There are masks and hammers in the foyer. We're taking out all the plaster and lath. Try to avoid the moldings and the cupboards."

"All right," Forrest said, and turned to retrieve a mask and hammer.

"So, Forrest," Grandma spoke over the creak of resistant nails a couple moments later. "Where'd you hike from?"

Forrest positioned himself next to Grandma Peach in front of a large expanse of exposed lath. "Echo Lake," he responded, not quite meeting Grandma Peach decibel for decibel. "It's right near South Lake Tahoe."

Vika spoke up, "When did you start?"

"July 2," he responded, quietly.

"Must have been hot," Grandma Peach remarked. "Are you section hiking?"

Forrest yanked an entire board off with one push of the hammer. "Well," he started, "I didn't know the trail existed till about then. A buddy of mine told me. Said it might be good." He paused to pull the nails out of the board and drop them in a bucket. He tossed the wood onto the pile in the center of the room. "So far I ain't been disappointed." He shrugged and yanked another board out.

"Well, stay as long as you'd like," Grandma Peach said. "We love the company."

"Thank you, ma'am," he said quietly.

AN OLDER WOMAN, IN HER FORTIES, Vika guessed, appeared on the lawn that afternoon, pack still on her back, feet planted, dreads pulled back, in the very center of the grass. There was no car driving away and no dust in the air to tell them that a car had just been in the area.

Suddenly, she was just...there. As far as Vika could tell, she wouldn't have moved all day if no one saw her. Maybe she didn't know what to do, there wasn't a door to knock on after all. Then again, maybe she had only been there a moment. While Vika wondered, the woman noticed Vika in the window, and of course she couldn't just stand there and continue staring.

Quasi stirred from his pile of newspaper he had made his bed in the corner of the room. When he saw Vika head for the door, he went from sleepy to hyper in about two and a half seconds and tore down the stairs.

Vika saw the woman awkwardly pat the diva of a dog, though her smile was warm.

"Your dog is so friendly," she said when Vika stepped out onto the porch.

"Oh, he's not mine. But yes, he is," Vika corrected, as she stepped onto the lawn and crossed to her. The woman's shirt, made of a colorful, South American pattern, stretched like cotton across her taunt, well-built, tanned body, her wrists adorned with bracelets of earthy-colored beads. She wore sandals on her feet. Long, flowing pant legs billowed out sporadically when they caught the wind.

"So you're hiking the PCT?" Vika asked.

She looked up from the dog. Her eyes were hazel and the prominent crows feet put her at maybe further on in years than Vika initially guessed.

"Yes," she said. "The state of Washington. I still have a bit in Northern California to do, around Lassen Park to Shasta, but I'll save that for next year. There was a fire in the area when I tried it four years ago. Right after I retire. I'll leave the AT for my retirement hike." Her voice was not necessarily smooth, or scratchy for that matter, but it possessed such a genuine tone that Vika couldn't help but be entranced.

"Oh, we haven't had any section hikers through yet," Vika said, hoping she used the phrase accurately. "Glad to have you. You can pitch your tent in the lawn, or sleep in that coop," she pointed. "There are bunk beds and armchairs in there."

"Oh, the lawn's fine. Just fine." Her smile was just as genuine as her voice and Vika had no doubt that she would be as fine as she said she would. "I'm Newton," and she straightened to shake Vika's hand.

"Nice to meet you," Vika answered, introducing herself. Her hand was leathery, but her grip was just as sincere as her voice. "Well, Forrest, Dane, Grandma Peach, and I are heading into town tonight in about half an hour for dinner, if you'd like to join us. The food at the diner is very good."

"Sounds wonderful, I'll set up my tent in the meantime," Newton said graciously and turned.

"All right, I'll let you go set up."

Newton set out across the yard and Vika walked across the lawn to the camper. "We have a new hiker," she told Grandma Peach.

"Wonderful!" she said. "Did you tell him about the diner? We have plenty of room."

"Yeah," Vika said, "I told her, and she's coming."

"Oh, it's a *she*. Excellent. Where is she sleeping?"

"She's putting up her tent right now over on the other side of the driveway, I think."

"Good, good. Does she want some tea?" Grandma Peach asked enthusiastically.

"I, um, don't know. Do you want me to ask her?" Vika inquired, already knowing the answer.

"Oh, well, yes. It'll be a nice pre-dinner beverage," Grandma Peach said and already started filling the teakettle with water.

Vika hopped down the stairs in search of the hiker, who conveniently, was pushing the last of her tent stakes into the ground. Quasi sat under a nearby tree watching.

"I think we'll be leaving in a couple minutes," Vika said as she walked up to the woman.

"Oh, that's fine, just fine," she said with a smile.

"Would you like to have a cup of tea with me and Grandma Peach while we wait for the guys?"

"Oh, I love tea," she said, placing her pack in her tent and zipping it closed.

They walked back to the camper together, Quasi trotting along at their heels just as the whistle of the teakettle sounded. "Ginger or chamomile?" Grandma Peach asked as they ascended the stairs.

"Ginger, please," Newton replied.

"Ginger it is," Grandma Peach said and poured a cup of hot water. She dipped the tea strainer into the mug. "You can call me Grandma Peach."

"And you can call me Newton."

"Nice to meet you, Newton. Have you settled in? Do you need anything else?"

"Oh, thank you. This is more than enough," she answered, the tempo of her speech even and slow. Vika poured her own mug and plopped a chamomile bag into the hot water.

"We have extra blankets in here," Grandma Peach offered.

"That's very kind of you. I have a good sleeping bag, though."

"Well, if you change your mind, you know where to find us," Grandma Peach said as she removed the tea strainer from the mug and placed it in the sink. She set the cup on a saucer on a table next to the loveseat. "Please, sit and enjoy."

Newton thanked her and Vika sat in the small bench for the kitchen table, sipping her own cup of tea.

"How is the trail, dear?" Grandma Peach asked the hiker.

"Breathtaking," she answered. "Challenging, long, sunny." She sipped her tea. "Delightful," she gushed, "just delightful."

"Did you start at Mexico?" Grandma Peach asked.

"No," Newton answered, turning to look at her. "I've been section hiking for six years now. This year I am doing White Pass to the border."

"Oh, congratulations, dear," Grandma Peach said and Vika echoed.

Dane's voice sounded through the screen, "Ready to go?"

"We'll be right there, dear," Grandma Peach told him.

"Yep," Vika added, "I'm starved."

"Whose tent is that?" he followed up.

"It's mine," Newton said as she stood from the loveseat. "Is it in your way? I can move it—"

"No need, just curious. Well, let's load 'er up," and he walked away toward the bus.

Two minutes later, Dane, Grandma Peach, Forrest, Newton, and Vika rode to dinner at a little diner on the edge of town. They filed off, greeted the hostess by name and were seated in Grandma Peach's favorite booth. Vika ordered a salad and was surprised to hear her order echoed by the hiker.

"Not going for the burgers, huh?" Dane also noticed.

"Burgers? No," answered Newton, "On the trail, I actually crave citrus and the fresh green stuff. A lot of hikers do."

Forrest agreed, his hands clasped on the table. "I thought about drinking a bottle of orange juice for about sixty straight miles."

Grandma Peach nodded. "I thought Candle Maker was going to eat an entire bag of apples by himself in one sitting."

"How is the trail?" Dane asked.

"Extraordinary," Newton replied. "There was a little snow on the passes in Washington. Adams was covered."

"That's no fun," Vika said, as she leaned back to let the waiter place her meal in front of her.

Newton shrugged. "Just a different standard. My grandmother used to say, 'There are three responses to every situation: to accept it, to enjoy it, and to be enthused about it. The rest is madness.'" She laughed. "I had a hard time with that for about the first week, and then I decided with the snow, I could make my own trail. It became fun again."

"And Goat Rocks," she cooed. "My goodness, what a view! It was…words couldn't describe it…incredible. The trail was clear of snow. Some of the path leading up to it was under snow, but the knife edge was dry."

Grandma Peach leaned forward on the table. "So tell us, Newton," she said, "what is it you do when you're not hiking?"

"I teach."

"My wife used to teach kindergarten," Forrest said.

Grandma Peach brought a hand to her chest. "Women after my own heart. I used to teach as well. Much differently, I assume, it was a one-room schoolhouse in northern Minnesota."

"Teaching, just the same," Newton responded. "I teach science. Eighth grade."

"What a nightmare," Dane said.

"What got you hooked on teaching?" Grandma Peach ventured, ignoring Dane's comment. Vika had to agree with him, though. The middle-school years were like the 13th floor. Bad luck for everyone; better to just leave it out completely. Leave out the pimples, the awkward growth spurts, the braces, and the Friday night dances. Especially the Friday night dances.

"To tell you the truth, I never thought I would be a teacher. It was a very affordable way to travel, and then I fell in love with it."

"You mean the summers?" Vika asked, taking a sip of her water.

"No, no," Newton said, "I started out teaching English in South Korea and Thailand." She sat leaning back against her seat, a serene smile on her face, shoulders relaxed, and hands folded in her lap. "I didn't get a job in the States until years later. Ironically, I worked summers for the first five years." She turned to Forrest. "Where did your wife teach?"

"In the town we grew up in, Silver Hook, California?" He looked at her as if she might know it.

"That sounds wonderful," Newton smiled. "Were you high school sweethearts?"

Forrest looked down at his hands. "No, ma'am" he said, through a chuckle. His cheeks turned pink. "No, ma'am, she was four years younger than me." He looked up and shrugged, "We didn't know each other until she came back from college."

Their food arrived in a parade of waiters and the conversation slowed its pace.

"I miss teaching," Grandma Peach said nostalgically, "especially the little ones. Oh, they said the most adorable things."

They finished their dinners and stayed for another round of drinks. Grandma Peach eventually got the group moving outside when she spotted Newton trying to stifle a yawn.

"Well," she said, "it's getting late and Quasi's probably getting anxious."

The entire table looked appreciative of the decision and shuffled out the door, not necessarily quickly, but no one stopped to look for a bowl of after-dinner mints at the hostess stand either.

The dew had already set by the time they returned to the Dancy property and the air was chilly. The group filed out of their bus and headed to their respective sleeping quarters almost immediately.

Vika followed Grandma Peach to the camper and rummaged through her luggage to find her favorite oversized sweatshirt and wool socks to cozy up in. When she padded out to the kitchen, Grandma Peach was pulling vegetable after vegetable out of the refrigerator, a pot of water set to boil on the stove.

"Hungry already?" she teased.

"Oh, no, dear, I think I'm going to make a couple of salads."

"For anything in particular," Vika queried, "or just because?"

"I figured," she answered, pulling three boxes of pasta from the pantry and setting them on the counter, "it'd be good to have the food around. The hikers will be coming by more frequently, and Heaven forbid I don't have anything to feed them!"

Vika smiled, yes, Heaven forbid. "What would you like me to do?"

"Oh," Grandma Peach waved her hand, "relax tonight. I can do it."

"Grandma Peach," Vika began, "I'm here, let me help. I'd be happy to."

"Well," she thought a minute and looked at her pile of ingredients, "you can cut the green pepper. And maybe the mozzarella. How are you with cutting onions?"

"I'll get right on it."

CHAPTER 9

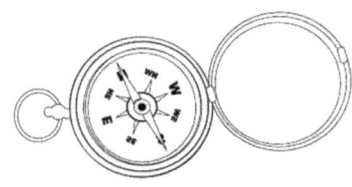

EITHER GRANDMA PEACH WAS PSYCHIC, or she knew hiking patterns like sailors knew the trade winds. The next afternoon, while she was finishing red velvet cupcakes for "just in case," a small Toyota pickup stopped at the end of the driveway and two hikers jumped out.

Later that evening, Grandma Peach and Vika sat with their new company around two picnic tables Dane dragged out from somewhere—probably the barn, everything came from the barn—on top of which the salads sat next to the hamburgers and hot dogs that came off the grill.

"Now how in the world," Grandma Peach began in a concerned voice, "did you get the name Cougar Bait?"

The hiker, about the same height as Vika, wore her short, black hair pulled tightly into a ponytail with the aid of numerous bobby pins and a headband. Her clothes were dirty and her brown eyes were bright, her legs pure muscle that disappeared into colorful gaiters.

"In the Sierras," she began, taking a sip of the iced tea, "I stopped treating my water." Grandma Peach sucked in air between her dentures and she began to pet Quasimodo with a little more haste.

Cougar Bait had a crooked smile. "I know, I know, anyway I got Giardia and I happened to be behind Thud the morning that it kicked in. I fell farther and farther behind and I felt like cougar bait stumbling over rocks and taking rests every five minutes. I probably looked like a pretty easy snack. The name just stuck."

Vika had heard mention of Giardia before, but it was still mostly a mystery to her. "What is Giardia?" she finally inquired. No better person to ask than someone who's experienced it.

"Intestinal disruption and eruption," Thud answered.

Cougar Bait spooned macaroni salad into her mouth and nodded.

"Ew," Vika answered making a face. Though she only had herself to blame—she was the one who asked.

Thud snorted.

"I had to walk eighteen miles in 90-degree heat through the smoke from a forest fire to the next highway so I could hitch back into town and get some drugs," Cougar Bait said. "It drained my energy, too. My God, it took me four hours to go six miles. I was drooling all over the place because it took too much energy to keep my jaw shut while I was walking. I would scout for trees that were close enough to the trail that I could lean on them without my feet leaving the trail."

Thud rubbed his hands over his face once, and then clasped his hands together and leaned back. He let the tension out of face, but he wasn't fooling anyone. Vika bet it would've been difficult to watch your hiking partner succumb to a disease right in front of you.

"But hey," Cougar Bait went on, "you know what they say: You haven't lived until you've dry-heaved out your ass."

Vika gagged as Thud shot Cougar Bait a look. "No one says that," he told her. "That's disgusting."

Vika couldn't imagine, not that she wanted to.

"Sure puts a perspective on things," Cougar Bait smiled. "Now when I have a bad day, at least it's not *that* bad."

"So how long does this put you out for?" Vika interjected before it turned into a fight; Thud looked restless.

"Off the trail? About a day," Cougar Bait answered. "Some people it's more, like five or six days, but all you really need are meds. I guess a couple more days if you want the test to be sure it's Giardia."

"A *day*?" Vika asked, dumbfounded. "Is that healthy? Shouldn't you let your body recover a little bit?"

Cougar Bait shrugged nonchalantly, obviously having fielded this question numerous times before. "Even with Giardia, a thru-hiker's body is pretty strong. Fast recovery. High tolerance for pain and discomfort and you can't lose ten days worth of miles." She cocked her head and looked skyward, as if thinking if her last comment made sense. "Well, I guess you *could*, some people do, but we didn't want to. I'd get out of shape, and we'd try to make the miles up later anyway. That's a lot to make up."

She pushed herself up from the picnic table and walked over to the grill, grabbing a third hot dog. She came back and started loading her new find with every condiment in reach. Vika stared. She didn't know if she was more speechless about the Giardia conversation, or the fact that this skinny girl in front of her was downing more calories in a single sitting than she normally would in an entire day.

Cougar Bait looked up and smiled. "It's a different mindset on the trail," she said, grabbing a handful of chips. "I was always terrified about Giardia before this trail. But then you get on and you hike. And hike. Suddenly, you're not going to stop for anything. You feel strong and invincible and you won't let yourself be put down by a goddamn protozoan." She took a bite of her hot dog. "I never said we were a very logical bunch."

"Speaking of the bunch," Thud remarked, taking advantage of the switch in conversation offered, "who've you had come through already? Only the forty milers, probably, right?"

Vika answered, "Yes, well, you've met Forrest and other than him, New Pants was the first one through—"

"Oh, New Pants!" Cougar Bait exclaimed through a mouthful of food. She chewed and swallowed. "Such a nice guy! He was doing forties when he passed us near Seiad Valley—"

Thud chuckled, "He passed us twice, remember? Passed us once, had a couple beers in town and passed us again."

"On that damn climb!" Cougar Bait looked back to Vika and recounted, "we were chugging ice cold Gatorade with a Trail Angel who drove up there and New Pants practically comes bounding out of the woods. He was super chatty. I guess that happens when you hike for so long by yourself. How was he?"

"Good," Vika told her. "He got to the border at the end of July, I think."

"Good for him," she said.

"For sure," Thud added.

"Who else? Sasquatch and that crew, did they come by?" Cougar Bait wondered.

Vika nodded. "Yeah, about ten days ago."

"We've been reading their entries for the past two and a half months," Thud explained around his burger. "We tried to catch them for a little while, and then lost some ground in Northern California when she got sick."

Dane wandered over in his usual work clothes and plopped his plate of food on the picnic table. He swung one leg over the bench with a groan and eased the other over before cracking a beer and taking a sip.

"How's the trail?" he asked the hikers as he combed back his thin hair with both hands, which fell back into his eyes nearly immediately.

"We love it," Thud answered.

"Well, the snow's finally melting," Cougar Bait expanded. "The Sierras were pretty dry and Oregon was the worst, for sure. I hear we're going to hit some on Glacier Peak and then we'll be in the clear."

Dane nodded. "That's what my sources say," he confirmed as he went to take another sip of beer. "You been doing OK on the snow? We have some ice axes kicking around somewhere. They're old, but they work if you want to borrow them."

"Thanks," Thud answered. "We should be fine, though. We've had lots of practice by now."

"Glacier Peak really isn't that bad," Dane answered with a nod. "Ever since they re-routed the trail on the west side of the mountain."

Their conversation paused as people scooped up food from their plates.

"What are you working on?" Thud gestured to the house twenty yards away.

Dane spoke around a mouthful of pasta salad. "What *aren't* we working on?" he responded and washed the food down with beer. "Plaster and lath is stripped on the first floor. We'll be taking out electrical and plumbing next. Then," Dane paused, not knowing what came next and looked at the house for answers. "Hmm. Oh, right, I'm knocking down a wall on the first floor and a couple on the second and I just picked up three radiators today. They were in the trash—can you believe that? I got an old dresser out of the trash last week, too."

"Sounds like quite the project," Thud said.

"Says the one who's walking 2,600 miles," Vika jested.

"True," Cougar Bait agreed.

Thud was still looking at the house. "What are you going to do with it when it's done?"

"It will be a hiker hostel," Grandma Peach said as she leaned forward as though she were letting them in on a secret.

"No kidding!" said Cougar Bait. Thud looked pleasantly surprised.

"Mmm-hmm," Grandma Peach nodded, her eyes shining. "The coop won't cut it long term. Maybe we'll keep some of it open for overflow, but we're going to have about twenty beds in the house."

"Really? That's incredible, I would love a tour of it. You know, if it's safe," Cougar Bait said.

Thud gave a quick nod. "Me, too," he said. "Will you live here, too?"

"Oh," Grandma Peach waved her hand at him, "I have my camper. Dane sleeps in the barn."

Cougar Bait snorted.

"It's true," Dane said. "Get's a little drafty in the winter so I'll have to do something about that." He chewed on some macaroni salad and then turned to the hikers. "Well, I started to pull out some of the wiring a little earlier. If you want to work on that in about twenty minutes," Dane suggested.

Thud's eyes opened with surprise. "Yeah? OK, sure!"

"Boys," Cougar Bait muttered.

Vika half-smiled at her, and knew Cougar Bait would be right next to Thud removing the plumbing and electrical in twenty minutes. The opportunity to help build a hostel for future hikers was just too appropriate for hikers to pass up.

Vika was right: A short time later, Dane led the way into the house, followed by Thud, Cougar Bait, and herself. Dane started the tour on the first floor, past the walls that had come down, by the gutted bathroom, and through the cabinet-less kitchen. Vika had no idea where they went, but she surmised they probably went to the barn—everything went to the barn.

"Careful around the cords," Dane said from the front of the line. The other three of them carefully stepped over the extension cords that snaked through the walls. A handful of power tools leaned against the back wall of the dining room, next to a powerful stand-up light. Dust was everywhere, even though she had seen and participated in strict vacuuming rules, and so she supposed it was a permanent effect of construction.

The group returned to the front of the house and went up the stairs. Though stripped on the ground level, plaster and lath still held fast to the two-by-fours by the time they reached the top. Slowly, Vika shifted her gaze from the stairs to the living room and out the window. She saw Grandma Peach carrying bowls of salads into the camper, Quasi trotting at her feet. Two antsy chickens pecked at the ground at the base of a maple tree on the far side of the yard. She stepped back from the window and left the room.

At last, they made it back to the foyer for some gloves, some wire cutters and set to work. Dane did a little demonstration, and slid off a small porcelain tube and held it up. "Save these please. Just put them here, in the box. Carefully. They're all original.

"Everything's off, I wouldn't want any of you poor bastards to light up like a Tesla coil." He turned toward the kitchen. "Happy cutting!"

They worked until sundown that night, pulling and piling the wires in the corner of the room. Some came easily, some snagged on every sliver sticking out. They hung up their wire-cutters in the foyer after they finished.

THE NEXT MORNING, THE HIKERS were up before anyone else and were busy packing their packs, stirring oatmeal over their stove, with their knit hats pulled down nearly over their eyes and their legs tucked up tight underneath them.

Vika walked across the dewed grass. The cool droplets slipped off the blades and made her feet slide around in her flip-flops. She pulled her old flannel shirt tightly around her as she climbed the steps to the porch to set up the coffee pot. "Should be ready in about ten minutes," she said in a sleepy voice to Cougar Bait and Thud.

"Thanks," came the replies.

Vika went back into the house to change into some sturdier clothes for more work on the house, since she didn't have to report to the store until the next day. When she came out and left Grandma Peach to read her newspaper and sip her coffee, Cougar Bait and Thud were sitting on the porch drinking coffee, their packs small and compact, leaning against the porch.

"When are you guys heading out?" Vika asked, the sleep still evident in her voice.

Cougar Bait raised a shoulder and let it drop. "Soon. Gotta get back on to make it to the border before classes start."

"Dane should be up soon to take you," Vika said looking towards the barn. "I'm surprised I haven't seen him yet."

"That's all right," Thud replied. "It wasn't a bad hitch to get here and you guys have done enough for us already. This place is amazing."

"You sure?" Vika said, pouring her own mug.

"Positive," came Cougar Bait's reply.

They left shortly after that. Packs on their backs, faded and worn. Shoes held together by duct tape, shirts with dirt lines on them outlining pack straps. And they walked away as though they were walking toward paradise.

To live the vagabond life, Vika thought, is a curious thing. She felt a little prick in her chest as she watched them step off the driveway and onto the road. With a slight dread, she knew this experience was going to happen over and over again, like it did with New Pants, Sasquatch, Candle Maker, No trail Name Jason, Newton…the list was getting lengthy. Hikers would come, they'd stay for a day or two and then they would walk on. She took a deep breath and pulled those thoughts in, tied them in a little box, carefully placed them on a high shelf in the back of her mind and hoped they wouldn't fall off before she was ready to retrieve them.

As Vika surmised, Dane was indeed up, though he had already made it to the basement to adjust the jacks in the house. He emerged in jeans and a Pink Floyd T-shirt.

"It's easier to lift a house after it loses two or three tons of weight, I'll tell you that." He climbed up on the porch for coffee and sat in the swing, taking up nearly the entire span of it.

"Working on the same thing today?" Vika asked, taking her own seat on the bench.

"Yup. And tomorrow if it's not done. Where'd the hikers go?" He looked around the yard as though he expected them to have moved their tent in the middle of the night.

"They left," Vika said, "about five minutes ago."

He nodded, his gaze fixed on the driveway.

Several beats later, he pushed himself up and walked toward the entrance to the house.

"I'll join you soon," Vika said, twirling her phone in her hands. "I'm going to call home quick."

"Sure," Dane responded, his voice already echoing through the foyer.

She swiped the screen on her phone and looked through her contacts and she stared. She stared so long the screen went black and she had to do it over again.

Her thumb hovered. She bit her lip. She could feel her palms sweat and she thought that was ridiculous. She had nothing to be worried about and she pressed the call button before she thought too much more about it.

Alex answered on the third ring, "Vika." Vika half-smiled. Her brother's intonation rarely changed, but when he said her name like that, he was pissed.

"Where the hell are you?"

"I'm in Stacklen, Washington. It's really nice, you should come visit me!"

"Mom almost killed *me* last weekend because *you* wouldn't answer the phone," he exploded. "She wants you home."

Vika rolled her eyes; she couldn't help it. "Well, I'm not coming any time soon. Grandma Peach is so sweet and Dane, well, Dane's a little weird, but he's all right. I'll be home by Thanksgiving."

"Vika," her brother said, his patience wearing thin, "just call her."

"I did, Alex, and it didn't go so well. What else am I supposed to say? I had a car fire. I'm stranded here," Vika spoke, defensiveness sneaking through her voice. "I live with people she's never heard of and probably wouldn't approve of. Strangers come all the time to set up their tents here." She paused, and then repeated, "What do you want me to tell her?"

There was silence on the other end.

"Seriously, Alex. You know she'll fly out here and drag my ass home before I can explain that I *like* it here."

Alex again didn't respond, at least not right away. "Why didn't you ask mom and dad for money for a plane ticket or something? Why didn't you ask *me*?" He didn't sound angry, he sounded hurt.

"Alex," she said, unable to conceal her confusion, "you don't have money like that and besides, it was my problem. I had to get out of it myself."

"So instead of asking family to help you, you're staying with strangers. How are you going to get home anyway?"

"I work at a store in town."

"Are you serious?" Alex sounded stunned.

"Just short term—"

"You even got a job because you didn't want to reach out?"

"Alex, come on—"

"If you wanted to go on a little adventure, you didn't have to make it seem like you were running away from home."

"Alex, I wasn't!"

"We would have helped you." Vika rolled in her lips and bit down on them. Alex continued, "But it sounds like we're pretty low on your list."

A spark flared in Vika. "What the hell, Alex? You know that's not even close to true."

"Thanks, Vika," he responded. "You know what, my shift starts soon, I better go."

"Fine," Vika said. "Hey, Alex, I expected this from Mom, not you."

"Well, I didn't expect you to ditch town and leave me to try to cover for you. Everyone thinks I know what you're up to, but I don't. Because you didn't tell me. But go, have fun. Talk to you…whenever." Alex said.

"Alex," Vika's eyebrows bunched and she stiffened as she waited for his response. "Alex?" She looked at the screen of her phone and saw the time blinking across the bottom. She cursed and shoved the phone in her pocket. Vika stared into the lawn without seeing it, and tried to figure out how that call took such a wrong turn. She just wanted to talk to her brother, but he was clearly on a different page. First the conversation with her mother, and then Alex, added to Dane's…perspective and the constant stream of people drifting in and out of her life, and Vika felt as though she had lost control.

She heard a hammer hit a wall somewhere in the house and it made her jump. She stood and walked into the house to find her own hammer.

The downstairs was plaster-free, but the upstairs still needed work. She grabbed a mask and hammer and ascended the stairs. Plaster sagged in some sections of the closest bedroom, and was completely missing in others. There were scratches on the hardwood floor, and much of the faded paint from the window molding had flaked off and collected with dead flies against the screen.

The room was small. Small enough that there was not room for two people to stand in it with a swinging hammer. She counted on that fact. She counted on no one venturing into her territory to ask her if she was OK, if she needed anything, if she had the time. She knew she would be alone until she removed all the plaster in the room. Carefully, she secured her mask over her nose, cocked the hammer and let it smash into the wall.

She never thought she would be a frustrated pillow puncher, but there she was, destroying a wall to let out a little tension. Again.

She replayed her conversation with her brother and she hit the wall harder. Of all the people she would have thought to have her back, it would have been him. BAM! But he just tells her to call her mother. BAM! BAM! They both knew that she wouldn't understand—what did Alex call it? Oh, yeah. Her 'little adventure.' BAM! She felt red creeping into her line of vision, and she shook her head. BAM. BAM. BAM. Her shoulder ached dull, subtle requests to take it easy if she didn't want to be in pain the next day. Vika ignored it.

Her arm swung over and over into the wall. She worked with the desire—no, the need—to strip the thick, old, useless plaster from the wall. Strip it so she could build on a blank canvas. She wanted a medium to create new ideas on an old foundation. Her arm wielded the hammer with the power of this possibility and smashed a hole next to the window. She imagined the new paint colors as the old colors exploded when her hammer connected, and she imagined how the furniture would fit into the room. The lath splintered and she imagined the crystal door handles, the people who would inhabit it. Another chunk of plaster burst into dust as it hit the floor and she imagined the hobbies they would have, the ideas that would be created and she swung harder.

A cloud of white encompassed her and she slowed to a stop, her hammer swinging heavily at her side. She leaned against the doorframe and slid down until she was sitting, her knees crunched up to her chest. Her work looked like a hungry shark had come through and tore apart the walls. She wiped at the dust on her leg. She tried to take a deep breath, but it felt like someone banded her ribs down and wouldn't let in air. She pushed her legs down flat on the ground, tilted her chin up and tried again. She breathed deep, but her ribs were tight and the air *whooshed* right back out. All she wanted was some *air*!

Vika didn't know which way was up, a feeling that had gained strength the last couple of months. She felt as though she needed this time in the mountains to figure out what she wanted to go back to, what she *craved*.

At the same time, she felt like it was wasting. Time, that is. Surely a random construction project in Middle of Nowhere, Washington, only provided a gap in her résumé. It was like a leprechaun employed by society kept tapping her shoulder with a little stick, telling her to get a move-on and to think about the comfort provided by job security. The faster she got on that, the leprechaun argued, the faster she'd be comfortable.

God, she wanted to break that stick.

Vika closed her eyes. She envisioned her blood pumping through her veins, bright, red, one cell at a time. She envisioned her lungs opening up, even the bottom most sections inflated and breathed again. This time, air filled her and it calmed a bit of the anxiety rolling around in her belly.

CHAPTER 10

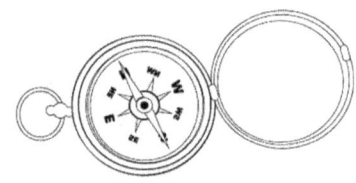

THE FOLLOWING SUNDAY, BUZZ, Chicken Shit, Forrest, Vika, Ted, Patty, Grandma Peach, and Dane sat around some card tables in the dining room of the house since there wasn't enough room in the camper, with a delectable chicken sitting in the center. Dane had given instruction the night before that no one was to work on inside of the house Saturday evening through Monday morning because, "plaster dust is not a seasoning. I don't need you all shitting blocks and ruining the toilet out back."

Vika helped him move tables out of the barn, the first time she had set foot inside it. When she stepped through the door, her first impression was of a bachelor pad, plain and simple, but it was littered with books instead of beer cans, canvases instead of dirty clothes, and blueprints instead of fitness magazines. She slowed to take in the paintings, most of which were series of mechanical contraptions, some of engines, some of spokes on the dirt bike, some of an old typewriter. All were layered with paint, subtle lines, though no doubt of where one subject ended and another began, and Vika was impressed. The paintings were realistic, and full of color. She knew there wasn't a touch of black in any of them, the way the colors came alive and glowed. Some were close, some far, and Dane hadn't neglected any part of the canvas, or any part of the subject. Mixed in were unfinished paintings, and it looked as though he was working simultaneously on about six. A couple canvases sat as pretentious anomalies to the others, cute cottages next to streams, barns with excessive Christmas decorations, and even a seascape. Gorgeous by themselves, they looked misplaced in the setting.

"Did you paint all those?" Vika asked.

"Sure did."

"Those buildings, too?" she prodded.

He looked at her sideways. "Like Mr. Da Vinci and Mr. Santi, I'd like a retirement fund, too." He stopped in front of some long buffet tables. "Grab this end and pull, I'll get the other end."

On the way out, she spotted a corner designated for hiker boxes, stacked five high and two thick. Colorful markers or tape adorned each one to be easily identifiable. The same deliveryman had been dropping off the boxes more frequently, and only a couple hikers had come through to pick them up. Dane had tacked a spreadsheet onto a nearby expanse of open wall with the date they had come in, the ETA of the hiker, the pick-up of the hiker, and the name of the picker-upper. Vika hadn't gone through the boxes for a hiker yet, but she knew Dane had IDed everyone asking for a box.

"Though you'd have to be one sick son of a bitch to steal food from a hungry hiker, and you'd deserve any hell brought upon you," he'd said.

FORREST VOLUNTEERED TO HELP Grandma Peach prepare the chicken, a stroke of luck Vika was appreciative of. It was golden brown, oozing juices, and the smell wafted through the entire yard. There wasn't a front door to keep Quasimodo out and he whined incessantly until sitting next to Grandma Peach, begging as though he hadn't been fed in a year.

The chicken was cut, the meal was served and the wine was poured. Dane lifted his glass and said, "Here's to the Pacific Crest Trail."

Everyone lifted their glasses, some people said, 'here, here,' some people just took a sip. Then forks started flying, knives and plates connected with a clank, chatter flowed, potatoes passed, a piece of meat fell to the dog, unnoticed by most, teeth sank into the rich, juicy slabs, and chairs squeaked as people adjusted their posture for better access to food, drink, or conversation.

Vika smiled. With aching muscles, she was more content than she had been in a long time. She watched Dane and Buzz talk as though they had known each other for years, while Chicken Shit and Forrest swapped stories about truck driving.

The memory of Vika's conversation with her brother had gone from vivid to dusty, the Trail of Deception as just a blip on the radar, hardly distinguishable from static—at least during the majority of the day. It faded enough that she could exist firmly in the dining room in Stacklen with these people, instead of partially here and partially in hypothetical places with hypothetical contacts for hypothetical jobs.

She felt...relaxed. For the first time in about a decade. Give or take.

"So I said no again," Grandma Peach's voice pushed into her thoughts. "He still wouldn't take it. I eventually put the engagement ring in a box and mailed it to him."

Patty looked amused and aghast. "I bet he was heartbroken!"

"Well," Grandma Peach shrugged, "if he was, at least he had the sense not to mail it back."

"Well, Ted," Vika heard Patty say to Grandma Peach in a low voice as she leaned in, "never proposed! *I* was the one who asked *him*!"

"Oh," Grandma Peach looked sympathetic, "sometimes they need a swift kick." She took a dainty bite of chicken and caught Vika's eye.

"When I was your age," she said, "I was married and had a baby already."

Vika managed a nervous laugh. "I wouldn't know what to do with a baby." She wouldn't be ready to settle down for the next ten years, she figured. She rarely even thought about it. In the distant future, another life, sure, but on a realistic timeframe? Never.

"Oh, I don't think anyone does, dear," she said.

"Hey, Ma!" Dane called from across the table.

"Sweet Jesus, he is going to call me like a dog until the day I die," she muttered, and then she raised her voice, "Yes, dear?"

"Did you see the paper today? Ted says there's a big fire in central Oregon. Right near Mt. Jefferson, I guess."

Grandma Peach looked startled. "No," she stuttered. "No, I didn't hear. How big?"

"A couple thousand acres are up right now," Ted said from beside Dane. "It looks like they don't have much of it contained, though, I think it said about ten percent. The PCT goes right around Jefferson, doesn't it?"

"Yes," Grandma Peach said uneasily. "Oh, my. I hope everyone is all right. Have they said anyone has been hurt?"

Ted shook his head, "No."

Patty reached out and patted Grandma Peach's hand. "I'm sure they're shuttling hikers around it."

Chicken Shit spoke up, "Yeah, they're pretty good about that stuff. Last summer in Colorado, they airlifted out a bunch of us, we didn't even know a fire had started."

"Oh, no," Grandma Peach said, more distressed. "They might not have any idea! How far is the nearest road?"

Buzz shrugged, "Thirty miles or so? That's right around Santiam Pass, right?" He looked toward Chicken Shit for validation, but Chicken Shit shrugged.

"It all runs into a blur," he defended. "I know it was after the Three Sisters and before Hood."

"I think about thirty miles was the longest stretch," Buzz said with more certainty than previously. "They'd know about it pretty quick. There'll be signs all over the place."

"Oh, good, good," Grandma Peach said.

"Who shuttles the hikers around?" Vika asked.

"What dear?" Grandma Peach looked up, caught up in her own thoughts.

"The PCT hikers, who shuttles them around?" Vika repeated.

"Trail Angels in the area, I suppose. A lot probably hitchhike around. Jerry! Jerry McCloud! That's the name of a Trail Angel near Eugene. Oh, I don't know where his number is." She scrunched her eyebrows again and Vika knew she was visualizing the junk drawer in the camper next to the armchair, imagining the pages of the address book inside. "Well, if I don't have it, Milly will."

"Well," Patty patted her hand again, before Grandma Peach stood to call her friends, "you can't do anything about the hikers now, Grandma Peach. Sit down and let's finish this delicious dinner you've made. The hikers are very well-connected, they probably knew about the fire the second it started."

"Yes," Grandma Peach sank back into her chair. "You're right. What would I do from here right now?" She placed her napkin carefully on the side of her plate. "Who wants a cupcake?"

A general agreement went through the tables and Grandma Peach went to get the cupcakes, her eyebrows still knit together, while Vika walked out to the porch to start a pot of coffee.

The talk of the wildfire in Oregon faded to the back and Chicken Shit and Buzz entertained Forrest, Ted, and Dane about an encounter with a particularly aggressive rattlesnake north of the San Bernardino Mountains.

"He struck on my hiking pole so high," Chicken Shit was saying, "one of his teeth nicked my pinky."

"He screamed like a little girl."

"My finger was numb for two days."

"Lucky bastard," Dane said shaking his head.

Buzz snorted. "Lucky? That's an understatement. The guy has a horseshoe up his ass." He leaned forward. "That mess with the Colorado fire? The day before, he was camped five feet from a tree that went down from a lightning strike."

"I was sleeping, thought it was the beginning of World War III," Chicken Shit said.

Forrest cocked his head. "The same bolt that started the fire?"

"Now wouldn't that be something!" Chicken Shit roared, laughing.

"Same storm, different bolt," Buzz clarified. Then he looked back at Chicken Shit, "What else?"

"Broke my leg last year," Chicken Shit added. "Didn't see anyone for three days on that trail before I broke it—it was the CDT in southern Montana. Then, I broke my leg and half hour later, a Boy Scout Troop walked by. They had all kinds of useful shit."

"Your karma must be amazing," Dane said.

Chicken Shit shrugged, "I buy the random person a coffee in the drive-thru every once in a while."

"I KNOW THERE ARE SOME TRAIL ANGELS near the fire," Vika said to Grandma Peach the next day after work as she climbed the steps to the bus, "but wouldn't it be fun to go down to Oregon and help shuttle?"

"Oh, Vika," Grandma Peach answered, "it's so far away and Dane—"

"He doesn't have to go. I've been driving the bus more so we could take turns."

Grandma Peach stared at Vika at least a full minute before she answered. "Well, yes, I suppose," she said slowly, though still doubtful about the plan. "We'll have to ask Dane if he needs the bus, and call to see if there's any room in the campground. I'll have to go grocery shopping, and cancel my piano lesson with Jo, and..." Grandma Peach stopped and scrunched her eyebrows. "Yes, I think we should go," she finished.

"Yes," Vika said excitedly. "Absolutely. I'll go ask him when we get back."

They drove up the driveway to the sound of a jackhammer. Well, maybe a jackhammer, Vika couldn't really tell. She had only heard them in movies.

Grandma Peach parked the bus and said, "Come on, Quasi, let's go look for that number." Those two headed for the camper and Vika set out to find Dane and whatever he was doing. She walked around the back of the house to a door, which led directly into the basement.

She found him jackhammering, all right. He wore those same aviator goggles he was wearing the day she landed in their yard. His teeth were gritted as he controlled the machine, his entire upper body bouncing with the rhythm of the hammer. Big, black earmuffs blocked some—certainly not all—of the sound, and Dane had yet to realize Vika stood outside the door. After about two minutes, Dane turned off the jackhammer, breathing hard, pulled off his ear protection, and pushed up his goggles.

"What a workout!" He said to no one but himself, still unaware of Vika's presence.

"What are you working on?" Vika asked.

"OH!" he yelled and turned, surprised, clearly trying to speak over the pounding in his ears left over from the jackhammer. "WHAT?"

"WHAT ARE YOU DOING?"

"THE FLOOR. GOTTA GET A NEW ONE. THIS ONE IS SHIT."
Vika tried to keep her face straight and nodded.

"Are you going to knock that down, too?" She asked, pointing to what looked like a giant block of cement.

His voice lowered finally, even if still on the slightly elevated side. "The cistern? No, keeping that. We're keeping it off the grid as much as possible. Maybe put up some windmills on the back forty. Well, I guess it would actually be the back six."

"Dane," she went on, changing the subject to the matter at hand. "Today, Grandma Peach and I were talking about the big fire in Oregon and—"

"The fire Ted was talking about yesterday?"

"That's the one. Would it be OK if Grandma Peach and I went down there for five or six days? You know, shuttle people around it?"

"To Oregon, huh?"

Vika smiled.

"Where are you going to stay?" he asked.

Vika thought a moment. "Grandma Peach said something about a campground in…Sisters?"

"Sisters? I know the one," he answered. "Well, I don't need the bus for anything and the pack is still south of here—right around the fire, actually. You know how to use the vegetable oil, right?"

"Actually, no, I haven't—"

"I called up Mr. Chen this morning, he's giving me about twenty gallons of grease and it's already clean. You'll smell like Kung-Pow chicken, but it should get you a ways anyway."

"OK," Vika responded slowly. "What do I do with it?"

Dane looked confused. "It's the fuel. Just make sure it's warm and liquid before you put it in the tank. Put it in a tray on the engine and it will heat up nicely. Don't break my engine."

CHAPTER 11

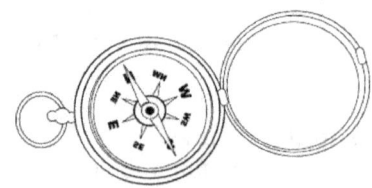

THEY LEFT EARLY THE NEXT MORNING to head south. Grandma Peach was on the phone the night before, talking to her contact in Eugene to get details and names of Trail Angels he knew. The trail was closed, Jerry told her, from Santiam Pass to Olallie Lake, and many hikers were hitching around by way of Sisters, Oregon. It was a sizable town—at least in the summer—a relatively easy hitch from the trail and many hikers took the time to venture into town to resupply. It helped, too, that Sisters had a phenomenal bakery.

The skies were clear on the drive and they made it to the area by midafternoon. The exceptional planner she was, Grandma Peach had called the campground and reserved one site for the bus, and another three tent sites for the hikers they expected to pick up.

Before going into town, the two women figured it would be the best use of time to make a run to the trail head and see if any hikers were around to shuttle. As they bounced up the road, Vika could see a low and dense thundercloud against a bluebird sky. They rumbled over bridges with dry creeks underneath, kicking up dust, dust, and more dust. At last, they pulled up to the top of the pass and parked at the trailhead.

There wasn't a hiker in sight.

The two climbed out of the bus and were hit with a wall of heat. The air was still, the bugs and birds were quiet. Vika looked towards the trail, hearing only the crunch of Grandma Peach's orthopedic shoes as she walked towards the billboard. The dirt was sandy-dry and it sifted into her shoes as she took a step, the plants around her short and sturdy with harsh ends, a defense against the lack of available water. Across the road, lava rocks comprised most of the landscape, though a couple hardy trees managed to twist their way through the rough terrain.

Vika stood there. It was hot. It was sunny. She watched the smoke cloud over the mountains, trying and failing to comprehend the impact of the fire beneath it. Wildfires in suburban North Dakota were about as common as clean snow on a New York City Street. A breeze slid across her face and she squinted against the bright sky.

She stared and as she stared, a single, perfectly formed, and perfectly charred-black maple leaf floated down from the blue sky, slowly, silently, to rest inches from Vika's right foot. Somehow, it had remained flat, each of its eleven points intact and pinching off in perfect symmetry. A chill went up her spine as she bent over to pick it up. She brushed a finger gently along the edge of the leaf and it crumbled into black flakes. She turned her hand over to look at the soot on her fingertip, at the evidence that tied together news stories and reality.

Grandma Peach's footsteps came towards her and Quasi ran up to smell her leg.

"Any notes?" Vika asked, placing the leaf on a nearby rock.

"No, nothing," she answered, looking around at the quiet campsite.

"That's weird," Vika said. "I expected at least fifteen hikers to be waiting for us. This is just about the exact middle of the pack."

"Yes, it should be," Grandma Peach replied.

She had hardly gotten the words out when a rumble came from behind a group of trees a short ways down the trail. Grandma Peach and Vika turned their heads simultaneously towards the sounds of shifting packs, conversations, and hiking poles on rocks as hiker after hiker came around the bend.

Tanned and covered in dust and dirt, each one was alert, excited, and heading right towards them.

They reached that awkward distance where someone needed to say something.

"I think we're the hiker trash you guys are looking for!" one guy called out.

"I think so, too, dear!" Grandma Peach called back.

Quasi, who had been squeezing out as much pee as he could muster on the nearby bushes, trees, and lone blade of grass, looked up and ran to greet them. He got some quizzical stares and one girl kind of squealed and backed up, but the bright blue collar apparently made him domestic enough to get a few pats. He basked in the attention and wound through legs and hiking poles as the group walked toward Grandma Peach and Vika.

Eventually, they were close enough to shake hands.

"Hi," said the guy who first called out. "I'm Two Packs." He put out his hand. "We were keeping cool in a little grove of trees over there."

"Well, nice to meet you, Two Packs," Grandma Peach said, "and everyone else." She looked past him to the thirteen people standing behind him. "I bet you guys are looking forward to hot food and some showers!" she continued. "Everyone going to Sisters?"

There was a ripple of agreement though the crowd and some thank-you's mixed in.

"All right," Grandma Peach directed, "let's get a move-on! The bus is air-conditioned!"

The hikers tried to act normal, but Vika could tell by the raised eyebrows and quick shuffle that this was an unexpected bonus.

The hikers chattered as they filed in, taking spots on the couch and when that was full, they sat on the floor. Some made polite conversation with Vika and Grandma Peach, and some spoke amongst themselves.

"Have you guys been shuttling for long?" Two Packs asked.

"No," Vika answered from her perch on the engine cover. The smell hit her slowly, but very insistently, though she managed to keep a blank face. It was the smell of sweaty, active bodies that hadn't experienced a stick of deodorant in months, under clothes that had their own…flare…of several hundred miles. She tried to breathe through her mouth instead of her nose. "We just got in this morning. You're actually our first run."

"Right on," Two Packs answered, nodding enthusiastically. "We really appreciate it."

"You won't have the pleasure of meeting Purple Rain," someone said loudly from the back—a 20-something man with an unkempt mop of curly brown hair and a scruffy beard, deep brown eyes to match.

Another hiker said loudly, "That idiot is hiking through, isn't he?"

Two Packs turned to him and shook his head in disapproval, "Yeah, he went through a couple days ago, though, so he's probably way on the other side by now. He said he fought forest fires before and he was going to night hike the section so he could see it."

"I thought that moron grew up in Indiana."

A chuckle rippled through the bus, and one hiker called out, "Corn can burn, too!"

"You mean pot?" a female voice teased.

"Yeah," Vika said sarcastically, "bummer we missed him. How did he end up on the trail?"

Two Packs shrugged, "His roommate planned on thru-hiking but he got off after two weeks or something because he sprained his ankle."

"What? Who was his roommate?" a hiker shouted from somewhere in the mix.

Two Packs turned to the hiker asking the question. "Rolls Royce."

"No way! I didn't know that! Why would a stand-up guy like Rolls Royce put up with that much bullshit?"

The curly haired hiker laughed. "Rolls didn't ask him or anything, he kinda just tagged along on the hike. They roomed together back in Dallas. Friend of a friend kind of deal. Man, you should have heard ol' Rollsey complaining about him. He threw out garbage on the trail all the time. Pissed everyone off."

"Rolls said his diet was always, 'some kind of meat fried in butter and beer that he could put in a taco shell.' Then he'd pour the grease down the drain all the time and Rolls Royce had to pour this acid down the drain after it. Said it exploded once and ate a hole in the wall. He fixed it up before the landlord found out."

"That's disgusting," said a girl with blonde streaked hair and suspicious blue eyes sitting in the corner of the couch.

"He sounds lazy," Vika said.

One of the hikers shrugged, "He probably had nothing else to do."

"Yeah, so watch out," Two Packs told Vika. "He's planning on stopping by Stacklen when he gets north."

The girl in the corner of the couch huffed. "He's a harmless pothead," she said to Vika.

"OK, Someday," the curly haired hiker turned to her, "maybe to you, but I've seen him walk out of restaurants without paying at least three times. The pothead part isn't the problem—the fact that he's a dick is." He turned back to Vika. "Just keep an eye on him when he's around."

Vika gave a curt nod. "Will do," she assured him.

Someday sat quietly on the couch, watching the scenery pass by out the window. She folded her hands and kept them her lap, her ankles crossed. She wore black shorts with bright green trim, and a gray T-shirt that had worn thin where her shoulder straps rubbed against her collarbones. Blonde wisps had fallen out of her weather-beaten braid, but a thin headband held them back and out of her face. She seemed closed off to the conversation going on around her, a small, occasional smile the only sign she wasn't completely lost to this world.

They pulled into the campground a short time later and the hikers filed out. Someday was the last to get her things together and step down into the heat.

The campsites were in separate areas, but only a two-minute walk from each other and Vika could see hikers packing in as many tents that would fit. There were a couple other sites spotted throughout the campground, and the thru-hikers mingled from one site to another.

Vika wrote up a rough itinerary for the next couple of days she and Grandma Peach planned on staying in the area. It gave times for shuttles to Santiam Pass and Olallie Lake twice a day, one in the morning and one in the evening, and a "town run" every day about noon. She climbed the stairs to the bus and upon getting approval from Grandma Peach, taped a copy to the dashboard. She introduced herself to some hikers and informed them of the bus schedule, but found most of them had gone out to feast on hot meals. Vika noticed her own stomach was rumbling.

Finding food was always a good way to acquaint oneself with a new town, and after dropping the rest of the fliers in the bus, she found a deli barely a ten-minute walk from the campsite. She saw Someday at a far table sipping tea. Vika ordered herself a sandwich and coffee and walked over with her buzzer to where the hiker sat.

"Someday, right?" Someday looked up, surprised Vika remembered her name.

"Yeah," she smiled. She pulled an empty plate towards her, clearing off the other half. "You can sit if you'd like."

"I'm Vika," she introduced herself. "How long are you planning on staying in Sisters?"

She shrugged and twirled the string of the tea bag around her finger. "I'm thinking just a day. I'd like to keep moving."

"Well we're doing a run to Olallie Lake tomorrow at about eight if you want in," Vika mentioned as her buzzer went off in her hand and she got up to grab her food. "Excuse me."

She grabbed her food and wove her way back through the tables. "So," Vika said, sitting down again, "how's the trail?"

"Oh," Someday's smile fell just short of her blue eyes, "it's good."

Vika took a bite of her sandwich. "Yeah?" she questioned, and chewed. "You don't sound so sure about that."

Someday shrugged, "It's good. Three Sisters Wilderness was really good."

"You've been hiking with Refill, right?" Vika asked.

Someday nodded, looking down at her tea.

"The Cascades are gorgeous," Vika said, trying a different tactic. "It'll be a great way to end."

Someday took a sip of her tea in response.

"You are going to the end, aren't you?"

Someday scrunched her eyebrows together and took a deep breath. "The thing is, we're not the same pace," she said slowly, "me and Refill. She likes the scenery and I like to push myself."

She quickly looked around the room to make sure there weren't any eavesdropping hikers.

"I've been trying to push her but at the end of the day, she won't walk any faster and I just wait longer." She fiddled with the tea bag string.

"Why don't you talk to her about it?" Vika suggested.

"I have tried. I've suggested we could alternate sections from city to city my pace then her pace, but the thing is, she can't. Or won't."

"You might have to change the way you think about the trail."

Someday's eyes turned hard. "I have tried. And I think I did a pretty damn good job of it for 1,900 miles. That's a long way to hike someone else's hike. She's dictated the entire thing for the simple reason that she walks slower than I do. I get bored. I've been getting *bored* on a 2,600 mile hike because I'm waiting."

She let out a frustrated sigh and continued, "When I was mentally preparing for this, I thought of it as a physical challenge first and foremost. Scenery, contemplation, philosophy, whatever you want to think about, all of that was second for me. It was important, and a huge part, but it was still second. When I wake up in the morning, I think about miles first, and then whatever else. It's 2,600 miles; you *have* to put it first, don't you?" She looked confused, as though she wanted to explain what she was thinking, but afraid to at the same time because if she verbalized everything, she almost certainly would have to do something about it. "Out on the trail, you don't exactly have time for rocket science, you know? If my brain is not getting exercise, I have to exercise my body, enough that I don't care my brain is getting fat and lazy. When neither is happening, I feel like a waste of space."

Vika bit her lip and approached from a different angle, "Why are you still hiking with her?"

"Because we started together! We planned the entire hike together," Someday looked close to tears. "I'd feel like the biggest jerk if I stopped hiking with her. I keep thinking I can change my attitude." She rolled her eyes. "I can't imagine what my parents would say. Actually, yeah I can. That I abandoned her. That I'm selfish. That her parents must hate me for leaving her."

"To be honest, you look like you're on the verge of an ulcer. You'll be abandoning her anyway if you have to get off the trail."

Someday was looking at her now, eyelashes wet and clumping together. Someday didn't tell her what the worst part was. She didn't want to make it seem as though she were trying to pit Vika against Refill. She didn't hate Refill. She didn't want to talk behind her back. The truth was, they were having a bad day about two weeks ago, fighting about the pace—Someday wanting to go faster, Refill wanting to do her miles and set up camp by 5:30 p.m. In the fight, Refill let it slip that she never cared about a thru-hike, anyway. She said she wanted to hike and she wanted to explore out west, but she said she never cared if they made it from border to border.

If Refill was going for a hit that hurt the most, she nailed it spot on. Someday was mad as hell at her. At herself, too, because she felt so used and taken advantage of. She had saved and planned for months to thru-hike, and the entire time she did so under the false pretense that Refill wanted the same thing. She wished she could let go of it and keep hiking. Embrace the, "it is what it is" philosophy.

But then she'd sit there, getting bored waiting for Refill, and an evil little voice in the back of her head would whisper that maybe she would've been able to hike her own pace from the beginning, if only Refill had the balls to tell her that before they made this commitment together. She could have saved so much drama. She wouldn't be waiting, and she might enjoy hiking through Oregon.

Of course, then she would feel bad if she put the majority of the blame on Refill, when she felt that in the end, *she* was the one who couldn't figure out how to appreciate the hike and decided to use Refill as a scapegoat. Then she thought of the ulterior motives again and became livid, and then guilty again…

All that up and down, among other things, pushed Someday to a near meltdown. She knew Vika was right. She'd hate the trail soon enough if she continued on that emotional rollercoaster and she'd quit. Her only hope was to change things. And she knew that meant hiking without Refill.

Vika sat quietly, sipping her coffee, watching tension cross through the hiker's face in waves. She swallowed her food and spoke carefully, "You know what they say, 'Hike your own hike.' It's not too late to start. Switching things up might even be more exciting and help you get to the end."

Someday smiled and let out a half-laugh, half-sob. "I've been telling myself that since we crossed the Oregon border." The two sat in silence for a few moments.

"We'll be fine, right? Hiking separately? We're in the middle of the pack. We probably won't have to hitch alone. We've been hanging out with Trot and Starsky; I bet she'll keep hiking with them. I know Time Warp is in front of me a day or two and he did the road walks around the closure. I think he's going about the pace I want to go, so I could catch up." She puffed out a determined breath. "You're right. I deserve to hike my own hike, too."

Vika ate her sandwich and let the girl justify her decision.

"Oh, maybe I should plan some mail drops while I'm here in a town with a decent grocery store and then I won't have to worry about that. I'll have to tell Refill soon." Her gaze dropped.

Vika finished her sandwich and they walked together out the door.

"If you need anything else, you know where to find us," Vika said to the worried hiker. "We're the only bus in the campground."

"Thanks," Someday said as she slowly turned and started heading in the direction of the grocery store. Vika turned towards the campground, not envying in the least the conversation Someday had to have with Refill.

She passed a chocolate shop shortly after and didn't even slow down as she passed through the front door. A bell tinkled at her arrival and the smells of sugars, chocolates, subtle fruits, nuts, and coconuts stampeded her nose.

Ten minutes later, she walked out with two boxes—one for herself and another for the hikers to justify her splurge.

Vika carried an armful of the chocolate assortment to the site and the treat was met with enthusiasm, as hikers scurried over and inhaled three or more at a time. Two new thru-hikers came from the opposite side of the campground.

"What's this?" one of the new hikers said, gesturing to where the tents were set up. "Look at all that green! You guys parked it on some dead grass with a bunch of rocks and a Charlie Brown Christmas tree. Shame, shame."

A middle-aged woman Vika knew as Cheshire spoke up, "Want to know where I slept last night? In a grove of trees overlooking a mountain lake with beautiful blue water in the middle of the Three Sisters Wilderness." She laughed, "Then we come here listening to RV generators and pop our tents on lush green grass and get kicked off because, and I quote, 'even one night might kill it.'" She shook her head with a grin and continued, "Makes you wonder what luxurious means. I swear, if towns didn't have ice cream, sometimes I wouldn't even bother."

The counterpart of the new hiker team plopped down his pack with one hand and holding a melting chocolate in the other, started in on a story.

"So there we were, waiting for a ride for," he gave an exaggerated shrug, "probably forty minutes, right, and this Jeep going the opposite direction turns around and pulls over. This brunette chick gets out and we're like, what the hell? A single girl picking us up—that usually doesn't happen—and then we got closer and saw this girl was ripped. I mean *ripped.* In a hot way. She could kick both our asses."

"So we were riding in the car and talking, you know, normal first conversation talk, Buffalo Bill asks her what she does for a living and she says, 'I do triathlons.'" He laughed out loud and clapped his hands. "Just like that! 'I do triathlons.'" He laughed again. "So we asked her about it. Clearly. Who wouldn't? Did she say she used to swim for the National Team, Bill?" He looked at his hiking partner for confirmation.

Bill nodded, "Yeah, tore her shoulder up pretty good and started running and biking when she got dry docked."

The first hiker looked out at his audience and continued, his eyebrows raised and arms out, "Did you know that triathlons are an Olympic sport? We did not, but apparently they are. She was in Beijing in 2008 and in London in 2012." He took a deep breath and put his hands on his hips. "Man, we got picked up hitchhiking by a hot Olympic triathlete."

"Did you get her number?" Cheshire teased.

"We should have," they said at the same time.

CHAPTER 12

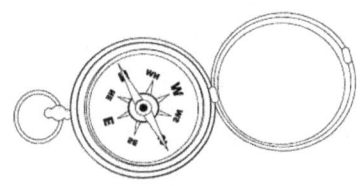

AFTER THE CHOCOLATES had been polished off, Vika looked up and saw Grandma Peach talking with about five other people, all looked to be in their 60s, maybe some of them were a little younger. A man, whom she didn't know, cooked outside of the bus on a grill they did not own. Grandma Peach caught her eye and waved her over.

Vika walked up to the group and Grandma Peach took her by the arm. "Oh, Vika, dear," she said, "I want you to meet Bill and Joyce. They're Trail Angels from Ashland."

Grandma Peach led her to a married couple who looked to be in their mid-50s. "Hi, how are you?" she greeted them, putting her hand out for the man to shake. He was smaller than Dane, but then again, everyone was smaller than Dane. He wore a pale blue T-shirt that had *Myrtle Beach* written across the chest, tucked neatly into his khakis. His wife, standing by his side, sipped a cup of tea. Ginger, from the smell of it, Grandma Peach's favorite and no doubt her suggestion. She wore her gray hair short and styled, and everything else about her was simple and polished.

Vika smiled and shook hands with Joyce.

"Grandma Peach said you've been staying with them a while in Stacklen. How do you like it?" Joyce asked, her grey eyes focused and a touch intimidating.

"I like it a lot," she said. "I've really gotten the hang of everything by now. The house, the motorcycle, all of it." She laughed and they politely chuckled.

"That house sounds like quite the project. We'd love to see it sometime. Of course, probably not in the next month or so, seeing as we have about thirty hikers a day," Bill explained. "Joyce here, she loves changing our house around. I can't imagine what she would do with a clean slate to work with."

Joyce laughed. "It would be a dream come true!"

"Well," Grandma Peach said, "we're still on deconstruction right now. We won't have walls for a couple months so you have plenty of time."

"Great!" Joyce answered.

"You said your niece is looking after your house now?" Grandma Peach asked.

"Yes, she's working at the school over the summer and she's staying with us. I'm sure she has her hands full about now, but it was the weekend so she was home and we were able to come up and shuttle. I haven't been to this part of the state in years, right Bill?" She looked at her husband for help placing it. "When was the last time we came up here? Oh, well, you went with Ted and the boys on that scout trip. ...Hmm, oh! I know what it was! Mom and Cindy and I came up for that quilt show here five, six years ago." Looking back at Grandma Peach again she said, "Yes, it's been a while."

"Me, too," Grandma Peach answered, "but the Sisters are just as beautiful as ever."

"They sure are," Bill responded and Joyce nodded. They moved simultaneously to let a couple of thru-hikers behind them move to talk with some other Trail Angels at the site.

Vika brought her gaze back from the distraction. "Have you hiked the trail?"

"No," Joyce answered for both of them.

"Oh," Vika answered and after a moment asked, "What made you want to be a Trail Angel?"

Joyce looked skyward and shrugged. "It's fun," she said with a grin. "It keeps me young."

Bill leaned forward and joked, "Have you seen these guys?" A corner of his mouth pulled up. "They'd be under an inch of grime if someone didn't let them use their washing machine every once in a while."

Joyce nodded in concession to her husband and turned to ask Vika, "Are you in school?"

"No," Vika answered, chewing the inside of her cheek as she wondered how best to describe her situation. She figured she'd be telling the story plenty this summer so she might as well get used to it. "No, I just graduated in May. I was on a road trip and had a little car trouble."

"She blew it up," Grandma Peach interjected.

"What happened? I'm glad you're OK!" Joyce was appropriately shocked, while Bill looked quizzical.

"Thanks," Vika said. "It started out more like a slow-roasting fire and I was out for at least five minutes before it got to the gas tank."

"Oh. Oh, well, glad to hear it." Joyce looked expectantly at Vika to continue and she did.

"I was walking on the side of the road, trying to get to a town and Grandma Peach drove by in the bus. She picked me up took me to the house, and well, I've been there ever since. I work at the little shop in town, too."

"How nice! Funny how things work out, isn't it?" Joyce said, and instead of waiting for a response, she continued, "Did you know about the PCT before?"

"Nope," Vika replied. "New Pants was at the house the day I arrived. He gave me a rundown."

At the mention of the name, the two thru-hikers behind Bill and Joyce turned around, raised the beers, and cheered, "New Pants!"

The shorter one spoke up first, "He finished right?"

"Yes, dear," Grandma Peach told them, "on July 30."

"Beast!" said the taller one loudly through the crowd. "He's a beast!"

They talked briefly about the other hikers who made it through Stacklen. When the hot dogs and burgers started coming off the grill, the groups of people shifted and Vika found herself in a semicircle of different thru-hikers. They talked about the trail—the fire mostly—and some hitchhiking stories.

"Three of us rode twenty-one miles in a truck bed camper," said a tall, thin guy named Stilts.

Spurs across from him laughed and said, "I don't have that one yet! The guy who gave us a ride here told us to lie down in the back of the truck. He must have been on the job but hey, we appreciated it."

"Both of those were about twenty times better than the ride Antares and I got outside of Truckee." Vika looked at the black-haired girl with two burgers on her plate. "She was drunk, completely wasted. Ugh, I was so pissed. We didn't know when we took the ride, not until half a mile down the road they each cracked open a beer and offered us some. They had a little Chihuahua that shook the whole time, too. He was either on crack or terrified out of his damn mind." She shook her head and chewed her burger. "Of course, any road around the trail winds around like you wouldn't believe, so we didn't really have a safe way to bail, either. Ugh, I was so pissed," she repeated.

"So what did you do?" Vika asked.

"We sat there. After about six miles there was an intersection and we told them we had to get out. I wanted to get out earlier. I mean, it really wound around, like I said. Antares was terrified, too." She paused and playfully jabbed him in the side.

"Got some burgers and hot dogs here!" someone yelled from one of the Trail Angel sites. Hikers chatted and shifted towards the food as they told their stories.

"I got a half dozen new blisters from the shoes I'd had sent to me in Ashland," said a hiker who had moved into earshot of Vika as the crowd flowed.

"Ah, that's too bad," his friend replied as he gave him a pat on the back.

They were almost to Vika when she said, "We have a first-aid kit if you need anything out of it."

The hiker with the blisters looked up as he limped by. "Ah, that's all right," he said, "I have blisters under calluses, blisters on top of blisters. There's not a lot that can be done." He shrugged, "I drain them every once in a while, that's about it. I have a pair of new shoes waiting for me at the post office here. At least, I hope so."

Vika opened her mouth to try and say something back when another hiker came from the left and clapped the blistered hiker on the shoulder.

"You're disgusting," he said with a smile.

"Trapper! What's going on! I haven't seen you since Kennedy Meadows," he said.

"Yeah, I've been hot on your tail for the last three hundred miles. Are you going to grab something to eat?"

"Hell yeah. Where's Gumbo?"

"Giardia. Shit himself down six more pounds and his wife made him go home."

The blistered hiker made a *tsk* sound. Trapper shrugged and took a sip of the beer he was holding. Their voices started to mix with the other hikers as they moved toward the food and away from Vika, but she heard, "Probably for the better. He would have walked until the buzzards started circling."

The crowd shifted behind Vika. "I'm not the one that sent the p-cord home because it weighed too much," she heard a hiker say.

"I hang a bear bag every night," another hiker answered.

"Well, the p-cord went home, and a bear ate our food two days later."

"Tough break."

A third voice joined the discussion, "I haven't hung a bear bag the entire trail."

"Me neither."

"In the desert, I used my food bag to elevate my feet."

"Great, so when the bears start roaming the camps for food, we'll have you all to blame."

"What the hell, guys? Hang your food."

"Yeah…I probably won't."

Vika moved through a group and up the stairs to the camper. She grabbed a sweatshirt for when the sun went down and walked to a circle of hikers sitting around a campfire. She pulled up a plastic chair and sat down with her own bottle of beer.

"Windigo Pass was awful," a middle-aged hiker named Swish said, as he put a bottle to his lips and took a sip of beer. "I didn't get a single break. Constant vigilance. I would wipe my arm off, and by the time I got to the other arm, at least twenty were already lined up. I had my bug spray can out constantly. I'm so glad we're out of mosquito country. I don't know how Manifesto made it without bug spray, I tell ya."

Vika pulled up a chair and popped the top off her own beer bottle.

"He started walking at five when they woke him up," another hiker said, "and kept walking at four miles an hour all day long."

Swish chortled, "I guess at least with those big miles he made it through quick enough, even if he was a mosquito chew toy."

"You're talking about the only species I would love to make extinct," Stilts said as he pulled up a chair next to Vika. "I sprayed the swarm following me every once in a while, slow 'em down. And they *hummed*. There were so many of them, when I was lying in my tent, I heard a constant *hum*. I had nightmares about that."

A female voice added to the discussion, "I sprayed down my ass before going to the bathroom."

"Hey," another hiker called, "what about the elk in the Three Sisters Wilderness? Did you guys see them?"

"Sure did! They were everywhere. One of them was eating grass right next—and I mean *right* next to—my tent yesterday morning."

Vika relaxed into her chair, content with listening to the stories, being part of the hiking culture if only for a little bit. She wondered if she could do it. She wondered if she'd want to.

SOMEDAY WALKED UP TO THE BUS later that evening while Vika and Grandma Peach sat, talking with Bill and Joyce, ready for the shuttle run that would be twenty minutes later. Vika pushed herself up and met the girl on the edge of the campsite. Someday was distracted, flustered, and flushed when she approached, her arms piled high with boxes. She put them down on the ground and shook out her arms. "I have one for Timberline, Trout Lake—I'll have to hitch for that one but it's either hitch or get five days worth of food at Cascade Locks—and White Pass. I'll buy food in Cascade Locks when I go through," she rushed. "That should get me to you guys again and I'll finish up my resupplies in your town. You have a decent store, right? I'll have to get another for Stehekin." She thought a moment, "No, I'll do Stehekin now."

She was excited, and shuffling around boxes, fiddling with their position.

"Yeah," Vika answered, "it's not the greatest convenience store, but during the summer it has a hiker section. You should be fine. It might be a good one if you want anyone from home to mail stuff out. We take packages."

Someday looked kind of fidgety. "Oh, good."

"Did you tell Refill about your plan yet?" Vika asked.

Someday shook her head quickly and wrung her hands, "I'm going to do that now. She'll want to go grocery shopping soon. That'd be weird if I waited for then to tell her. 'Oh, by the way, I already went. I'm not going to be hiking with you.'" She shuddered and swallowed hard.

"OK, well, I'm going to go do that," she took a deep breath and wiped her hands on her pants.

She bent down to pick up the boxes.

"You can leave those here," Vika said, bending to help her. Someday looked up, a touch of relief noticeable within all the tension that stretched the span of her face.

"Thanks," she said, as she stacked the last box on top. "Thank you for everything. If I kept hiking with her, I don't know if...I don't know... I'm—"

"You're welcome," Vika said easily, avoiding repeating the conversation they had in the café. She turned towards the bus and Someday followed. They quickly put down the boxes and returned outside. With one last look, Someday raised her eyebrows as if to say, "Here I go," and turned to walk across the campground in search of a breakup.

She didn't come back by the time Vika and Grandma Peach were to do their evening trailhead run, and Vika stacked the boxes carefully next to a bookshelf in the bus. Four hikers were going up to the lake, two were going back to the Pass to do the road walk, and six got off at the grocery store as they headed out of town.

They said goodbye and good luck, and the hikers started off.

The bus was quiet on the ride to the other side of the fire. The air was dry and hot as they bounced swayed along over the road.

It wasn't quiet for long, though. When Grandma Peach pulled up to where the trail crossed the road, about fifteen dirty thru-hikers waited patiently for the ride they read on the billboard was coming.

The two hikers who were going to do the road walk stepped onto the dry soil, while the waiting hikers shuffled onto the bus. More were tired than not and the conversations filled the bus more slowly than during the more energetic morning run.

Just as they had shuffled on, the hikers shuffled off the bus once they arrived at the campground and squeezed their tents in where they could find a spot. Some joined the groups of people around the fires, while others climbed into their tents as soon as they were set up.

Vika looked around for Someday, but she was nowhere to be seen and her tent looked dark.

Someday sat reading at a picnic table when Vika woke up the next morning and emerged from the camper. She wore the same black and green shorts she had on the day before, but had pulled a black puffy jacket over her torso and she secured her hair in a new braid. Her pack rested against the table supports next to her, fully zipped and clipped, and fastened for hiking. Her head hung over the book, ankles crossed and under the bench in such a way that she leaned forward, her elbows locked into her sides to keep in as much body heat as possible.

Vika stepped down into the grass and felt the cool water droplets slide over her sandaled feet, as she pulled her dark fleece up around her neck to block against the chilly morning air. Someday flipped a page in the paperback as Vika wound through tents to get to her. She swung a leg over the bench, and then pulled the other through and sat down.

"We have your boxes in the camper," Vika said.

"Oh, thank you! I'm so sorry I forgot I left them until I got into my tent and by then it looked like you guys had already turned in for the night."

"No worries," Vika reassured her. "They were probably safer and drier with us anyway. The post office doesn't open until later, so we'll just mail it after we to the run this morning."

"Are you sure?"

"Positive."

"Thank you, thank you," Someday said, clearly relieved as she pulled out some folded bills.

"There's coffee in the camper," Vika continued. "It'll be ready soon if you're interested."

"Sure," Someday nodded and shoved receipt between the pages in her book. Vika had seen thru-hikers come to the house with books, and some of them had doctored them pretty well. They would cut off the chapters they had read so they wouldn't have to carry around the extra weight.

"How are you?" Vika asked.

Someday shrugged, "Fine. Sarah brushed it off like it was no big deal. I know she was pissed, but she didn't say so."

"I'm sorry," Vika offered. "That must have been tough."

Someday shrugged again, "Yeah, but it got to the point where I had to do it. It'll work out."

Vika nodded and stood. "I'll go get that coffee. Cream or sugar?"

"Neither please."

Vika returned with two cups of the steaming beverage, one black and one a light beige, loaded with the extras.

"We'll be leaving in about forty-five minutes with whoever's ready to go," Vika said as she passed a mug and sat down again. "Everyone knows the deal is eight o'clock sharp."

Alas, they left at ten after eight, six hikers including Someday occupied the furniture of the bus. Some looked like they could use a couple more hours of sleep, some emanated energy, clearly rejuvenated by the food, showers, and good cheer of the town of Sisters. They all talked about the trail.

"I can't *wait* until Goat Rocks," one hiker said.

"I heard Northern Washington is going to kick our asses," another put in.

"I'm looking forward to Timberline."

"Hell yeah, man. Hell yeah. Belgian waffle buffet."

"Isn't that where they filmed 'The Shining'?"

"I think so."

And so the conversation went, hikers excited to hike. Grandma Peach pulled off the road on the far side of the fire at Olallie Lake and about two-thirds of them filed out to say goodbye, thank you, good luck, and see you in Stacklen. Quasi bounded around them and barked his goodbyes as he received a couple pats. Vika was excited for them to continue, but in a different way than she felt in Stacklen. Here, there existed the possibility that they would meet again. In Stacklen, she felt as though every time she said goodbye, she said goodbye forever; it was likely true.

Someday hung back until the other hikers had left and came up to give Vika a hug. "Thank you," she said with a squeeze.

Vika hugged her back hard. "Stay safe. Hike your own hike, and call if you need anything. Anything, OK?"

Someday nodded and turned to go, pulling in a deep breath. She shifted the weight of her pack and took her time adjusting the length of her hiking poles. Then she planted one foot in front of her, and then the other. She glanced back and gave a tight smile before she disappeared around some trees.

Vika was nervous for her and hoped she'd catch up to the other hiker soon. She stood at the trailhead and watched the empty path her friend had gone down. The crunch of small feet shuffled up to her from behind.

"She'll be OK," Grandma Peach said. "Starting is the hardest part. Static friction and kinetic friction and all that, or whatever nonsense my son blabbers about. Anyway, your friend there, if she's strong enough to start out by herself, she's strong enough to get wherever she wants to go." Grandma Peach patted her on the arm, and Quasi peed on a rock. Vika gave a tight smile.

They drove back to Santiam Pass and slowly descended into the already stifling heat, Grandma Peach, Vika, Quasi, and the remaining road-walking hikers all stood together there for a moment, staring down the vacant trail, the sun beating down on them. Similar goodbyes and good lucks were given and they started off.

A minute later, a bout of laughter sounded, followed quickly by the *tink* of hiking poles against rock that coincided with an adult gait. One figure emerged from the grass covered lava rocks, two others on his heels. They all stood above six feet tall, with shaggy, bleach blonde surfer hair, and as they moved closer, Vika noticed they all had light blue eyes and the same nose.

Not one of them could have been more than a 160 pounds. Blond beards covered most of their face, and bright, clear blue eyes were glowing with excitement. Their faces were tan with faint sunglass lines across their noses, and their tanned, dirty, defined legs boasted strength with layers over layers over layers of muscle and they approached with an easy stride. All of their feet were shoved into sneakers, with tape here and there stuck on their shoes, in attempt to keep their feet on the inside, but even so, she could see one of the hiker's socks clear through the torn mesh on the top.

Quasi was the first to voice a greeting and one of the guys bent to pat him.

"I'm Tic," said the first hiker in the group.

The other two introduced themselves as Tac and Toe.

Tic, Tac, and Toe loaded into the bus, full of energy and obviously relieved at having a ride that would deliver them to a shower, laundry, and hot food.

Grandma Peach put the bus in gear and eased it out of the parking spot.

They settled back into the couch.

After a couple moments, Tac asked, "So what brings you to Sisters?"

Vika answered, "Grandma Peach's son, Dane, owns a house in the North Cascades—"

"The Darcys'?"

"Dancys'."

"Right, we've heard of that house."

"Yeah," Vika continued, "we heard about the fire and wanted to help shuttle."

"And you drove from Northern Washington?"

"Yep."

"What other hikers have you guys had at your place?" Tic asked.

There hadn't been too many and between the two of them, Vika and Grandma Peach were able to name them all. "Forrest is still with us," Vika added.

"Forrest? Oh, man, good for him!"

"Yeah, we were worried he'd have a heart attack on the trail."

"He was a big guy. Is he still big?"

"No," Vika answered, "he showed us a picture of him when he started to hike. He's down about thirty pounds."

"Thirty pounds…" Tic said out loud. "When did he get in?"

"About a week ago."

"A week! Forrest is holding up to his name. It's not like we've been screwing around."

"Too much."

"Yeah, too much."

"What do you mean about his name?" Vika asked, as her eyes shifted constantly among the brothers sitting exactly the same way on the couch, leaning forward with their forearms across their knees.

"We named him. He would go and go."

"Like Forrest Gump," Toe said.

His brother Tic added, "But he wasn't running like in the movie."

"Man, he was so slow. He just never stopped," Toe continued.

"Especially at Tahoe. He would start walking at dawn and stop, well, no one knew when he stopped."

"It was almost like he didn't. We never saw him at his camp. He passed us once at midnight."

"Didn't talk much, either, like Forrest Gump."

"We had just come from the Sierras and we were doing 30s pretty easily and he was hiking about the same mileage, it just took him more hours in the day."

"He wore jeans for the first 150 miles."

"He was still wearing jeans when he got to Stacklen," Vika said, unsure the significance of that detail.

"Really?"

"Tac asked him why he wouldn't stop," Toe told them.

"Especially since he'd just started. The guy didn't look like he was in shape."

"That worried us, you know?" Tic said. "We were kind of ahead of the pack and there weren't a lot of other hikers out. What if he had a heart attack or something? Twisted his ankle, anything. He didn't look like he could hold his own in the woods."

"We said that to him, that he ought to rest a little more and take care of himself. He said he couldn't. He couldn't stop—"

"His wife died of cancer," Tic added.

"She died?" Vika blurted, at the same time Grandma Peach made a sound of sympathy. Vika quickly thought to the conversations she'd had with him, and he had always talked about her in the past tense. That also explained why she never saw him talking on the phone, mailing anything home—no one was waiting for him.

"Yeah," Tac answered, "the year before, on July 4."

"He wouldn't go into town. He had his neighbor mail out all his food. He said if he got in a town he would never get back on the trail and the trail was the best thing that happened to him in the past year."

"Which was why he kept walking and never stopped."

"I think he wanted to be so exhausted he couldn't think."

"We hiked together, kind of, for about a month."

"Yeah, we'd see him on the trail every three days or so."

"That was comforting."

"Mmm-hmm, because we got off for a couple days to go to a brew fest in southern Oregon, and by then we were pretty confident he could make it."

Vika managed a nod, and from the look on Grandma Peach's face, it seemed as though she was hung up on the news as well.

CHAPTER 13

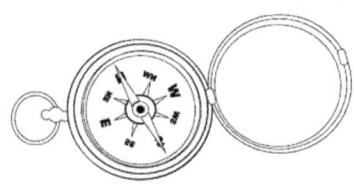

THAT SAME DAY, VIKA WAS READING in a camp chair while Grandma Peach sat knitting in the chair next to her, when a guy walked up to them; beard, tan, skinny legs—the usual thru-hiker look. Vika didn't recognize him from the bus.

"Hi," he said, clearing his throat, "so I heard, um, that you guys have a house in Washington." He cleared his throat again, "and well, I was wondering, um, if you need any help?"

"Help?" Grandma Peach raised her eyebrows, knitting needles frozen midstitch. "Honey, it needs a new roof, new plumbing, new wiring, new insulation, and there's a twenty-foot hole in the foundation. We need all the help we can get."

The guy gave a brief smile. "That's good to hear. Well, not good that there is that much work, but I can help. I've worked with my uncle laying blocks. I'm pretty good."

Grandma Peach squinted at him and said, "That's very nice of you dear, but you still have five hundred miles to go before you get in our neck of the woods." She stitched and pearled.

The guy twisted his hands, "I'm done. Done hiking, I mean. Sisters is the end for me." He held her gaze but Vika thought it was a challenge for him, given the way he clamped his jaw shut.

Vika watched as Grandma Peach studied him. She stared at his face a long time as he fidgeted, and then let her gaze drop, past his dirty shirt, and dirty shorts, down to where his foot tapped and shuffled against the soil.

She brought her eyes back up. "OK. Then," she said, "we'll be leaving in two days."

"Yes, ma'am. Thank you." He turned to go.

"Hold on," she stopped him. "What's your name, dear?"

"Oh," he said with a nervous chuckle, "Slip An' Slide. Or David. Either one." He stuck out his hand for her to take.

"OK, Slip An' Slide. I'm Grandma Peach. See you on Thursday." She shook his hand with one of hers, and patted the top with the other.

He turned and awkwardly walked away.

Vika watched him go. She watched the tension in his shoulders and the slight limp in his stride. She wondered if he was in a similar situation as Someday, or was sick, or injured. The list expanded the longer she was exposed to the hiker life.

He walked through the campground waving at a couple of people, and then he passed the tents and walked out on the other side. She watched until he crossed the street and disappeared behind a house.

Vika looked down at her book but the pages were suddenly uninteresting to her. She closed it with a sigh.

"I'm going to the bakery," she told Grandma Peach.

"You can't fix them all," Grandma Peach said as she stitched and pearled.

"What?"

"Will you pick me up a cinnamon roll, please?" she asked, glancing up to give Vika a warm smile. "I think they're the best cinnamon rolls I've ever had."

Vika raised her eyebrows, but Grandma Peach gave no inclination she was going to revisit her previous statement. "Sure," she answered, and set out at a slow and steady meander in the general westward direction.

She ordered the food and sat to eat. She tried to savor each bite but they never lasted as long as she wanted them to. Before she left, Vika took another pastry to go for herself because she simply couldn't resist and went for an easy stroll through town. She saw packs lined up by the library, some she recognized, and some she didn't. She had no doubt the owners of the packs were inside stinking up the computer room to get on the coveted internet to update their online journal, blog, email loved ones that they made it through yet another leg, and maybe order new gear.

Her feet took her to the door of the post office where she found a registry and flipped open the first page to read the thoughts of hikers who've passed through. The entry belonged to New Pants and she felt camaraderie with him as she read the short and sweet note, thanking the town of Sisters for the exceptional hospitality. She continued reading on, some of people she knew, and some she didn't.

Found a swimming hole. Not as good as Desolation Wilderness. Almost froze my balls off.—Gandalf

Great town! Waiting for Smack and Chief.—Stargazer

Laaaavvvvvaaaaaa!—Krakatoa

Pretty cool terrain, just hot and dry. Going around the fire now—I hate to say it but the smoke makes for some pretty stellar sunsets. Met some AWESOME Trail Angels from Stacklen! Thanks Sisters!—Fiddlehead

"Once upon a time/

"I went for a hike/

"Covered in dirt and grime/

"Sometimes I wish I had my bike."—Lasso

SAW A COUGAR! BE JEALOUS!!—Lil Bit O' Salt

Already ate an entire pie at the bakery. Going back for another.—Time After Time

Lil Bit O' Salt: WHERE WAS I???? Hitched into town on a horse and buggy.—Tom Tom

SHE READ AND READ AND READ, and finally, when she had had her fill of reading, she continued on through town and saw a couple more ragged packs sitting outside an outfitters and across the street she could see hikers milling through a used bookstore a little further up the road. She walked by a thru-hiker sitting under a tree on the lawn of a craft store.

"Mom, we are fine," she heard him saying. "The fire was really far away, they were just being cautious."

This wasn't the first time Vika overheard this phone conversation over the last few days, and she also knew that in some cases, it wasn't entirely true.

"We're in Sisters…no…Mom…*Mom!* Someone picked us up and we drove around it…Well, don't believe everything the media says," he said. "Yes, Three Sisters Wilderness was phenomenal and thank you for the candy bars…My feet are fine…Yes, I've been getting enough food—we just ate at a really great Mexican restaurant last night."

Vika kept walking and the conversation faded into the noises of the traffic and window shoppers. She knew it was her turn to make a call. She hadn't called home in—well, since her mother had yelled at her the last time. She bit her lip and pulled her phone out. Across the street was a little area with a fountain and a statue of someone and a plaque underneath. Town hall maybe? She didn't know, but it looked like public domain. She crossed the street and sat on the bench.

Vika scrolled quickly through her contacts and hit send.

"Vika!" her dad greeted her.

"Hey, Dad," she said, "just calling to say hi."

"Where are you?"

"I'm in Oregon. What's new in Jessup?"

"Same old, same old," he answered. "I'm working on a deal that will take me to September, at least. So, Oregon. They have bears, right? Keep an eye out, will you?"

"Sure, Dad." Vika heard a new voice in the background.

"You're mother's here and she wants to talk—"

"Hello, Vika," her mother sounded distant and as though she were speaking through clenched teeth.

Vika swallowed. "Hi, Mom. Tell Dad I said goodbye, I guess."

"Where are you now?"

"Um…In Sisters, Oregon."

"With who? *With who, Vika?*" her mother's voice didn't sound quite so far away anymore. In fact, Vika pulled the phone away from her ear a bit because she sounded close enough to reach through the phone and throttle her.

Vika cleared her throat and answered, "With Grandma Peach. Did Alex tell you about them?"

"Who? The hillbillies? Vika, I want you to come home right now or—"

Vika started to feel the back of her neck heat up and felt her throat close. "They are *not* hillbillies, Mom. And what? I come home or what? You're going to come get me?" Once again, the conversation was spinning out of control.

They both knew it, and they both let it.

"I will! I will come to Washington, or wherever the hell you decide to go next with those people, and I will bring you home!" she spat the words out.

"No!" Vika raised her voice, "No, you won't and I don't want you to. I've already told you that, I don't understand why you don't trust me."

"Oh, my god, Vika," her mother sighed. "You are acting like you're four years old. Whatever I did to make you want to run away from home I'm sorry."

"I did not run away from home! I'm—"

"Is that what you want? I'm sorry. You'll come home now?"

"I don't want or need an apology. I'm healthy and I'm happy and this is my choice."

Her mother sighed dramatically and continued, "Martha, the one at my work? She says her cousin is curator at a museum in Cincinnati. I can't imagine it's very big but it could be a good start. She says she'd put in a good word for you."

"Mom—"

"I told her you were visiting an aunt in Seattle. On your father's side."

"Stop it."

"What? You don't want a job? You don't want a house? You don't want to build a life? Instead, you want to smoke weed around a drum circle for the rest of your life."

"Stop it."

"What, Vika? You don't want me to help you? Fine."

"Fine."

"Fine." She paused, a loud, loud pause. "You know one day, you're going to have to grow up."

"Growing up has nothing to do with the things you just listed."

"Oh?" her mother's voice listed. "I'm sorry, did you go to school for philosophy? My mistake, I thought it was art history. And now you're gallivanting around God knows where, wasting your degree."

Vika bit the inside of her cheek. "I'm just saying there is more out there than a forty-hour work week."

"Oh, Vika." Her mother laughed out loud and sounded almost cheerful when she responded, "You'll thank me in fifteen years when you have a comfortable pension, your kids have green grass to play on, and you can take a vacation each year." Vika's mother became quiet. "Why don't you want that? Your father and I have worked so hard to set you up for success, and you just...run off."

"Mom," Vika said, "it doesn't work like that."

"What are you talking about?"

"It's just not that linear anymore. Of course, I appreciate everything you and dad have done, but there are a whole new set of obstacles from thirty years ago."

"Oh? What's this new confirmation bias you've talked yourself into? That people should abandon real life any time things get hard?" Vika shook her head and stayed silent. She heard her mom take a deep breath, and then continue as though it were any old conversation, "Alex has an interview with a tech company in Chicago in a few days. He had one with a marketing firm in last week but he didn't get that job. Maybe you'll talk to him about it? He could read over your résumé."

"For what?" Vika was taken aback. "He hasn't taken an art class in his life."

"Maybe he can give you some tips."

Vika curled her fingers around the phone. "Yeah," she answered. "Sure."

"By the end of the week?"

"Mom, I'm not coming home right now."

"But at least your résumé will be ready when you come to your senses."

"I have to go, Mom."

"Fine. End of the week, Vika. You hear me?"

"Sure, Mom. Talk to you later."

Vika stared at her phone, eyes wide and *mad*. So mad she could feel her pupils dilate, and her lungs squeeze shut. Her back stiffened and her skin prickled. She was states away and still couldn't escape this cat and mouse game of what she should and shouldn't be doing. And worse, her mother not only consistently brought Alex into it, she brought the Dancys into it, too. She could throw around anything she wanted to about Vika and it would hurt, but to blindly attack the people she was beginning to feel were family was unacceptable. Her mother didn't understand anything other than work and schedules.

Anyway, she had hikers to transport, so she had no time to dwell.

Still, she looked down at her phone to see if her mom called back, but she hadn't. If stubbornness were hereditary, she definitely received that gene from her mother's side. Neither would call the other for days, maybe a week or two, when upset.

She pressed the heels of her hands into her eyes for a moment, and then pushed herself off the bench.

It was quiet when she returned to the campground and she found Grandma Peach and Quasi inside the bus. Even with the air conditioner, Quasi lay quietly on the rug, spread out, tongue lolling out the side of his mouth. He opened an eye and raised his head an inch when Vika made her entrance.

"Are you all right, deary?" Grandma Peach asked as she looked up from the murder mystery she was reading.

"Yes," Vika answered, doing her best to avoid eye contact.

"You sure? You look tense."

"I just spoke with my mom," she explained. "It didn't go so well."

"Do you want to talk about it?" Grandma Peach asked calmly.

Vika brought her eyes up quickly. "No, thanks."

Grandma Peach watched her for a second and gave a slight nod. "Anyone else need anything?" she asked.

Vika shook her head. "I think it'll be quiet for a little while. Most of the hikers are either sleeping, doing laundry, or at the grocery store or the library."

"OK," Grandma Peach said, looking over her glasses and gesturing to the counter. "I made some cookies for whenever people come around. You should have one," she winked at Vika. "They're good."

Vika didn't exactly feel like a cookie, but she was doing her best not to build a gray cloud in the middle of the camper, so she walked over to the plate and slid one out from under the plastic wrap. She took a bite.

"Mmm," she said. "They're still warm." She took another bite. "Oh, my god. These are delicious!"

Grandma Peach smiled, "What did I tell you. Have another." She just might, Vika thought, they were good enough to ease the memory of the phone conversation with her mother.

That evening Grandma Peach and Vika made another trip to the trailhead and back to the cookout frenzy for second night in a row. Then for the third. Some hikers were there for all three of the days Vika and Grandma Peach were there—either using it as an excuse to socialize, wait for other hikers, or treat injuries—but most of the hikers who came into town were back out on the trail within a day and a half.

ON THURSDAY MORNING, Grandma Peach and Vika packed up to wait for the last load of hikers before driving back north to Stacklen. Slip An' Slide was on the bus with his pack fifteen minutes early, quietly waiting and seated on the floor at the end of the couch. Hikers talked as they shuffled in and the bus rumbled out of the campground at exactly 8:02. They all puttered down the road leaving a cloud smelling of fried food in their wake.

As they made their way up to the bakery, two hikers jumped up from the curb they were sitting on and stuck out their thumbs. They climbed on as another exploded out the door of the store with a coffee in one hand and a pastry in his mouth. He jogged across the street and climbed up the stairs.

"Thanks," he panted and sat down next to Vika, who perched on the engine cover near Grandma Peach.

"Where's that chick you were hiking with?" a voice came from the back.

"She ditched me," the voice Vika recognized as Refill's shot back.

"What?"

"Yeah," she said, "she left two days ago. Said I was too slow."

"She said that?" another female voice piped up.

"She just wanted to hike her own hike," Vika called to the back, with the hope that using a hiker motto would quickly dampen any accusations.

"Yeah, you told her to hike without me," Refill said, glaring.

Vika straightened and looked at her without blinking. "I said she should hike her own hike. If that was at a different pace than—"

Refill snorted, "What do you know about hiking anyway? You wouldn't know the inside of a pack from the outside."

"Look," Vika started, "just because—"

"She abandoned me," Refill snapped, "and you told her to."

"All right, girls," Grandma Peach started.

"I don't have to be a hiker to know when someone is using someone else."

"Using? You think I was *using* Anna?"

"Girls!"

"Absolutely! You completely ignored—"

"I SAID ENOUGH!" Grandma Peach bellowed. Vika jumped. She didn't know Grandma Peach could bellow, but there it was. Vika felt her cheeks heat up and she focused her gaze at the metal window frame of one of the windows. She could feel the glare of Refill on her face still. She hated confrontation, even more than she hated crying.

So it was a mystery to her why she brought her gaze up and stared back.

The rest of the ride to the trailhead was quiet with sporadic, quiet conversations here and there. Some looked at Vika, some looked at Refill, some pretended they were asleep. Slip An' Slide caught Vika's eye and he smirked.

The *nerve*.

When Grandma Peach parked, Vika went down the stairs with Quasi. Grandma Peach stayed on the bus near her seat, but Vika saw her unbuckle and stand up. Hikers went by saying thank you, shaking her hand, and they did the same to Vika as they descended the stairs. She did her best to smile politely. When Refill exited, neither said a word. She walked on by and down the trail.

Finally, the hikers had gone and Vika climbed back in. She sat down on the couch, next to Slip An' Slide, who had relocated from the floor.

Grandma Peach lurched onto the road and Vika settled into the cushion. "Make yourself comfortable," she said. "It's about six hours."

Instead of acknowledging her advice, Slip An' Slide said, "Soooo, what was that about with you and Refill?"

"What? So you can laugh at me again?"

"Laugh?" Slip An' Slide's eyebrows raised and that same smirk pulled at the corners of his mouth. The *nerve*.

"Yes, that!" Vika said, gesturing to his face.

"I'm not laughing!" Though the moment he said it, a chuckle escaped. He pulled it in and took a deep breath. Vika stared on indignantly. "Sorry. I didn't mean to. I thought it took a lot of balls—"

"Balls?"

"Refill's kind of known for being a bitch, and a lot of people felt...bad for Someday. I thought it was cool that you said something."

"Cool?"

"Am I talking really quietly or are you just hard of hearing?"

Vika bit back a retort and shrugged instead. "Thank you."

"You're welcome," he answered.

Slip An' Slide took a deep breath and leaned into the cushion before letting his eyes drift shut. He stretched out his long legs and crossed his arms across his chest. Vika took that opportunity—after double-checking that his eyes remained closed—to let her gaze wander over the scenery.

His shirt was a light blue button-down and a vee of tanned skin showed at the top of his chest. She could see the outline of a well-toned upper body underneath the fabric, a little bit of an anomaly among the hiking population. She had heard this phenomenon called Dinosaur Syndrome, where the hikers walk and walk and walk until their legs become massive and their arms shrink with lack of use. But somehow, his arms still looked strong and, like most hikers, were tanned to an even chestnut color that complemented his light blue shirt perfectly. A white band encircled his wrist, along with a colorful braid that looked like a child's craft.

Gray running shorts covered his legs and bony knees overlapped where his legs crossed. Worn, torn, ratty shoes covered his feet and he looked completely comfortable.

Vika did a last once over and settled into the cushions in the same way and let her eyes drift shut.

Neither opened them until they bounced into the parking lot of a gas station for a break.

Two hours later, Quasi woke them with his excited barks for the familiar dilapidated Victorian and the nine Henriettas pecking through the yard.

Vika felt the power of the familiar, too, and breathed deep the Stacklen air she found she missed.

Slip An' Slide moved next to her as the bus slowed to a stop. He planted his hands on his shorts and moved to grab his pack. She watched him stand and together, they walked down the stairs into the stifling, midafternoon air. Vika felt her entire body slow with the presence of the heat, even hotter than the previous five days in Oregon.

Quasi was already tearing after the chickens, unfazed by their annoyed squawking. She brought her gaze up from the crazy dog and saw Dane sitting on the porch munching on a blue Otter Pop.

"Want one?" he called and tapped a cooler with the tip of his boot. "I already ate an entire box. I didn't mean to, but then, I didn't expect it to be six thousand damn degrees."

"Sure," Vika said back. She turned to Slip An' Slide. "Want an Otter Pop?"

"I love those things," he said and they closed the distance to the porch.

Slip An' Slide put his hand out and introduced himself.

"Figures," Dane remarked nonchalantly. "My mother can't go anywhere without picking up a lost hiker. How long you going to be around?"

Slip An' Slide cracked his knuckles. "Couple days?" he guessed and cracked them again. "Sorry, sir, I'm not exactly sure."

Dane gave a brief nod. "Well that's what we're here for," he said, "for 'not exactly sure.'" He took a bite of his popsicle. "Look at that one," he said, gesturing to Vika, "she's the definition of 'not exactly sure' and we took her in."

Vika opened the lid to the cooler and gave her best theatrical glare over the top of it. Then she looked down and pushed aside the ice.

"Don't look for any red ones," Dane said to the top of her head, "I ate them all."

She pulled out a purple one and Slip An' Slide reached around her to grab a green one.

"Purple?" he said. "And I thought I had you pegged."

She cut off the end and took a bite. "I never have to worry about them running out," she said, pushing the ice around in her mouth.

"Are you interested in working on the house?" Dane asked Slip An' Slide after a moment.

Slip An' Slide nodded enthusiastically, "I spent the last two summers laying block with my uncle. Vika, and er—"

"Grandma Peach, dear," Grandma Peach interjected as she wandered up and pulled out a red Otter Pop.

"Dammit," Dane muttered.

"Vika and Grandma Peach," Slip An' Slide continued, "said you still have some foundation work to do?"

"We do," Dane said suspiciously, "I'll show you around the basement in a little while. I can't move right know. I'm afraid I might stroke out."

Instead of touring the basement, Vika led Slip An' Slide to the hiker coop and let him settle in. Forrest lay on top of his sleeping bag wearing jeans as usual, one arm flung over his eyes and snoring softly. Vika was grateful he was snoring or she might have suspected that *he* stroked out.

"Go wherever you want," Vika said quietly, "no one comes in or out except for the hikers sleeping here and Forrest is the only one other than you right now. I'll be in the camper if you need me." She backed out the door quietly.

It was hot, but Vika was restless and she wandered up the stairs to the house where Dane was eating another Otter Pop.

"You are going to give yourself one hell of a sugar crash," Vika told him.

He shrugged in response. "A small price," he said and took another bite.

She wound through the two-by-fours into the living room, and then through the dining room and into the kitchen. It wasn't long before Dane moseyed on into the room.

"Are you almost done pulling up the floor in here?" he asked, looking at where she had worked.

Vika nodded, "I just have this little section near the door."

"Good," Dane said, bending over to pick up and inspect a piece of the aged plastic laminate. "Ted's coming by tomorrow morning to help with some of the plumbing in the bathrooms, and Forrest used to work as an electrician. I've got him wiring upstairs. My order of slate is coming in soon. We'll have to wait until the basement is done but with Slip An' Slide down there, it shouldn't take much longer."

Dane began to walk away but abruptly stopped. "One other thing," he said. "Would you maybe want to give Cassie a call and see if she wants to visit?"

"Me?" Vika reeled at the change in conversation.

"Yeah, well, she won't talk to me."

"Dane, she's your daughter. Ask her yourself."

"You're about her age. You have a lot in common. Just ask her."

"We've never spoken. We have nothing in common. We're the same age, that's it."

"OK, well, ask her if she could make it up in say, two weeks?"

"Dane, I'm not asking her."

"One phone call, one—"

"Dane, if you want her here, you're going to have to ask her herself. If you really don't want to talk to her, ask Grandma Peach."

"Cassie won't talk to me," and with his evasion of Grandma Peach, Vika surmised she would tell Dane something very similar to what Vika told him five seconds before, or already had.

"She won't talk to you because you haven't apologized to her!"

"Apologized?" He looked genuinely shocked and Vika fought hard to resist an eye roll. "What do I have to apologize for?"

"Dane," Vika sighed, "you insulted her boyfriend—"

"I wouldn't have if he wasn't an idiot."

"Dane! From what I heard, you complained about her school, you made snide comments about her apartment, you—"

"Snide comments," he snorted. "No, I didn't."

"You did. And she probably won't come out here until she's confident you're not going to attack her again."

"I did *not* attack her!"

"So you have a better explanation for why she won't talk to you?"

Dane glared at her. "She's stubborn," he finally said. "Got that awful trait from her mother."

"Yeah," Vika muttered, "her mother."

"Like Pulitzer and Hearst we were," he said. "I'm not apologizing,"

Vika shrugged, "Then you probably won't be seeing her soon."

"You are no help. None," he said and turned to leave.

"If," Vika started loudly, and Dane paused but didn't turn around. "If you wanted to apologize, you could say that you were upset she brought her boyfriend without warning. Because you were upset, you said some things you didn't mean, and if she were to come back—maybe without her boyfriend this time—you two can catch up, and you're really interested in her life in Seattle. If you wanted to apologize."

Dane stood there for a moment, his hulking back covered in a gray T-shirt, and mumbled something Vika couldn't hear. He then left out the way he came without glancing back.

Vika shook her head and turned back to remove the rest of the laminate.

"IT'S EASIER TO FIX A HOUSE if you're not dead," Dane said to Slip An' Slide after Slip An' Slide remarked about the number of jacks in the basement later that day during the grand tour of the foundation. "There's some Gatorade in that cooler there. If you have to piss, there's a compost toilet in the coop and porta-potty in the back. Or at least walk to the edge of the field. Quasimodo loses his mind when too many strangers piss on his turf. Runs in lots of circles and starts shitting in the camper. Weird fucking dog," he shrugged momentarily at a loss for words, but really, Slip An' Slide didn't need more than that. To psychoanalyze the ugliest dog ever was probably above his pay grade, Vika thought.

"So you've worked with blocks before?" Dane asked.

"Yep," Slip An' Slide answered, "with my uncle for a couple summers. He owns a company that does that kind of work."

Dane gave a noise of acknowledgement, even if not one of admiration. "You know how to use this?" Vika watched as Dane gestured to a box with some twine, a couple little hammers, and that thing with the air bubble in it people used to level stuff with. She saw her dad use it once for a bookcase he put in her room in like fifth grade. She was pretty proud of herself for remembering that.

"Sure do," Slip An' Slide answered.

Dane looked at him sideways and Slip An' Slide remained staring at the tools, either unaware—or unconcerned—of Dane's doubt.

"Because we don't cut corners at the Dancy house," Dane said.

"Yes, sir," Slip An' Slide said, in a way that suggested he was more unconcerned than unaware of Dane's doubt.

"Literally and figuratively," Dane added for good measure.

"Yes, sir. Full corners."

"That's right. OK," he said, satisfied Slip An' Slide wasn't there to sabotage his foundation, "I'll be down here by seven tomorrow. You can join me whenever you'd like." He turned and made his way out of the basement.

"Is he always like that?" Slip An' Slide asked.

"Um," Vika started, "you'll have to be more specific."

"I mean, he's going to be breathing down my neck the entire time, isn't he?" Slip An' Slide asked.

"Oh," Vika said, "yes."

"That should be fun."

"He'll ease up after you prove yourself," Vika reassured him.

"Dane? You think so?"

Vika thought a second. "No," she conceded, "just kidding."

After he sifted through the tools and inspected the wall, they walked together to the porch and Vika poured them both a mug of tea.

"So," Slip An' Slide said after a beat, "Dane lives in the barn?"

"Mmm-hmm."

"The hikers live in a chicken coop, chickens live in a different coop, you and Grandma Peach live in a camper, you all sometimes live in a bus, and the only house on the property is uninhabitable?"

"Yes."

"Huh." Slip An' Slide leaned back into the cushions of the swing. There was another question—at least—on the tip of his tongue, and a couple times it looked to Vika as though he formed an entire idea, but then it would fade. After a little while, he asked, "Why do you guys have this porch?" He took a sip of his tea.

"What do you mean?"

"Nothing else of the house is done, except the porch," Slip An' Slide pointed out.

Vika shrugged as she thought about the exact question she had asked Dane when she first arrived. "So there is a dedicated spot to relax." She thought a moment, and then mentioned, "When I asked Dane about that, he said that 'the porch is the most fundamental architectural structure of human sanity. If you don't need a porch, you're either not sane, or not human.'"

"Ah."

"I'm quoting. He likes to make grand, all-encompassing statements," Vika said, staring out into the yard.

"Hmm."

"Sometimes he can be a real jerk," she added with a shrug.

"Noted."

"Sometimes it's really hard to figure out what he's talking about. Let alone argue with him."

Slip An' Slide sipped his tea and eyed Vika above the rim. "Sounds like an interesting dude."

Vika continued to stare, a couple chickens having made their way into her line of vision. "Yep."

A rumble of a truck broke the quietude and kicked up dust in its wake.

One hiker climbed out of the cab and three climbed out of the bed. The driver got out briefly and gave a quick wave to Vika, who waved back. He looked familiar though she couldn't place him. Then again, everyone looked familiar in a town of 1,700 people and she worked at the only store.

She heard a frenzy of thank-you's and good lucks, hands were shaken and the driver got back into his truck and pulled away.

The four hikers trudged up to the porch and Vika thought she may have to make more coffee.

"Is this the Dancys'?" one hiker, a girl maybe a year or two older than herself, asked.

"Yep," Vika answered, standing up. She walked down the stairs and put out her hand for the hikers. "I'm Vika."

She shook the hand of the girl who first spoke and introduced herself as The Liberator, who turned to shake Slip An' Slide's hand.

"This is Rut," she said about the guy who stood next to her of about the same age, "and that's Matchstick." She pointed to an older man who looked to be in his 50s.

The fourth in the party shook hands with the driver of the truck and swaggered on over and stuck his hand out.

"Night Burglar," he said, with a half smile and a drawl to melt the coldest heart. Vika smiled and Slip An' Slide nodded his greeting.

"We have the coop over there," Vika pointed, "or you can set up anywhere in the yard."

"I'll take the coop," The Liberator said and jabbed a thumb towards the pack on her back. "I wiped out in a creek this morning and my tent's soaked."

"Oh, we have some extra sleeping bags, too, and all the beds have blankets and sheets in them. I know Grandma Peach has some extra blankets somewhere," Vika rushed. "Are you doing OK?"

"Thank you. My bag's actually fine. It was only a little wet and I was able to dry it out at lunch. My *knees* on the other hand—" Vika glanced at her bare knees and saw both bruised pretty well and a cut on the left one, "they're a little sore."

Vika looked down at them. "Do you want some ice?"

"Nah," The Liberator waved it off, "I took some good ol' vitamin I."

Vika raised an eyebrow. "Vitamin I?"

"Ibuprofen. Rut here made it look so easy. 'Just one little three-foot jump,' he says. He flies over like a gazelle. I, probably looking more like a rhino, ran off the end, land on the rock—moss-covered, mind you—my feet slipped out and I landed on my knees and slid off. Hence, the wet tent." She shook her head.

"Funnier than hell," Night Burglar piped up, smiling. "I wish I filmed it or something. That would have gone viral in about five minutes."

"Nice," Slip An' Slide put in.

"Oh, shut up," The Liberator shot back, rolling her eyes at Night Burglar. "You can sleep outside."

"Oh, ouch," Night Burglar retorted. "Sleeping outside, imagine that."

"I'll sleep in the coop, too," Rut said to Vika, ignoring his the bickering of his compatriots and he turned to walk across the lawn, "Thank you, this is great."

"No problem," Vika answered. "Do you guys want to go into town tonight? There are bikes over in the barn for whenever you want. I have to go pick up my paycheck anyway, so I can leave whenever in the bus. I'll get some ointment for your knees, too."

"Really, they'll be fine."

Vika paused. "Please? It'll make me feel better to know you won't get a crazy mountain infection."

The girl gave an exaggerated shrug, but it was accompanied by a smile and she finally conceded, "Yeah. Sure."

"Great. So do you guys want a ride?"

The hikers looked at each other, no one taking the initiative to make the decision.

"Are we staying here tomorrow?" Rut finally asked the other hikers.

"How about a half-day?" Night Burglar suggested.

"So at least the morning," The Liberator put in.

"I'm out early," Matchstick said, "I have to get back on the trail."

"Let's all just go tonight," The Liberator decided and turned to Vika and Slip An' Slide. Vika noticed it was more to Slip An' Slide than to her and to her surprise, a little ball of unease flared up inside of her. "If that's OK."

"Sure," she said, keeping an even voice. "Where do you need to go? The post office is closed tonight."

"None of us have packages," Night Burglar said tentatively, looking around at his hiking partners, verified with three shakes of the head, "so we just need the supermarket and the laundromat if it's close."

Vika nodded, "They're right next to each other."

"Perfect!" The Liberator said and turned to her hiking partners. "Rut, do you want to take care of the shopping? I'll do everyone's laundry at the same time."

"Sure," Rut answered.

"Yep."

"Works for me," Matchstick added.

"We can be ready in as early as fifteen minutes," Rut said to Vika, getting everyone moving.

"All right," Vika responded, "we can meet here." She turned and led the way towards the coop, hearing the shuffle of the hikers behind her. They spread out immediately, quickly staking out their own domains.

"There are some clotheslines around the woodstove and over on the other side if you want to hang up your tents or anything," Vika explained and turned to let the hikers settle in. Slip An' Slide was sitting on the porch and got up when she approached from the coop.

"When are we leaving?" he asked as she walked towards him.

"In fifteen minutes. You don't have to go if you don't want to," she said.

He shrugged. "I will," he said, "I don't have anywhere else to be and bonding time with Dane can wait until tomorrow."

"You sure?" she teased. "I'm going to check in with Grandma Peach before we head to town, though, see if she needs anything."

Grandma Peach was stirring vegetable soup at the stove when they climbed the stairs to the camper. Quasi sat next to her visibly drooling, as he resisted even a glance in Vika's direction, only able to afford a miniscule ear flick.

"Got some new hikers, have we?" Grandma Peach asked without turning around.

"Yep," Vika answered. "We're going into town soon. I was just wondering, do we have any extra blankets?"

Grandma Peach paused her stirring and looked up out the window, concentrating. "Blankets! That's what I was trying to remember. Right, Quasi?" She turned to Vika and recalled, "We have a small box of them, maybe five or six. They're in my closet in the back left. I was going to stop at the thrift shop in town the other day and stock up, but clearly I forgot." She put the spoon down in a small dish and walked by Vika to get her purse off the table to dig out a bill.

"There you are, dear. That will get you some. Of course, I always run it through the laundry before I give it to hikers, but I assume you'll be heading to the laundromat anyway?"

Vika nodded. "Is there anything else you'd like me to pick up while we're in town?"

"No. Thank you, dear," she smiled and patted Vika on the arm. "Do you want the other blankets as well?"

"Sure," Vika said. "One of the hikers landed in a creek earlier. She said she was OK, but I'll bring them just in case."

"Oh, my," Grandma Peach said, "Yes, you'd better take them." Vika moved to the back of the camper to retrieve the box.

"Thank you," Vika said as she squeezed by Grandma Peach and the dog towards the door. Grandma Peach hummed in return.

"Would you like to be my taste tester?" she heard Grandma Peach offer some of the soup to Quasimodo as she closed the door to the camper and made her way back to the porch to wait.

Ten minutes later, the four hikers, Slip An' Slide, and Vika loaded on the bus. Since they walked with only the essentials—and the essentials needed to be laundered—they all had on some sort of mix and match of rain gear and tank tops, or spandex shorts—clearly clothes that were seldom worn. Rut sat in full rain gear.

Vika pushed her foot down on the clutch, gave a little gas, eased the clutch, gave a little gas, eased the clutch, and she lurched the bus ungracefully out the driveway and even more obnoxiously down the road. Her top speed hit about twenty miles an hour on a slight downhill, and roared at a million decibels, give or take a few. Luckily, the tiny town was located a scant two miles away.

It felt like twenty, sitting on a jet engine.

She pulled up close to the laundromat, and spotted that the back end was still well into the road.

She flung the doors open and The Liberator climbed out with a laundry bag in each hand.

"All right, guys," she said to the rest of the hikers, waiting for a car to go by. He gave her the finger with a blast of his horn and she tried not to let her face turn red. "There's a community parking lot a little ways up this road. I'm just going to park there and let you all out. We'll pass the supermarket on the way."

"That'll work," Matchstick said.

Vika lurched into first and the engine whined down the road. She bet a lawn mower would beat her. She bet it would be quieter, too.

She let out a small sigh of relief when she saw the lot was almost empty. The bus crawled up to the side of the road—still so damn loud—to where Vika parked like a jerk, taking up six spaces, without even feeling bad about it.

It took two hours for them all to run errands and meet back at the bus. The Liberator was the first to return to join Vika, clean laundry in hand.

"Got everything?"

"Oh, yeah," The Liberator said easily. "Everything goes in the wash and everything goes in the dryer. If it can't go in the dryer, I don't wash it."

Vika laughed at her casual attitude and changed the subject. "What made you want to hike the PCT?" she asked as the hiker settled into the couch.

The Liberator raised a shoulder and let it drop as she adjusted her posture. "I like the mountains," she answered. "What about you? What made you want to be a Trail Angel?"

"It was an accident," Vika confessed.

"An accident?"

"Yeah," Vika continued, "I was trying to get to this place called Lake Chelan—"

"Oh, yeah. Stehekin's on that lake."

"Yep, and my car, well, I had a car fire and Grandma Peach happened to be driving by and picked me up."

The Liberator let out a laugh. "You're kidding."

"Nope," Vika shook her head. "That was weeks ago, and I haven't left." They sat quietly for a couple moments.

"So how did you get your trail name?" Vika asked.

"Oh," she said, "there was snow in Northern California and a bunch of spruce trees were bent over, stuck in the snow kind of. They were only caught in the snow a little, so I pulled them out."

"Are you talking about all that snow we had to walk through?" asked Night Burglar as he climbed the stairs, a five-star grin across his face. "Hey," he said to Vika.

"Hey," she said back.

"Yeah, Vika was asking about my trail name," she said.

"Ah," he said and put some grocery bags down next to the laundry, stretching his legs out once he took a seat next to The Liberator. "She spent more time doing that than navigating."

She directed an exasperated look at him. "We got here, didn't we?"

"No thanks to you."

"I heard there was some snow in Oregon, too," Vika said.

"Yeah, it wasn't too bad by the time we got there, and dried up quick after we left."

"That's got to slow down your pace, doesn't it?" Vika asked.

"Yeah," The Liberator explained, "night hiking is pretty much out because there is no trail to follow, really. Plus, walking on snow takes more energy."

"Especially postholing all over the place," Night Burglar said as he jutted a thumb at his hiking companion while looking at Vika.

"What is postholing?" Vika asked about the new hiker vocabulary.

"Sometimes when you're hiking over snow, you're also hiking over fallen trees or rocks on the trail that have air pockets next to them. Every once in a while, your foot breaks through the snow and falls into that air pocket. Usually, I only postholed up to my knees, but a couple times I went in up to my hip.

"We'd be going only eighteen to twenty miles on the really rough days. I broke a pole and I think Rut bent one when he postholed somewhere."

Shortly after, the other two hikers boarded the bus and they headed back to the Dancy estate.

THE HIKERS WENT TO THE COOP, but Vika thought a cup of tea would do her well and she made her way to the porch. She sat heavily on the swing and leaned back against the cushion, her mug clutched between both hands. Three quarters of the way through her tea, she heard footsteps from inside the house and only an instant later, Dane stood in the doorframe. He took two slow strides and lowered himself into the chair to sit for a moment looking out into the yard. Together they silently watched the fireflies blink. A bullfrog croaked in the distance and katydids ground their legs against their bodies. Layers of sounds pulsed from the grass, from the shrubs, and from the trees. The house behind them creaked as it too settled for the night after a long day's work.

For a while, Vika thought that he sat only to listen to the natural resonance of the yard when he cleared his throat and broke his silence. "I think sculpture is harder," he said, thoughtfully.

"Excuse me?"

"Sculpture, definitely harder. Why the hell do you think I paint? You can paint over mistakes but with marble, the first chisel is the point of no return."

"I disagree," she countered, "the perfect coloration is harder than no color at all. It could take weeks, years, to create the perfect hue. Sculpture is grid and method."

Dane made a sound of disapproval. "The sense of weight has to exist in sculpture. From all sides."

"A lot of painters painted figures from all sides to prove they could." Like you do, she wanted to add.

He sat in silence next to her unmoving, and they watched the fireflies. She tried to hold in a grin. She had zero doubt he believed painting to be harder of the two because in his words, why the hell would he choose painting?

"She'll come if I apologize to her?"

Vika jerked her head slightly in surprise of the sudden shift. "I think so," she said.

"That's all? I just have to apologize."

"Mmm-hmm," she answered, "but Dane, it has to be a sincere apology. You can't say, 'I'm sorry your boyfriend's a dumbass.'" She paused to smile, "Even if it's true."

A laugh bubbled up and erupted from Dane. She allowed her pride to swell a miniscule amount. A genuine laugh from Dane made for a small victory in her book.

He gave a curt nod. "That will stay between you, me, and these two-by-fours."

He pushed himself up from his chair. "Good night, Vika."

"Dane," she stopped him, "don't wait until next season."

CHAPTER 14

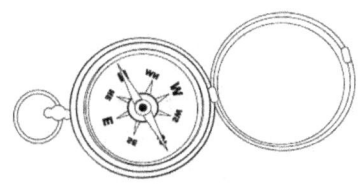

SLIP AN' SLIDE/DAVID WAS GOING TO LEAVE on Thursday. Then again on Friday. Saturday morning he woke up and asked Dane if he could continue working in the basement.

He wasn't going anywhere any time soon.

"Do you really like construction that much?" Vika asked when she found him in the basement.

Slip An' Slide shrugged, "I'm used to walking thirty miles a day. I can't sit still right now."

This always amused Vika. She imagined if she were to hike for months at a time, she would want to sit down after she was done. Put on some sweats, make some hot cocoa, and sit down. Maybe read the paper, watch her favorite show. If she had to wash the dishes, she'd do it sitting down. Mop the floor? Chairs have wheels. She guessed she would have to compare notes if she ever walked for thousands of miles.

"Don't you miss home?" she asked Slip An' Slide.

"A little," he answered, hefting a cement block next to the half-constructed wall and muscles and tendons rippled up his forearms as he transferred the weight. Slip An' Slide pulled up his gloves before grabbing the next one, as he seemed to be making a stack of blocks closer to the wall to work with. Vika noticed some of the jacks that had been holding up the wall when she first arrived at the house were either removed as the wall was constructed, or modified to have blocks around them. Lights from the ceiling gave enough light for Slip An' Slide to work, but most of the illumination entered naturally via the twenty-foot hole in the foundation. Rabbits, chipmunks, and woodchucks went in and out, along with bats, a chupacabra, and probably one of the last few black rhinos.

Vika observed that the hole, though roughly the same size, had moved down the wall as new wall went up and older wall came down.

"Then why won't you go?" Vika asked.

Slip An' Slide pinched out a pseudo-smile and grabbed another block. "Eager to get rid of me, huh?"

"No," Vika answered quickly, maybe too quickly, "just curious. You keep saying you're leaving, and it's not a big deal, but then you...don't."

He held her gaze for a couple seconds, his eyes hard, and then turned away from her and answered, "I don't want to yet." He grabbed a bag of mortar and dumped it in the wheelbarrow.

"Where is home for you?" Vika asked conversationally.

"St. Louis," he stated.

She was about to press him more, but he turned on the hose, to drown the dust, to drown out her voice, and the voices in his head.

She watched him, his shoulders working overtime to mix the mortar to the right consistency. When he finished, he plopped some on a wooden slat with the trowel and walked to the half-constructed wall, all the while ignoring Vika.

Slip An' Slide wanted her to leave. She was too persistent to ignore completely and too pretty to want to. But he wanted to be by himself and concentrate on the wall. He wanted to be by himself for the rest of the day, maybe week. That's why he pushed Dane to work on the foundation, because no one went down there. The work was tedious, not a lot of people could do it, and it was cold and dark. Dane showed up sometimes to make sure he was doing decent work, but he never pried into his personal business.

He flipped a chunk of mortar like it was a pancake.

Then there was Vika. Wandering down just to bug the hell out of him, it seemed. He couldn't tell her that he was going home to, well, nothing. No job, no money, no girlfriend. If he were lucky, his little Honda Civic would last until he stayed in one spot long enough to care about finding a new car. The engine was almost shot and the only place he should drive it to would be a demolition derby.

He knew his friends wouldn't give him a hard time about the trail, about not getting to the end. They had been supportive from the beginning. Maybe they thought he was a little nuts, but most people encouraged his dream regardless. And if he went home, he would still have to tell everyone. Many people, many different places, many times the explanation. Every time he'd tell someone that he cut out early was another time he'd have to remind himself that he didn't make it. Another time his own words would ring in his head for hours.

It was a lot of crow and he wasn't ready to eat it yet.

Then there was Vika, trying to force it down his throat.

VIKA WATCHED HIM place the mortar and block, look at the level, tap it with a hammer, look at the level, tap it with a hammer. He paused to adjust very gingerly the string he used to mark the height of the row, his brows pulled together so tightly they almost touched. Then he leveled and tapped, leveled and tapped. She watched him set two more blocks as he continued to ignore her.

Eventually, she admitted defeat and retreated out of the basement and into the sunlight. She asked Dane what she could do outside and was quickly put to work picking up sticks and weed whacking near the buildings. She wondered how she offended Slip An' Slide. He took the defensive side to almost every question she asked him. Well, she thought with an uneasy shrug, you couldn't be friends with everyone.

Much of the rest of the day she spent in the garden. The blueberries were near the end of the season as were the blackberries, while the veggies were taking shape. It wouldn't be for a couple weeks they'd be able to get much yield out of it, but she still managed to find a couple ripe onions and squash.

Even if Vika's knowledge of vegetable growth was limited, she could weed without being told. The sun was hot on her back as she pulled at grasses and plants that invaded the boundary of cultivation. Down the bean line she went. Then around the potatoes, the zucchini and squash, and the tomatoes. Sweat was dripping down her forehead, sweat that she had wiped away numerous times and wouldn't be surprised if she found dirt smeared all the way across her brow.

She finished weeding the cucumber line as Dane crossed the lawn towards her.

"Are you trying to instill fear in other weeds thinking about growing in the garden by yanking those out like that?" he asked, standing close by, hands on his hips.

"I just," Vika huffed, "I don't get it. Sometimes. I don't get it. I don't get the hikers. I don't understand how they can put their lives on hold. They halt their entire career."

"It's all relative," Dane replied.

"I was just asking him a question."

"Some questions aren't as simple as they seem."

"If it didn't work out, why do hikers hang around? What do they have to gain?"

Dane responded, though his voice was harsh, "We need the hikers and people like them to believe in something so fiercely that they create a new standard, a belief in something that is so devastatingly powerful they are unable to return to the life as it existed before. For someone to stop and re-group is not a bad thing, Vika.

"Your generation goes and goes and goes. School, internships, college, more college. By the time you get out, you're a hundred thousand dollars in debt and you can't fuck around because you have loans to pay off. So you look for a job, and you get one—maybe—and if you do, by the time that happens, it's about time to get married and have kids.

"Do you have time to live? Explore? Hike thousands of miles? Some of the most creative years—and the stupidity to do it—is suppressed by this insane pursuit of a job. To what end?" he asked as he took a step forward. "To what end? You think you're going to become a doctor because you think you're *supposed* to? Got news for you kid. There are a couple thousand people waiting to take your spot in med school because they think they're supposed to, too."

"But I don't want to be a doctor," Vika said.

"The good doctors are the doctors who become doctors because they can't stand not to be," Dane plowed on, ignoring her remark. "The doctors who try to be teachers, mathematicians, accountants, but somehow by the pure, ingrained desire to be a doctor are brought back. It might start with a miniscule glimpse of medicine but it's not enough. They do more training, more school, because they *have* to, with every fiber of their being. Like the need for food or air.

"It's the artists who create works because ideas bounce around in their heads so goddamn vehemently that they barge out on a canvas on their own damn accord! The architect who doesn't sleep because his new idea has taken over his body and his mind. His tools measure, his pencil sketches so quickly out of a completely uncorrupted need to create *that* building.

"We *need* people to forget about...*rules*...and explore and push themselves as though the sun is going to blow up at any second. Like these hikers," he said gesturing around the empty yard. "Even when their focus seems to strip them down to *nothing*, when they wake up dirty, tired, hungry, in pain, and realize they're not even halfway, they shimmy out of their sleeping bags anyway, pull on their jackets, shove all their gear into packs, stand up on tight muscles, and say, 'Hell yeah I'm ready for a 12-hour day.' These hikers walk to the trail in tattered clothes, sunburned noses, duct-taped shoes, and are excited.

"You see, these people simply can't exist without being themselves. Sometimes, the sweat, the work, the mental perseverance in a strange indefinable way, feels like relief, like purpose. Show me them and I will show you what we should all strive for."

"You believe that? You believe everyone has that much freedom?" Vika had risen and was facing Dane, humoring him for a minute.

"Yes," he answered without blinking.

"How?" Vika asked incredulously. "How is hoping for that illusion better than focusing on a solid education and a good job? How is it different?"

"You answered your own question. That *is* the first focus!" He leaned forward enthusiastically, eyes bright. "A diploma can be important, but it should not be what your life depends on. The importance of learning is a concept even a seven-year-old can think about. That is a start: Go to school and learn. Eventually, that knowledge will evolve and will, hopefully, lead to a realization that there is a choice. You choose the knowledge to pursue."

"You can choose to go to college for different things," Vika said.

He gave Vika a look that was as close to malice as she had ever seen on Dane. "The *choice* to pursue knowledge is the difference between formal and informal education. You think you can sail across the Pacific by reading Moby fucking Dick?" he roared and Vika took a step back in response.

"Experience, Vika! Experience! Life!" He waved his hands in exasperation. "It's worth just as much if not more than a diploma! A college is a college is a college—different information with the same life philosophies, and it's not for everyone."

"But to play the game—"

"There is no game! If you think there's a game, you've already lost! If you think there's a game, you've capitulated to someone else's rules, and guess what? They don't have a fucking idea what they're talking about."

"What happened to love, money, and nepotism?" Vika said as she threw her hands up. "What happened to ending up jaded and crying?"

Dane stared, his blue eyes searing straight into her. Vika held her ground.

"What are *your* rules, Dane?" Vika pressed. "What is *your* game?"

He stepped back and broke eye contact. "Be a doctor if you want," he said, circumventing her question, "be an art historian. Sell hot dogs on a fucking street corner. It doesn't have to be big. It doesn't have to be grand. It just has to be true. What is true for you? What are you here for? What are you trying to learn in Stacklen? Do you even know your options?"

Vika flushed and opened her mouth but nothing came out. She glared from embarrassment.

"Of course not! Because you've been in a goddamn tunnel since you were five!" he shook his head and looked away for a moment.

Vika pulled her eyebrows together and bit the inside of her cheek, blinking away surprised tears. Her head spun and her face flushed.

"I am not in a tunnel." Each word came out in staccato through gritted teeth.

"When you can tell me what is true for you, you can comment on what is true for other people. Until then, if a hiker wants to stay, a hiker can stay."

"What is true for *me*? What is true for *you*? You can't even talk to your own daughter! Her boyfriend at Easter? I bet she puts up a front to piss you off because she tried to be just like you but you didn't accept her then, either." Vika snapped her mouth shut about as quickly as Dane recoiled.

Dane recovered more quickly than Vika and retorted, "As you said, you've never met her!" He let the best of his temper out, "I've always accepted her. I don't agree with her all of the time, but I have always accepted her."

"No," Vika said firmly, "because whether you like it or not, she has grown up in a society you have resisted and so her reality is different from yours."

"You're wrong. Values still remain the same—"

"I'm not saying values are different, I'm saying that the tools to build them are different, and if you want to understand your daughter, you need to learn how to use them."

Dane had gone from friendly to angry to disappointed throughout the course of the conversation and she couldn't pinpoint where he was at that moment, but she thought she heard it somewhere between defeated and irate. "Don't tell me I don't understand my own daughter," he snarled.

Vika felt her stomach drop, somewhere between ashamed and contumacious.

They stared at each other for a couple seconds, until Vika blinked and looked away.

"I'm sorry," she said, barely loud enough to hear her own voice.

"I have to go clean up," he said with poison in his voice.

Vika stood in the garden after he left, staring at the cucumber line, blood roaring in her ears. She checked over her shoulder to make sure he had gone into the house before she started towards the camper so she wouldn't have to pass him.

"I heard you two arguing from all the way in here. Quasi was in a tizzy," Grandma Peach said from her armchair as Vika climbed the stairs. "I hope Dane didn't upset you, dear." Vika turned to face her with the best smile she could muster.

"Of course not," she said, "he's just very opinionated."

Grandma Peach smiled. "That's my Dane. He got that from his father."

CHAPTER 15

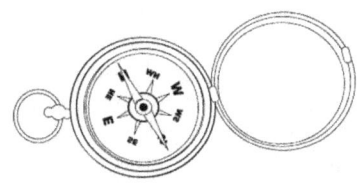

"THANKS," VIKA GRUMBLED as she piled six hiker boxes on the lawn.

The deliveryman, Randy, raised an eyebrow at her.

She had tried not to grumble, she really did, but the conversation with Dane the day before was festering in her mind. Damn, she'd have to rein it in in the future.

"Have a good day, Randy," she said and managed a smile.

"Yep," he replied, stone faced, his fingers drumming on the steering wheel, "you, too."

She carried the boxes over to the barn door and knocked. When Dane didn't answer, she put the boxes near the door.

She slept fitfully the night before, tossing and turning, thinking of the argument in her sleep. Vika needed fresh air and, unfortunately, most of the air over this property was high with tension. She could practically hear it sizzle and crackle above her as though in the bowels of a lightning storm.

A chicken squawked and Vika jumped. Her feet stumbled on the uneven grass, and then on the uneven stone of the driveway and finally, she was on the pavement of the road heading towards town.

God, she was mad.

"What does he know anyway?" she said to herself.

A tunnel? What was he saying? She was not in a tunnel.

She kicked a rock. It skipped on the asphalt and bounced off another rock into the weeds.

She walked some more and wished she were taller. It wouldn't take her so long to get where she wanted to go, if only her legs were longer. At five-two, they didn't have much stretch, but on she walked. Maybe she could have started the walk a solid two hours earlier in the day, but there she was, as the sweat stains under her boobs could attest.

She passed a street and the houses got closer and closer. She passed another street and another. On the fourth, she turned down. She had only been to Smith's house once, so she hoped she got it right. The modest garden looked familiar and she caught sight of a little welcome sign in Italian. This was his, she was sure of it. The paint was faded on the house but it was far from decrepit; it looked well lived in.

Only seconds later, she was standing on the porch knocking on the door.

"Vika?" Smith asked as he opened the door. Though he was in casual clothes, he still had his shirt neatly tucked into khakis fastened by a brown belt. Bifocal glasses rested on the tip of his nose, and the book he was reading he held open in his hand. The wingtips he wore to work sat on a mat near the entryway, exchanged for a pair of slippers.

"I think I want to go hiking."

"You what?"

That's about what she was asking herself as well. Hiking? She didn't know the first thing. It probably had something to do with these godforsaken existentialist tendencies she was suffering from.

Instead of voicing this to Smith, she repeated herself. "I want to go hiking." She decided it was best leave out *I think*. It was more convincing that way. She hitched up her chin.

Smith scrutinized her. He pulled an old price sticker out of his pocket and shoved it into the pages of the book and took off his glasses. "Come on in," he said and placed his book on a small table next to a set of keys.

The house was small, and cozy. The furniture was colored with earth tones for the most part, but a bright stool here and end table there added a flare of personality to the house and likely the presence of a female occupant. She recognized Mediterranean knick-knacks and remembered he had said he had been to Florence numerous times. Pictures of family sat quietly and firmly around the living area.

"Is that your wife?" Vika asked, pointing to a frame that held the photo of a beaming couple in front of the counter of a dessert shop, one of which was a younger Smith. The woman was gorgeous, long dark hair cascading down her shoulders, a smile that reached her eyes, holding a small plate with a slice of pie artistically decorated between them. Together, they looked as though they owned the world.

Smith flicked back a glance with a quick nod. "Sophie."

"Where is she?" Vika couldn't help but ask.

"She heard you were coming and ran out the back."

"Thanks, Smith."

"I can't keep her schedule straight," he shrugged. "On the weekends, she's always having lunch or going to a play with this friend or that group," he answered.

Over the dining room table was a six-piece painting of a red velvet cupcake, on different sized canvases that spanned the entire wall.

"Did she work at the bakery with you?" Vika asked, stopping to appreciate the art.

"Who, Soph?" Smith called from the next room. "We owned it together," he called to her, "twenty-three years. I baked cakes. She did pies. We both did pastries when we had to."

Vika walked again and found him in the kitchen. Cluttered was not the word to describe it, as everything clearly had a very specific place whether it was next to the toaster or on top of the refrigerator. Vika also knew if she searched for any baking appliance she wanted, it was somewhere within the four walls of the room. She wondered when was the last time he or Sophie used them.

"Water? Iced tea? Hot tea?" he asked, face behind the silver door of the refrigerator.

"Iced tea, please," she answered as she boosted herself up on a stool at the counter.

He poured two glasses and pulled a stool to sit across from her.

"Did you walk here?" he asked, eyeing her hair and the way that she drank half the glass in one gulp.

"I did," she said, "which makes me think I could do that. Walk, I mean. In the woods. You know, hike."

"Hike," he echoed. "And what exactly made you want to hike?"

She shrugged, looking at her glass. "I just thought it'd be fun. To…I don't know…experience new things. I hear about hiking all the time but I've never done it."

"Who would you be hiking with?" Smith asked, keeping his voice surprisingly neutral.

"Well, I don't exactly have a partner yet, but I'll find one."

"Did you get into another fight with Dane?"

"What?" she practically squeaked. "Why?"

"Why?" Smith looked at her suspiciously. "Because the last time you did, you walked into work pouting and said you Gatsbied the Ninja Turtles. If anything more absurd could come out of your mouth, it's that you, 'think you want to go hiking.' Why do you let him get to you?"

Vika slid some condensation off of her glass with her thumb. Smith took another sip, waiting. "Because I'm afraid he's right." It wasn't even a whisper. It was a thought, but a thought that somehow she knew Smith heard because he sighed and leaned back.

"What makes him right?" he asked.

She stared at her glass. "Because if I'm driving around wherever the hell I'm driving around—or *was* driving around before I blew up my car—I'm looking for…I don't know. I'm thinking there's something better."

He shrugged in response.

"Right? I must be looking for something else. Something meaningful, you know? What I'm really supposed to be doing. Even if I can't tell you what it is. Even if I can't tell *myself* what it is. I wouldn't have left if I had everything I wanted, right? I figure the mountains are a good place to look for whatever it is that's missing." she frowned.

"Well, I don't know," Smith scratched his ear, "that's a little—"

"Existentialist?" Vika laughed.

"Yeah, over the top, whatever you want to call it. Dane's just very opinionated, that doesn't mean you have to listen to everything he says."

"No, but he—"

"I've seen you deal with a lot of people at the store and you deal with more at the house. With most of it you smile and nod, but Dane says something and it eats away at you, and I mean *eats*. I think you need to figure that out first before you go walk into the wild blue yonder."

Vika took a sip of her iced tea.

"I've done some hiking myself," Smith said after a couple moments. "Of course, much more when I was younger; I can't hike now like I once did."

"You did?" Vika wondered surprised. "Where did you hike?"

"Oh," Smith said, looking past her into his memories, "around here some, like the Olympic Peninsula, my wife loves the Olympic Peninsula. Soph loves the ocean. We spent quite a bit of time in British Columbia, too." He paused and smiled, "I didn't hike like these kids do—the one who go through your yard—but I can tell you, if you're out there long enough, you have plenty of time to think. The things that were kind of fuzzy before might become crystal clear. Good or bad."

Vika looked up. "That's what I'm hoping. I need time to think and nothing else."

"I said might. It *might* become crystal clear."

"I know what you said," Vika answered, a little more pep in her voice. "Thanks, Smith." She slipped off the stool and pushed her glass across the counter.

"Well now, Vika," Smith started, "you still need to go with someone." But she was already walking around the peninsula to give him a hug.

He patted her on the back awkwardly when her arms wrapped around him.

"Thanks, Smith," she said again. "I have to get to the store. My shift starts in ten minutes."

"Vika," Smith warned as she moved towards the door.

"I'll tell you all about it when I get back."

"Vika," he said, "Vika!" She was halfway down the sidewalk and gave him a wave over her shoulder.

"Take someone with you!" he called after her. "It's a lot easier to think when you're not getting mauled by a bear!"

"Bye, Smith!" she cried out over her shoulder and saw him with his hands on hips standing on his porch, a scowl on his face.

VIKA PUNCHED OUT FROM THE STORE six hours later, bounced down the front steps, and started down the road. It was a fast walk, much faster than when she had set out that morning, as she thought about joining hikers on the trail. She was nearly running by the time she turned down the driveway, past the front entrance of the house, around the back and into the basement just as the first stars were illuminating in the sky. The lights were on and she knew she'd find Slip An' Slide. He was sitting on a cement block with his back to her, staring at the wall and sipping a beer. His arms were draped over his legs, his head tilted slightly up, unmoving except to accommodate the beer.

He stared.

The wheelbarrow and trowels were cleaned of mortar, though broken pieces of block littered the floor amidst some empty iced tea cans, pieces of wood, a beer bottle, and some random tools that lay around him.

"I've heard Stehekin has a pretty good bakery," she said to his back.

She watched for a tell, but he remained perfectly still as though she hadn't spoken at all.

"I've heard that, too," he finally answered, as he continued to stare at the wall. Vika realized then it was the wall that he had finished. Not a hole could be seen in the entire foundation. She looked around and wondered how long he had been sitting there.

"We should go," she said at the same time he stood up and turned to look to at her. He passed her a beer and she took it.

"I hear the ferry ride on Lake Chelan is really nice," he said.

"That'd be fun," she said, cracking open her can, "but I was actually thinking maybe…if you wanted…we could hike up there."

He stared hard at her and Vika could tell he was trying to determine if she was being serious. She took a sip of her beer as she waited for an answer and appreciated the slight distraction.

He finally broke eye contact and took a sip of his own. "No," he said.

Vika's heart jumped at the force of the word. Of course, she half expected that answer but it sounded much more harsh when he said it out loud.

"I think it's about 90 miles from Highway 2 to Stehekin," Vika went on. "We could take the ferry back from there if you want."

"Vika," Slip An' Slide said, "I got off the trail for a reason."

"Which you won't tell me," she responded and saw his mouth open to counter, so she rushed on, "but I was thinking it could just be a hike. No pressure of border to border. Most of the pack is behind us so we'll have the North Cascades to ourselves."

"You don't have any hiking gear," he said.

"How do you know that?" Vika asked indignantly.

Slip An' Slide answered with a single raised eyebrow.

"OK, fine," she huffed, "I don't. But I'm sure Dane has some for me to borrow, right? I mean, he has everything."

"Ask him if he wants to hike," Slip An' Slide said through his beer.

"I can't—I don't want—ugh, no."

"Why do you want to hike anyway?" Slip An' Slide asked.

Vika shrugged, letting her eyes drift over the new wall again. "Because I never have. Because I've been around hikers and I wonder what it's like." She brought her eyes back to his. "I like learning new things. Experiencing new things." She twisted the tab on her beer can absentmindedly and it snapped off. "Sure you don't want to go?" She hopefully half-smiled at him.

Slip An' Slide answered with tense sigh.

Vika gave a slight nod at the answer. "All right," she said, "I have to go ask Dane if he has extra gear for me."

"Don't go by yourself," he called out to her back as she walked out of the basement. He was right, if she didn't find a hiking partner, she shouldn't go. The most camping she'd done was roasting marshmallows in a campsite near Mt. Rushmore next to their family's camper.

But something was telling her to go, and she believed it. God help her, she believed it with every cell in her body. She cursed herself. A chicken pecked at her feet.

"Run," she told it. "Your number might be up in a couple days."

She thought about the hike again. It was just walking, after all. It couldn't be that hard, people did it all the time.

Vika wandered over to the light in the barn and as she did, the clank of metal on metal confirmed her conjecture that Dane was inside. She spotted him through the door, hands full of grease, with his thin hair pulled back into a ponytail. He wore a ratty T-shirt with equally ratty shorts and sneakers, whose original color had long since been replaced by grass stains, grease stains, berry stains, paint stains, and who knows what other stains.

He turned down the music when he saw her and against her better judgment of interrupting whatever mood he was in, she stepped over the threshold into the building. A couple canvases sat against the far wall. She could tell it was the motorcycle that was standing in the center of the room, a series of paintings with different color palettes but the paint tubes on the easel were all screwed shut.

"Yeah?" he said, holding a wrench in his hand.

Vika took a mental deep breath, trying her damnedest to dissociate the present conversation with the one earlier in the day. "I was thinking about hiking in the mountains a little bit and was wondering if you had any extra gear?"

"What mountains?"

Vika blinked. "What—Um, those ones," she said and pointed a finger out the window to where they cracked up through the horizon. They looked jagged and intimidating.

"Why?"

"Well," she said with a smile in attempt to ease the tension, "it's all anyone talks about around here."

Dane stared.

Vika stared back. "I thought I would test myself and try something different."

Dane's expression remained the same but he picked up his chin slightly. "You're going to get lost out there."

"No, I won't," she answered. She tried to hold his gaze but her eyes slid away and she couldn't bring them back. So there she stood looking at the motorcycle he was tinkering with. "I want to see what's out there," she shrugged.

"You have maps?"

"I'll get them."

"You're not going if you don't have maps."

Vika brought her gaze back. "I'll get them," she repeated. "I can ask Slip An' Slide for gear if you don't have any; he hasn't been using his recently."

Dane squinted at her, and then flicked his eyes to the corner of the room. "Sure, I have gear," he said eventually. "You might find some stuff in that trunk. What do you need?"

"Everything."

Half an hour later, she walked with her pack back towards the camper, through the lawn that had settled into the darkness. She had a stove, a pack, and some other stuff she hoped to remember its purpose. She had some rope—oh, not rope, Dane almost had a heart attack when she'd said that. *P-cord.* She didn't know what the 'p' stood for, but she didn't think it'd matter much.

She walked around the corner of the house.

A lighter, a compass, a—

"So you're really going?"

Vika jumped and gasped at the sound of Slip An' Slide's voice in the darkness. The flame of an insect repellant candle jumped around on the little table next to where he sat on the porch, no doubt drinking a beer.

"Jesus Christ," she said, "you scared me."

"Most people call me Slip An' Slide. Or David."

Vika rolled her eyes in the dark and walked toward the porch. She stayed in the grass and answered, "Yes, I'm going."

"By yourself, huh?" He leaned forward and rested his arms on his thighs. She was wrong, she thought, eyeing the mug. He was drinking tea, not beer.

"Not if you decide to go," she edged.

"Nope," he replied, "but I will teach you how to use your stove."

"You don't even know what kind of stove I have," she argued.

He shrugged, "Doesn't matter. You don't know how to use it, do you?"

She glared. "I can figure it out."

He leaned back. "Sounds like a fail-safe plan. Going to do that with all your gear?"

He took a sip of his tea.

She made a few snide comments inside her head then slung her pack off her back and rummaged through it for the stove. "Fine," she said. She found it and handed it to Slip An' Slide.

"Oh, wow, this is old. So you got anything else for me?"

She gestured to his hand, "You asked for the stove. There it is."

Slip An' Slide looked from the stove up at her, a smirk pulling at the corners of his mouth. "There's this thing—it's called fuel—and for anything to burn—"

"Yeah, yeah," she muttered, already pushing aside the tent in her pack, looking for the canister she remembered Dane handed her. She grabbed it and held it out as she climbed up on the porch and kneeled down the same time Slip An' Slide dropped to the floor of the porch.

"Thanks," he said. "The stove screws on here, you have to open this valve here, and prime it like this," he showed her how to twist this just so, not too tight, but have everything sealed and then he pulled a lighter out of his pocket and flicked it. The stove caught and made a sound like a tiny rocket ship preparing for takeoff.

"Huh," she said, "can you show me again?"

He did and she tried it once.

"Whoa there, killer!" he said, chuckling and grabbed her hand to ease it on the valve.

She rocked back on her heels, away from the stove. "Can I ask you something?"

"Shoot."

"What does the 'p' in p-cord stand for?" she asked.

He held her gaze for a second. "Parachute."

"Oh." After a beat, she followed up with, "What do you use it for?"

"Are you serious?" he responded deadpan.

"Um." She didn't think Dane told her. If he did, she definitely couldn't remember. "Yes."

He rubbed his hands over his face. "It's to tie up your food so the bears don't get it."

Of course she knew there were bears in the mountains but she kind of thought of them on a different plane. In a different world within this world. Or that there were boundaries they respected. Her gut flipped. "Oh," she managed.

"We're going to have to practice this, too, aren't we?" Slip An' Slide asked.

"If you want."

"And risk you using your food bag as a pillow?" Slip An' Slide asked without a hint of humor.

He shifted on the ground. "So how long are you planning on going for?" he inquired, fidgeting with the quiet stove between them.

"Well, I would go Highway 2 to Stehekin. I think it's about 90 miles, so, five days?" she said.

"Take an extra day of food. Just in case," he said. "It's around Glacier Peak Wilderness, an area around Red Pass and Fire Creek Pass, I think. It's really beautiful up there, I hear. It's awesome all the way to the border but that's like a 200-mile trip. I had a buddy do a section from Snoqualmie Pass to the border two summers ago. He said it was some of the best hiking he's ever done."

She nodded and fumbled with the stove as she tried to disassemble it. For having only two main parts, it sure was a bitch.

"Well, you should have good weather. It's supposed to clear up in about two days and stay that way for a while. That should be plenty of time."

She nodded. "Yeah, that's what I figured," she said as she unceremoniously shoved the stove into her pack. "All right, it's about that time for me to turn in. Thanks for helping me with the stove."

"Mmm-hmm." He stood at the same time she did. He remained standing, watching her as she crossed the grass to the camper.

"SO YOU'RE REALLY DOING THIS hiking thing?" Smith asked her as they talked in front of the cash register.

"Where you hikin'?" asked the customer, as he held out two dollars in callused, cracked hands for the coffee he came in every morning between 8:13 and 8:22 to buy.

"A little section of the Pacific Crest Trail. Not far from here. Maybe up to Stehekin," she responded, fifty-three cents at the ready.

The guy nodded. Vika couldn't remember his name; maybe she never knew it in the first place. "That's nice country up there. I go huntin' with my buddy. He has a cabin up there." He pocketed the fifty-three cents. "Shot me an elk last season."

Vika, at a loss for anything to say, went, "Cool." Not that she necessarily found elk hunting cool, but out it came anyway.

"You mean Jeff Clark?" Smith asked.

"That's the guy," Coffee Drinker confirmed.

"The cabin on the lake?" Smith asked.

"Yup. Been there?"

"Three or four times. My wife and his wife are friends," Smith said by way of explanation.

"Ah." He took a sip of his coffee and adjusted the hat on his head. "All right, well, you two have a good day, and good luck with the hikin'."

"Thanks," Vika said, "you have a good one, too."

The bell tinkled as the door closed behind him.

Smith looked at the array of scratch-offs. "Give me..." Smith waved his money as he thought. "Two number sevens."

"Wow," Vika teased, "venturing into the unknown."

Smith grunted, "Consider it inspiration."

She smiled as she tugged the tickets along the perforated edge and scanned them. "Good luck," she said.

"Who are you going with?" Smith asked.

"Slip An' Slide," Vika lied. She was still trying to talk him into it but he hadn't committed. Yet.

He stared at her for a second before grabbing a penny from the penny dish. "That's good. It wouldn't be very wise to do it yourself. How well do you know this Slip An' Slide fellow?"

Vika gave Smith a sideways look. "Slip An' Slide? Well enough."

"Are you sure? I don't want you getting into...trouble," Smith said, looking at his tickets.

"Slip An' Slide? You don't have to be worried about him."

"No? Has Dane talked to you about him?" Smith prodded.

Vika looked incredulously at him. "*Dane?*"

"My point exactly," Smith said. "Someone has to vet this guy. Maybe you can bring him around here some time and I can interview him myself."

"Um," Vika said, torn between being moved or amused by his concern. "Thank you," she settled on, "but I trust him."

"Just be careful."

"I will."

"And sleep with a knife in case that doesn't work."

"A—" Vika bit her lip and shook her head. "OK, Smith, I'll keep that in mind. Maybe it'd be better to do it myself," she suggested, knowing it would annoy him, "but you don't think I can."

He scratched off a ticket, and from his blank face, Vika guessed it wasn't a winner. He moved on to the second ticket. "I think you can do anything you want," he countered. "But first you have to learn how to go about doing it, though. You have to learn how to pay attention to weather, to sounds, to animal signs. Or guys twice your size.

"The most successful adrenaline junkie calculates risk. He—pardon me, *she*—does not ignore it or is immune to it."

"Of course. I *have* calculated it."

"Vika," Smith said firmly, "you haven't even been exposed to all the variables, yet."

"Well," Vika shrugged, "Slip An' Slide is going with me anyway."

"Right."

Vika gestured to the tickets. "Win anything?"

"Not a cent."

"Maybe next time."

"Maybe," Smith answered. Then he tossed the tickets in the trash and started towards the kitchen. "I'm making tiramisu for dessert. Want a little extra?"

"Smith! Do I want a little extra? Oh, my god, you made my day."

Smith smiled. "I'll save some for you and put it in the fridge in the back. Don't let Jill see you, though."

"Oh, absolutely," Vika nodded, "Thanks!"

"Those calories will do you well before this hike. All right, I have to go make some tuna fish sandwiches before I get in trouble. Think about the risk. All of it."

THE REST OF THE DAY, Vika did. She thought about risk while she cashed out customers, she thought about risk when she washed the cooler doors, and she thought about risk when she re-filled the coffee pots. She thought about the risk of going alone, she thought about the risk of going with Slip An' Slide, and she thought about the risk of not going at all.

She concluded that Slip An' Slide was going hiking with her.

Now the problem lay in the convincing of said party to join her at the trailhead.

Vika punched out at ten after three with more audacity than a reasonable plan. It was drizzling outside, slow but steady, and she ran across the parking lot to the bus, tiramisu packaged and in hand.

She drove the bus faster than she had ever driven before, raindrops flying off the side as the windshield wipers cranked back and forth on high.

Vika pulled into the driveway and almost into some pallets, the contents of which were indistinguishable under what looked like a lot of plastic wrap, though, honestly, there could be a giraffe waiting for her in the backyard and she wouldn't be surprised. Vika ran straight to the barn to find Slip An' Slide.

He wasn't there. She ran into the house and heard Dane's voice explaining electricity to an audience. She rushed into the room and found Slip An' Slide, Forrest, and Dane.

"Sorry," she said as they turned to look at her. "Um, I," Vika cleared her throat, "Slip An' Slide, can I talk to you for a moment?"

Vika saw him think about it, but after a beat, his footsteps sounded behind her, and Vika felt her audacity slipping away.

"Slip An' Slide," she began. He stood there looking at her. "Well, I, um—"

"Spit it out," he said. He seemed taller than she remembered. And a little grumpier.

"Will you please go hiking with me?"

"No."

"Look, I don't know what to look for. I don't know anything about weather patterns, I don't know anything about sounds—;"

"Sounds?"

"I don't know anything about animal signs. The risk is too high for me to go alone."

"Then don't go."

"The risk is too high for me not to go. I've been in a tunnel, I want out!" she said fervently.

"What?" Slip An' Slide looked genuinely confused.

"A tunnel. Well, Dane thinks so anyway. That pissed me off a little, I mean, would I be out here in the first place if I were in a tunnel? No. Well—whatever," Vika sighed. "Regardless of tunnels, I need to go on this hike. I need to see for myself what's out there for me. So, please, will you go with me?"

"Look, I don't know what you're talking about, but I have yet to hear what I get out of this," Slip An' Slide said as he turned to go back to the lecture on direct and alternating currents.

"Wait," she said, feeling like a jerk, "I don't know what you'll get. I don't, and I'm sorry for not asking you about that sooner. But I know that you don't want to go home, wherever that is, and I know that you love the mountains. Just because you didn't do a thru doesn't mean that you can't ever visit them again." She held her breath, waiting.

He sighed and looked at the ceiling. "I have to go," he finally said, and went back to the kitchen to where Dane and Forrest were.

She stared after him, refusing to let that be end.

She turned and walked across the wet yard to the camper to think of a plan. Grandma Peach was humming while she washed the dishes with Quasi asleep and curled up on the rug at her feet.

Vika kicked off her wet shoes, put the tiramisu on the counter and made her way to her suitcase to pull out dry clothes. Once she was changed, she went back to the kitchen and opened a drawer to pull out a fork.

"Do you want any tiramisu?" Vika asked Grandma Peach.

"No, thank you, dear," she answered.

She pulled off the plastic wrap and stuck her fork in for a giant bite. Vika's jaw twitched from the sweetness as she bit down on the soft layers. She closed her eyes and held the dessert in her mouth for a moment to savor it.

Vika had to think of something that Slip An' Slide wanted. Something that he could get only on the trail. She took another small bite of the dessert. First, she had to figure out what made him get off and then she could figure out how to get him back on. Maybe. Though, the people who likely knew the answer were a couple hundred miles south on the trail at the moment.

Slowly, Vika walked across the area to the loveseat and sank into it. For a few minutes, Vika ate, Grandma Peach washed dishes and hummed, and Quasi slept on.

"Grandma Peach?" Vika said, poking at the last of the bites in the bowl. It was beginning to seem questionable that she would figure it out before the snow started to fly.

"Yes, dear?"

"Can you drop me off at the PCT on Highway 2 the day after tomorrow?" she asked quietly.

"Sure, dear," she said, with a glance over her shoulder to Vika, "Slip An' Slide, too?"

Before she could answer, there was a knock on the door. "Come in," she called and the door almost immediately bounced open and in walked Slip An' Slide.

"Fine," he said. "God, you're stubborn."

Vika looked up. "Most people call me Vika," she said.

Slip An' Slide shook his head. "You're impossible. But fine, I'll go hiking with you."

Vika's eyes went big. That turned out to be a lot easier than her half-formulated plan. "You will?"

He gave a tight nod.

She sprung up from her seat and gave him a hug. It was like hugging a wooden board. "Thank you!"

"Only because I'd feel bad if you die out there. And I'm going through your pack before we hike."

"That's a little personal, I mean—"

"You'll do everything I say."

"Well, maybe not everything—"

"Those are the conditions," he said, "unless, of course, there is more risk with me doing this."

Vika scrunched her nose at him and her distaste for using her own words against her. "Fine, you can go through my pack."

"No cotton," he said.

"No cotton," she repeated.

"No cans of food," he said.

"Not even beans?" Vika asked.

Slip An' Slide looked at her.

She might be visiting the small outfitters in town, she thought to herself. Get herself some of those ready-made meals. Just add water.

CHAPTER 16

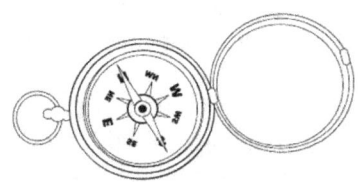

IF VIKA KNEW SHE WAS GOING to wake up at six o'clock the next morning to the sound of heavy machinery in the area, she wouldn't have set an alarm. Groggily, she rolled out of bed and padded into the kitchen to pour herself a cup of coffee.

"What is Dane doing?" Vika asked Grandma Peach, who was reading a book with a cup of tea close by, having already showered and sat in her camper-sized armchair.

"Oh, I don't know, dear," she said, unfazed. "It's a rare day when I do. His father was just like that."

"He was?" Vika asked, reaching for the coffee pot.

"Oh, yes," Grandma Peach answered, flipping the page in her book, "always into this and that. I would come home from school and he would have built a cabinet, fixed the driveway."

"What kind of work did he do?" Vika inquired.

"Well," Grandma Peach answered thoughtfully, deciding to close her book and remove her reading glasses from her nose. "He stayed at home with the kids when they were little."

"He was a stay-at-home dad? Was that popular?" The cup of coffee with a scoop of hot chocolate mix dulled the irritation of Dane's racket and a doughnut dulled it even more. Besides, Vika had to pack for hiking and she thought she'd be productive with the extra time.

"Oh, no, dear. Not at all," Grandma Peach shrugged, "But it worked for us then. It's probably what sent him to the grave earlier than me, but neither of us would want a do-over. When they went back to school, he went back to his job as a car mechanic." She gave Vika a warm smile and put her glasses back on her nose and opened the book again.

Vika licked the powder off her fingertips and thought about how easily the entire family defied convention. A couple minutes later, she grabbed the backpack from Dane she had shoved under her bed the night before, her coffee nearby on a shelf attached to the headboard.

"Oh, my," Grandma Peach said an hour later, as she spotted the gear Vika had then dumped on her bed. "What have you got there?"

Vika looked at the pile, trying to remember all of Dane's explanations. "Gear," she said, quite convincingly she knew exactly what she was talking about, "for my hiking trip."

She sifted through the stove, the p-cord, the fuel, a headlamp, the tent, the poles, stakes, a massive orange poncho, matching orange rain pants, a sleeping bag, a sleeping pad, and a lighter. There was a wrap, antibiotic, safety pins, and a bottle of aspirin in a small first-aid bag.

Vika pulled out her suitcase and started to go through it for clothing. She packed enough underwear and socks for each day plus one, two bras, and a pair of jeans—Tic, Tac, and Toe didn't seem too fond of them when they spoke of Forrest, but she didn't have anything else and so into the pile they went. She wanted to get a shirt at the outfitters but she had to have another to change into. And a long sleeve, a hoodie in case she got cold— just one of each. She didn't want to over-do it. Of course, she had to have clean pajamas, too, so she threw those into the pile.

Next, Vika moved into the bathroom to grab her toiletries and brought them back to her other supplies. Carefully, she stuffed the pack, shoving her pajamas in the top pocket. She snugged the straps tight and looked at her finished product with pride.

It wasn't even very heavy.

Satisfied, Vika changed into her work clothes and went into the yard to help the boys. Forrest stood at the edge of the excitement watching Dane shut off the excavator and climb down.

"Well that looks good, at least," Dane said, pulling his 1930s goggles to the top of his head and planting his hands on his hips while looking down into a trench. Vika, having seen few freshly excavated trenches in her time, silently agreed.

She looked at Forrest who stood only a couple feet from where she was standing. "How's it look, Forrest?"

Forrest shrugged, unconcerned. "Straight enough," he answered.

Vika leaned in. "And what, exactly, is it straight enough for?"

Forrest wore an expression resembling amusement. "He's digging for electric and gas."

"Ah."

"Vika!" Dane called from the other side of the trench, his hands still on his hips, "want to drive the excavator?"

Vika shook her head. "Thanks, but no thanks, Dane," she called back. "I don't think that would be a good idea."

He belly-laughed and responded, "The blackberry patch might not catch you this time. I guess I'll do myself!" The engine fired up again only seconds later.

Vika walked around the house the long way to avoid Dane and the giant claw attached to the machine he was driving. She found Slip An' Slide on the far side, shoveling gravel from a pile next to the barn into a wheelbarrow.

"What are you up to?" Vika asked him.

"Backfilling that last wall I finished," he said, continuing to shovel.

"Oh," Vika answered as she watched him for a moment then added, "I finished packing my pack."

He gave her a half smile as he rested the shovel against the pile of stone and picked up the handles to wheel his load away. "How much am I going to have to take out?" he teased.

"Not that much, I don't think," Vika answered. "I didn't put in anything I don't really need for four days."

"OK," Slip An' Slide said, but his voice was doubtful.

"WHAT IS *THIS*?" HE CRIED later, after they had finished backfilling the wall, as he pulled…and pulled…and pulled her towel from the outside pocket.

"It's worn down quite a bit. It's not that heavy," Vika defended.

"No."

"What if it rains? I can use it—"

"If it rains, wear the poncho. If this is wet, it'll weigh five times as much."

"Fine," Vika shrugged as he tossed it aside.

"Shampoo?" Slip An' Slide held the bottle up to her. "Where exactly do you think you're going to need shampoo? In the 40 degree lakes?"

Vika flung out her hands. "We're going to Stehekin. I thought I'd bring it along for that."

"No."

"No? I'm not expecting to shower on the trail, but when we're back in civilization—"

"We'll buy it there."

Vika rolled her eyes. "Fine," she repeated.

"Same goes for conditioner," Slip An' Slide said as he tossed a second bottle aside. Next, he held up her deodorant.

"I'm taking that," Vika hissed.

"No, you're not," Slip An' Slide retorted.

"*Yes*, I am," Vika glared at him and shot out her hand to grab at the small pink stick. He grabbed it back just as quick.

"Hey!" Vika yelled and tried to grab it again but he pulled it out of her reach.

"OK!" Slip An' Slide chuckled, trying to swat away her hand. "Fine, you can take it."

"Then give it!"

"Wait!" he said again, as she attempted to swipe it away again, "Wait, I'll give it back to you, just one second."

"What?" Vika asked, folding her arms across her chest. Slip An' Slide grabbed a pocketknife with his free hand and opened it to the biggest blade on the contraption. Vika's eye widened. "What are you doing?" she asked.

He answered by flipping off the cap to the antiperspirant and rolling it up.

Her eyes widened with horror and her hands reached out to take it again. "*What are you doing with my deodorant?*" she shrieked.

He elbowed her away as he moved the blade to the edge of the stick. "Stop! You're going to make me stab myself!"

"Well, I wouldn't," Vika shot back, "if you weren't trying to *cut up my deodorant*! Give me that!" She reached for it again despite his warning and grabbed the soft material as the blade slid through only to come away with a handful of *Rose Blossom*.

"Oh, my god—Slip An' Slide!" she shrieked again, walking quickly towards the bathroom, tossing the chunk in the garbage and washing her hands. "What did you do that for?" Vika yelled at him as she stormed out of the bathroom.

"Losing unnecessary weight," he countered calmly. "Now you can take it."

"Are you serious?"

"Yes, Vika," Slip An' Slide said, "I go on this hike if I go through your pack. That was the deal. I am not going to listen to you whine about how heavy your pack is, and guess what? I know how to pack a pack. We're doing it my way."

"Unbelievable. You're unbelievable," Vika complained, "and now my hands smell like soapy roses."

He opened the large pocket on the top and pulled out her clothes. He closed his eyes and took a deep breath, as though it would make the jeans in his hands disappear. Without a word, he raised his eyebrows and held them up.

"I don't have anything else," she said, by way of irritated explanation.

"Well, find something," he answered. He pushed aside more clothes. "Vika," he sighed, "this is all cotton. Except for your long sleeve. You can take that, everything else, no."

Vika spread her hands wide. "I don't have anything else."

"A T-shirt and a pair of pants," he said, "that's all you need."

"For five days?"

"Yes, and what are you doing with all of these socks? Oh..." he said, pulling out a pot. "What is this?" His voice was terrifyingly quiet.

"Um?" Vika looked at the pot. "This is a rhetorical question, right?"

"This weighs at *least* three pounds—"

"So," Vika sighed, "I'm going to take a wild guess here and say it's not going."

He shook his head. "Give Grandma Peach her pot back."

He finished with the large pocket and unzipped the top pocket. "You don't need pajamas either."

"I thought I'd keep my sleeping bag as clean as possible," she explained.

"Not with flannel pants, you're not," he said, "maybe with something a little more lightweight."

"I don't have anything—" Vika paused. "I have some spandex leggings."

Slip An' Slide shrugged and Vika saw his jaw twitch. "Those will work," he said, "and you'll need a hat." He looked at the two piles for a beat. One, the gear he allowed her to take and the 'gear' he did not. The piles were almost the same size.

"Where were you going to put the food?" he asked with genuine curiosity.

"There was still space," Vika retorted and pointed to the pack. "Here...here...oh, here and here..."

Slip An' Slide shook his head. "OK, well, we still have to go shopping. Do you want to go now and we'll stop by the outfitters and you can pick up a T-shirt?"

"Yeah," Vika responded, "that works."

They went to the outfitters first and Slip An' Slide had to steer her away from the packaged meals.

"You just have to add water!" she said as he dragged her to the women's clothing section.

"There's a lot of food that you just have to add water," was his rebuttal, "and we'll find it for a lot cheaper."

"Huh," Vika said, "have you ever had one of those meals?"

"Yes."

"Were they good?"

"Delicious."

"Then we should get one."

Slip An' Slide looked at her. Vika smiled back. "My treat," she said, "do you like chicken?"

They walked out fifteen minutes later with a new T-shirt—light blue with a sketch of a tree in navy going up the left side, really cute, Vika thought—and those fancy zip-off pants, and one package of freeze-dried chicken fettuccine Alfredo with veggies.

They walked down the street to the supermarket and Vika followed Slip An' Slide through the aisles as he threw item after item into the basket. Sometimes he would ask if she preferred berries or seeds, chewy or crunchy granola bars, savory or spicy rice, peanut butter or chocolate spread.

"Is that a real question?" she had asked. He smirked and put the chocolate spread in the basket.

CHAPTER 17

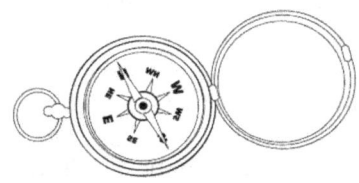

GRANDMA PEACH OPENED THE DOOR to the bus and unbuckled to give them each a hug. "Careful kids," she said, "watch out for bears and mice." Ugly Quasi barked at their feet.

Vika hugged her hard and scratched Quasi behind the ears. "We will."

She climbed down with her pack and tried to ignore the butterflies in her stomach. The sun shone on them in the parking lot of a ski resort, a handful of clouds sprinkled along the horizon. What if she couldn't do it? She chewed the inside of her lip and went through motions of checking her pack. That was pretend, though, because she had no idea what she should be checking for. At least it kept her hands busy for a minute.

Slip An' Slide was tightening his waist belt, adjusting the straps, and adjusting them again. If Vika didn't know better, she would have thought he was doing the same thing. As she watched him, she became more and more aware of differences between them. He stood about a foot taller than her, and the few weeks that had passed since he left the trail did nothing to diminish the muscles that roped his legs. Scabs and scars decorated his shins and his arms and legs had maintained their bronze color, stark against his light-colored clothes. His hair, shaggy and blonde, grazed his eyebrows when he looked down.

Vika, on the other hand, stood on legs that hadn't seen the brutality of a mountain trail, pale and smooth with their lack of miles. Borrowing the idea from Someday, she had picked up a pair of black running shorts to hike in, and the breeze that swept by left a little trail of goose bumps on her skin. Her shoes were new and clean, and the handles of her trekking poles felt foreign in her hands.

She pulled on the bottom of her blue shirt as she waited.

"Ready?" he finally asked.

She adjusted the headband that held back her auburn hair and nodded.

She thought maybe that the first step on the trail would be somehow glorious, enlightening, *something*. But really, day hikers and their dogs occupied the trail for the most part, with the occasional overnight hikers. The trail was just…dirt. It wasn't gold, or blue, or marked with "PCT" in every rock. No, it was good old-fashioned dirt that looked a lot like the dirt in North Dakota. A rogue weed hung over the trail and Vika pushed it aside with her leg as she walked by. Her ankle rolled off a small rock on the trail and combined with the new weight on her back, she almost went headfirst into the grass.

"What are you, new?" She could hear his smile.

"Hey now," she replied with her own smile, aware it was probably the first of many stumbles to come.

A handful of tiny gnats buzzed around her head, interested in the sweat that was already creeping out near her hairline. She swatted them away and kept walking. The first miles were easy enough, as it was decently flat as it wound around the foot of the mountain.

Then they started to climb. Vika knew the even grade wouldn't last forever, but in some magical universe, she kind of hoped it would. Rays of sun found their way onto the trail as they hiked amid the trees. The air smelled of pine and her feet slipped an inch or two when they stepped onto small piles of needles that had collected along the path. She could hear birds above her, but couldn't easily spot them.

Slip An' Slide insisted on hiking behind her so they wouldn't separate, but she felt like she was holding him back. He insisted she wasn't and that they'd be ending up at the same campsite anyway. So they went, Vika sweating buckets and Slip An' Slide patiently hiking behind her, taking pictures.

The grass on the side of the trail was replaced with harsher plants, weeds, and bigger rocks. Breaks in the trees became more frequent and she caught glimpses of the mountains stretching upwards, in the direction they were heading. With every step, the noise of the parking lot and the highway became merely a memory and Vika felt she was actually immersed in the wilderness. Their plans had become reality and it was terrifying.

They stopped for a snack break at Lake Valhalla and they commented on the amount of people out for the weekend, or "weekend warriors" as Slip An' Slide called them. A man walked by as they were putting their food bags back into their packs.

"That pack has to be at least fifty pounds," Slip An' Slide muttered. There were three stuff sacks hanging off the back, in addition to his sleeping pad and what looked like half of a kitchen set.

Vika playfully slapped his arm. "Be nice," she said, "maybe he's carrying extra stuff for his kids or something."

Slip An' Slide snorted, "Doubt it. You'd probably look like that if I didn't pack your pack for you."

"I would not!" she said, though she silently acknowledged the truth in that statement and inwardly cringed at the memory of asking Slip An' Slide if she should bring an extra pair of shoes. He full out laughed at her.

"The heavier your pack, the more you like camping," he had said, "the lighter your pack, the more you like hiking."

She looked out onto the lake, at the grey rocks that slid into the water on the far bank, at the ripples that traveled across the surface intermittently, pushed by an occasional breeze, and at the depths of the lake that disappeared into a sunken log and indefinable blueness.

There was no beach. It was grass, and then water. Sometimes, it was trees and then water, or rocks and then water. She watched a mother about twenty yards down the bank, perched on a rock, reach over and pull the socks off a young boy. They dipped their toes into the water at the same time. He shrieked and pulled them out, grinning and rubbing them. It wasn't fifteen seconds later when he did it again, his mother watching in amusement.

"Well," Slip An' Slide said as he shifted next to her, "let's get a move on. Your feet still OK?"

Vika hefted her pack onto her knee and slipped her arm into it. "Yeah, they're fine."

"Good. If they start to get really hot or start to rub, tell me, OK?"

Vika waved him off. "Yeah, yeah. You've said that like five times already."

"Well, I'm serious. If you get blisters, you'll have to hike with them, but it's a lot more comfortable if you don't have to."

The truth was, the idea of massive blisters and associated infections she could get while she was miles away from a road scared the hell out of Vika. She was paying quite a bit of attention to her feet. His feet were still tough from the 2,000 miles he put in already that summer, but hers were not weathered.

She looked up at him. "I'll tell you if they're bothering me."

They continued on and the traffic thinned. No more did they pass day hikers or weekenders. They stopped once so Slip An' Slide could put duct tape on a hotspot of hers. She protested, of course, not wanting anyone to touch her dirty, sweaty foot, but the red spot that had the potential to become a full-blown blister. Hell, *she* didn't want to touch it, but he didn't trust her to do an adequate job.

"I can do it," she said, as he washed off her foot with water from snowmelt, trying to grab the handkerchief from him.

He swatted her hand away and said nothing in response.

"Betty Friedman just rolled over in her grave," she grumbled.

"It's Friedan," he said, yanking some tape off his water bottle, "and this has nothing to do with being a housewife."

She snorted. "Just the big strong man taking care of the damsel in distress. Pretty much the same idea."

He raised an eyebrow at her. "So you think I'm big and strong?" he drawled, wiggling his eyebrows while carefully smoothing the duct tape over her heel.

"Oh, God," Vika muttered.

"Make sure that reaches above the back of your shoe." He tossed her sock at her.

"Yes, sirree," she saluted.

He shifted to shove his water bottle back into its pocket and pulled out the maps in the same motion. He stretched out against his pack, flipping between two of the sheets. The wind softly rustled the pages.

"I think we can make it to Pear Lake for tonight," he said after a moment. "What do you think?" he asked.

"How far is it?" Vika tugged on her sock and reached for her shoe.

"About five more miles. There's not a ton of elevation change, and most of it is down, anyway." He looked at home sitting across from her, leaning on his gear, one knee bent and pulled up, the other leg stretched out straight while he studied the maps. One hand absently brushed a bug off his well-toned arm.

She raised a shoulder and let it drop. "Yeah, that sounds fine to me," she answered as she pulled the laces tight. He nodded at her and slipped his arms through the straps on his pack. Vika stood and picked up her granola bar wrapper to stuff it inside the top pocket. She hefted her pack up on her back and gave Slip An' Slide a thumbs up.

Vika was beginning to understand the popularity of the PCT. It had opened up since leaving Steven's Pass and the scenery was, in a word, gorgeous. There were spruce trees here and there, but for the most part, she could see for miles and miles. Rivulets flowed from mounds of snow down and over the trail. The air was cleaner than it was in Stacklen and the sky was bluer. Her heart thudded in her chest and she inhaled slowly and fully. She had to turn her head this way and that to see the mountains around her, and wished her eyes could open wider so she could see more at one time. Plants crept up and around each nook and cranny of the terrain, soaking in the sun, leaving exposed earth only directly on the path they walked along.

The rocky grey peaks of the mountains in the midafternoon light were defined against the blue backdrop, not at all like an impressionist's rendition of nature with blended colors. These lines were uncompromising and firm—calculated almost.

She saw the vegetation a short distance away bend and turn lighter in color as a gust of wind rode the downhill of the mountain, pushing the grasses and small trees as it moved through. The air picked up the fragrance of wildflowers and enveloped Vika and Slip An' Slide in the aroma before continuing across the landscape. Vika looked closely at her surroundings to try and identify the sources of the new smells. Flowers she couldn't name, in every color she could imagine, bordered the trail.

She wanted the Earth to stop spinning and freeze for a moment.

Instead, she stumbled over a rock.

"Sorry," she said, "I was looking around a little too much, I guess."

"Nah," Slip An' Slide murmured, "you can't look around too much. You can't look around enough." He paused for a beat, and when he started, Vika could hear the nostalgia in his voice. "I was just before Kennedy Meadows and went to set up camp behind a cactus. I found an almost perfect snakeskin. It was about five-feet long with a split in the middle from where the snake pulled out. You could even see the eyes!" He snickered in amusement as he held out his arms to show the size. "Makes you wonder what kind of amazing shit is within three feet of you at any given time out here. Try not to sprain your ankle, though."

She hoped she didn't see a five-foot snake, but she hoped they'd see a bear. From a distance, of course. The thought of a bear up close made her stomach turn, as it should, and she figured that was just good survival instinct.

They walked on and the air got cooler. They bounced up above the treeline and walked through fields of shorter plants, the leaves thick and small, and the stems sturdy. The views opened up and Vika looked out over the rolling hills that spiked into rocky slopes and reached up to a jagged peak. Snow remained nestled in the shaded gullies and pockets on the rock face.

The bugs faded back somewhere, Vika couldn't remember exactly where, but they had disappeared in the higher elevation.

Her leg muscles were tired, though she expected nothing less and luckily, the hotspot Slip An' Slide tended to earlier remained a hotspot and hadn't turned into a blister. Her back was aching and she rolled her shoulders to try and ease some tension to no avail. She'd have to stretch it out at camp. God, it was like someone poured acid right in between her shoulder blades. The layer of sweat on her entire body she wasn't too fond of either, and she'd have to use that lake to wash some of it off before she climbed into her sleeping bag. The thought of it was just too gross.

They found the spur trail to the lake shortly after, and along with it, an empty campsite. According to Slip An' Slide anyway. To Vika, the "campsite" looked like a moderately flat area between some trees.

The lake was beautiful. It was clear and blue, and Vika spotted a fire on the far end of the lake, though the other camp was concealed by a grove of trees.

Slip An' Slide immediately got out a filter and his water bottles. He chugged one to empty it and went down to the lake.

Vika opened her pack and looked inside. She pushed some stuff around and finally found the tent and pulled it out. She laid it out on the ground and stared at it. There were holes along the edge of the tent material, where she imagined the poles went but how? And didn't they have to clip—

"Are you waiting for it to set itself up?" Slip An' Slide wondered as he walked up behind her.

"I'm getting there. Give me a second," she answered.

Slip An' Slide chuckled and wandered over to his pack. He took out a pot, a lighter, a stove, fuel canister, and some other little contraption. "We'll eat a dinner you have," he said, pouring water into a pot.

Good, she could get out dinner. She couldn't set up her tent, but she could get out dinner.

"Sure thing," she said as she abandoned her tent and sifted through her food bag. She tossed some bags of rice his way.

Vika didn't even try to help; his hands moved so quickly, twisting this, turning that, and eventually flicked the lighter and blue flame shot up from the stove. He carefully placed the rice and water on the heat and stood up. Within thirty seconds, their dinner was cooking and she had no idea what he had done to make it happen.

"All right," he said, brushing his hands on his pants. He wore the same pair he had on the in California and Oregon, ones with the bottom hems shredded where they met the back of his trail runners. Grass stains streaked along the outside of his right leg, and Vika could see a tear in the fabric amidst the green marks on the khaki material. "I can help you with that."

"Is that going to tip over?" Vika asked, gesturing to the large pot of their dinner balanced on tiny supports.

He looked back at it as though the thought hadn't crossed his mind. "Let's hope not," he responded and reached towards her gear. "Let me show you."

He adjusted the tent over the footprint and kicked away a couple sticks as Vika watched. With a flick of the wrist, the pole segments snapped together and he easily fitted them into the grommets. Within three minutes—and a stir break for the rice—her tent was up.

"Wow," she said, impressed, even though she knew he had done it countless times. "You're like a tent ninja. Thanks."

Slip An' Slide smirked, "What was that? The sound of Betty Friedman having a conniption fit?"

She gave an exaggerated eye roll. "It's Friedan, you ass."

While Slip An' Slide divided the food, Vika dug through her pack to find her jacket and a hat. She had been hot all day, but the sun was making its way behind the mountains and it made the sweat in her shirt cold.

The rice was surprisingly good. But there was a lot of it. She poked her spork at the pile and took a spoonful.

"I don't know if I'm going to be able to finish this," she said.

Slip An' Slide shrugged. "Whatever you don't eat, I will. Trust me, on the trail for a week or so and you would have no problem. I used to bring instant potatoes and mix them in with the rice. I slept like the dead." He shoved a spoonful—sporkful?—into his mouth.

"I bet," she answered as she lifted her jacket up to her ears using her shoulders, huddling up a bit. She spooned in some more rice.

When they finished their dinner, Slip An' Slide showed her how to clean her pot and he stuck it in the food bag.

"Can you find a rock about the size of your fist?" he asked, as he shuffled through his gear for the p-cord.

"I might not know much about the woods, but I do know what a rock looks like," she said, setting out in search of one. She kicked up some leaves, sifted through some sticks and at last found the perfect stone.

Slip An' Slide quickly tied the p-cord around it and handed it back to her. "See that tree there?" They began to walk away from the camp. "The one with that branch that sticks out about twenty feet from the ground?"

"Yup."

"Throw it over that one," he said.

She stood at the base of the tree and fed out some of the cord. She pulled her elbow back and threw. The rock sailed a good five feet below the branch and landed in some bushes.

"Wow," Slip An' Slide said, "that was ... good?"

"Oops," Vika responded.

They found the rock and the end of the p-cord and went for try number two.

Vika bounced it off a tree next to the branch and the rock popped out of the little harness Slip An' Slide had tied around it. It took another four minutes to find another rock.

Vika pushed back Slip An' Slide's tanned hand when he handed it out to her.

"How about you try?" she suggested. "It'll take me all night."

He shrugged and pulled his arm back. It sailed through the air in an arc, clear over the branch and dropped slowly on the other side. "Here," he said, holding onto the cord, "you take this and don't let go. Or we'll have to do that all over again."

"Got it," she said.

He took their two food bags over to where the rock dangled in midair. He removed the rock and quickly replaced it with the bags. "OK," he said, "let's hoist."

It was embarrassing how bad she was at pulling up the food and Slip An' Slide didn't hesitate to take over. Vika vowed to try harder the next night. The bags would also be lighter.

"Sorry," Vika said.

"For what?" Slip An' Slide looked at her as he tied that end of the p-cord to a nearby sapling.

"I feel kind of useless."

Slip An' Slide shrugged. "You'll get the hang of it," he said, finishing the knot. "Tomorrow you can cook dinner."

"That might take a couple tries," she confessed, "but I'll do my best."

Slip An' Slide grinned and shook his head. "You would be in tough shape if I didn't come."

"I probably would have turned around after about three miles," Vika agreed.

They headed into their respective tents only minutes later. It was early, but they were both tired, and Vika had forgotten all about bathing in the lake. She slid into her sleeping bag and tugged her hat down to her eyebrows. She pulled out her headlamp and a book, but she started to drift off before she finished the first chapter.

VIKA WOKE THE NEXT MORNING to Slip An' Slide telling her to wake up, start packing, that he had breakfast ready, and she should probably keep her hat accessible. Light flooded her tent and it was only 6:30.

She rolled out of the tent still half asleep. Slip An' Slide was sitting against his pack, all other evidence that he had slept the night there erased. He smiled at Vika, leaned over the stove and calmly stirring a pot of...something.

Vika apologized for not waking with the alarm.

"I don't set one," he replied, "I just get up with the sun."

"Oh," she said, an explanation that made her feel a little better. "Seriously?"

He laughed. "The water is almost done," he said, checking the pot. "You can pack up your sleeping bag and stuff and then we'll eat."

"Sounds good," Vika answered. "I'm starving." The big dinner she ate the night before had burned off quickly.

It took her roughly four times as long as Slip An' Slide to pack up, she figured, but she got it done. She plopped down her lumpy, lopsided pack and sat down as Slip An' Slide handed her a plate of maple brown sugar oats.

"I got up in the middle of the night," she said, making conversation. "My God, the stars were amazing!"

He grinned. "I didn't see them last night, but they were definitely something in California. When I slept on Hat Creek Rim, I woke up twice during the middle of the night thinking it was morning. There was a full moon then, too, so it was really bright. The second time it was like 3:30 so I just got up then and started hiking. Didn't even need a headlamp."

"You started hiking at 3:30?" she asked through a half-chuckle. "Is that normal?"

Slip An' Slide smiled. "Sometimes," he said. "It depends on the motivation. I like night hiking every once in a while because the night can be more calm than the day. When you're standing out on the Rim, the stars go on forever. The constellations pop right out at you even if you don't know the names of them, and the Milky Way seems to bring as much light as the moon." He paused and glanced up at the now-blue sky, "It's just you, some crickets, and a sky full of stars. Everyone is asleep and it's like taking a deep breath of fresh air. Like you just discovered one of the world's best kept secrets."

"Mmm," Vika said. "Maybe we could do a little night hiking on this trip?"

Slip An' Slide shrugged. "If you want," he said. "In the case of Hat Creek Rim, it was just known for being hot. I was doing myself a big favor by avoiding going through it at high noon. There is not a natural water source for 30 miles, so some Trail Angels put out water caches. Obviously, you don't want to drink it dry so you have to pay attention to your water supply."

"Oh, yeah!" Conversations at the house surfaced in Vika's mind. "I think I've heard hikers talk about that one. Most people said that the reputation was worse than the actual experience."

Slip An' Slide laughed. "Yeah, sounds about right. I think a couple people were caught off guard, though. Time Warp said he was miserable and went the last eight miles without water."

"Time Warp? Someday mentioned him, she said she was going to try and catch up."

He snorted. "Good luck. He's a cool dude but totally unpredictable. One day I saw him and he's only done three miles and it was seven at night. I camped with him, actually. He said he didn't feel like hiking that day." He scooped some oats into his mouth. "It wasn't even a really good site, either. I've definitely stopped before I planned to around a swimming hole, killer views, or bad weather, you know? This site he found…" he shrugged at a loss for words, even if only to speculate. "Other days he did forties without breaking a sweat."

"Well, I hope Someday catches him," she scraped the bottom of the pan as she spoke, "because if not, she'll be hiking alone."

"Eh," Slip An' Slide responded, "doubt it. She'd find someone or someone would find her."

"You think so?"

"Absolutely."

"Good, because I don't think she should hike alone."

"Why not?"

"Why?" Vika stuttered. "Isn't it dangerous for girls to hike alone?"

He looked at her pointedly. "Vika," he began.

"OK, OK," she started, letting the unspoken ideas drop between them, let alone her entire plan to hike by herself, which she figured it was more of a threat than reality anyway. "She's smart. You think she'll be fine, though, even if she ends up by herself?"

He nodded, "Yes."

They cleaned up the dishes and topped off their water bottles.

Vika was excited to start hiking, and she could tell Slip An' Slide was, too. The mountains didn't disappoint.

She never imagined herself outdoorsy before. She wasn't one for the wilderness, but this felt so good.

They moved along for a good two hours and stopped for some trail mix and cheese. She never ate cheese like they did, passing the brick back and forth, breaking off a chunk and passing it back. There was something liberating in idea of calories entirely as fuel and less as potential love handles.

They passed people on the trail and everyone told them that the scenery only got better from there.

She didn't believe them. She saw mountains, streams, wildflowers, blue skies, what else could be missing? So she smiled, nodded, and walked on.

Slip An' Slide watched her closely, Vika thought to make sure she was enjoying herself. Lucky for her, she didn't have to pretend.

"Hey, Slip An' Slide," she said when she caught his eye on a switchback.

"Hey, what?"

"What do you do in the real world?"

"This is the real world," he answered.

"You know what I mean."

He paused and Vika anticipated his answer. "Heating and cooling."

"Ah. What did they say when you went on the hike?"

"I quit."

"You quit?"

"I knew I'd be out here for four or five months, I had to."

"Oh," she said quietly, understanding his extended stay—part of it, anyway—at the house in Stacklen. He didn't have a job to go back to.

"What do you do?" he asked, interested in changing the subject.

"I went to school for art history," she answered, the dry, mechanical answer she had been giving since graduation.

"Art history," Slip An' Slide said, "that makes complete sense."

"What is that supposed to mean?" Vika asked, trying to fake offense, and looked over her shoulder at him.

He shrugged. "It just seems like you. Studying in a basement somewhere, brows furrowed."

Vika laughed. "Oh, my god."

"Big glasses, a flavored latte."

"Stop," she rolled her eyes, still smiling, "just stop." She walked a couple more steps. "But yeah, that's pretty much my deal."

"I knew it."

"Until I Gatsbied the Ninja Turtles."

"You what?"

"Do you think Da Vinci would be an engineer if he were alive today?"

"What?" Slip An' Slide sounded all kinds of confused with that one word. When Vika didn't reply, he pressed, "Who told you that? Dane?"

Vika huffed. "Why does everyone ask that?" she muttered.

Slip An' Slide didn't answer right away, "OK, forget Dane. Do you think you'll still do art history?"

"Hmm," Vika thought back to the classroom, "yes. Well, maybe not." She huffed again. "I don't know. I like the paintings, but I'm not so keen on the studying in a basement somewhere, you know? I'm not quite ready for that yet. I like this freedom right now."

Slip An' Slide conceded, "I know what you mean."

"I want to do something that I can't stand *not* to do. I love Renaissance paintings, but there's more to them than art."

"So wouldn't that just make them more interesting?" Slip An' Slide still sounded confused.

Vika kept walking in front, looking at the trees in front of her. "Yes," she finally said, "it should."

THERE WAS STILL SOME SNOW at the tops of the peaks and water flowed over the trail in some parts. Every once in a while, the snow extended down over the trail, and Slip An' Slide showed her how to kick the side of her foot into the snow to keep from slipping. Vika took a deep breath. The sun was out, and the air was still. By all accounts, it was a calm, beautiful day in the mountains, all except for this bit of snow. She stared at the footprints from Slip An' Slide's walk across the snow-filled chute. The snow, having been melted, re-frozen, condensed, melted and frozen again, shifted like tiny beads where he disturbed them, but none slid down the side of the mountain, as she feared. Even so, the first time she sunk her foot into the snow, she made the mistake of looking down and pictured herself skidding, grappling, twisting, fighting, images rush by— which way is up?—as snow shoves up her running shorts, twists the navy tree printed on her shirt, digging under her fingernails and SWOOSH— over the side of the cliff she goes.

She froze and looked up across the stretch of white. "Nope," she said, "not doing it."

Slip An' Slide reminded her that rest, food, and salvation were on the other side.

"Just keep your downhill ankle rolled in," he said.

"Keep your downhill ankle rolled in," she echoed. "I don't even know what that means! I friggin' hate the snow."

"Friggin'?"

"I don't say the 'F' word."

He laughed. The nerve! she thought.

"You'll be sorry if I disappear over that cliff and the buzzards eat me," she said, kicking her foot into the snow.

"Yeah, yeah. Quit whining."

She looked at the snow again and told her leg to take a step. Only problem was, it didn't listen.

"Are you coming?" Slip An' Slide asked, more entertained than annoyed.

"I'm trying!" she responded. Breathe, she told herself. In through the nose, out through the mouth.

Slip An' Slide must have seen it, because his voice changed. "The snow's soft, you'll be able to dig right in," he said. "Do you want me to come out and meet you half way?"

"No," she said, "then you'll be in my way."

"OK," he chortled, "one step. Just one. Kick in to the snow ... there you go. Solid? Now bring your other foot around, slowly and kick. Good."

"Oh, my god, this is hard." She had every muscle clenched with the effort to balance herself perfectly over her planted foot. Her foot shifted and she shot her arm out to catch herself, her fingers clamped into the snow like a vice and she held her breath. Her muscles became even tighter. Her hand was already feeling the cold of the snow push through her skin and she knew it would be painful if she stayed like that for too long, yet at the same time, the heat from the sun warmed the back of her neck.

Her ass muscles were like little boulders and—oh—was that—yes—she felt definition in her bicep! Pride bloomed inside her and gave her the confidence to take another step. She kicked her foot in and took another.

"Now was that so hard?" Slip An' Slide asked when she grabbed his outstretched hand and she jumped off of the snow.

"We better not have more death chutes to walk over."

He nodded, "I'll try to keep it to a minimum."

They walked along through lush, green vegetation, high on the mountain and gloriously above treeline. She could see in some parts how the trail wound over a saddle and along another set of mountains, and she was overwhelmed with excitement about getting closer, standing in that spot she could see in the distance, a view of a ridge she hadn't seen yet. The trail went down a little into a saddle, as they talked about nothing and everything -- car engines, forest fires, "The Simpsons," "The Life of Pi," whether or not someone someday will find out if pi is rational, and if apple pie, blueberry pie, or raspberry pie was better.

"Huckleberry pie!" someone yelled from their right. Vika jumped and looked to where the voice came from and spotted a green tent nestled in a grove of spruce trees. A skinny guy with a scraggly beard waved to them. Vika couldn't tell if he was normally that dark-skinned, or if there was an extra layer of dirt covering him head to toe.

Ignoring the thought, Vika looked around at the sun starting to travel over the far side of the ridge, the miles and miles she could see in every direction, the lupines and pink flowers lining the trail. The mountains looked picturesque, with a touch of danger added as the impending darkness threatened to rouse all the creatures that dominate the deep, dark, forests of fairy tales.

She nodded towards his tent. "This is quite the camping spot you found there."

"Yeah," he said with an even bigger grin, "too bad the view is horrible."

Slip An' Slide laughed out loud. "Where'd you hike from?" he asked, as the hiker picked over a barely-there spur trail up to them.

"Mexico," he answered, "and you?"

"We've been at the Dancys' in Stacklen. Just came out to see what all the North Cascades hype was about." Slip An' Slide put out his hand to shake. "I'm Slip An' Slide. I hiked Mexico to Sisters. I've been in Stacklen for the last couple of weeks." Vika saw his jaw twitch as he explained.

"Right on!" the hiker said, "I'm Modifier." He turned to Vika and they introduced themselves. "I've heard of the Dancys! They're new right? I actually had family come out so I headed west for the night, but I would have loved to meet them. They're, like, building a house or some shit, right?"

"Yeah," Vika answered. "Dane bought an old Victorian and is fixing it up to be a hiker hostel. Hikers have been helping out some as they go through."

"Right on," he nodded his head in approval. "I'll have to make my way down there some time. I grew up outside of Seattle and have hiked these mountains since I could walk. The Sierras get all the hype but man, nothing beats the North Cascades in my opinion." He paused. "Are you going to the border?"

"No," said Slip An' Slide, "just to Stehekin."

"Right on," Modifier said again. "I've actually never been, but I'm planning on taking my last zero there. I mean, it's Stehekin, you know? You gotta."

"We might see you there. We'll probably hang out for a few days," Vika said, "then we're taking the ferry back to Chelan." She slurred the word, unsure of how to pronounce it and doing her best to mask the attempt.

"Who's that?"

"Lake what?"

"What?" She looked from Modifier to Slip An' Slide, and then repeated, " ... Chelan?"

"That sounded like the name of an explorer. Something like... Machellan?" Modifier said.

"No! Magellan!" Slip An' Slide exclaimed. "That's it! I've been trying to think of his name for two days, since the first time she said it!"

Vika watched the guys bounce the conversation back and forth at her expense. She glared at them.

"He sailed down the Mississippi, right?"

"Oh, I thought it was the Hudson River."

"I don't know, I haven't taken history in—" Modifier looked skyward as he counted.

Vika took that opportunity to hiss, "He circumnavigated the globe."

"No, he didn't."

"I think she's making that up."

"The Straight of Magellan?" She said, like *that* kid in the front row of class.

Two blank stares answered her.

Slip An' Slide muttered with a grin, "Big glasses and flavored latte, studying in a basement..."

She chuckled and looked skyward. "How do you say the name of the town?" she changed the subject.

"Shuh," Slip An' Slide said, and held out a hand as a cue for her to repeat.

"Shuh," Vika echoed.

"Lan," he finished. "Like 'pan.'"

"Shuh-lan." Vika locked it in her brain for future reference to avoid similar circumstances.

Meanwhile, Slip An' Slide looked at the map and at his watch. "Are you feeling OK?"

Truth was, Vika was getting tired and she almost suggested they stay with Modifier for the night. She shrugged, "I can keep going, but I'd kind of like to camp soon."

"I'm thinking we can camp on that saddle up there?" Vika followed to where he was pointing. At least it was visible and it was nearly at the same elevation they were standing. Vika agreed. She couldn't wait to get out of her shoes—her feet were starting to throb.

They bid farewell to Modifier and started to walk again, the sun dipping lower in the sky and a breeze chilled the sweat on her back. A little stream of runoff trickled down over the trail, conveniently providing dinner water and an extra liter or so for each of them to start out the next morning.

At last, they reached the saddle and Vika almost fell to her knees to thank all the gods she could think of. She didn't think she'd last another step.

Just like the night before, Slip An' Slide had dinner on the stove by the time she had taken off her pack. Unlike the night before, she could barely walk. The last couple of days had caught up and her feet were swollen, dirty, and refused to properly support her weight. She limped around, trying to set up her tent and get all her stuff inside.

"Ugh," she said as she eased herself down to the ground next to Slip An' Slide at last.

"You OK?" Slip An' Slide asked as he divvied up portions.

"My feet are killing me," she answered.

"Blisters?" he wondered, concern lining his voice.

Vika shook her head. "It feels like a truck ran over them."

"Oh," he said, his attention going back to the food. "Massage them before you go to sleep tonight."

She gave a noise of understanding.

Her dinner went down more smoothly than the night before and sleep crept up on her more quickly than the night before.

"You look beat," Slip An' Slide commented on the obvious. "I'll wash up, you can climb into your tent."

"Are you sure? I can—"

"I'm sure. Sleep well." He reached to grab her bowl.

She pulled herself up as he stepped away into the woods with a water bottle to clean up the dishes.

Her sleeping bag felt like heaven when she snuggled in and was asleep before it was completely dark out.

CHAPTER 18

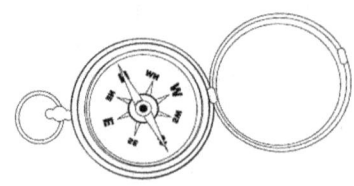

VIKA PACKED FASTER THE NEXT MORNING, but not by much. It was cold and she wanted to get moving to warm up. As they hiked, the sun crept up in the sky and lit the mountains in reds and yellows, while blues and purples persisted where it was still shade. Dew weighed ferns down over the trail and the water droplets slid off the leaves and coldly down Vika's legs as she walked through them. The plants were a vibrant green, so green that they seemed to emit the color from their leaves. Vika paused to close her eyes for a split second and she thought that if energy were tangible, she would be caught still in a spiderweb of glistening, pulsing, humming strands. When she opened them again, she saw clear rivulets of water tumble down the rocks and the birds flit from shrub to shrub.

It was almost too much for her to comprehend. She was sure she had the biggest, stupidest, awestruck grin plastered to her face. Luckily her pack sat high enough that Slip An' Slide couldn't see it. She hoped.

They had camped high and they stayed high for a while. There were small dips and climbs here and there, but nothing too extreme for her leg muscles. Vika continuously scanned the ridges, the woods, looking for wildlife.

That was about when she heard a scream. Was it a scream? Maybe it was a whistle but she should probably—

There it was again!

Vika whirled around to face Slip An' Slide. "What was that?" she asked frantically.

He shrugged, amused. "A marmot."

"A marmot?" Vika asked. "What is that?"

"A big rodent."

"Ick."

"They're two-toned out here—light brown waist up and dark brown below," Slip An' Slide gestured. "They look kind of like the woodchucks. They're cute and they're really curious so they'll stay out until you get pretty close sometimes. We'll for sure see one at some point. A buddy of mine petted one once. Dumbass."

"Well, that doesn't sound safe."

"He did stuff like that all the time."

"Still not safe."

"Yeah, I would advise against petting wild animals."

"Maybe just the baby bears," Vika said.

"Oh, of course. Pet all the baby bears you want."

"You'll fend off the mother for me right?"

"Not a chance."

"Glad to know you have my back."

"Any time."

They kept walking and the screams echoed across the mountains every once in a while. Vika imagined if she were a marmot and she lived here, she'd be shouting across the mountains and bubbling streams as well. There was certainly more than one, though. Just when she thought she was getting close, the call would be from the mountain over and she would walk on, hoping that one popped up in front of her.

Then, there it was: a whistle close enough to be seen. The two stopped simultaneously and scanned the scree slope they were hiking by.

"There it is!" Slip An' Slide said at the same time Vika cried, "I see it!" A little brown head poked up by a larger rock about thirty yards up from the trail. They stared at one another for a couple seconds and the marmot, as though to get a better look at them, hopped up on the rock and put his ear to the wind. He turned this way and that, antsy at their presence but curious enough to remain visible.

"I want to get closer," Vika whispered to Slip An' Slide as she unzipped the pocket on her hip belt to pull out her phone. "Just for a picture. Don't worry, I won't touch it."

She slowly sank her foot into the crushed rock and cautiously climbed. The marmot froze and watched her as she made her way to within ten yards. She held up her phone and took a picture. The marmot turned. She took another and the marmot turned again. She could have sworn it was posing for her. The rock was shifting under her feet and she moved one for better stability, but at the same time, her planted foot slid and she threw out a hand to catch herself. The marmot screamed and dove into its hole. Little marmot screams replied from far and wide, and Vika imagined dozens of marmots running for cover, warning their little ones about crazy humans.

"They're going to eat us!"

"Hiking pole my ass, that looks like a SPIT!"

"They'll sell our fur on the internet!"

"And make key chains out of our feet!"

"No, that's—not—that's—"

"Did you see those shorts with those shoes? AN ABOMINATION!"

Vika gave one last glance to the now-bare rock, quieted her mind of imaginary marmot conversations, stuffed her phone back in her pocket, and gingerly climbed down the slope. They walked on, Vika ecstatic from her wildlife encounter, wondering if she would see another marmot—or maybe another animal. Something bigger. Slip An' Slide was always close by, and so if they did run into something, at least she would have him to tell her what to do.

They walked along ridges and over saddles. They wandered below treeline for a very short while, and then back out to what seemed like the top of the world. The trail snaked along a mountain for a while and at last, they found themselves standing where the trail traveled though Red Pass.

The last time Vika saw that much snow, it was January in North Dakota.

She thought back to the little strips of snow they had passed over, but this wasn't a little strip. This was the entire side of the mountain. Of slick, dangerous snow. Her stomach dropped and her breathing came quicker.

"Uh, Slip An' Slide?" Vika started.

"Yeah?"

"What do we do?"

"Lunch?"

Vika paused and felt the emptiness in her own stomach, but she was not about to get distracted by the problem at hand. "I mean about the snow."

"What about it?"

"That's pretty solid. How do we get around it? Do we turn around?"

His expression was priceless. "Turn around? What kind of thru-hiker are you?"

"Not one."

He smiled. "Come on, North Dakota. We're walking over it."

"Walking…Slip An' Slide. No. I might be from North Dakota and my blood is thick as tar during the winter, but that doesn't mean I hike through snow. Remember yesterday? Oh, God. Do we have equipment? Don't we need those spike things on our feet? And rope. What about rope?"

"Crampons? OK, Jon Krakauer, this is not Everest. We are glissading. It's soft enough. You'll be able to dig in pretty good. Let's do it after lunch, though, I'm starved. It looks like we'll be glissading into treeline, anyway. Might as well eat with a view."

"What's glissading?" Vika asked, dreading the answer a little.

"Like sledding. Without a sled."

"Oh." That didn't sound too bad.

They had peanut butter and dried cranberry sandwiches, with trail mix and a chocolate bar. Slip An' Slide pulled out the maps to study and Vika leaned back against her pack and closed her eyes. The marmots must have stayed in their holes; she hadn't heard one in a while. She went through the trail in her mind. A year ago—hell, a couple months ago—she never would have guessed she would be here. Hiking and liking it. She used to think the woods were dirty. She used to think that the Met was the most peaceful place on Earth. Yet, here she could feel her actual soul getting a scrub down, she thought as she relaxed behind dark eyelids. The air seemed lighter and cleaner, no doubt it was, the sun shone brighter and existed as pleasant illumination and warmth, instead of the oppressiveness she felt in the cities, where the sun bounced of every concrete slab that made up the sidewalk, every car and truck, every street sign, telephone pole and building. The North Cascades were a far cry from 5th and 82nd.

She was vaguely aware of a hum sounding to her left. It became louder suddenly and faded just as quickly, though still present. She let her eyes flutter to let light in slowly and she sat up. Quickly, she spotted the source, a giant bee buzzed near a spruce tree. An odd looking bee, for sure. Well, maybe, a bird?

Vika squinted. A hummingbird? She had never seen a hummingbird in the wild before. It was a charcoal color and the wings were two blurs on the sides of its tiny body. It flitted quickly around the cones of the tree and zipped over to inspect Vika. She held her breath, mesmerized. The tiny bird looked directly at her and cocked its head to the side, much like a dog would. She held her breath. The hummingbird darted back and forth and then turned. It whizzed right between Slip An' Slide and the map he was studying. Then, like a base jumper running off a cliff, it dove down over the rocks as if to say, "Yes, this is the perfection of flight. Watch this!"

She watched the edge of her view, long after it had disappeared, waiting for it to come back. Only when Slip An' Slide moved to pack up did she check herself into reality and also packed up, but she did so distracted, keeping an eye out for her flying friend.

He looked at the maps again. Eventually, when Slip An' Slide was confident he knew what to aim for, they stood and walked to the edge of the snow.

"Keep your knees flexed," Slid An' Slide explained, "like shock absorbers. You're just going to sit down and here," he said as he handed her his hiking poles. "Hold these like so, use them to steer, but it'll be a pretty straight shot to that island there—" He pointed to their first meeting place, about a third of the way down the north side of the Pass before the trees.

"Won't you need them?" Vika asked.

"No, no," he answered confidently, "I've done this a ton. All right, you ready?"

Vika fidgeted. "Can I see you go first?"

"Just go. You'll be fine."

"C'mon, I've never done this before. Let me just see you do it."

Slip An' Slide shrugged and sat down. "Fine. Remember, knees bent, dig your heels in, got it?"

"Mmm-hmm."

He pushed forward, stuck, pushed again, and got going, painfully slow.

Vika breathed out a sigh of relief. Slow she could do. Rocketing down the side of a mountain on her ass she could not. She sat down and pushed, and stuck and pushed and stuck and pushed. Then she hit a steeper slope and off she went. Her heels dug into the soft snow and sprayed little fountains of slush all around her as she passed Slip An' Slide. It was fast enough to give her a start, but not enough to lose control. She picked up her feet a little and went faster. A shadow of a rock poked through the snow and she leaned hard on her poles and successfully steered around the threat. She kept going, settling into her speed, and saw the island where they planned to regroup approaching quickly.

She dug her heels in and slowed substantially. She came to a complete stop fifteen feet from land. She hmphfed and stood to walk the short distance before turning to watch Slip An' Slide, who was hauling down the hill, a ridiculous grin on his face. He pushed himself up and skied the last twenty yards to the landing.

"How was it?" he asked, out of breath but eyes gleaming.

"Coldest wedgie of my life," she answered through a smile. "So much fun though. Where's our next stop?"

Slip An' Slide laughed, "It's getting going that's the hardest part. Hmm, let's see. We need to end up on the other side of this drainage, so let's go for that spot there." He pointed, "The one with the two or three bushes and the boulder on the right side."

"Got it," Vika said. She walked to the edge and was about to sit down when Slip An' Slide ran passed her and jumped, landing on two feet and crouched over like a ski jumper feet parallel and facing straight down the hill. He bounced over the uneven snow and just when Vika thought he was doing really well, he pulled up a little as he tried to regain balance. His stomach muscles contracted and brought him back, overcompensating a bit and his arms flew out. Sure he lost it, Vika clapped her hands over her mouth, but suddenly he had righted himself and continued skiing. Then one foot got in front of the other, his torso twisted and he ran two steps, desperate to stay feet down, head up, and it worked! He was skiing again. Though as before, that lasted only seconds before he spun around in a 180 and finally wiped out. She could hear his laugh over her own and she sat down and pushed off.

Gaining speed quickly, she closed the distance.

"Coming in hot!" she yelled over the scrape of her heels on the snow and she hit the dirt with both feet and collided with him.

"Sorry," she said, laughing, looking down at him, her body flush with his, "I didn't mean to knock you over." She became more aware of their position when she inhaled and she let her gaze skim over the blonde scruff on his jaw, down to his shoulders that he had shrugged up and kept tense when she collided.

She brought her eyes up to his and saw he was looking up at her, a little peeved, she thought. "Better me than a rock," he grumbled, but the glance to her mouth and back up to her eyes gave away his façade of nonchalance. She took a moment longer than she needed to push away from him. It was a moment too long for Slip An' Slide, and he put a hand on her waist to gently roll her over and up into a sitting position.

He combed a hand through his hair, and then helped her to her feet and pointed down hill. "Let's follow this drainage a little longer, the trail goes right next to the creek. I figure we can aim for there," he moved his hand as he spoke. "Try not to aim for *me*," he said wryly. "Then we'll bushwhack a little to find the trail. It shouldn't be too hard."

They glissaded together, pushing, racing, and heckling each other to where Slip An' Slide directed. The trail was clear as a beaten footpath. Vika navigated around some snow piles and rocks, with Slip An' Slide close behind until their feet were firmly planted on dirt. They walked through the trees, enormous spruces that towered over them. The trail wound down the ravine some, wandered over a creek, and then came back over half a mile later. They walked for a little while longer, until both their stomachs were grumbling.

The trail flattened and they hiked until they found a campsite only yards from the creek. Without a word, both of them walked over toward the fire pit and let their packs slide off their arms to quietly thump on the ground.

Vika stretched to the left and then to the right. Slip An' Slide had already opened his pack and held his tent. He watched her stretching and hesitated, fiddling with the tent in his hands. "It's supposed to be pretty cold tonight," he said.

"It is?" Vika sighed. "I woke up a couple times the last two nights shivering. I slept with a hat on, too." She bit her lip.

"Well," he started. Glanced at Vika. Looked down. "I mean," he tried again, "you could, if you wanted, I mean—"

Vika smiled, "Save myself the trouble of putting up my own tent?"

He looked directly at her. "Yeah. Maybe you'll be a little warmer."

"A little warmer," she repeated, "sure. Thank you."

She gave him an easy smile and then turned her face away to bite it back before it grew. She then pushed the tent in her pack aside to find her sleeping bag. She set it on top of her pack and moved to help him set up his tent. They had it up in a matter of minutes and Vika unpacked some of her gear into Slip An' Slide's tent, while he busied himself preparing the dinner.

"What are we having?" she asked, sitting down close next to him on the log for a bench.

"Tortellini," he answered, "with spinach, I think."

"Mmm," she answered, "sounds good."

They ate and talked easily. They laughed when they should have, cringed, awed, and gasped when they should have and stayed close enough to touch throughout the entire meal. She watched everything he did and said with a renewed interest, her eyes noticing how he pulled up only the left corner of his mouth when he started to smile, how his hands stayed wrapped around his bowl except for when he told her a story of bushwhacking. He gestured to mimic how he climbed back onto the trail over fallen trees, rocks, and through vegetation on a route that was shorter as a crow flies, but took three times as long than if he were to walk around on the trail.

They told each other stories until the sun went down, the stars came out, and Vika's teeth started chattering. Vika so desperately wanted to ask him why he got off the trail, why he got back on, and why he wouldn't go home. Somehow she sensed he expected those questions, as a stiffness passed through him every time there was a pause in the conversation.

"Come on," Slip An' Slide said softly, an arm tight around her, "you're cold, let's get you settled in."

Instead of settling in, though, Slip An' Slide leaned over and kissed her. It was a single graze along her lips. Her back straightened and she sucked in air with the surprise of it, and her gasp got caught in her throat. She felt him pause and smile, both of their breathing slowed.

"You OK?" he asked against her lips.

She nodded without pulling away. "I didn't expect that."

"Mmm," he breathed, that left corner of his mouth still toying with a smile. "Can I do it again?"

"I'll have to think about it," she said, her voice quiet and even.

"That so? Can I get a timeline or something?"

Vika laughed and responded by pressing her lips against his. His hand came up to her face and traced her jaw line, and when Vika's mouth opened in response, he deepened the kiss and pulled her closer. She brought her arms up around his neck and shifted to eliminate the space between them. When that wasn't enough, she gripped his jacket to guide him into the tent.

THE NEXT MORNING WAS WARMER than the last couple, maybe because Vika slept so close to Slip An' Slide, or maybe not. But she liked to think so.

They hiked low for a while and then—as per laws of the universe—the trail that goes down must come up, and up they climbed. Just when she thought she couldn't climb anymore, the trail took a turn to the west over a creek and leveled off some. The trees thinned and Glacier Peak emerged from the woods above them. Clouds rolled in, though luckily nothing fell from the sky. They slogged over snow and rocks around the mountain and even a few marmots emerged from their holes to scream hello.

Vika and Slip An' Slide talked, took pictures, and watched the clouds around the mountain. Well, Slip An' Slide watched the clouds. Vika watched Slip An' Slide, unsure what he was looking for.

Vika's mind drifted back to the conversation with Dane about the tunnel. She grunted to herself as she remembered how he told her that she didn't know what she was doing in Stacklen, what she was looking for. How she had to get "experience, Vika! Experience! Life!" Her stomach dropped with renewed anger. Who was he to pass so much judgment, anyway?

Regardless of Dane's accuracy of her tunnel existence, he couldn't argue the same anymore, that was for sure. The mountains had served some purpose. They chipped away at her boundaries, but as the walls came down, clarity of her next move became fuzzier. Did she go back east to a museum? Did she stay in Washington longer? Did she travel somewhere else?

Her travel, the hiking, made the world seem more accessible than she had thought before. What a burden, she thought sarcastically.

Vika bent her head and saw rocks pounded into the dirt from countless footsteps that had stepped before her. Her mind drifted and the smell of pine stirred up memories of decorating the tree for Christmas with Alex. Since they were the same year in school, their elementary years provided the same holiday craft supplies, so there was double of nearly everything on the tree. He designed his always with precision and patterns, while she decorated hers with glitter, markers, cut-out patterns, and anything else she could get her hands on. She sighed. She missed her brother. He didn't even know she was in the mountains.

Vika watched Slip An' Slide's pack shift as he walked along in front of her. He stepped over rocks in the trail, around or over sticks, and maintained a steady pace. She kept up with him and for this stretch, and they kept their thoughts to themselves.

THEY SLEPT IN THE SAME TENT that night, and the hand that rested on Vika's hip held her close.

When they started to hike again the next morning, they again remained below treeline for a while and eventually started to climb. And climb. And climb. Vika was proud of herself as she kept going, just another minute, and since that wasn't so bad, she went for another minute and another. Sweat was prickling out of her hairline and slid down her forehead, through her eyebrows and off her eyelashes. She wiped them twice and came to realize quickly that she could be wasting precious energy wiping and might as well let the sweat pour down her face.

Vika would have liked to say that just as she felt like giving up the grade leveled out. Unfortunately, that wasn't the case. She stopped twice hoping it would flatten just around the bend, but alas, it was only up.

Clouds moved in over them, and Slip An' Slide explained that big mountains sometimes made their own weather. He had bluebird skies the days before and after Jefferson, but on Jefferson, he was caught in a hailstorm.

Eventually, finally, it flattened out. It had rained recently and made the mountain a little more mysterious. Eerie. The greens looked greener, the flowers richer, and on the bark of trees, she saw yellow, red, and purple instead of brown. It was enchanting, really, how the water pulled out colors. How everything appeared to be more alive. The air smelled of wet foliage and when Vika breathed in, she captured lungful after lungful of unpolluted mountain air.

At last, the shrubs disappeared, too, and old snow covered the trail. It covered ten-foot sections, and then fifteen, and then, before she knew it, the trail disappeared entirely. She was utterly lost without the patted dirt, though Slip An' Slide seemed to be well versed in predicting the direction the trail traveled. To Vika, they wandered aimlessly over snow banks and she was surprised every time she saw a trail post.

Slip An' Slide never looked surprised. He just kept on walking.

Until he stopped and turned in the middle of a snowfield. "Hmm," he said, "do you see any markers?"

Vika thought they were lost for sure. "No," she answered, looking around as well.

"OK," he responded, taking a couple steps to the left. "Keep on going up to that bluff there. I'm going to head over here to see what I can see."

She looked at the ground, looked up and around. "Shouldn't we go back to where we last saw it?"

"Nope."

"Slip An' Slide. Then we can figure out which way it went," she said, her voice getting a little higher with fear. It made her nervous to walk aimlessly.

"You'll never pick up a trail by standing in the same place. You have to keep moving somewhere," he called as he started out in search of the trail.

"What if we get lost?" she shouted after him.

"You're not lost, you just took a temporary hiatus from the trail," he yelled as he increased the distance between them.

She groaned in frustration and turned to look in the direction her personal Confucius asked her to. She was almost to the bluff when she almost stepped on something in the snow. Letters? Definitely footprints.

"Slip An' Slide!" she called, "I found some footprints!"

She waited while he made his way over to where she was standing, and she carefully walked around the prints.

"What did you find?"

Vika let the shadows catch the snow. "Um...Hep-A Thru-Hiker. Eats...now? Eat Snow." She squinted against the glare. "It says, Help A Thru-Hiker: Eat Snow. I'm willing to bet they're going the same way we want to."

The two or three sets of footprints seemed to be going in almost the same direction they were heading, and the two of them set out to follow. With enough caution not to miss a marker twenty yards in any direction, Slip An' Slide clarified.

They made it to dry land and on the trail in time for lunch. They descended down Fire Creek Pass in early afternoon, and since it sloped a little steeper than Red Pass, she appreciated the soft snow for her to dig her heels in on the glissade.

The steep grade was killing Vika's thighs and she decided to take a break on some rocks. Slip An' Slide glissaded in next to her and pointed across to the next mountain.

"I think I know where we're going next," he said.

She followed his finger and saw green on the side of the next mountain. It faced them across an enormous valley, the bottom of which was not visible. The side they stood on was open and snow covered with rocks and occasional trees, while the entire side of the other mountain was a dark green, with a lighter shade of green zigzagging its way all the way to the top.

"No," she said, as she slowly comprehended she was looking at switchbacks. "You're not serious, are you? We have to climb that?!"

"Looks like it," he said, more in awe than of dread, the latter being more attune to what Vika felt. "Think we can make it to the top to camp tonight?"

Vika knew that was coming. She didn't like it, but she knew it. "Sure," she said dejectedly. "Why not?"

Slip An' Slide clapped her on the back and smiled. "Don't get too used to saying 'why not,'" he teased. "You'll be doing forties before you know it. Besides, it'll hurt a lot less if we do it now than if we do it at seven o'clock tomorrow morning."

Vika couldn't argue with that. Her muscles were loose and malleable even if they were tired. If the last couple of mornings were any indication, she'd be stiff and sore at daybreak.

AN HOUR LATER, THOUGH, she regretted the decision. They still hadn't made it to the bottom of the mountain they started on, and every step she took down translated to another step up on the other side—a little bit of her soul cried.

They walked and walked, over logs, pushed aside plants, and picked their way carefully over the rubble where some of the trail had washed out. Her thighs burned with the downhill pace, and she pictured the cartilage and ligaments in her knees grinding and straining in their struggle to counteract the pull of gravity.

"I can't believe I'm going to say this," she said through gritted teeth, "I think uphill is easier than downhill."

"Oh," Slip An' Slide answered, "for sure."

She celebrated a small victory when the trail flattened out at Milk Creek and Slip An' Slide brought out some trail mix.

"Gimme some of that," Vika said, sticking out her hand.

"Take all you want," Slip An' Slide held the bag open for her, "Make it lighter for me on the way up."

"Well," she said, scooping a handful, "in that case, this is my good deed for the day. Chalking up the karma."

He shook the bag in front of her. "Have at it," he said.

She tossed back a handful of peanuts, pretzels, and M&Ms, at the same time Slip An' Slide swung one of his hands sideways and released bits of food down the embankment.

"What was that?" Vika snorted.

"I don't like raisins."

"What?" Vika asked, flabbergasted. "So? Eat them anyway."

He raised an eyebrow. "No."

"Why," she breathed, "did you pick that mix then?"

Slip An' Slide shrugged and answered, "'Cause you said you'd eat it." He reached into the bag and scooted some of the dried fruit out of the way. "Old petrified grapes are disgusting. The ones with the sugar on them are OK."

"Ah, yes, the healthy version."

"Your pack must be pretty heavy, carrying around all that sarcasm."

"Doesn't weigh as much as those raisins."

Slip An' Slide shook his head.

"Watch out," she pointed as she watched him pick through the food. "You don't want to accidentally get rotten grapes."

He pulled his hand out of the bag and dropped some pretzels into his mouth. "Rotten grapes, huh? Does that mean you have wine tucked away in your pack?"

Vika chuckled as she watched him. "I wish," she sighed.

He pinched his fingers along the plastic zipper and stuffed the bag into his pack. "Ready to get going?"

"Ready." Vika brushed her hands off on her running shorts and pushed herself up.

THE TRAIL ON THE OTHER SIDE of the creek started in the trees and remained there for a while. This worried Vika because her feet were dragging and they hadn't even made it to the green zigzags that they saw from Fire Creek Pass.

Then there was a plant about the same height as Vika, with huge leaves about the size of her face and thorns poking out from the stem. It hung over the trail and they pushed it aside as they passed.

Then there was another of the giant fern-looking plants. And then two in a row. Then three, and four, until they looked in front of them and the plants grew so close together and so high, they obscured much of the trail. "I think we found the green," Slip An' Slide said.

Vika had her arms in front, to push them aside and spot the trail. Their pace slowed to a crawl as they pushed aside plants and took a step, pushed aside more plants and took another step. The trail had been carved out of the side of the steep slope, switchbacks going back and fourth—Vika lost count somewhere around eight—and narrowed to about ten-inches wide.

If she stepped off the trail, would she go far, or get caught in the nearly impassable vegetation? She didn't want to test it.

And so they climbed, switchback after switchback, up the mountain. Slip An' Slide had taken the lead, and he warned her of rocks and fallen trees in the trail. He walked carefully in front of her, but even so, a calculated step missed the trail and Slip An' Slide fell forward to catch himself on his hands and one knee while his other leg dangled off the side. Vika gasped and froze. He stayed there for a second, and then kicked his foot out of the plants and pushed himself into a standing position.

They continued like that, battling obnoxious plants for another hour and a half, until they emerged above treeline at about 5,600 feet. Vika hoped to be steps away from the end of the climb upon reaching direct daylight. She was wrong. And though spectacular, the view did little to ease her aching body. Her pack seemed to be getting heavier, her feet hurt and stumbled over the terrain, and her stomach growled for her dinner of rice.

"Where is this campsite?" she asked, trying to sound merely curious.

"Maybe two, two and a half miles. You OK?" Slip An' Slide asked from in front of her.

She sighed, "I'll make it."

"We can stop and take a rest."

Even though she dearly wanted to, she wanted to set up camp a little more. "No, let's just keep going."

"If you're sure."

They kept walking, in tired silence for the most part. They wove through gullies and over rivulets. There was an echo of a rushing creek, though every time they rounded a bend, the water trickle was not the cascading image Vika had conjured in her mind. After about the third one, she wondered if the noise was the collective water traveling down the mountain.

Then they rounded a bend and the water flowing down the mountain spanned ten-yards wide. She heard Slip An' Slide slow down behind her, and turned to see him unclip his chest and hip belts.

"We might as well fill up on water here," he said, swinging his pack to the ground and sliding out his water bottles.

Vika imitated his motions in response, though without the grace of a veteran hiker. "Is there a campsite around here?" she asked, looking for the telltale fire pit but didn't see one.

"I think in about a half mile, maybe a little more." She groaned and sat on the ground, her pack still strapped to her body. "According to the maps it looks like it's on a ridge. Good spot to watch the sunrise, if you're ready for an early hike."

Vika wasn't thinking about the next morning yet, though she had to admit it sounded nice in theory. She shrugged. "That sounds good."

Slip An' Slide filled up her water bottles and helped her back to her aching feet. They continued on in the general northward direction, over small patches of snow, and luckily the trail was clear at the spot the spur trail split off. Vika stopped in the middle of the intersection and gave each possible direction a thorough visual investigation.

"Hang on," Slip An' Slide said, looking down at her feet. "You're standing on something."

Vika jumped to the side with a small shriek, images of a number of wildlife—and wildlife scat—but she saw nothing, except for maybe a couple scratches in the dirt.

"It says... hmm... oh, maybe we shouldn't camp here."

"What?" Vika said, looking at the ground where Slip An' Slide was staring. Then she looked around for a sign. When she didn't see one, she turned to stand next to him and followed his gaze. Sure enough, those scratches said BEAR with an arrow pointing down the spur trail toward the campsite they were looking for.

"Damn," said Slip An' Slide quietly.

"Damn is right," Vika said, surprising herself at how unthreatened by the possibility of a several hundred pound animal with four-inch razor sharp claws—she'd read that somewhere. If she weren't so tired, she would have surprised herself even more when she heard the next words that came out of her mouth, "Shit, Slip An' Slide, I'm so tired. We could check it out. Who knows how old the sign is. We'll just hang our food far away and high. Far away." As it was, she just wanted to sleep.

Slip An' Slide looked surprised, and the left corner of his mouth pulled up in amusement. "Yeah. OK," he answered slowly, "let's go check it out."

They walked down the trail a bit and had to step over some candy bar wrappers torn and pushed into the mud. If Vika were a betting person, she would be willing to bet it was the work of the bear they were warned of. At least there were no shredded hikers—or gear—nearby. The next twenty yards of the trail that led to the campsite was thankfully free of litter from wildlife and the campsite was spotless.

Vika shrugged and looked toward the west. The sun was hanging just over the mountains, oranges and reds bleeding out across the horizon, teasing them with imminent darkness. Vika turned toward Slip An' Slide. "Well, every site we've stayed at so far theoretically had bears, right? This is as good as any."

He chuckled, "I've slept in worse spots. This will be fine."

"Fine," Vika echoed, "yeah, too bad the view is shitty."

The mountains had turned purple, deep and rich in front of the endless orb above them. The light that broke through the branches of the grove of trees they stood in glowed orange, as though they were caught in a gently smoldering landscape. It lasted for only a couple minutes, but Vika sat entranced by both the visual exhilaration as well as a curious warmth she felt down to deep in her rib cage.

Slip An' Slide moved around her, pouring water into a pot, and lighting a real flame among the illusions. She pulled the tent out of his bag and went to set it up. The ground was packed from routine foot traffic, but soft enough that she could push the stake into the earth with the heel of her shoe. She had seen Slip An' Slide set it up enough times that it only took her a few minutes to fit pieces together and work the ends into the grommets.

Slip An' Slide had just taken dinner off the stove as Vika secured the last stake of the fly.

The sun dipped under the mountains and she felt a pang. Similar to the unease she felt when she dropped off a hiker after they had stayed with them, shared their stories with them, and inevitably, ruthlessly, continued on.

The smell of barbecue chicken and rice gently pulled her from her daydreaming and into the present moment. Which were remarkably similar. They might even be the same. Though her daydreams never before smelled like BBQ chicken and rice.

Slip An' Slide daydreamed beside her, staring through the pine needles as he ate his rice. Vika saw the corners of his eyes tense as he squinted into the sky. "Your paintings look like this?" he asked.

She followed his line of sight over the stove, past their packs and gear strewn about, across the campsite, along the spine of the tent and into the air. Her gaze darted like the hummingbird, through the scattered plants along the ground, up through the green needles, to free fall through sky under the first stars, in front of an amaranthine backdrop.

"No," she answered. She inhaled through her nose, the cool, evening air filling her lungs, the smell of flora around her lingering, and the sounds of birds nestling in for the night. A breeze swept through their site; a couple trees creaked in response. "My imitation of the third-dimension isn't the same as this."

Slip An' Slide nodded next to her.

When Vika pulled out her sleeping bag later, it was warm to the touch, as though it had just come out of the dryer. It took her a moment of confusion before she remembered they had their bags laid out to dry at lunch. She crawled in to the cozy sleeping bag warmed from the sun and snuggled in right up to her chin as Slip An' Slide followed.

They slept without the presence or the fear of a bear—which might at well be the same thing—forgetting all about the sign in the dirt.

She woke up to the most offensive snort in the world and rolled over to shove Slip An' Slide for disturbing her dreams. Then it came again. Vika's nose was pressed into his chest and the snort came from behind her...oh, God—

She held her breath, eyes wide without seeing, and froze.

That...thing snorted again. "Attractive," came the sleepy voice of Slip An' Slide.

"That wasn't me," she hissed.

"Huh?" He shifted next to her.

"It's coming from outside," she whispered, scooching closer.

"Oh, shit," he replied, his voice a little more awake. "I think the bear's back."

"A bear?" Vika tried not to cry.

"Well, stop pushing me," Slip An' Slide said, "you're going to push me right out of the tent."

"Sorry."

The sound of sticks breaking sounded outside.

"HEY!" Slip An' Slide yelled and the sounds stopped.

Vika swatted at him. "Stop! What are you doing? Now it knows we're here!"

She could feel Slip An' Slide look down at the top of her head, which she had taken care to conceal almost entirely in her sleeping bag.

"It already knows we're here. That's why it came."

"Oh, fuck, we're going to die. Fuck, fuck, fuck—"

"I thought you didn't say the 'F' word."

"I save it for dire fucking circumstances," Vika shot back, realizing the bear encounter she had hoped to experience was notably *not* so great in reality. "Like, perhaps, when I'm about to die."

"So you want your last word on this Earth to be 'fuck'?"

"Seriously, now? We're talking about this right the fuck now?"

"You have to work on the context, though, that last one…eh—"

She shoved him in the shoulder. "WHAT DO WE DO ABOUT THE FUCKING BEAR?"

"Relax, we're not going to die. It probably is just looking for the food bag. HEY!" he yelled again and Vika squealed and hoped she wouldn't wet her sleeping bag.

He shifted more and Vika realized he was getting out of his sleeping bag.

"What do you think you're doing?" she whispered harshly.

"Getting my headlamp."

"You are *not* going out there," she managed, and understood exactly why her father had locked himself in a cabin while that bear broke into his car all those years ago. She wished she had a cabin like he did, instead of the flimsy piece of fabric as a barrier.

"Oh, no way," Slip An' Slide said, "at least, not yet." He blinked the light on and kept it in his pack. He took out a pot and his spork and started beating the hell out of it, while yelling.

"Playing the drums now?" she screeched.

"I'm just making noise. Keep your head down." There was a crashing noise as sticks broke, branches slapped trees and each other, leaves were upturned, boulders rolled, and the Earth shook. "Hear that?"

"It sounds like Bigfoot and twelve of his fucking friends! We're going to die!"

"I told you, we're not going to die. I think it's running away," he said.

Slip An' Slide pulled back the fly and carefully popped his head out. "Looks clear," he said.

Vika tried to pull in some air. "You sure?" Her voice shook.

"Yep," he said, "it's gone and our food's still here. Nice."

"Oh, Jesus Christ," she sighed and pushed back the sleeping bag.

"I think it was a bear, actually."

CHAPTER 19

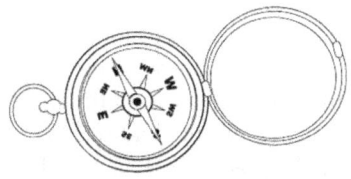

IT TOOK VIKA AN HOUR to fall back to sleep, yet she stirred first at dawn, the fly of the tent barely glowing from the rising sun and she rolled over and closed her eyes again. The second time she awoke, the tent was light and her heart skipped, thinking she had missed a mountain sunrise and silently cursed herself for going back to sleep the first time. She shimmied up the mat, keeping her sleeping bag snug up around her shoulders, and she blew her hair out of her eyes as she reached for the zipper. She eased it up a couple inches, Slip An' Slide breathing heavy next to her, and pushed her face up to the opening to scan for bears. Relieved, she saw only blue and knew there was time for her to get to the ridge before the pinks, yellows, and other warm colors slipped across the sky.

She groaned and stretched her aching muscles, and Slip An' Slide shifted in his sleeping bag. "Did we miss it?" he mumbled, his voice gravely with sleep.

"No," Vika whispered, "we have plenty of time."

They moved together, dressing, packing and eating, slowly waking. The bear seemed like a distant memory.

A few stars and planets held on well into daylight, as though in an incredible persistence of survival, but they eventually faded as the sun won the sky. The two of them sat and waited looking eastward, savoring their breakfast.

At last, a tiny crescent of gold burst over the side of the mountain and they watched the rest of the sun rise quickly after.

Vika felt that same warmth she felt the night before deep in her rib cage. The energy spread through her limbs, out her toes, through the soles of her shoes and rooted her to the ground, to the mountain, to the moment. Her heartbeat quickened, and she felt her body revive. A part of her felt small and insignificant, and part of her said that the smallness and insignificance meant that she had complete and utter free will.

Her muscles twitched with a desire to hike and they began moving.

Marmots screamed across the landscape as they woke and emerged from their dens.

They hiked down, with the aid of another series of tight switchbacks, and moseyed on down to the Suiattle River for a couple miles. They had a snack on the footbridge and proceeded to mosey back up the other side.

Eventually, it leveled out and they wound up and over some small knolls, through some small valleys and had lunch at a lakelet. Then into the trees they went again, talking about Thomas Cole, Thomas Eakins, and Thomas Frenel, a friend of Slip An' Slide's who had nothing to do with art. In fact, he didn't even like art and Vika couldn't remember how he happened into this conversation.

It didn't matter to her. The conversation was effortless.

The trail set out slightly down into a picturesque valley and ended. Or disappeared or something. Whatever happened, Vika saw boulders stacked on boulders, next to and behind other boulders. It didn't help that they were almost covered in snow, too.

"Well," said Slip An' Slide, "I guess this is the 'rocky area' in the maps."

"So," Vika huffed and looked around, "how do we do this?"

"Step on rocks you can see. Check them before you put all your weight on them. I think we're supposed to stay at about the same elevation so let's plan on…" he bit his lip and looked around. "There. See that weird-looking tree that's half-dead poking out through the rocks? Let's meet there. I'm going to go ahead and see if I can spot the trail on the other side."

Vika nodded and they both stepped out onto the new landscape. It wasn't as hard as Vika first thought, and soon she was navigating rather steadily through the terrain. As expected, Slip An' Slide hopped, jogged, and jumped his way much more quickly to the tree and beyond.

Vika made her way to the outcrop with the funky tree and waited. It wasn't long before Slip An' Slide called to her from about twenty yards away.

"Come this way!" he shouted, waving her over. "The trail is there!"

She followed his finger and didn't see anything resembling a trail, but she trusted him and started out in the same direction.

Anyway, she was having fun scrambling over the boulders using all fours. She was never too keen on heights—a survival instinct she'd always insisted, not a fear—and this particular terrain allowed for the illusion of rock climbing without the threat of falling to her death or worse.

She picked her way the rest of the way to Slip An' Slide and sure enough, wound up on the trail.

"Maybe we should find a campsite soon," Vika suggested as they pushed aside shrubbery to where the trail was slightly more defined. "I mean, we have an extra day's worth of food, right?"

"Well, I don't know if there's good water close to here. Hemlock Camp will definitely have a good site. It's only about four miles away."

"Four miles!" Vika sighed. The feeling from the night before was returning and the miles at the end of the day were getting tough. The energy she felt with the sunrise that morning had burned up a while ago. Her toes felt swollen and raw in her shoes and she noticed now more than ever the pressure points of the pack on her hipbones and her clavicles. She knew it was all superficial and hardly worth mentioning, especially to someone who put up with that kind of pain for a good two thousand miles.

Even so, Slip An' Slide picked up on her discomfort. "OK, let's try to get two more miles, and we'll stop for dinner on the trail. See how you feel. Maybe it'll help you push to Hemlock Camp, and we'll be that much closer to Stehekin."

She nodded, not wanting to spend the evening whining. "OK. I can do two miles."

The next two miles wasn't exactly torture, but it was close. Luckily, there was virtually no elevation gain. Her legs seemed detached from her body, though, and they impressed her when they kept a consistent pace. It was slower than earlier in the day but it was consistent. As a matter of fact, her feet set the pace so well that Vika ignored the grumblings in her stomach for fear that her feet wouldn't find the pace again if they stopped.

After a while, however, her stomach became louder than her logic and she spotted a nice flat area that would serve perfectly as a dinner stop.

As with every night before, Slip An' Slide had dinner—this time teriyaki noodles—boiling within minutes. She had to admit, it was kind of nice to eat on the trail. It was still warm and she didn't have to find her jacket and hat to eat dinner with.

Slip An' Slide flipped through the maps. "If we're where I think we are, we have a little over a mile to go to Hemlock Camp. If you want to try for it."

Vika spooned a mouthful of noodles into her mouth and chewed slowly. She gave a brief nod, "Yeah, I think I can make it."

Slip An' Slide grinned. "That's my girl."

When they started up again, Vika's feet throbbed as she stood and the blood rushed to fill them. She hobbled a couple steps. She thought maybe she spoke too soon, and maybe she'd start looking for a campsite again. While she thought this, she had hobbled a couple more steps. And a couple more.

"Shit," she breathed, "my feet are killing me."

Slip An' Slide walked behind her. "Just keep going. Make sure you're taking steps like you normally do."

"Easy for you to say," she managed through gritted teeth.

"That happened to me too the first—eh," he shrugged, "two weeks I hiked the trail. It's suggested for thru-hikers to get shoes half a size bigger than they normally do, because most people's feet will swell."

"Doesn't make it hurt less," Vika responded, trying to straighten her back and take a normal stride and wincing at the pain.

"No, but it does mean that nothing's wrong. Even if it hurts, I'm serious, walk like you normally do. If you change your gait, you'll start to put stress on muscles, ligaments, and tendons that you normally don't. Then you actually *will* have an injury. The more you walk on it, the easier you'll... break them in. The pain will go away soon."

Vika let out a whoosh of breath when she stepped on a small rock and felt it through the sole of her shoe. She had to admit he was right, though. Her feet hurt less and less with every step. Not a lot less, but enough for her to think that it wouldn't be so bad if and when she took another step.

It took longer than Slip An' Slide suggested, but at last, Vika walked a decent pace. Soon after, the sound of rushing water poured through the trees and infiltrated every space.

Vika walked faster. Every tree they passed, she expected the trail to head straight across the creek, but they followed it downstream for half a mile before it was clear they were finally going to cross. While Vika hoped—envisioned—another handy little footbridge for the crossing, the open creek proposed one final challenge before they could rest.

"This is going to be cold," Slip An' Slide mumbled as he inspected the disappearance of the trail into the creek and the emergence on the other side, fifteen yards away.

He started untying his shoes and Vika asked, "You're going barefoot? Wouldn't it be easier with shoes to grip?"

"Probably, but I'm not putting on wet shoes in the morning. You can if you want."

Vika looked at the rocks, some with green moss flowing downstream with the current, much like hair blowing in the wind. It was probably twice as slick barefoot. Then she thought about putting on cold, wet shoes the next morning.

Slip An' Slide stood and held his shoes in one hand while he waited patiently for her to decide.

She held out a pole for him. "Here," she said, "take one, I'll use the other." Then she bent to untie her shoes.

She thought her feet hurt before. The first step was cold. Ice immediately shot into her veins, growing through her toes, through the top of her foot. The second step was painful and she involuntarily let out a yelp. She pushed her feet forward, taking as much time to test the rocks for stability and no more. Numbness imprisoned her toes, but they still functioned as she wished as she watched them through the clear surface of the water. Her shins had lost feeling as well, a red line cutting across them horizontally, the line of demarcation between wet and dry. Silent versus screaming. Warm versus unbearably cold.

Slip An' Slide closed in on the far bank and hopped up on the side. He bent at the waist and curled his toes under his feet as he squeezed his eyes shut.

By then, she was halfway across the creek and thought for a second about running the last couple yards. The idea shattered with a fleeting image of her tripping and getting all of her gear wet instead of just her skin or her shoes.

Her feet emerged bright red on the other side and for a few moments, she felt nothing. Then she felt fire. The fire that only comes when it's too cold for nerves to process. The cramping that comes with it, too, and the cursed knowledge that there wasn't anything she could do about it but wait for her blood vessels to open and let warm blood back in. God, it hurt and she groaned. She realized she looked exactly like Slip An' Slide had only moments before, bent at the waist, toes curled underneath, and eyes squeezed shut. The air on her legs felt like sauna heat, but it worked slowly and her legs and feet screamed as though the warm blood was high pressure and toxic. She wondered if she would ever feel her toes again. At last, what felt like days, the throbbing eased.

Just behind Slip An' Slide hung a sign, "Hemlock Camp."

"We're here," she said, out of breath from the pain, "and not a moment to soon." She walked by him towards the camp, still holding her shoes in her hand. Little bits of dirt and spruce and hemlock needles stuck to her damp feet but the soles of her feet remained numb—she didn't feel them.

Branches lined little pathways to separate sites, all surrounding benches carved into felled trees around a communal fire pit. A sign on a tree said "toilet" and was accompanied by an arrow that pointed up the hill and, Vika surmised, behind the only tight cluster of trees around.

Slip An' Slide had followed and investigated on his own. "This spot looks pretty good," he called, throwing down his pack.

Vika stepped over branch dividers and put her pack down next to his. "Not bad," she said.

"Glad we made it here?" he smiled.

"Yes."

They set up camp quickly before the sun went down and climbed into the tent.

Vika tried to fall asleep and shifted against Slip An' Slide, but she still couldn't find a good spot. She shifted again and groaned.

"Stop moving, babe," he said against the top of her head.

Vika groaned again, "My feet feel like they're about to explode."

"Here," Slip An' Slide said, pushing his legs under hers, eyes still closed, one arm still resting over her waist. "Keep your feet up a little on mine. It might drain out some of the fluid."

She snuggled up closer and he held her a little tighter. He was right. It felt better. Not perfect, but good enough that she could get some sleep. She slept like that for a while, but woke up sometime during the middle of the night with her throbbing feet on the ground. She looked around to get oriented and found her face in Slip An' Slide's back.

She gently shoved him and he groaned.

"Can I have your feet again please?" she asked through the pain.

He rested a second and then flipped over quickly and pulled her in. "Yeah, sorry, babe," he said and almost immediately started snoring quietly into the top of her head.

Vika woke the next morning alone and to the smell of pancakes. She thought she was experiencing olfactory hallucinations and scooched up in her sleeping bag to poke her head out of the tent.

Sure enough, Slip An' Slide sat hunched over the stove using a spatula to scrape a flapjack off the bottom of the pot.

"Pancakes?" she said, rubbing her eyes.

"With chocolate chips," Slip An' Slide answered with a grin.

"I don't remember packing that."

"You didn't," he said, "I did. We had to have something special on the last morning, right?"

Vika smiled. "I'll be right out."

She wiggled back into the tent, pulled on her T-shirt and shorts and slid a jacket over her head. To her pleasant surprise, her feet, though swollen, hurt only mild to moderate, a marked improvement from the night before. Minutes later, they each had a small stack on their plate.

"These are the best pancakes I've ever had," Vika said through a mouthful.

He chuckled. "Remember that when you're not suffering from hiker hunger."

"Nah," she said, hardly audible, "I feel like I died and went to heaven."

Only ten miles, explained Slip An' Slide, to the bus stop where they could get a ride into Stehekin. Vika smiled to herself. She'd come a long way to think in terms of "only" ten miles.

The pancakes gave her motivation, but her feet resisted the hiking, swollen and sore. Her ankle and foot didn't have the flexibility of her normal load and brake gait, and she felt as though she was walking in ski boots. She hobbled for the first half mile of the day until eventually her ligaments, tendons, muscle fibers, what have you, surrendered and stretched. They quieted their screaming, and settled for a nagging, but dull—and more importantly, manageable—protest.

The trail followed the creek down, a slight downward grade and easy for the most part. The trees were tall and wide and their massive roots poked through the earth in the trail. They switched up small knolls and back down the other side. Patches of undergrowth sprouted here and there, as they navigated through the green with their feet hidden underneath.

Vika and Slip An' Slide spooked a mule deer along the way, and it bounced away on seemingly spring-loaded legs. They took a single break for a snack and continued on their way. Vika thought about the end over and over and then intentionally pushed it out of her mind to live in the here and now. The end, though, would mark a hundred miles of hiking trail she covered and that was no small deal, even if it was only a section of the entire PCT. From North Dakotan suburbia to the North Cascades.

They rounded a curve in the trail and Vika stopped short.

"What's that?" she asked suspiciously, pointing at a lidded bucket tied to a tree.

Slip An' Slide stepped next to her, following her finger. "Looks like a little trail magic."

"What now?"

Slip An' Slide didn't answer, instead he walked towards the bucket. He twisted and pulled and eventually the lid popped off. "Nice," he said.

Vika peered over the side of the bucket and gasped. It was full to the brim of energy bars, candy bars, and little snack packs of a variety of chips.

"Who put this here?" she asked in awe.

Slip An' Slide shrugged.

"Why did they put this here?" Vika prodded, determined to get a word out of Slip An' Slide somehow.

"'Cause they wanted to," he answered.

"Who's it for?"

"Thru-hikers."

Vika reached in and pushed aside some bags, and pulled out a small registry. The first page was a story of the provider, a thru-hiker of a couple years before. She had been about to quit when she took a zero day at a

Trail Angel's house. They had helped her fall in love with the trail again and she went on to complete the 2,600 miles. The bucket was her way of paying it forward.

"Want anything?" Slip An' Slide asked.

Vika stared for a second at the goodies. "Nah," she said as she stuck the notebook back into the bucket, "I'll save it for the thru-hikers."

Slip An' Slide fastened the lid back on and they continued walking.

"Does this happen a lot?" Vika asked. "You know, the trail magic?"

"Yeah. Well, a decent amount. Nothing beats a hot day in the desert and a trailside cooler full of cold soda."

"What was your favorite?"

"A couch," Slip An' Slide answered almost immediately.

"A couch?"

"Mmm-hmm. Right on the trail. It wasn't even at a road crossing, someone had hauled it up from somewhere. With a little coffee table in front with a bunch of new magazines. And soda. There's almost always soda."

Slip An' Slide continued with a few other recollections of magic as they switched down a small hill and crossed a bridge. They paused for a couple moments to stare at the blue churning water below them and when they finally reached the other side, they found themselves on a gravel road.

Slip An' Slide gave a cheer behind her and smacked her pack. She couldn't help but smile. "We're here! You hiked a hundred miles! And you only complained a little."

Vika gave him a look and playfully shoved his arm. "Barely. I barely complained."

"That's what I said," he countered with a smile and started walking up the road to a bulletin board.

Vika rolled her eyes and followed. Suddenly, her feet didn't seem to hurt at all, and the memory of the pain earlier that day was dulled with time.

"I'd do it again," she said to his back as she caught up to him.

She could feel his grin, even though she couldn't see it. "One too many and never enough?"

"Something like that," she looked around him to view the bus schedule and then looked at her watch. "We won't have to wait too long, it looks like."

"Nope," he said, "I think we have to find the actual bus stop, though. I don't think this is it."

He looked both ways, and then as though he mentally flipped a coin, chose right and began walking. Vika's shoes crunched on the gravel behind him as she thought about a nice warm shower. No, hot. A scalding shower, she thought, and she'd wash her hair at least four times. Who knew what was in the rats' nest she hadn't combed since they left Stacklen six days before. Six days was a long time. She also thought her legs got really tan, but she should have known better. With her pale skin, she never tanned. She burned various shades of red instead. Sure enough, when she crossed the stream the evening before, she discovered the change of color in her legs as the grime from the trail washed away in the water. She shuddered at the thought.

She might need steel wool to get all the dirt off.

The road opened up into a parking area and a family of four sat at a picnic table, with two mountain bikes leaning against the end of the table. One leaned against its kickstand a couple feet away, and another lying on its side in a nearby patch of grass. Both parents were looking intently at a map on the table, while the girl, Vika guessed to be in her midteens, looked faithfully at her smartphone with a frown, which likely meant she couldn't find service. The boy, holding a stick, poked at the corner of the table and little flecks of wood shot off and disappeared into the stone road.

Slip An' Slide and Vika crunched their way over in the vicinity, unclipping their belts as they walked and tossed their packs down almost simultaneously on the ground next to a log-carved bench. They sat down and Vika's stomach let out a terrible rumble.

"Hungry there, killer?" Slip An' Slide asked. "Don't worry, we're stopping at the bakery first."

"I could eat an entire pie right now. I would eat until nothing else would fit in. My portion control is abysmal."

He laughed at her, and then nodded towards the road. "Here's the bus." It rumbled up the incline and made a U-turn in front of them. Slip An' Slide leaned over, "Though if you do eat a whole pie, I have a couple ideas at how to burn it off."

"Maybe you'll have to show me later."

TO HER DISMAY, THE BUS WAS PACKED and she suddenly became very self-conscious about her hygiene. She squeezed her arms down tight to her sides and looked around for two seats next to each other. Her dismay turned to horror, as she realized not only were there not two seats next to each other, there wasn't a single seat by itself. Up her gaze went, to handles on attached to a rail for standing passengers.

Her groan was audible. Slowly, slowly, she reached up and silently apologized to everyone on the bus. Slip An' Slide wandered up next to her and swung his arm up to grab the strap as though it were any day on a bus ride. She was impressed with his ability to push aside the obvious and roll with the punches. Or rather, be unfazed at making everyone else roll with *his* punches.

"What's so funny?" Slip An' Slide asked her as he leaned back onto his heels.

She bit the inside of her cheek. "Nothing."

"Nothing?" he didn't believe her.

"It's just, it's really crowded in here and I bet we smell pretty bad."

"So?"

"So? We're packed in here like little sardines with our arms up in the air. It's kinda gross."

"Well, until someone offers me a seat, this is the deal. And we look pretty badass."

"If by badass you mean dirty, then yes, we look very badass."

A little bit later, the bus slowed and stopped. Everyone jerked a bit with the motion and people stood.

"This is our stop," Slip An' Slide said, starting to turn towards the door. They squeezed their way between the seats and the passengers who remained on the bus and stepped down onto lush green grass. Vika took a couple steps, having already forgotten what a lawn was like. The Dancy lawn grew in decently, finally, after months of regular mowing, but didn't compare to this. Not a single weed in sight and flowers, tiered by natural height, bordered much of the yard.

They climbed up the wooden stairs to the front entrance of the promised bakery and stood at the end, at least twelve people from the front. At last, they ordered and brought their cupcakes and pastries outside to eat at some of the lounge chairs. She almost immediately shed her socks and shoes and burrowed her bare feet into the soft grass. It amused Vika to have finished a hike and choose to sit outside. Given, the environment differed greatly, as did the company, but the principles remained the same: to be outside in the fresh air.

She sat back and took a bite of a triple, quadruple, chocolate truffle cupcake, or whatever it was. She finished her treat slowly and closed her eyes as she let her body rest.

"Well look what the trail spat out!" A voice jarred her back to reality and she squinted against the sun to spot a figure about her height, which wasn't saying much. The girl had blonde hair that reached her chin—too short to be pulled back into a ponytail and instead was kept back by a pink bandana she used as a headband. She was petite, but the angles that defined her face were sharp, and wiry muscles roped her entire body. "Hey, Toolbox, look at the hiker trash I found!"

A guy, on the short and stocky side with a baby face, appeared out of the left side of Vika's field of vision, chomping on the biggest pastry heart she had ever seen. He walked with a quick pace and a straight face up to Slip An' Slide and stuck out his hand.

"I'm Toolbox," he said.

"Slip An' Slide."

He nodded and quickly moved to Vika. "Vika."

"Slip An' Slide and Vika," he said, fidgety, "nice to meet you."

The girl had sauntered up to the group as well. "I'm Princess."

"More accurately," Toolbox said through his pastry, "the Motherfucking Princess."

Princess shrugged and asked, "Where are you two coming from?"

"The Dancy house in Stacklen," Vika answered. "Slip An' Slide did Mexico to Sisters and then he came up to help us work on the house. We're taking the ferry back tomorrow."

"No border?" Princess asked, eyebrows raised.

"No," Slip An' Slide said, "not this year. We have to get back to the house. The pack's coming soon. Where'd you guys hike from?"

"Shasta," Toolbox said and took another massive bite.

Vika looked at him for a moment, wondering if he would continue. Instead, he pulled a beer out of his pocket and cracked the top. It started to fizz over and he moved quickly to slurp it up before it spilled over.

It was Princess who answered, "We did Mexico to Shasta last year. We wanted to do a thru, but we fucking ran out of money and never would have made it to Canada. We started where it goes over I-5 near Shasta mid-June, and well, here we are! At the tiniest fucking town in America!" She raised her arms out wide, putting the scenery on display. "So are you staying in town for the night?"

Slip An' Slid nodded, "At a little inn on the lake."

"Right on," said Princess. "We're in a little cabin set-up. Our neighbors think they're out on the fucking frontier and I'm like, this is the most civilization I've seen in ten goddamn days. And Seattle's like two hours away, I mean, get real. Maybe three hours? I don't know. It's fucking close."

Toolbox stood next to Princess, legs planted, short legs thick with muscle one hand in his pocket, one on his beer. "There's a big bonfire down on the lake tonight, I guess. You guys should come."

"Yeah!" said Princess before either Slip An' Slide or Vika could respond. "Private thing, but he's inviting all fourteen people who actually live here."

Vika slid a look to Slip An' Slide to try to read his reaction to the invite. He looked at least a little interested. Vika nodded, "Sure. It sounds like fun."

"Great!" Princess said, taking a swig of Toolbox's beer. "It's just down the main drag there. Past the post office, past that outfitter, restaurant, tourist building, and then it's maybe another couple hundred feet. Past the docks."

"OK," said Vika. "I'm sure we'll find it."

"It's a fire. Walk towards the flames and you won't have a problem," Princess shrugged. "Well, we should go. We rode these bikes out here and there's been a pig roasting on a spit all afternoon for dinner. Looks fucking disgusting, but smells like heaven. Toolbox, you ready to go? No drinking and driving." She settled on the bike as Toolbox pounded the last couple of sips. "God, my ass is killing me," she muttered.

With enthusiastic waves, they pulled out of the yard and turned toward their cabin.

"Well, she's..." Slip An' Slide raised an eyebrow, "talkative."

Vika raised her own eyebrow. "Talkative," she echoed. "Yes, she's definitely talkative."

They finished their sweets and caught the next bus into town, hardly an hour later. It swayed and bounced down the gravel road, and Vika found the only two available open seats on the bus. Vika enjoyed the cross breeze from the open windows and caught snippets of the commentary the driver spoke about the town.

She felt good. She had just hiked a hundred miles and with no major hiccups. She could feel the fluid building up in her feet again, her legs ached and had already assumed sleep mode, but nothing that wouldn't heal shortly.

A little cabin stood—hardly—in a small field and the driver said it housed a family of eight. Talk about lack of privacy.

Her mind drifted as they passed. Back to the jagged skyline of the mountains, back to the little creeks that flowed down the ravines, back to the blue skies, the purple lupine, and the greenest, happiest grass she had ever experienced.

She smiled to herself. If she thought the grass was happy, she was losing her mind. But to her, in that moment, it made sense. The grass was fed by mountain water, up five thousand feet closer to the sun, and the color practically pulsed from the leaves. From the soil, up the roots, through the veins and nearly exploded from the surfaces of the plant. The grass on the mountain grew long and wild, natural, appropriate.

Appropriate? Who was she to say what grass was appropriate? Maybe the manicured, pesticide sprayed lawns in her development back in North Dakota were appropriate. Each blade was exactly the same length, as though a tiny little seamstress walked through with a tiny little pair of scissors and a tiny little measuring tape and *snip*. Precisely 2.78 inches long.

She thought again. Well, yes, in fact, the lawns *were* appropriate. The regimented state of the grass reflected the regiment state of the lives of the people who lived in the house. Morning came and people stretched and moaned as their battery-operated alarm clock beeped the standard beep. There would be one individual in every block—never more, never less, only sometimes the same—who would think about not punching in that morning for no other reason than to sleep longer. But he or she would eventually heave a sigh and push back the covers. They always did. There were mortgages to pay. Food to buy.

After a shower, a low-fat breakfast that would undoubtedly lead to a regrettable midmorning snack, they grabbed their pre-made lunch in the fridge, a warm cup of coffee in a thermos, and locked the door behind them as they left. Some went north, some east, some south, and most west. Pleasantries were exchanged with the front desk administrative personnel at their respective places of employment, and then to one last sip of stress-free coffee before the computers booted up. Across the city, the state, the entire Midwest, Eastern Seaboard, Western Seaboard, and everything in between, the hum of electricity powering the unintentional pursuit of singularity was heard.

The regimented grass was for regimented people. That made sense. That was appropriate. The wild grass was for wild people. Beards grew long, bodies went unwashed, and just as the greenery bent and stretched towards the sun, each human guest looked and listened, turned and inhaled toward an invisible yet so profound to be almost tangible feeling of clarity. The pulse of the wilderness echoed in visitors' chests cavities until their hearts beat to match the rhythm of nature.

The mountain grass bore itself to its co-inhabitants, living and not. Whether they conjured up poisons to ward off predators, or they flaunted bright colors and shapes to attract pollinators, all of it evolved for survival. Vika felt as though the hikers she met bore themselves in a similar way, not for survival in a literal sense, rather for the survival of their intellect. They could not pull punches. There had to be a fight. A constant fight to grow, to share resources, to create a life even bigger and brighter and even more curious than the one before.

The bus lurched to a halt and snapped Vika out of her funk. She shook her head. God, it sounded like something Dane would say.

She didn't want Dane in her head.

CHAPTER 20

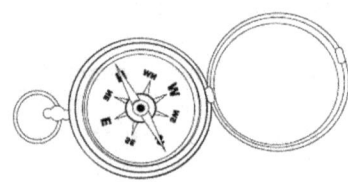

SLIP AN' SLIDE PUT A HAND on the seat in front of him and pulled himself up. Vika followed him quietly, pushing her tired body and now tired mind down the aisle and off the steps.

A breeze greeted them and white sailboats spotted the blue water. The sun pinged off the surface of water, sending shards of light outward and making them squint. Vika and Slip An' Slide stood together for a moment in front of the piles and watched a young couple kayak by, while an older, tanned man wearing only lime green short shorts and sunglasses paddleboarded in the opposite direction. An arm pushed the door of a nearby floatplane open and, a moment later, a man crouched to step out onto the dock. A headset hung around his neck, and his hair looked as though it spent its entire life in a salty breeze, blonde and wavy near the ends, dark at the roots, and sticking out on all sides.

On the opposite side of the narrow lake, mountains reached up out of the water and ended sharply where they touched a clear blue sky. Vika thought back to the photo she had taped to her dashboard – the photo of Lake Chelan that entranced her all those weeks ago. This, right here, was the entire reason she had set out from North Dakota in the first place, and boy, it didn't disappoint. Vika remembered a few nights previous when Slip An' Slide asked her if her paintings were like that. No. Not there, and not here on the edge of Lake Chelan. That extra dimension possessed all the differences between idea and adventure, and while both were crucial, each had become stronger in the presence of the other.

Vika squinted against the brightly speckled lake, and could spot some small washouts along the mountains. There was no beach, no docking area, just the mountains that started below the surface and reached skyward. The mountains looked intimidating, but not threatening. They looked challenging, but not impossible to climb. They looked fierce, but not vengeful. They looked as though they were not for the faint of heart.

Slip An' Slide let out a low whistle as he looked out across the lake.

"Ditto," Vika murmured.

They stood next to each other for another moment, until Slip An' Slide said, "Want to see our place for the night?"

"Absolutely," Vika answered, turning away from the view, but all too ready to pull off her sneakers and, this time, leave them off for a few days. She wanted to walk around and see the tiny town, but first, a shower. Now that she was around people regularly again, the dirt felt dirtier, and she was pretty sure if she took her hair down, that it would remain in a rust-colored braid affixed from the grime.

They scrambled up steps carved into the dirt, reinforced by logs. The screen door, nearly weightless, swung open on a skimpy wooden frame.

A big yellow dog looked up with large brown eyes from his place on the rug near a small waiting table. He was big, but the gray around his mouth and across his forehead aged him. Disinterested, he laid his head back on his paw and his eyelids fell closed again. A woman in her early thirties, Vika guessed, emerged from a room in the back and stood behind the desk.

"Can I help you?" she asked. Her voice was bright as she looked from one hiker to another. Her dark, curly hair was pulled back into a ponytail, a couple stray wisps floating around her blue eyes.

"Yeah," Slip An' Slide stepped forward and pulled out a small dry bag and pulled out a credit card, "I made reservations about a week ago? My name's David. McIntyre."

Vika bit back a smile at the strangeness of hearing his real name.

"All right," she answered slowly as she started to type the information into a keyboard. "OK, David, can you fill out this sheet for me please and I'll get your key."

Slip An' Slide took the clipboard and went to sit down at the table with the old sleeping guard dog.

"Were you guys on the trail?"

Vika nodded, "Yeah, we hiked up from Stacklen."

"Oh! I know where that is. I was going to say you two are pretty early to have come from Mexico. How's the hiking out there?"

Vika smiled at the woman, who seemed genuinely interested in their adventures. "It was good. There was some snow on Glacier Peak and on the passes..." she paused and looked back at Slip An' Slide for help with the names, but he was scratching away on the piece of paper.

"Red Pass and Fire Creek Pass?" the woman offered.

"Those are the ones."

She nodded, "I've only hiked little bits of the trail around here and parts of the PNT, but I try to send trail conditions to Trail Angels south of here so the hikers know what they're walking in to. Actually, someone, New Pants I think his name was, said there was a new Trail Angel house in Stacklen, but I don't have their information."

"The Dancys! I'm staying there this summer! I met New Pants a couple weeks ago," Vika said in surprise.

The woman's eyebrows went up and her mouth fell open just a little. "Small world."

"Yeah, well, here, let me write down my email and Grandma Peach's. It's Dane's house, but he hardly ever goes on the computer," Vika said, as she reached for a pen and flipped over an itinerary sheet on the desk.

"Are you family, or—?"

Vika looked up from the paper. "With the Dancys? No, I was driving through and had some car trouble. They let me stay for a couple days and then I didn't leave. This was actually my first time hiking. Come to think of it, this is my first time west of the Rockies."

The woman laughed as she slid the paper with Vika's email off the table and pulled up the cash in the cash drawer to place the paper underneath. "That sounds like me about ten years ago. This guy I was dating moved out to Colorado to, I don't know, ski, hike and screw everything that walked." She shook her head at the memory.

"I had never been out of New England and it was new and fun for a little while, and then we broke up and I didn't want to go home. A buddy of his had mentioned this town so I moved and worked here at the inn. When the last owner sold this place, I was the first in line. My husband and I have been running it for the last four years."

"Good for you!" Vika said.

"And you! Not a lot of people pick their first hiking trip to be a hundred miles through some of the most rugged terrain in the Lower 48."

Vika raised a shoulder and let it drop. "Slip An' Slide—er, David—is really good, so he helped me pack." She laughed, "He said I couldn't bring a pillow."

The woman leaned over the desk like she was sharing a secret and said, "On my first trip, I brought two pots and a saucepan." She cringed at the memory.

"Vika would have brought those, too, and more if I let her pack herself." Vika jumped slightly, unaware Slip An' Slide stood beside her, holding out the completed paperwork.

The woman took it and grabbed a key off the desk. "Well, if you did bring all that, you'd learn quick enough not to on the next hike. Thanks, you two can follow me." She walked out from behind the desk and they saw where her pressed blouse ended, biking shorts began. They were spotted with mud and the farther down her leg, the thicker the mud. Her thin bicycle shoes clicked on the hardwood as she led the way down the hall to the base of the stairs. She stopped at the bottom and turned with an apologetic expression.

"You guys are up the stairs, second door on the right. I'd walk you up myself, but you caught me right after a ride and I don't want to track mud all over. Breakfast is at eight in the dining room, there," she pointed, "and there are snacks, coffee and hot water available all day. Dinner is at six every evening except Friday, and the kitchen is open for you to cook between eleven and three every day, and until eight on Friday."

Vika and Slip An' Slide nodded together. "Sounds great," Vika said, "thanks so much!"

"No problem. Enjoy your stay!" She turned to leave. "Oh," she said and swung back, "my name is Liv, if you need anything. My husband's name is Tim."

They trudged up the stairs and Vika twisted the skeleton key in the lock. The door creaked open and they stepped in. The room was, in a word, adorable. A single, queen-sized bed sat in the middle, a multicolored quilt covering it. A loveseat rested near the open window, light curtains riding on a cross breeze. The floor was hardwood, and an old-style dresser and matching vanity filled the wall next to the window.

Vika didn't take time unpacking, but quickly found the bathroom and pulled off her dirty attire. She stepped into a steaming shower a few minutes later and let out a sigh. She stood there, feeling the water pound through her resilient braid, and watching dirt run off her legs and swirl in little eddies around her feet. She let her head fall forward for the water to loosen the muscles at the back of her neck, tight from six days of wearing a pack.

After what seemed like an hour, she grabbed the shampoo and lathered her hair. When she finger combed it, strands upon strands of hair came off, entwined in her fingers. She pulled at the end of her hair, and another clump of auburn strands slid off into her hands. She combed some more, and when she figured all that was going to come out had come out, she grabbed the washcloth and scrubbed. And scrubbed and scrubbed. At last, her skin felt pink and raw, her hair was no longer weighed down by God knows what, and her muscles were warm and loose. She turned the water off and grabbed her towel. She moved slowly, relaxed, savoring the cleanliness, and stepped out into the room.

Slip An' Slide smirked at her. "Save any hot water for me?" he drawled.

"None," she smirked back.

"Figures," he mumbled and trailed his fingers across her arm as he walked by into the bathroom.

Vika walked barefoot across the floor and realized with a sinking feeling she had exactly zero clean clothes. Everything she brought, she walked into town wearing. She groaned out loud. First stop, she thought as she pulled on her dirty outfit, the gift shop. She could at least get a new T-shirt there, and probably a stick of deodorant.

Slip An' Slide was a lot faster about his shower, and getting back into dirty clothes didn't seem to faze him in the least. They walked down the stairs, passed the sleeping dog and walked out the door into the setting sun.

There wasn't much to the town, but everything they needed they found easily. Vika hobbled on her aching feet next to Slip An' Slide in some cheap flip-flops she bought along the way, down to the waterfront with their burgers and ice cream in hand. They sat on the edge of a dock and Vika slipped off her sandals and settled her feet into the cool water, hoping to manage the swelling a bit. The lake turned to glass as the sun fell behind the mountains and Vika shifted into Slip An' Slide for warmth.

"We don't have to go to the campfire if you don't want to," he said against the top of her head.

"Eh," she reasoned, "we're halfway there. We could stop by for a little bit, but I don't think I'll last very long."

"OK," he said easily, "let me know when you're ready to go."

"M'kay," she answered.

It was another twenty minutes they sat there, watching little ripples build up across the lake, running along and disappearing into the sand, not a single white cap in sight.

A shiver went up Vika's spine and she said, "A fire might be nice right about now. You ready to go?"

"Yep," Slip An' Slide answered, pulling his legs up underneath him to stand. He offered his hand to help Vika stand. They wandered down the road Princess had mentioned, and it wasn't before long they felt the bass of an outdoor sound system and saw orange light dance through the trees. As they go closer, they realized "campfire" was a bit of an understatement. The pit was at least ten-feet across and wooden palettes were thrown on the pile at least the same number of feet high.

Well, Vika thought to herself, she wouldn't have to worry about getting cold.

People milled around everywhere, most in their mid-twenties, drinks of every color in their hands. Under a tent was the DJ, blasting music across the lake, and just a little farther, Vika could make out a makeshift bar, with prices of different drinks scrawled in magic marker across some poster board. The man behind the bar looked to be about fifty, dressed in a Hawaiian shirt and sunglasses.

"Want anything to drink?" Slip An' Slide leaned down to her and spoke loudly over the music.

Vika nodded "I'll come with you," she yelled back.

The man in the Hawaiian shirt was handing them their beers when, from behind, they heard, "Vika! Slip An' Slide!"

They turned and saw Princess weaving through the crowd, Toolbox looking around, sipping his beer, following the tiny, loud-mouthed girl in front of him.

"Glad you could make it," Princess said, "and find the bar. It just started picking up, the music's fucking loud but I think people will hang around for a while. I already did three shots of the Stehekin Slam Dunk. I don't know what the fuck was in it, but it tasted like a goddamn pine tree. You two should do one!"

"Sounds good," Vika said through a smile, "but maybe later."

"So I was just telling Toolbox here how we've walked through so much snow on this trip," Princess motored on. "Last year, when we went through the Sierras, we walked across like a twenty-foot patch of snow on Sonora Pass. Drier than a motherfuckin' bone. On this trip, I think I've walked more on snow than not. Fire Creek Pass was a bitch. Oh traction, I wish I had some. I fell on my ass like three times, and one time I slid about forty feet. I was like, FUCK!"

"You should see her shoes," Toolbox said. Reflexively, both Vika and Slip An' Slide looked at her feet, but she had sandals on instead of the shoes she hiked in.

"They're not that bad," Princess brushed him off. "They have zero fucking traction, but they worked just fine."

"Just fine?" Toolbox said incredulously. "You put twelve-hundred miles on them and every time you tripped on a rock your foot popped out the top, through the mesh that stopped actually being functional three-hundred miles ago."

"Yeah that was a pain in the ass. But they were broken in and didn't give me blisters."

Toolbox snorted. "Broke the fuck in. Sure. If that's what you want to call it."

"Oh, and then that one climb, just passed Milk Creek maybe?" Princess went on, ignoring Toolbox's last remark. "Those fucking plants!"

"The switchbacks that were covered in the six-foot-tall weeds?" Slip An' Slide ventured.

"Those are the ones," Princess said animatedly. "Oh, my God, I felt like I was transported to Jurassic Park. No wonder raptors were such goddamn assholes. I'd cut a bitch, too, if I got slapped in the fucking face by a giant ass fern every time I turned around."

Vika laughed. "No kidding. Then to make matters worse, our campsite had a warning about bears."

"Well, Christ on a cracker, I wrote that!" Princess said, amazed. "Where did you end up camping?"

"We stayed there, at that campsite. We—"

"No shit! There you go! You know you're a thru-hiker when you say, 'Fuck it—we're sleeping with the bears tonight! Hope they don't eat my goddamn food.'"

Slip An' Slide's mouth was parted in amusement.

"Oh, and then," without waiting for an answer, Princess continued, "there was that little cove of trees. I wanted to sleep next to the other guys, 'cause, fuck, we saw the bear right before we called it a night. I had my tent already set up and then we saw that motherfucker and I'm like hell, I don't want to get eaten by a fucking bear. I'm so close to Canada. So I pull apart my tarp up on the ridge and I set it up in the trees closer to everyone, but it was on a goddamn hill. I rolled around, slid off my mat—I was sick of that bullshit in about thirty seconds. I went over to Toolbox and told him to move the fuck over, I was climbing in."

"Did it hang around for you?" Slip An' Slide interjected.

"Yeah," she huffed. "It poked around a little. Good thing I slept with my chocolate. It could eat anything except my Dark Chocolate Bits. That bitch would have to pry that bag out of my cold, dead hands."

"Oh, my God!" Vika exclaimed. "It might have."

Princess raised an eyebrow. "Please," she scoffed. Vika silently conceded she had a point.

"Anyway," Princess continued, "it didn't go after the food or anything. It was more like a walk through. Actually, the only wildlife trouble I've really had was mice. Those fuckers ate my couscous. Oh, and then there was that bird near Etna."

"The bear visited us, too, actually. Slip An' Slide made a bunch of noise and it ran away."

"Fuckin' bears," Princess shook her head.

Princess ordered them all another shot of the Stehekin Slam Dunk and she was dead on, it tasted like a pine tree. People around them packed in and the group of four made their way back to the fire. A table sat on the far side of the fiery pallets, stocked with the makings of s'mores, with roasting sticks leaned up against it. Those, being only about two and a half feet long, rested unused, more danger to the roaster than was worth it, since to get close enough, one would essentially have to walk into an oven. Instead, partiers had duct taped marshmallow sticks to canoe paddles, longer sticks, shovels, and anything else they could find. There were a couple of guys who secured about five marshmallow sticks on the end of a ladder. One guy stabilized the bottom and the other guy lowered the top down nice and slowly with the aid of a climbing rope, roasting six at a time.

Slip An' Slide and Vika stayed for a while longer, chatting with the other two hikers, but sooner rather than later, Vika's bones became heavy and she slid an arm around Slip An' Slide's waist.

"What do you say we head in for the night?" she asked.

"Fine by me," Slip An' Slide answered and steered her in the direction from which they came. They saw Princess and Toolbox talking with a small group of people, no doubt about the trail and Vika pulled away.

She reached out and touched a hand to Princess's arm, who turned. "We're going to head in for the night. If we don't see you tomorrow, good luck and congratulations! It was really nice meeting you."

They all hugged and shook hands, and Slip An' Slide once again held on to Vika as they made their way together through the crowd, away from the music and the fire and onto the dirt road from which they came.

It was a quiet walk, comfortable in each other's silence and they covered the distance quickly.

The air cooled rapidly as they walked away from the fire and Vika snuggled a little further into Slip An' Slide's side. The porch light of the inn was still on and several dozen bugs swarmed the fixture. The wooden stairs creaked as they dragged themselves up them and through the door. The kitchen and front desk were dark and they tiptoed their way to the second floor.

"SLIP AN' SLIDE," VIKA STARTED, watching him shuffle through his pack. She was rummaging through one of her dry bags on the bed. "Why did you get off the trail?"

Slip An' Slide looked up over the top of his pack and stared at her. "Um," he began, standing up straight, "I was tired of it, I guess. Why are you asking me that now?"

Vika shrugged and said, "I don't know. After hiking a little, I'm just curious."

"Oh." He bent over and went back to pushing things around in his pack. "Well, I started losing interest in Northern California and gave myself two weeks to change my mind. I ended up staying on for three weeks with a little extra hope, but it wasn't happening."

He shrugged. "Nothing dramatic. Just got bored. Maybe I'll finish it someday. Or do the whole thing someday. But not now."

Vika nodded and watched him. "Makes sense. No use in torturing yourself. But," she couldn't help herself, "if it were that simple, why did you not want to go home?"

Slip An' Slide glanced up and immediately looked away, and Vika knew he was starting to pull into himself and she silently cursed herself.

Moments later, to her surprise, he brought his gaze back to her and visibly forced himself to relax. He stood up straight, holding a shirt in one hand, his toothbrush in the other.

"It wasn't simple," he said, sighing. "I planned this hike for two years. I spent hours—probably hundreds of hours—researching everything. Packs, food, water treatment, footwear, everything. But in the end, I couldn't hack it." He looked down at the toothbrush. "I knew I had to get off, but I couldn't really figure out why."

Vika had her own toothbrush in her hand and was rolling the top of her dry bag down to fasten it.

"I hung around with you guys because," he stopped to look up and smile at her, though it didn't reach his eyes. "I wasn't ready to tell everyone yet." His hands went out to his sides, palms up and gave another shrug.

"So are you happy with your hike?" As she asked, he leaned back against the doorframe, still gripping his shirt and toothbrush in his hands, but he managed to weave his arms through each other and cross them on his chest.

He looked past her to focus on the dresser as he answered, "It was the best I could have done this year."

"Are you just uncomfortable telling everyone because you're afraid of what people will think?" Vika asked.

"No," Slip An' Slide said loudly, "no, no. I've never really worried about that to be honest."

"Then why?" Vika prodded.

"I..." he paused. "The thing is, when you tell someone else, you have to say it out loud." His gaze dropped to the floor and he tossed the shirt back onto the top of his pack. He brought his hand up to rub the back of his neck. He left it there while he continued, "Even though I heard it in my head, saying it makes it so much harder to listen and comprehend. Vika, *I* care about what I do and there's something final about saying it out loud. It makes it true. For me to not even be able to explain why I was getting off the trail...I don't know. It was too hard."

Vika noticed it was still too soon to use the word "quit." They sat in silence for a while, processing those words, when Vika spoke up.

"2,000 miles is a huge accomplishment—"

His head rolled back, *thunked* against the frame, and he clamped his jaw shut. "Never gets old," he mumbled.

"What never gets old?" Vika stood up straighter, working the muscles in her own jaw.

"The 'good job at trying, here's a participation trophy,' condolences."

Vika scoffed, "That's not what I meant."

"Really?" He was looking at her full on now. "What did you mean?"

"I meant...I just meant," she stammered, her eyes skirting around the small room in hopes that an antique or piece of furniture would help guide her conversation. "You should be proud of walking to Sisters. You should—"

"I should what?" he interjected. "Look. It's fine. Good job at trying."

"Slip An' Slide—"

"I'm telling you what it sounds like." He pushed himself off the doorframe and stood, feet apart, to face her. "I've told *myself* that. You know: Great first effort. You've done more than a lot of people ever will." He shook his head slightly. "Forget it. It's not something I'd expect you to understand."

"Then tell me!" Vika walked around the corner of the bed and stood a few feet away from him. Slip An' Slide dropped his hands to the side.

"Why? Why do you need to know? Why are you pushing so hard?" He sounded completely dumbfounded and a little angry.

"So I can help you!"

"Help me? I don't need—Vika—" he sighed audibly. "It's hard and confusing because while you're out there, you do things you never thought you could do, you see things you never knew existed, you meet the best people, you hone skills you didn't know you had."

"I know that," Vika countered.

Slip An' Slide scrubbed his hands over his face. "You've gotten a taste. But every time you mention that I made it 2,000 miles or to Sisters, or wherever, you're still missing the point."

Vika's eyes were wide, and a blush had crept into her cheeks. Her mouth was parted as though she was about to say something, but no words came out.

Slip An' Slide was oblivious to her reaction and continued, "The hardest thing is to be in the middle of that process and getting wrenched out of it. You could be 500 miles in, 2,000 miles in, or right at the Canadian border. And you're expected to pull a 180 on your lifestyle. Just pack up and go home. And I didn't think I could handle that change yet. My mind is still in the mountains."

Slip An' Slide slouched back against the doorframe, deflated from the confrontation. He gave her a crooked smile. "The mountains make sense to me, Vika. I don't want to leave yet."

Vika stood at the end of the bed, her gaze fixed on a spot on the floor, and she chewed the inside of her lip.

"So, question for question," Slip An' Slide said, interrupting her thoughts. "Why did you drive away from your North Dakotan suburb?"

Vika didn't look up, but she answered, "I wasn't getting hired anywhere and decided I could use a road trip."

"Have you ever gone on a road trip before?"

"Well, no."

"So, what made you go on a road trip?" Slip An' Slide waited a quick moment for her to answer and when she didn't, he added, "Running from something? Bad job? Bad relationship? Why didn't you go east? That's where you were applying for jobs anyway, right?" The tension started to build up in his shoulders again, and he had jammed his hands in his pockets. Vika recoiled from the onslaught.

"I'm...I'm not running *from* anything."

"No? Then where were you running to?"

She floundered. The conversation she had with Dane pounded in her ears. They were both right: She had zero direction. She didn't know what she was going to, but she was pretty sure she wanted to experience something other than climbing ladders in the art history world. Was that running from something? She had thought she was just taking a break, but maybe it was running. Her mind was racing, and nothing was clear.

"I," she bit her lip. "I...wasn't going anywhere specific. I just took a break." She shrugged.

Slip An' Slide looked at her, waiting for more, but Vika felt backed into a corner and kept her mouth shut.

"See? Pretty hard to explain something you don't understand yourself, isn't it?" Slip An' Slide asked. Slip An' Slide stared at her a second longer for a response, but Vika closed her mouth and her eyes slid away from his.

He grunted, taking her silence as a blow-off, and popped the cap on the toothpaste tube as he walked into the bathroom. She knew he was pissed, but she didn't know how to fix it.

THEY SLEPT IN THE SAME BED that night, but Slip An' Slide's hand on her hip was clenched with tension. By morning they had separated completely.

It wasn't long after they had woken up that they were out the door. In search for coffee, Vika told herself, and nothing to do with the alternative—being in a room alone with Slip An' Slide without anything more to say about the night before.

They drank their coffees quietly and walked around the small town again, but without too far to go, they found themselves back on the bus. They stopped at a waterfall to oooo-ahhh and take some pictures with the rest of the tourists.

By early afternoon, they had done the entire loop again and, with nothing left to do to escape talking to each other, walked towards the inn to ask Liv about any events going on.

On their walk, they saw Modifier on the front lawn of the post office. A large white hiker box lay opened next to him and food lay sprawled all around him. He was sitting with his legs in front, a smaller box in his hands, and his cheeks full.

"Want a cookie?" he asked them through a mouthful. "They're delicious." He chewed and chewed, his cheeks not getting any smaller. His grey synthetic shirt looked like it might make it to Canada on a prayer, and his pants had streaks of stains on them, the hem of one side torn, a loop hanging down over his knee. He wore sandals that put his sock tan line on display and even though he had found a shower in the tiny town, dirt still clung to his feet.

He pushed himself up and walked over to them. "I tell my mom not to send them, but she knows they're my favorite," he swallowed as he explained. "Chocolate and coconut and macadamia nuts." He shoved another cookie in. "Only problem is, I have to eat them all here so I don't have to carry them, you know?"

Vika looked into the box. "There's at least two dozen cookies in there!" she exclaimed.

"Want one?" Modifier held the box out. "I'm telling you, they're the best damn cookies around."

"Sure," she smiled and reached into the box. "Thanks."

Modifier held out the box to Slip An' Slide, who also took one.

"Mmm," Vika responded after taking a bite.

"I know, right?" Modifier smiled a smidge of chocolate stuck on his front tooth.

He put the box down and wiped his hands on his pants. "So what did you guys find to do around this town?"

Slip An' Slide took a breath and looked at Vika, "We rode the bus. Went to the bakery."

"Three times," Vika added, "and there was a bonfire going on last night, we met up with two other hikers."

"Oh, yeah?" Modifier said. "Which ones?"

"Toolbox and Princess," Vika answered.

"Right on." He looked past Slip An' Slide to the water. His expression changed. "That would make for some sick kayaking."

Vika followed his gaze. "Want to go?" she suggested. She didn't know the first thing about kayaking, but hell, she didn't know the first thing about hiking and she made it a hundred miles. She thought back to Slip An' Slide's 'why not?' comment a couple days before.

Slip An' Slide looked at her and Vika barely made out a slightly raised eyebrow. She couldn't make out exactly what it meant, but stiffened at his partially concealed scrutiny. She had made it to Lake Chelan and she wasn't going to let the fight she had with Slip An' Slide get between her and the lake.

Modifier thought about it for a moment. "Sure, I'll go."

"They have a bunch you can rent out from that building on the water," Slip An' Slide said.

"Let's do it," decided Vika.

It was beautiful on the lake and even though the water was a little choppy in the middle of the day, they made it quite a way down the shore and back. She watched the paddles as they sliced in and out of the water, creating miniature whirlpools behind them. Birds and bugs flew around them and every once in a while a fish swam below them. Luminous silver bounced off of the waves and, even with sunglasses, the sun's reflection was bright.

About halfway down their track, they paddled to a little cove. A small stream ran down the side of the mountain, colliding with the water of the lake in a pool of white bubbles. Vika pulled up close and watched, mesmerized by the moving water. The path down the rock changed constantly, slipping and sliding horizontally across the rock face, pulling on little bits of moss that had built up on the side borders. She stuck out a hand. It was cold. She paddled back to the guys, who were currently discussing lightweight gear.

Without stopping, she paddled past them to inspect some plants along the bank. Little fish darted in and out of the reeds, and a frog croaked from a location she couldn't pinpoint.

By the time they hauled the kayaks out of the water, it was late afternoon and all stomachs accounted for were grumbling,.

The three of them ordered burgers and hotdogs from a food cart and sat on the water to eat. Though there was talking going on for much of the day, little of it was between Vika and Slip An' Slide, and he felt distant to Vika as she sat next to him and popped open the little container of curly fries.

Modifier excused himself after dinner, to catch the last bus to a hotel on the road towards the trail.

"The kayaking wore me out," Vika said, picking at the crumbs at the bottom of the container.

"Me, too," Slip An' Slide said. "You have a little red on your nose."

Vika groaned, "I don't tan. I burn."

THE NEXT MORNING, AFTER WAKING from a night similar to the one before, with only slightly less tension between the two; the sun was up, the sky was blue and the ferry down the lake was waiting. They packed up their packs, thanked Liv and Tim and walked the short distance to the dock.

They stayed on the deck. Slip An' Slide was prone to seasickness, and thought going below wasn't going to help matters much. It was a clear day and small white caps broke across the lake. Couples curled up on the benches around the deck, talking excitedly, snapping pictures.

She wanted to snuggle into Slip An' Slide, but his posture kept her at a distance. Instead, Vika closed her eyes and felt the water push them up and down and side to side. The sun was warm, but the breeze was cool, and she breathed in deep through her nose. The air, though fresh, wasn't the same as in the mountains. It smelled of fish and algae instead of dirt and plants—a worthy contender—but the air on the lake had a hint of a diesel and just like that, the win went to the mountains.

A floatplane buzzed above them, only a few hundred yards off the lake.

Hmm, Vika thought. Wouldn't it be fun to learn how to fly a plane?

Getting lost in her musings, she shifted next to Slip An' Slide and was pleasantly surprised when he put an arm around her.

"This is fun!" she said.

"What?" Slip An' Slide yelled over the wind.

She turned her face towards him more and repeated, "This is fun! I've never been on a boat before!"

Slip An' Slide smiled tightly. "Yeah," he said, though the gray shade of his face begged otherwise.

In Vika's opinion, the ferry ride lasted far too short of a time. As Vika and Slip An' Slide ascended the ramp onto the dock, a breeze swept around the corner of the parking lot with a hint of fried cheese sticks. They rounded the corner and saw Grandma Peach disappear from the driver's seat. A moment later, she lowered herself onto the pavement and began walking quickly in their direction.

Vika could feel herself smile as Grandma Peach clasped her hands to her chest and Quasi bounced up and down at her feet, running over to sniff the garbage can, running back. He spotted the two hikers and ran flat out in a sprint towards them, making children squeal and mothers pull them away from his path. He ran so fast that the little blonde curl on the top of his head flattened between his ears.

Vika scooped him up and gave the ugly dog a hug, as he wiggled in her arms to try to get his face around to lick her face. She put him back down before he accidentally wriggled out, and he went up to Slip An' Slide, shaking his entire body in happiness.

Eventually, they were only feet apart and Vika opened her arms to hug Grandma Peach hard.

"Oh!" Grandma Peach said, giving her a once over, "You look great!" She turned to Slip An' Slide. "Slip An' Slide, how was it, dear?"

Slip An' Slide grinned, "It was good, Grandma Peach. It was good."

"Oh, I'm so happy for you," she patted them both on the arms at the same time. "Well, let's get you on the bus. I have all kinds of food, you can sleep if you want, and oh! I want to hear all about your adventures! But when you're ready," she added, "When you're ready."

They climbed the bus, Quasi sniffing at their heels behind them.

Slip An' Slide offered to drive, to ease his stomach from the boat, he said, and Grandma Peach and Vika sat on the couch with cups of tea Grandma Peach had brewed up while she was waiting in the parking lot.

"I went glissading," Vika said when Grandma Peach prodded her to get on with the stories.

"Oh, my," she said, "What's that? Tell me more."

CHAPTER 21

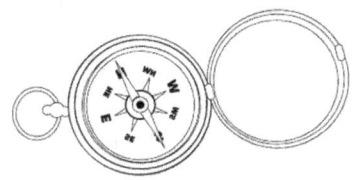

"JEEZ, YOU MISSED ALL THE FUN!" Dane greeted them in the lawn. "I poured a new floor!"

"What?" Vika said, sure she did not, in fact, miss "all the fun."

"The basement is nearly finished," Dane responded.

"Do you have much to take down inside?" Slip An' Slide asked.

"There's one beam rotted to shit downstairs and I have to knock out some walls upstairs. Good thing you're back for that," Dane said, with a huff that expanded his belly. "The wood's coming today."

"Sounds good," Slip An' Slide said. "Well, I'll be around. What are we doing in the meantime?"

"The weather's good enough, I thought we could start sealing the outside," Dane suggested. "More and more hikers will be coming, and it would be nice to have the house ready to paint. I'll work on framing inside when I have help. Hopefully we can be painting in a couple days, though." He started walking towards the house. "I had some construction guys come in and build the dormers up there," he gestured to the roof and Vika saw that under the thick plastic covering, a small peak jutted up where there wasn't one before.

He instructed them on which clapboards to keep on the house and which to take down so Vika and Slip An' Slide could get to work.

Detour, Dark Horse, and The Brit spilled out of a Prius at lunchtime, stretching out and apologizing to the driver about the smell. They introduced themselves to Grandma Peach as she raked up some recently cut grass, and she pointed to the flattest spot in the yard. Vika waved from her place on a ladder as she tried to pry loose a rotten clapboard, while Dane hung out the window, giving her directions. She wasn't very high, but it was enough to have her leaning her body on the ladder and weaving her free arm through the rungs to anchor herself.

The group of three plopped down their packs and the one she was later introduced to as The Brit rubbed his stomach. No doubt they'd be going into town to eat. There was a pizza place about two miles from the house that had an all-you-can-eat buffet. There were a handful of things that word traveled down the trail quickly for, Vika found out. Fires, gossip, a good bed, and buffets. Of course, the owners of the restaurant lost money every time a thru-hiker walked through the doors, but Stevie's Pizza had kept the buffet on the menu. The owner's wife liked to encourage the hikers to lounge until they were ready for their second round. Or third, fourth, fifth, sixth...

"They're just so skinny!" she'd say.

Vika gave one last yank at the clapboard, and it sprang off, nails spiking out from the bottom. She tossed it the seven feet to the ground on a small pile of identical boards. Cautiously, she climbed down the ladder, setting the crow bar against it. Vika assumed they already knew about the food, but it was an easy icebreaker so she wandered on over to the group.

"Hey, guys!" she called out. They turned their tanned faces her way and greeted her with equal enthusiasm. That was one of her favorite parts. They were always genuine—well, most of them—because they so appreciated a place to stay and hot food. "If you're going into town, there's a pizza place—"

"Stevie's Pizza?" the three guessed in unison. Vika laughed.

"We're prepared for the food buffet," Dark Horse assured her.

"Yeah," said The Brit, patting his stomach again, "I haven't eaten since breakfast. Saving up."

Vika had heard that before. "We have a few bikes around the back of the house," she said, pointing. "Some of them have some quirks so check them out before you ride them."

"Great!" Detour said, as she pulled her tent out of her pack. "That'd be perfect."

They returned a few hours later with canvas bags on the sides of the seats full to the brim with groceries. Vika, Forrest, and Slip An' Slide were still working on the clapboards, pulling off the rotten or split ones, while Dane divided his time between supervising and cutting boards when the wood was dropped off.

The delivery truck came by in his usual swirl of impatient exhaust and by the time Vika got to the driver's side door, Randy was already holding three large boxes. He glowered under his company-issued cap.

"Hello, Randy. How are you?" Vika asked.

He answered by shoving the boxes at her. "There's about thirty-eight more where that came from," he grumbled and reached for more he had stacked in the center, and tossed them on the ground when Vika didn't take them fast enough. He pushed the last few at her and they tumbled to the ground before Vika could get a firm grip.

"Hey! C'mon," she said, trying to pile them nicely on the ground, but Randy was holding out the pad. She reached out and signed it.

"Thanks."

"Yep, have a good day," she said as he already started to back out of the driveway. Then he slammed on the brakes and a hiker box flew out of the driver's side. Before it bounced in the lawn, Randy had already continued reversing. Quasi ran over to the rogue box and started sniffing it for the beef jerky that was likely inside. Vika shoed him and picked it up.

"What an asshole," she mumbled.

SLIP AN' SLIDE WAS CIVIL, but distant. She knew he was still mad at her for not being open or honest with him in Stehekin. She was going to apologize on the boat, but the wind was loud and there were always people close by. She was going to apologize the night before, but Grandma Peach and Dane wanted every detail of their trip, and then she was going to apologize while they worked on the boards, but Forrest was working in the same area and she didn't want to make it awkward with him, too, and then…well, Vika ran out of excuses and she still hadn't apologized.

She'd have to apologize after her shift.

"Well, look who's back from the mountains," the sound of Smith's voice boomed through the store. Vika drove the motorcycle to work and her hands still tingled.

"Hi, Smith," Vika said with a smile. "Did you hold down the fort while I was gone?"

Ted grunted. Vika couldn't distinguish if it was a "good morning" grunt or a "yeah right" grunt.

"Did you have fun?" Smith asked as Vika rounded the counter towards the registers.

"I did," she said.

"That didn't sound too convincing," Smith frowned.

"Oh, I did," Vika assured him. "It was beautiful. Really hard though. I don't know how these hikers can do that for four or five months straight."

"Ah," Smith hesitated, "did you go to the bakery in Stehekin?"

"Only four times," Vika grinned. "Smith, it was fantastic."

"Yeah, yeah," he grumbled, "I gave one of the baker's the recipe for the chocolate ganache on their chocolate layer cupcake."

"I had one of those! The ganache was the best part."

"Yeah, yeah," he repeated, but couldn't hold back a little smile. "Come on," he said, waving a five-dollar bill, "give me a winner before someone else comes in and takes it."

She laughed and walked over to the scratch-offs.

"Hang on, there," Ted said. "Count your drawer first."

"Oh," Smith joked, "the boss-man speaks. You'd better do what he says."

Ted mumbled something about insubordination.

"What?" Vika said, teasing along with Smith, though she had already popped open her drawer and pulled out the twenties to count. "You want Jill up here with you?"

Ted looked at her. "That's not funny," he said. "Food's coming today. Kate's not coming in for a couple hours so you'll have to start the inventory and mark the prices."

"Yes, boss," she said with a smile.

"Maybe I'll make you go in the coolers, too," he threatened. Or at least, Vika thought it was a threat. It was always hard to tell with Ted.

Vika feigned shock, "I almost got hypothermia last time I was in there."

"Tough," Ted said and left the counter.

Shortly after, as Ted declared, the food truck arrived and the front of the store disappeared under a dozen or so crates. Vika sighed and grabbed the inventory sheet to get started.

VIKA CHANGED QUICKLY AFTER she returned and approached the house in her construction clothes. She saw Dane hold a cut board out to The Brit and say, "Here, take this." The Brit looked at it with confusion.

"Where does it go?" The Brit asked when it was apparent Dane wasn't about to expand on that idea. Or had forgotten that The Brit required instruction.

"That will fit in a couple places," he said, "so one of those spots. Nails and hammers are in the foyer."

The Brit slowly walked away to look for equipment, his face still tense with puzzlement while Detour, who was standing nearby and heard every word, took the board and began comparing it to holes in the wall. By the third board, the team had a system down to nailing the clapboards in place and by evening, they had removed and replaced all damaged clapboards, leaving only the corners for the next day.

Forrest and Dane had gone into the house sometime in the late afternoon to formulate a plan of framing for the next day, though Vika had not heard any pounding.

It was nearly dark when the group finally turned in, muscles sore from the long hours, and it wasn't even ten o'clock when the last headlamp flicked off.

Vika placed her tea mug in the sink and grabbed a book on her way to her bunk, knowing the tents—and the occupants—would be on their way before she woke up.

SOMETIME DURING THE NIGHT, clouds moved in and cooled the air. Cool, but still dry. Dane handed out buckets of primer and directed Vika and Slip An' Slide to the side of the house that was sealed. They slapped the paint on, thick and fast with the brushes, while Dane nailed corner pieces to complete the outside. Vika heard Forrest working inside, or rather, preparing to work inside as he cut board after board. Likely, he was waiting for Dane to join him.
It took Dane the rest of the afternoon to finish the corner pieces, and three days for Vika and Slip An' Slide to prime the entire house. Clouds rolled over them, threatening to fill up and spill over, though none did and the paint was dry when the first drop fell.

Purple Rain came on the second day of the rain, complaining about the blisters on his feet and the actual rain. Grandma Peach offered him the first-aid kit and the bathroom in the camper. She counted sixteen Band-Aid wrappers he left in the sink and dirty footprints on the floor. When he came out, he handed Grandma Peach a pile of dirty, smelly clothes and asked if she would take them to the laundromat for him. He sauntered out the door before Grandma Peach got her wits together to tell him "no."

Vika had never seen Grandma Peach angry before, and it wasn't a pretty sight, that was for sure. She turned so red Vika was waiting for smoke to start coming out of her carefully permed white hair.

"Well, that's just—that's just—" Grandma Peach sputtered, holding onto the rank clothing. She opened the bathroom door and tossed them in. "RUDE!" she exploded. "Was the boy raised by wolves? I don't think I'll be offering him tea," she said.

Tea or no tea, he seemed unbiasedly inconsiderate. Going through his resupply on the lawn, he swatted at a curious chicken a little too hard to make it flop over on its side. Vika saw Dane's face turn to stone, which was much more terrifying than his angry face. She wondered for a second if he would march over there and break the hiker's hand. In the coop, Purple Rain took a top bunk for himself and the bottom bunk for his gear -- at least, for a day and a half until someone figured out no one was sleeping there and made him move it. His grocery shopping consisted of butter, beer and beef, all fried together in a taco shell, which made the coop smell to high heaven, and the congealed fat left in the pan remained a reminder of his presence.

One afternoon, he was smoking a joint on the porch and when Dane asked him to keep it away from the house, he flicked it on the wooden boards and ground the embers with his heel.

"Clean it up or I will drop your ass off at the trail!" Dane yelled, unconcerned with making or losing friends.

"Jeez, man," Purple Rain said, "chill out. It's just a little ash." Purple Rain bent over, though, and grabbed the flattened filter before he walked off to the coop, leaving three empty beer bottles on the porch for Dane to pick up.

The tables in the dining room were full for dinner that night, with the garden vegetables—roasted, fried, fresh, and baked into breads.

"Why did you start hiking?" the woman Vika remembered as Cheshire from the campground at Sisters asked the hiker sitting next to her. Vika strained to listen in across the table.

He shrugged. "I was applying for jobs. No luck," he answered. "I had about fifty applications and didn't get a single job."

Cheshire shook her head, "What is your field?"

"Physics. But I was applying to a job answering phones. There were ten spots, but thirteen hundred applicants."

Vika gave away her subtle eavesdropping with an abrupt, "What?"

The hiker looked over at her, only slightly surprised she had heard the conversation.

"What were the requirements?" Vika asked.

"High school diploma. They hired people with phone experience."

"And thirteen hundred people applied?" Vika asked incredulously.

He gave a slight nod, "A handful of times, I was one of a couple hundred applicants for jobs. Didn't get any of them, so I went for a hike instead."

"Makes you wonder what the other 1,299 people are doing today," a hiker named Hop And Skip said.

"Those twelve hundred other people are probably fumbling with two or three jobs to pay off their student loans," Vika said.

"To have only one job!" Dane's voice boomed across the conversation, "the new American Dream!"

Slip An' Slide shrugged, "I was lucky with student loans, but I have a friend who pays twelve hundred a month."

Vika turned to say to him, "I've heard about loans like that, too. Talk about budgeting."

"Everyone needs to move to Bakerstown," Purple Rain said. "I love it there.

There are so many jobs, I've had six since last October."

"Oh, my Jesus," Grandma Peach said under her breath next to Vika, who tried not to snort.

"Downsizing is for sure the new credo," the physics-hiker said, ignoring Purple Rain.

"No kidding," Cheshire put in, "and no better way to downsize than to hop on the PCT."

"Burchfield," Dane stated thoughtfully, "he said we have to return to nature." He looked contemplatively at the ceiling. "Or was it Hopper?"

"Few people are more successful at returning to nature than a thru-hiker," Grandma Peach said slyly. "Isn't that right, Dane?"

"Well," Dane shifted in his chair, "yeah, you guys are all right."

Grandma Peach smiled. "That's why he's building this house for you."

"Reconstructing," Dane corrected.

"Yes, dear," Grandma Peach said amicably. "He is reconstructing this place for you because he wants a place where adventure can live. A place where the embodiment of self-supporting adventure—hikers—can live."

"It was an interesting old house," Dane grumbled. "Couldn't let it go to waste."

"Yes, dear," Grandma Peach said and took a small bite of her chicken.

THE RAIN CAME DOWN LIGHTLY, but steadily, and the lawn was saturated and squishy by the following morning. Purple Rain was on his third shower when Dane suggested he may want a hotel room instead.

"*You* volunteered for this," Purple Rain said, wrapping a towel tight around his waist. "You should have assumed hikers would want to take showers when they came through."

"You're right. I volunteered. And now I'm volunteering to take your ungrateful ass right back to the trail. Would you like to ride on the roof or in the trunk?"

Purple Rain didn't make it to lunch, either having sobered up enough to seriously fear for his life and hitch out of dodge, or told by Dane that he didn't have any choice but to leave. Vika didn't know, but she saw him wander down the driveway, and turn left towards the trail in the far distance.

There wasn't any work to be done inside the house, other than helping Dane and Forrest with the last of the interior framing, and finishing the electric. Vika opted out.

While she and Grandma Peach ate lunch, a girl knocked on the door to the camper, the hood of her black raincoat cinched around her face, her eyes nearly covered, but the smile unmistakable. A guy with dark brown hair matted down by the rain and bright eyes the color of whiskey bounced up and down behind her, trying to fend of the chill. His own dark blue raincoat shielded him from the drops, and his hands were jammed into his front pockets. His chattering teeth told Vika the effort to stay warm had not quite paid off.

Vika walked down the steps into the rain and hugged her tight. Someday hugged her back just as hard. She looked happy. She looked strong. They both looked wet and cold though, so Vika broke the embrace and said, "Come on, there's a fire in the house you can dry your gear next to. We have clothes for you to change into, too." They had added clotheslines to the front two rooms of the house, which provided more room for drying than the coop.

She turned to Someday's friend and said, "You must be Time Warp."
He smiled and jerkily nodded, "Mmm-hmm. You must be Vika." He stuck out his hand and she took it.

She grabbed an umbrella from the coat rack near the camper door and slipped her feet into a pair of flip-flops. Together, the three of them dashed across the wet grass, up the stairs of the porch, and Vika held aside the plastic tarp they used as a temporary door for the two hikers to enter. She led them to the dining room and the woodstove. It was an immediate relief for both of them, Vika saw, as they pulled off their raincoats and hung up their damp sleeping bags in record time.

"How's the trail?" Vika asked. "Other than being wet?"

"Great," Time Warp said at the same time Someday said, "Gorgeous."

Someday pulled her fly out of her tent bag and water dripped down the fabric onto the carpet remnants they had laid beneath the lines.

"Sorry," she said. "Man, everything's so wet."

"Don't worry about it," Vika answered. "That's what we put the scrap pieces of carpet down for." She laughed. "We trade it out every couple weeks because it starts to smell a little funky."

"Oh, Vika," Someday gushed as Time Warp hung up her tent next to his, "Snoqualmie Pass to Stevens Pass was unreal. The weather was perfect that first day going through that section, and the mountains were mind-blowing even with the rain yesterday."

"Isn't that section like seventy-five miles?" The three of them turned to Slip An' Slide, who had entered behind them stealthily in the rain, and just as stealthily avoided eye contact with Vika.

Time Warp paused as he finished with the last clothespin and turned. "Hey, man, good to see you!" He took a couple easy steps over his gear and gave Slip An' Slide an enthusiastic handshake.

"Hey," Slip An' Slide greeted, pumping Time Warp's hand up and down. "How've you been?"

"Couldn't be better, couldn't be better." They broke the handshake and Time Warp gestured to Someday. "Someday said you came up after Sisters."

Vika slid a look to Someday during the slight distraction to ask the question silently. Someday caught her eye for a second, and when she pointedly looked at Time Warp for a split second and brought it back, Vika swore she saw a blush rise in Someday's cheeks.

"Yeah," Slip An' Slide said through a sigh. It was not a sigh that suggested he was irritated with Time Warp's knowledge, but a sigh that emphasized his exhaustion with the trail. "I just, I don't know, it was time for me to get off," he told him then turned his attention to Vika. "Vika and I did some of the North Cascades, though. We just got back a few days ago. Highway 2 to Stehekin."

Vika nodded enthusiastically, "I don't know much of what the rest of the trail was like, but you can't beat the North Cascades."

Time Warp sucked in air between his teeth, "The Sierras would contest that."

"They have their own...style," Slip An' Slide said.

"What a diplomatic answer," Someday teased.

"I try to be."

"What?" Time Warp said. "Everyone has a favorite."

Slip An' Slide paused, "If I had to pick, it would be the Sierras."

"That's right!" Time Warp said.

"From what I've seen, the Cascades have a little bit of an edge on the Sierras," Someday said, shooting an apologetic look to Time Warp.

"It's always raining!" Time Warp exclaimed.

"It's only rained like two days on us in Washington!" Someday shot back. "Even so, water trumps desert for me."

"It wasn't the *desert*," he retorted. "There were lakes all over the place. And c'mon, those rock faces?"

Someday spread her hands wide. "I don't climb, Time Warp. The Sierras were awesome, but northern Washington...you know... is a little...better."

Time Warp looked at Slip An' Slide and shook his head.

Slip An' Slide chuckled, "Did you guys really do that section from Snoqualmie Pass to Stevens Pass in two and a half days?" he asked.

Someday rolled her eyes. "Yes," she said, dragging it out.

"The maps we had," Time Warp defended, "said it was sixty-four miles."

"It was actually seventy-three, Time Warp, seventy-three," Someday filled in.

"Yeah, I'm not really sure where the miles were lost on the map," he shrugged. "We wondered why it took us so long to get to our landmarks.

"Whatever," he said, "we made it."

"Yep," Someday said cheerfully, "we're going to take a zero here. I haven't had one since Etna and we figure, with the rain, we might as well."

"Oh, good!" Vika practically squealed. "I'm so excited. You still have to stop in Stehekin, though, it was *unbelievable*."

"We will," Time Warp responded, "I have a package there anyway. So does Someday, right?"

He looked at her and she nodded.

"Perfect!" Vika responded, as Grandma Peach wandered in, nearly hidden under her rain gear and carrying a big black garbage bag.

"Oh, look at all those wet clothes," Grandma Peach tsked. She pushed back the plastic hood of her red raincoat and reached into the bag. "I just washed these," she assured the two hikers as she pulled out some wool blankets. "Take as many as you'd like, and we have replacement clothes in the coop out back. Not the one with the chickens, the one next to it."

"Thank you," Someday said smiling.

"Would you like something hot to drink?" Grandma Peach asked. "Tea?"

"We have coffee, too," Vika added.

"I would love some coffee," Someday said.

"I'm good with water," Time Warp replied.

"Wonderful," Grandma Peach said, "come join us in the camper whenever you're ready."

A knock sounded at the door and Slip An' Slide, Someday, Time Warp, Grandma Peach, and Vika all turned their heads to look in the direction of the entrance. It was odd, of course, because there was no door. Each fall of the person's fist must have connected with the molding, a solid connection and one that dropped to the floor in the foyer with a thud.

"The building inspector isn't coming until tomorrow," Grandma Peach said, more to herself than to the other four people in the room, as she began to take steps toward the front of the house.

Time Warp and Someday remained behind and pulled out the rest of their soaking gear to hang up to dry, Slip An' Slide asking about southern Washington, while Vika followed Grandma Peach.

The knocking stopped and through the plastic cover Dane had hung over the door to keep the rogue raindrop out, Vika could see a figure standing on the other side. The person was smallish, with something on his or her back, likely a pack. That puzzled Vika, knowing full and well that their sign inviting hikers to come in any time of the day was still intact and hanging up on the porch.

Grandma Peach pulled back the plastic tarp. The girl turned, her piercing blue eyes meeting briefly with Vika before moving on to Grandma Peach. Though she did, in fact, wear a pack, she was dressed in jeans and a hoodie. Her dark hair, Vika would say black if she didn't know better, was tied up in a mess. Drops of rain slid down her pale face and her wet eyelashes had stamped her mascara onto the skin beneath her eyes. She stood three or four inches taller than Vika, and so had to look even farther down to make eye contact with Grandma Peach. The girl pinched out a crooked smile.

"Hey, Grams," she said. "It's been a while."

"Oh, my," Grandma Peach managed quietly, and if Vika wasn't straining to hear, she would have missed it. Grandma Peach cleared her throat, "Yes, it sure has. Too long. Come in, deary, come in. You must be freezing." Grandma Peach looked flustered and shaky as she reached for the girl's hand and guided her over the threshold and pulled her into a tight embrace.

"Oh, my," Grandma Peach said again. "Forgive me, Dane didn't mention you were coming."

Cassie rolled her eyes and her smile faltered, but she played it off answering, "Dad? Forget something? Imagine that. Where is he, by the way?"

"He had to do a run to the store. I'm Vika," she said as she offered her hand.

"Cassie," she said, taking it. "Are you a hiker?"

Vika raised her eyebrows. "Me? No. No, I had car trouble and they were kind enough to let me stay while I sorted everything out." She continued, "Apparently, I need at least two months to figure that out..."

"Are you hungry?" Grandma Peach interrupted. "Cold? Wet? Oh, look at the bottom of your pants, they're soaked! We don't have much in your—er—style, just what we've picked up for the hikers. Well, maybe—Vika, dear, do you have clothes for her? I think she'd be about your size."

Vika doubted it, her legs were at least three inches shorter, but it was Cassie who jumped in, "I have an extra pair of sweats in my pack," she said and looked around. "Is there somewhere I could change?"

"Sure," Vika said, "my room, uh, I mean, there's one room up here that isn't used much. You can keep your stuff there." She started to follow Vika up the stairs. "There's another bed in the camper, too."

"Yes," Grandma Peach huffed as she followed the two girls up the stairs. "Of course you'll stay with us in the camper. The hikers, they wake up at all hours of the day and wander through or start working, and this is not a soundproof house to say the least. You'll sleep in the camper."

"OK, Grandma," Cassie said, and though Vika wasn't looking at her face, she could hear the smile in it.

"Are you hungry, dear?" Grandma Peach asked out of breath, as they all arrived on the top of the stairs and Vika pointed to the room on the right. "We could have Dane pick you up something. A sandwich? A burger?"

"I'm OK for now," Cassie answered.

"Are you sure? Stevie's has excellent pizza if you want that," Grandma Peach charged on.

"No really, I had a bunch of gas station food on the way here. I'm sure I'll be hungry in a little while for dinner if you want to do that," Cassie said patiently and, like a charm, Grandma Peach's hand, busy spinning a silver bead on her necklace, slowed to a near stop. Her chest rose and fell at a pace that was slightly less than panic-mode, and the two pairs of clear blue Dancy eyes came up to meet each other.

"Dinner," Grandma Peach agreed, "yes, OK, maybe we'll go to Stevie's then."

Vika looked up at her new guest and asked, "Did you see the camper when you came in?"

"Yeah," Cassie answered, "just behind the house over near the barn, right?"

Vika nodded and Grandma Peach called out as she began to descend the stairs, one at a time. "We'll be there. I'll put on a pot of water. You like tea, don't you? All right Vika, let's go, we don't want to keep Cassie in those cold, wet clothes for too long."

Vika held back a smile as best she could, but when she looked at Cassie with a comically raised eyebrow, she almost cracked up.

Cassie leaned over and whispered, "Is she always like this? I don't remember her like this."

Vika shrugged, "I think you surprised her."

"Vika!" Grandma Peach called from the bottom of the stairs, "help me boil the water."

The girls shared a look, knowing Grandma Peach stood down there waiting.

"OK," Vika called back, and then turned back to Cassie. "I'd better go," she said, "I have to go help boil water."

She caught up with Grandma Peach in the foyer and they walked quickly together across the wet lawn towards the camper.

"My," Grandma Peach said as she shrugged off her raincoat and hung it up carefully on a peg near the door. She slipped out of her shoes and into slippers without missing a beat. "I wish the rain would stop. For a little while at least. Let everything dry out," she said as she padded to the kitchenette and opened a cupboard next to the stove.

"Judy says the pump in her basement broke the other day and her son's been bailing it out every night. Do you think she'd like chamomile or cinnamon? Look, I have some raspberry peach. Why would I have gotten raspberry peach?" She pulled the box out and turned it in her hand inspecting, as if it had it written on the side.

"Oh, well," she shrugged and put it back. "So I said, 'Dane's really handy, you should have him take a look at it and maybe he can fix it.' At least temporary until she could hire someone, but she said no. Said something like her son would be offended because he said he could handle it. Men. They make no sense sometimes." She moved around the kitchen, pulling out mugs and tea bags and spoons and sugar and milk, the motions of her hand independent of her thought process, which, as far as Vika could tell, was not very linear.

"I'm sure she's very happy to see you," Vika said, as she cleared off some of her extra clothes from the bottom bunk and pulled out clean sheets and an extra blanket from the closet opposite for Cassie.

"What?" Grandma Peach looked up briefly at Vika with wide eyes—the color of which she shared with both Dane and her granddaughter. "Oh, yes. Yes, I hope so," Quasi wound between Grandma Peach's legs, picking up on her tension and feeding off of it.

"She is," Vika insisted. "Please relax, Grandma Peach. She's happy to see you and you're about to make both of you crazy by going a hundred miles a minute."

"Oh, posh," she replied, with a wave of her hand, "I am calm. I'm just excited. I don't need to *relax*." She accidentally slammed three mugs on the counter and opened a ginger spice for herself with shaky hands and stared at the other two. "Pfft. I'm just excited." She stared.

"I think you and I would both like chamomile," Vika said, keeping the smile out of her voice.

"Chamomile," she repeated, "of course." She opened up two bags of tea and set them in the mugs.

The door creaked and Cassie ducked in. "This is adorable!" she gushed as the door smacked shut behind her.

"Oh thank you, dear," Grandma Peach said. "Would you like some tea? I have chamomile here, but of course I have many more kinds, let's see—"

"Tea sounds fantastic," said Cassie, brushing by them to toss her pack on the bed before turning back to join them, "and chamomile is my favorite."

The beam that came out of Grandma Peach was almost palpable. "Chamomile it is," she said. "The water is almost ready." As if on cue, a whistle started low over the teakettle and quickly crescendoed to a shriek.

"Well!" Grandma Peach jumped at the noise, and Quasi barked. She quickly poured three mugs. Vika and Cassie took seats on the couch and Grandma Peach sat in a small armchair at the end of the counter.

Cassie eyed Quasi curiously. "Is that a dog?"

"Sure is," Vika answered. "He looks a little mangy, but he's nice."

"He's had all his shots," Grandma Peach reassured her.

"It looks like a raccoon that someone slapped a little ugly on," she said, somewhere between awe and disgust. "Why do you call him Quasi?"

"It's short for Quasimodo," Vika said, sympathizing with Cassie more than she expected Grandma Peach to.

"A raccoon, with what? Oh, Quasi, don't listen to them," Grandma Peach petted her dog, who only thought she was about to give him food and sniffed her hand expectantly.

The door creaked and Someday and Time Warp climbed the stairs.

"Oh, hello!" Grandma Peach said, "So glad you could join us, this is my granddaughter, Cassie, and, oh, forgive me, I've forgotten your names."

"I'm Someday, and this is Time Warp."

"Yes, now I remember," Grandma Peach pulled out two more mugs from the cupboard. "My mind isn't what it used to be. But I do remember," she pointed at Someday, "Coffee?"

"Yes, please, if you have some made up already. If not—"

"Oh, no trouble at all. I'll have it brewing right away." She turned to Time Warp to inquire, "What would you like, dear?"

Vika imagined Time Warp had never been called 'dear' in his life, by the way he stiffened just slightly. "Um, water's fine."

"No tea?"

Slip An' Slide entered and shrugged off his wet coat, slipping out of his muddy sneakers at the same time.

"No, thanks. I'm not much of a tea drinker, ma'am," Time Warp answered.

"Ma'am, huh?" Grandma Peach put one of the mugs back into the cupboard and reached into the refrigerator for a bottle of water. "How about you call me Grandma Peach? Here's your water."

He gave a tight nod.

"Cassie, dear," Grandma Peach said, turning, "how is your tea?"

"Delicious," she answered. "Why don't you sit for a bit? I think we're all pretty well settled."

Grandma Peach thought for a moment, and apparently coming up with nothing else that needed her attention, she picked up her own mug and sat down in the armchair.

Vika played with the tag of her tea bag trying to think of something to say, while Grandma Peach stared at her granddaughter with a look resembling panic in her face.

"Someday, Time Warp," Vika finally said through the silence, "how was Goat Rocks? I've heard—"

"Oh, Vika," Someday started and Grandma Peach looked visibly relieved. In fact, it seemed as though the entire camper breathed a sigh of relief at the break in awkwardness. "You have to go there. It was beautiful."

"I love Goat Rocks!" Cassie said. "I've hiked around there a few times."

"Have you?" Someday said. "You can see forever. I'd go back in a heartbeat."

"It was steep," Time Warp interjected.

"Well, yeah," Someday conceded, "you have to walk on a knife edge, but it wasn't that bad."

"That's what I thought in the beginning," Time Warp said, "and then it got a little knifier and a little edgier."

"It did," Someday agreed. She breathed a mix of sadness and said, "All of Washington has been breathtaking. I can't believe we're almost at the border."

"So what's next?" Cassie asked, sipping her tea. "Everest?"

Time Warp snorted. "No way," he said, "I'm not a fan of hiking on snow, and I'm not a fan of heights," he explained. "Hiking up ninety-eight snow-covered knife edges to get to the top of a mountain is pretty much my idea of a nightmare."

"Ninety-eight?" Grandma Peach said, aghast.

Time Warp stopped. "Oh," he said, "I don't know, I just made that number up. I'm sure it would feel like it, though."

Someday laughed, "We said maybe the Annapurna Loop. Or Camino De Santiago, there's one that goes across Northern Scotland, one that traverses the length of New Zealand—"

"One too many and never enough," Slip An' Slide said as he settled into the bench at the table next to Vika, a cup of steaming coffee in his hands.

"Like cocaine," Cassie said and Someday snorted a laugh.

"It's a grit addiction. What a hobby, right?" Time Warp added, though he seemed damn happy about his situation. "Where there's been a hiker, there's probably a trail, and if there's no trail, we could make one," Time Warp looked back to Grandma Peach. "We want to go abroad for a trail, though." Then he added, sliding a look to Someday, "The Annapurna Loop would be a great way to start."

"Where is the Annapurna Loop?" Vika asked Someday.

"Nepal."

"Wow!" Cassie exclaimed, her eyes wide.

"What a way to start," Slip An' Slide grinned.

"Nepal," Grandma Peach said. "Well, you be careful when you go there."

Cassie chuckled and Someday assured her they would be. "We've just talked about it," she added. "No plans yet."

Slip An' Slide looked at Cassie. "Would you ever do a thru?" he asked.

Cassie shook her head. "Probably not," she said. "I like hiking and camping, but not to that extreme." She looked at the rest of the group. "Have you guys done other trails?"

Time Warp answered first, "AT class of 2012. And I've done the Colorado Trail twice. Someday I'll get to the CDT."

Slip An' Slide looked over at his friend, a strange smile on his face. "2012? Did you know Bubbles?"

"No," Time Warp grinned, "I did it southbound, so I didn't really hike with anyone. Who is Bubbles?"

"My brother," Slip An' Slide answered. "He did a northbound."

"Bubbles?"

"He drank a lot."

Time Warp laughed. "He didn't come on this one with you?"

"One for him was one too many and more than enough."

"That's fair," Time Warp said.

"So, Time Warp," Cassie implored, "which one do you like better? The AT or PCT?"

"They have their own style," he answered almost immediately, unknowingly mimicking Slip An' Slide from earlier. He lifted his foot to cross over his knee and absentmindedly tapped his finger against his water glass in thought.

Someday made a face at him. "C'mon, you can't use that excuse!"

Time Warp looked at her like she had just suggested they eat only peanut butter to the border. "Why can't I say that?"

"We just went through this with the Cascades and Sierras. You have to pick one."

"What if I don't want to pick one?" Time Warp grinned, holding her gaze.

"Do it," Someday said, not returning a smile.

"Fine," Time Warp shrugged. He took his time sipping his water. "The AT."

"What?" Someday remarked loudly as she leaned forward towards him, her mouth open in disbelief. Vika watched her facial expressions in amusement. She had been quiet and reserved in Sisters, but around Time Warp she was an open book. "How could you pick the AT? You don't even get big views from that trail!"

Time Warp uncrossed his leg to plant his foot on the floor, and met her energy with his response, "You asked me which was my favorite! You've never hiked it, so how do you know what you can and can't see?"

"It's not nicknamed the Green Tunnel for nothing, is it?" Someday raised her eyebrows in a challenge and sipped her coffee.

Time Warp shook his head. "If you didn't want to know, you shouldn't have asked. The views aren't as big, and not as often, but there are more people. It's older, so there's a little more tradition, and," he shrugged, "it was my first one. It kind of got me hooked."

Vika chuckled at the exchange. "So, is it safe to say you don't have any interest in doing the AT?" she asked Someday.

Someday smiled at the irony, and sat back in her chair, her eyes on Time Warp a second longer. "Actually," she answered, as she shifted her attention to Vika, "I'll probably do it at some point." She sighed. "One too many and never enough."

WHEN THE BUS RUMBLED BY a short time later and the smell of fried chicken wafted through a cracked open window over the sink of the kitchen in the camper, Cassie excused herself to say hi to her father. Slip An' Slide took Someday and Time Warp on a quick tour of the house and the coop, while Vika made up the bunk for Cassie and Grandma Peach made some pasta salads.

CHAPTER 22

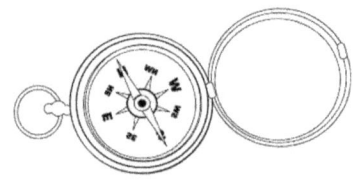

DANE, TIME WARP, AND FORREST started on the roof of the house the next day, a blue-sky background that promised progress. Dane, pointing this way and that, looked to be directing Time Warp over there, wait, no, over *there*. Vika had to hand it to Time Warp. He didn't seem the least bit perturbed and she knew Dane was doing his best perturbing.

Forrest looked like Forrest always had, in his jeans, T-shirt tucked in with a thin belt and a trucker hat and all the while, he ignored Dane. Vika guessed that he was the only one who could. Forrest wasn't doing it to be vindictive—he just went about his work quietly, and—more importantly to Dane—correctly. In other company, Dane might have interpreted that quiet nature as ignorance of the task, but Forrest moved around the roof, clearly deaf to the orders flying about, and this arrangement appeared to be completely acceptable to Dane.

There were a couple small scaffolding platforms around the building that had not been there the night before, which only meant that Dane and Forrest were up before the rooster crowed that morning. The larch boards stretched over the trusses and the copper gutters glinted in the sunlight. They had exactly…two pieces of slate nailed on.

As Vika watched over the sink sipping her coffee, Slip An' Slide emerged from the coop and ran his fingers once through his sandy tousled hair. He walked to the base of the ladder and then, as if his legs were heavy and his body still tired, he heaved himself up on the first rung, and then the second.

Cassie padded into the living room/kitchen area of the camper just as Slip An' Slide made it to the top.

"What's the deal between you two?" Cassie asked as she poured herself a cup of coffee.

Vika whipped her head around to look at Cassie. "Sorry?"

Cassie smiled with half of her mouth. "You watch him all day long."

Vika blushed. "I do not," she said, as her brain realized her face was red and turned up the intensity. Ugh, that was annoying.

Cassie sipped her coffee and looked for herself out the window. "If you say so," she said.

Vika turned her attention back out the window and fixed on Slip An' Slide automatically. She rolled her eyes to herself because, of course, Cassie was right. She did watch him, wondering what was going on in his head and how to get past the barriers he had thrown up. After a moment, Vika told her, "We were on the trail. And—"

Vika paused.

Cassie watched Slip An' Slide through the window, too, and raised a shoulder and let it drop. "You don't have to tell me if you don't want to."

"Well," Vika started, "it's a little complicated."

Cassie strategically used the cup to block her smile as she turned to look at Vika, leaning one hip into the counter. "Is this a 'what happens on the trail stays on the trail' thing? Because both of you are pretty terrible at that. He watches you, too, you know."

"Really? Well...I...um...we..." Vika stuttered. She put both hands to her cheeks and felt the heat come off of them. "We kind of had a fight our last night there."

"A fight already?" Cassie asked. "What kind of fight do you have after three days together?"

Vika shifted in slight embarrassment, "Well, in our defense, we knew each other for a couple weeks. It was about...the PCT and why he got off."

"Oh," Cassie answered. "Why did he get off?"

Vika sighed, "He got tired of it, but it was more about why he wouldn't go home since he's been off. He says he's not ready to explain it to everyone at home yet."

"Ah," Cassie replied, sneaking a sideways look out the window where the boys were pounding rock shingles to the roof. "Well, he shouldn't be sensitive about it. He practically stayed on the trail, and everyone who met him is going to ask probably what you asked when they go through."

Vika continued to watch Slip An' Slide. "Well, I may have also insulted him somehow. I think."

"If it's bothering you that much, just apologize for asking him about it," Cassie said, moving towards the bread cupboard to pull out her morning bagel.

Vika watched Slip An' Slide as he handed a piece of slate to Time Warp and the black keys inch their way across the larch boards of the roof.

Only problem was, she still didn't have answers to his questions and she felt as though she needed them as part of her redemption. She could tell him how her adventure began, but did intuition count for anything? How it all started with a couple pecks on a keyboard, searching for paradise, and how she left on blind faith that her Volkswagen and the wilderness that awaited her would have the answers for questions she couldn't articulate.

She took another sip of coffee. Slip An' Slide wiped the hair off his forehead with the back of his hand while Time Warp grabbed a slate from him. She saw them double-check the placement of the shingle before touching the hammer.

She thought back to how her Volkswagen expired in a fireball, but as for the wilderness, she had never come close to imagining the magnitude of its worth. And most of that experience, she owed to Slip An' Slide.
He deserved an apology.

Vika and Cassie left the camper at the same time and wandered over to see if Someday was awake. The three of them walked out of the coop and towards the house as Dane was yelling from his podium that there needed to be more overlap on the row that Time Warp and Slip An' Slide were about to lay, of course just as the hammer came down and secured the slate to the roof. Slip An' Slide said something unintelligible and yanked at the nail with the claw of the tool.

"A job well done," Dane boomed from the roof as he made his way to the ladder to come down, "is a job you don't have to do over!" He started to climb down and quick looked back over to the guys. "That chalk line," he said, "is for the top edge of the slate. Not where the nails go."

Dane finished climbing down the ladder as the girls watched Forrest discreetly make his way to Time Warp and Slip An' Slide, Vika assumed to explain the technique in less explosive ways than Dane was prone to do.

Dane stood in front of the girls, his huge form blocking half the house, it seemed, and combed his thin, chin-length hair out of his eyes, only to have it fall right down again. "Looking for work?" he asked, his blue eyes flicking from one to the others, his white teeth showing through his beard in a smile.

"Yeah, Dad," Cassie was the one to answer. "What have you got for us?"

"Insulation," Dane answered, "only until maybe one or two o'clock, though. We're going to have dinner in the dining room and I want the dust to settle." He began to walk towards the house and the girls followed. He led them to the back room, where he had mats upon mats of blue fluffy material lying around.

"I thought insulation was pink," Someday said.

"Fiberglass insulation is. That shit gets everywhere and itches like hell. This is recycled denim. I've never used it—that kid in Buffalo talked me into it.

"Both sides look the same," he continued, as he reached to grab a piece of insulation. "It's not rocket science," he said, "just shove it in the wall." He grappled with the length of the insulation, hauled it into the living room and—just as he'd said—shoved it between the two-by-fours.

"See? Nothing to it." He brushed his hands on his jeans. "I'd better get back up the ladder before they ruin the roof," he said without concern. "Wear masks and gloves. Push it around plumbing, behind electrical boxes, and anything else. Make sure the house is tight. If there's a space, cut off a little bit and shove it in the hole. Ends flush, got it?"

"Got it," the girls answered.

"Should we put it in the ceiling, too?" Cassie asked.

"Not on the first floor," he answered, "but on the second we will." Then Dane was gone, back to yelling about headlap.

The girls started out by carrying the full mats closer to the walls they were working on, and ripping off sections from there.

"Never thought I'd be helping build a house this summer," Someday said as she finagled the insulation around an electrical box.

"You're telling me," Vika answered.

"I never know what to expect when it comes to my dad," Cassie said.

"Is he in construction?" Someday asked.

Cassie shook her head, "Art."

"Art?" Someday repeated, as though waiting for the punch line.

Cassie nodded. "Mmm-hmm." She moved to the wall with a strip of the processed denim. "Most summers he travels around to art shows and sells his work."

"What kind of art does he do?" Someday asked, as Vika went about the room, only half listening to the conversation she was already familiar with.

"Everything," Cassie said, "architecture, landscapes. His favorite is machinery. Cars, motorcycles. He did a whole series on printing presses." She paused when her piece of insulation butted up to a light switch. "He says the observation and understanding of something mechanical is his self-medication. Otherwise, he'd spend all his time assembling the most unruly bastards he could find to storm the town hall as his customized system of checks and balances."

Someday and Vika looked up at Cassie, eyebrows raised.

"His words, not mine."

"I'm sure the time will come he'll fit it into his schedule," Vika said.

"No doubt," Cassie said. She then turned to ask Someday, "What do you do when you're not hiking?"

"I tag raccoons."

"You what?" Vika asked, amused, and realizing that she had never asked.

"I tag raccoons around Boston to monitor their push into the urban areas. Well, I did," she said, "in undergrad. I'm taking a gap year and next fall I'm going to work with a professor doing the same kind of thing around Detroit. It should be interesting."

"That sounds fun," Vika said.

"It is," Someday answered. "I love it."

"What does Time Warp do?" Cassie prodded.

Someday smiled at her boldness, "He is a judo coach."

Cassie's mouth fell open.

"Yep," Someday continued to answer her silent question. "He's really mellow when he talks about it, but he's nationally ranked and he's been all over the world to train."

Vika laughed out loud, "Of course, he has."

The girls moved quickly through the house, and by two o'clock, they had insulated the front of the house up to the kitchen entry.

THAT SUNDAY NIGHT DINNER, the company was eclectic. The rain continued to fall outside and Dane had set up tables in what would be the dining room, with blue insulation bulging out of the walls. It was warm with the wood stove in the room next to them and, as always, the chicken looked delectable.

Grandma Peach said grace, Forrest joined her, and Dane lifted his glass. "Here's to the Pacific Crest Trail," he said, like he did every Sunday, and took a sip of the merlot.

"Here's to the house," Time Warp said, lifting his glass of water. "It's pretty great what you're doing here."

Dane shrugged. "I'm just doing the same as you," he said, "hike your own hike. Live your own life. Build your own house. Don't let anyone under any circumstance do it for you, or you'll be looking at that fucked up countertop until kingdom come."

"*Dane*," Grandma Peach hissed, "watch your language at the dinner table."

"Oh, my god," Cassie muttered, shaking her head.

Time Warp and Slip An' Slide laughed and drank to that.

"I'll second that," Someday said, "here's to hiking your own hike."

CHAPTER 23

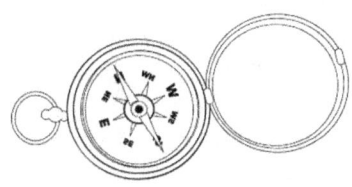

VIKA, CASSIE, GRANDMA PEACH, Slip An' Slide, Someday, and Time Warp were up with the sun the next morning, all prepared to ride in the bus to the trailhead to drop off Someday and Time Warp. Vika's stomach was turning. She could only manage a piece of toast.

"This sucks," Cassie said, as she sipped a cup of coffee as dark as her hair, next to Vika, who sipped her own.

Vika tried a smile. "That's an understatement," she answered.

Then, as if on cue, Someday and Time Warp knocked on the door for the coffee and eggs Grandma Peach insisted they have before they hit the trail again.

They left their packs outside of the camper, and shuffled in wearing light coats to defend against the morning chill.

Time Warp poured himself a glass of water, and Someday poured herself a cup of coffee.

"Thank you guys for everything," Someday said, and with that, Vika thought she might start crying.

"Yeah," Time Warp echoed, "this has been great."

"We're going to miss you," Vika choked out.

"Ahh," Someday said, her bottom lip sticking out, "you're going to make me cry." She moved to hug Vika. "There'll be lots of hikes to go on. We'll meet up on one of them." She squeezed her a little harder and let go.

Vika wiped at the corner of her eye. "One too many and never enough?" she chuckled.

Someday nodded. "One too many and never enough."

"OK," Grandma Peach said as she shoved between them. "Let's eat. We'll have time for goodbyes later." She plopped down the plates on the table, keeping her head down and her voice even.

Only when the very last morsel had been consumed did they slowly move to the bus.

"Send us a picture when you make it to the border," Vika said to Someday as they settled on the couch. "Grandma Peach and Dane are going to put them up over the fireplace in the dining room."

Someday nodded, "We will."

They made small talk for the rest of the ride to keep from thinking too hard about the looming departure of the hikers. But a scant twenty minutes later, the bus pulled into the small parking lot.

Gravel crunched under the tires. Grandma Peach parked the bus as close as she could to the trail and flung open the doors. Each member of the troupe descended the stairs.

Time Warp and Someday fastened their packs on their backs and walked over to the other four. Hugs were given, promises to remain in contact were made, and like every time before, the hikers hiked away. Vika felt as though someone dropped a lead ball in her stomach.

Vika was wiping the dust off soup cans when Smith came out to help himself to the coffee.

"Spill it," he said.

"What?" she asked innocently.

"There's something off about you." He pushed the large button on the top of the pot and coffee that looked like a bubbling tar roof squirted out.

"Ick," she said, "you're going to drink that?"

He swirled it around in cup. "It's going to need a little sugar," he grumbled. "When's the last time you changed this?"

"Last week," she grinned, "give or take."

He was still looking in his cup. "Huh." Then he changed his gaze to look up at her. "So?"

"It's lady business," she responded, hoping to halt the discussion.

"No, it's not."

"Do you really want to talk about it?" Vika asked him.

"If you're going to sulk like this for the next week, then yes, let's hear it," he said, dumping sugar into his coffee.

"Sulk?" Vika scoffed, though she knew it had a touch of truth. "It's just that we had a couple hikers at the house, one who I met in Sisters, and we just dropped them off at the trail."

Smith nodded.

Vika went on, "It was hard. I felt like I knew more about them in two days than I knew some of my college friends in four years. Then they just walked away."

"That's what they're here to do."

"I know, I know," Vika said. "It's just...so short. I've never really made friends so quickly, only to say goodbye so soon."

"Well," Smith suggested, "maybe you're more like the hikers than you expected. That's why you befriend them so quickly."

Vika shrugged again, "Maybe. The hike, the last couple of days, everything is making everything else more confusing. I don't know what the hell I'm doing."

Smith took a sip of his coffee as he thought. "So you went on a hike to find clarity and you're realizing it ruined your life instead. Am I getting this right?"

Vika laughed out loud, "Yep, pretty much."

He stirred in some cream. "Appreciate it, and then stop thinking about it."

"What?"

"Stop thinking about it. As a matter of fact, stop thinking in general. It solves everything," Smith said as he smiled at her.

She looked at him in curiosity, "That's your advice? Stop thinking?"

He shrugged, "You're young. You have time. Let a couple things play out. Do what you want for now and see where you land."

"Well, that's a new outlook," she ventured.

"And neither one probably works," Smith ended cheerily, "so what do you have to lose?"

IT TOOK HER WELL INTO THE AFTERNOON to finish everything she needed to at the store—her long talk with Smith didn't help—and on the way home, she swung by a garage sale to keep her mind occupied. She found a cute nightstand she was sure Dane could find a use for. She also thought the color would go nicely with a quilt Grandma Peach picked up in Sisters, and she did all of this without thinking about the motorcycle she rode there. It was a good thing Dane had wrapped some bungee cords around the seat.

Bungee cords, duct tape, and hiker trash: her life.

Vika was still out when Dark Horse, Detour, and The Brit returned. Dane explained later that a pickup rolled down the driveway with the three hikers in the back. He said Detour stood up to get out and promptly "fell over like a myotonic goat on the Fourth of July."

When Vika rode up, Detour was sleeping on her pad in the lawn and The Brit and Dark Horse were talking nearby.

Vika unstrapped the nightstand from the bike, and then walked by the hikers. "Is she doing OK? Why are you guys back?"

The Brit spoke up from the far side of the tent, "We hope so. We got in too late for the clinic, but she's got to get checked out tomorrow."

"What is it? Giardia?"

They both shrugged and Detour slept on. "Probably. She's been pretty out of it."

"Right. Well, how about I go make some Jell-O? Can she eat?" Vika didn't know how to help a person passed out with intestinal problems. "Oh!" she remembered, "we have a bunch of Gatorade, too. For when hikers get sick. I'll go get that."

The Brit nodded, "She'd really appreciate it."

Vika took the nightstand to the coop, before she made her way to the camper and immediately smelled something delicious and fruity. Grandma Peach was the only one to be found, and she stood in the kitchen, flipping through a recipe book on the counter, her teal-colored apron sprinkled with flour. Quasi trotted to Vika as she entered and Vika bent to pat him. She paused and he nudged her hand back onto the top of his head. As she scratched behind his ears, his eyes squinted, Vika gave Grandma Peach the update about the hikers and asked her if she had any Jell-O.

"It's already setting in the fridge," she said, "Cassie made some when they first came back."

"OK," she said. "Where is Cassie?"

"Helping Dane with the walls, I think," Grandma Peach opened the oven and pulled out a blackberry pie.

"That looks good," Vika said, her mouth watering.

"Dane stopped by the store for some ribs we'll throw on the grill later. This is dessert."

"Mmm," Vika said, "I can't wait." She pulled open the door of the refrigerator and gently agitated the pan of Jell-O. It sloshed around, still entirely liquid.

She set out across the lawn towards the sound of power tools, pausing to grab a pair of safety goggles in the foyer before proceeding on into the house. She found Cassie, Dane, and another hiker she didn't know.

The hiker held a small board against the wall of the living room, over the insulation. Cassie had the power drill and Dane stood back several feet, watching intently, giving orders consistently.

"Dad!" Cassie said, "I *know*. You've told me six times already!"

"A job well done is a job you don't have to do over," he said. "Now keep that drill straight."

Cassie rolled her eyes.

She couldn't see the hiker's face, and she could only imagine what her expression looked like.

Vika stepped into the room and into Cassie's line of vision, who looked over.

"Cassie!" yelled Dane. "Eyes on the wall!"

Cassie jumped. "My hands didn't move!" she said back. A few minutes later, she had the board secured to the two-by-fours and she pulled the goggles down her face, her dust mask still covering her nose.

"Want to put up some rock lath?" she asked insipidly. "The supervisor's a hoot."

"Hey," Dane defended, "a job well done is a—"

"Job you don't have to do over," Cassie finished. "We know, we know."

"I was just coming in to say hi," Vika said, "but sure, I'll help out."

Cassie laughed lightly. "I'm just kidding you. We've been at this a couple hours, actually. I think we're all about ready for a break. You can help us a little later."

Vika nodded and turned to the hiker to introduce herself.

"Medusa," she answered. She was heavier set, tall, with dirty blond hair that looked somewhere between curly and electrocuted. She wore a lightweight orange button-up and tan zip-off shorts.

"What is this stuff again?" Vika asked.

Dane walked up to them. "Rock lath," he said.

"What is that?" Vika asked. "It doesn't look like drywall."

Dane continued, "That's because it's not. It's for plaster."

"Ah," Vika acknowledged, "going old-school."

"Going quality," Dane responded without emotion.

Vika gave him a look as if to challenge the statement. He took the bait.

"What, did you think I was going to make a house out of particle board and plastic siding? What the hell did you learn in school?"

"Dad," Cassie scolded him.

"I never said that, but why not drywall?" Vika asked.

"Plaster's tighter. Stronger. The corners are more precise. The whole house is more soundproof. It's better.

"All right," he said, "I have to get the grill going soon, but I'd like to finish the kitchen walls tonight. It shouldn't take more than an hour." He walked away, brushing his hands on his pants.

"Why isn't he on the roof with Forrest?" Vika asked as the three girls made their way to the porch, dropping their gear off in the foyer in the way, and plopped down in the seats on the porch.

"Because," Cassie sighed, "he wants to train me on how to install the rock lath so I can 'supervise' that—well, and the insulation, I guess—while he's on the roof."

"I see," Vika answered.

Each poured herself a cup of coffee or tea and sank into the furniture.

Medusa played with the tea bag tag on the side of her mug. She looked out at the coop where they knew Detour slept inside. "She's so close," she whispered.

Cassie followed her gaze into the yard. "She'll make it. Even if she has to take a couple days, they're early enough to make it to the border with time to spare."

"Yeah," Medusa agreed, "but still. Have you had anyone else here sick?"

Vika shook her head as she thought. "No. No, but Cougar Bait said she got Giardia in California."

"Cougar Bait?" Medusa thought hard as she sipped her tea. "I remember that name for some reason...but I don't remember why. Maybe I just saw her in the registries."

Vika agreed, "She came through a while ago. She said she took a day off when she got sick. I don't think she slowed down much."

"A day?" Cassie questioned.

Medusa gaped at her. "Are you serious?" After a moment, she regained her composure. "Well, I'm glad it worked out for her, but it's not like that for everyone. My brother hiked the PCT two years ago and he did the same thing. He felt sick, went to the doctor, got his meds, and he went right back on the trail.

"It didn't stop, though. He went along for another 400 miles because he thought, 'the next day it'll be better,' or 'it's just my diet, I just have to get to the next town and buy a yogurt and some probiotic pills.'" She tossed her tea bag in the trash and poured herself some coffee. "Then he had a hard day and by the end he was dehydrated, hungry, and had lost about five pounds he didn't have to lose. He said he was on the top of a ridge in the Marbles and started to piss blood."

"Oh, my God!" Vika exclaimed. She remembered when her feet hurt, hell, her whole body hurt, but to be able to push her body that far? She didn't think so. "That sounds really dangerous, is he OK?"

"Well, he's fine now, but he said that was the most terrified he's ever been; he was 50 miles away from the nearest highway. It was the closest he's ever come to calling a chopper."

"Why didn't he? If he passed out or something—"

"Trust me, I've thought of all the possibilities and then some. It was a good thing we didn't know about it or we would have called the helicopter for him. He said he kept going because it didn't hurt. He said he was hungry, but his body didn't feel weaker and he could make it to the highway." She stopped to purse her lips and look skyward.

"I would have killed him myself if I were there and he kept walking. Anyway, he came home, but his gut was a mess for months."

Vika chewed on that thought. "400 miles," she whispered.

Medusa looked at her sideways. After a moment, she said, "There's kind of an unofficial mantra of a thru-hiker: You gotta keep walking. Tired? You gotta keep walking. Hungry? You gotta keep walking. Fire? You gotta keep walking. Blisters? You gotta keep walking. Snow? Fords? Giardia? You gotta keep walking. I can see the logic in most of it. If there is a fire behind you, if you have Giardia, what good is it going to do you to stop? But Jason shouldn't have kept walking."

They stared into the lawn, lost in their own disturbed thoughts when the delivery truck screeched to an almost halt in the road, and then swung into the driveway. Rocks kicked up and chickens ran for cover. Quasi picked his head up from an interesting scent near the garden fence and watched, ears forward.

The truck had hardly reached a complete stop when hiker boxes started flying out the side.

"Hey—" Vika started, as she approached the vehicle. A box with bright pink and green duct tape wrapped around it flew through the air and landed at her feet.

"Randy!" she yelled exasperated.

"I'm late!" came the agitated response from the back of the truck. "Goddamn it. When are these hikers going home?" A small box flew out at her and she caught it, grateful it was light.

"Careful," Vika huffed, "What are you—?"

He tossed another box on the ground and held out an electronic pad. "Sign, please."

"Randy, do you want to talk about this?" she asked, her voice as though she were addressing a child, and Vika could tell from the slight twitch in his eye it was enough to piss him off. She moved the pen slowly across the board.

"Want to know what today is? My son's birthday. I hired Godzilla to come to our house and where the hell am I? Out in the middle of these goddamn mountains driving around *boxes*. *For the second year in a row*." He snatched the pad back. "Thanks," he grumbled, climbed into the seat, and jammed the shifter into reverse. Without checking for traffic, he backed into the road, shifted again, and floored it towards town.

"What's his problem?" Cassie asked as she came over to help a stunned and flustered Vika pick up the boxes.

"Godzilla's at his house and he wanted to be there."

Cassie made a sound of sympathy, "That's a tough one to miss."

VIKA HELD ONTO THE BOXES and walked over to the barn. She heard music blasting from inside. She had heeded Grandma Peach's advice to steer clear before, as it was a sign that Dane was painting. This time, she was too worried that it would rain and ruin a hiker's mail. The bass of the song vibrated through the walls of the barn like a force field. Vika took a deep breath and decided to scoot in and out quietly, quickly, and, hopefully, unnoticed.

As stealthily as she could, Vika pushed aside the wooden door. Yellow light fell at her feet, and, as she pushed the door farther, Dane came into view, his hair pulled back into a small ponytail on the back of his head. The familiar smell of acrylic paints greeted her, along with motor oil and hints of hay. He had on old stained jeans and a CCR concert tee. He held a paintbrush in one hand and he stood about three feet from an easel—the contents of which Vika couldn't see. Dane stared hard at the canvas with his eyebrows pulled close together. An engine block sat on a sheet of cardboard on the floor in front of him, and Vika guessed it was his current model.

"You paint, right?" he yelled over Warren Zevon, but didn't take his eyes off the canvas. Vika's breath caught. She hadn't realized he noticed she entered and certainly didn't mean to get in his way.

"I'm not very good at it," she called back as she moved away from in front of the door to put the boxes down.

He made a face. "Not what I asked." The music shook the air around them.

Vika wrung her hands. "Sometimes," she answered loudly. "I play around with landscapes every once in a while."

"Good," he shouted back, still not taking his eyes off of the canvas. After another long minute, he broke his concentration, and looked, not at her, but to the corner of the room and pointed his paint-covered brush. "Grab that canvas. You have work to do."

Vika looked back at the door, thinking of Cassie and Medusa on the porch still.

"You're not waiting until the snow flies, let's go," Dane said.

Vika heaved a sigh and walked to where he gestured to grab a prepared canvas. He had pulled the material tight and stapled it across a frame. White gesso gave it a prime surface for painting and—

"Not that one," Dane called. "The one behind it."

Vika froze her hand on the smaller frame and moved it to the bigger one, identically prepared. It stood as high as her hip and half as long as the banquet table it leaned against.

She looked over her shoulder back at Dane.

"Come on," he shouted over the vocals. "Put it on that easel."

"Why can't I use the smaller one?" she shouted back. "What do you want me to do with this?"

"No." His attention was not on her, but on his own canvas, where he just whisked the brush across the surface. Vika couldn't see what he was painting still, but he had a canvas as big as the one he had just directed her to pick up.

She hefted it up and over to the easel on the far side of the room, locked it in place and stepped back. "It's ready," she said.

"Well," he answered, flicking his hand to the middle of the room where his paints were collected on a turn table, "get to work!"

Both of Vika's hands went up in confusion. "What am I painting?"

Dane let out an exaggerated sigh and for the first time since she walked in the room, looked at her. "I don't know," he said. "I'm not in your brain." He gestured to the canvas and shouted animatedly, "Paint what you feel!" He held both arms out and a smile shone through his beard.

"Is that what you do?" Vika yelled back.

"No," Dane's hands remained in the air, his smile held fast, and his eyes were still fixed on her. "I feel nothing."

Vika grunted and squeezed her eyes shut for a second in frustration with the lack of direction. When she opened her eyes again, Dane's full attention was on his canvas and his head bobbed to the music.

She wandered over to the stack of paint tubes and snatched up yellow ochre, dark green, and brick red to start. She hooked her fingers under the seat of a nearby stool and dragged it, metal scraping across the floor. She caught Dane's eye as he glared at her from around his canvas, and she smirked.

Vika snatched up a clean-ish rag next to the stool and draped on the top of her canvas to use to wipe off excess paint. Then she wandered over to a collection of brushes, pushed some aside, grabbed a few to her liking, and headed to the sink to get a cup of water. Eventually, her easel was set and ready to go, so she plopped herself down on the stool to stare at the white canvas.

She stared for a long time.

Images of the hike with Slip An' Slide flipped through the pages in her mind quickly, fleetingly, and she couldn't hold on to any of them. Her gaze fell on the engine block—a still life was better than subjects out of her memory—but she didn't have a single clue what parts she was looking at or how it worked. She could paint the house, but that sounded too much like work. Or she could paint North Dakota, maybe mimic an image she'd seen in school along the way. Without thinking about it, she squeezed some ochre out of the tube and onto her palette. She dipped her brush in the water, pressed it into the glob of yellow-brown paint and swirled it.

Vika felt the some tension in her shoulders release. When she painted, responsibilities, drama, and schedules fell by the wayside. She didn't think about ten years in the future; she didn't think about five minutes in the past. The paint was in the world now and it was going to dry. It deserved her full attention before it became obsolete.

Vika lifted her brush to the canvas and a brownish-yellow streak dashed across the canvas. Then another. She pushed out green onto the palette next to the ochre and did the same. Green streaks darted against, over, and near the yellow ochre, both of which were joined by the red only minutes later. She used the red lightly at first for fear of overpowering the canvas, but found herself going back to retrace lines and layering on new lines. Another trip to the pile of paints was in order and she picked up purple, cyan and a rich umber color. Onto the canvas they went. Some went boldly and some went lightly. Some disappeared as the perspective solidified only to pop up somewhere else. She moved the stool out of the way so she could walk back and forth across the space easier, and pull colors across her landscape. Time disappeared.

THE MUSIC MUST HAVE BEEN OFF for a while before Vika realized it, and when she looked up, Dane was sitting on his stool, a corner of his mouth pulled up as he surveyed her painting.

"What?" she asked, not particularly friendly.

He shrugged. "Nothing." His smirk didn't go away.

Dane planted his hands on his thighs and pushed himself up to stand. "You can wash the brushes in the sink in the corner," he said. "Let the painting dry here."

Instead of answering him, she stepped back and looked at her work. She squinted her eyes and tilted her head. Her eyes traced the dark silhouettes of the trees, the reds, yellows, and oranges that silhouetted them, the outlines of the purple mountains behind them. In place of the stove she and Slip An' Slide had used to cook dinner, she had dug a pit and lit a campfire on the gessoed canvas.

Dane cleaned up his own station before disappearing from view. A moment later, she heard the groan of the wood as the barn door closed behind him.

The acrylic had already dried and she reached her hand out to trail her fingers along the shapes and colors. She had never been very good at landscapes, and this was no Camille Corot, but this painting possessed a glow she had not achieved before. Her eyes followed her hand as it traced the trees, across a twig, and down to the forest floor, right to the spot a bear had stood that night.

She smiled.

Her fingers skirted over the roots, up another tree and into the sky. She subconsciously pushed against the painted air as though she hoped to fall into the canvas and tumble through the colors, and through the warmth of the setting sun she could again feel in the pit of her stomach. She could practically hear the insects buzz across the silent landscape, and feel a breeze jostle the needles of the trees.

Except, there weren't beetles in the wildflowers. She wasn't hiking through the mountains and there wasn't wind combing through the branches of the spruces. Her hand fell away from the canvas and her shoulders sagged. She knew someone else who felt exactly the same way.

BY THE TIME VIKA CLEANED UP, the sun had gone down and the dew had set. Vika walked over the wet grass and walked into the coop.

"Hi, Forrest," she greeted the hiker as her eyes adjusted to the light.

"Evenin'," he responded with a slight nod

"Is Slip An' Slide here?"

As Vika finished up the question, Slip An' Slide came around from a dividing wall.

"Hey," he said. "What's up?"

"Hi," she replied, walking up to him. He seemed larger, for some reason, his figure a little more imposing than she remembered. "Can I talk to you?"

"Sure."

"Back there," she nodded in the direction of the bunks, knowing his was in the back and it would provide the privacy she was looking for.

Slip An' Slide looked at her skeptically, and then gave a nod to talk behind the divider. Slowly they walked down the aisle of empty bunks to one of the last ones. She followed him, taking a deep breath on the way.

"It wasn't fair for me to ask you all those questions," Vika said quietly as she stood by his bed. Slip An' Slide didn't move next to her and only the insects responded.

After a moment, he asked, though she bet he already knew the answer, "What questions?"

"In Stehekin. The ones about the trail. Why you've stayed at the house. Why you didn't want to tell people."

Slip An' Slide shrugged, "It was fair. What wasn't fair was not answering *my* questions. You just brushed me off. It seemed to be a little bit of a one-sided conversation, to be honest, Vika. It felt like you were...studying me. Like one of your paintings."

Vika sat on the edge of his bed and Slip An' Slide raised an eyebrow at her. She looked down and pulled at the corner of the blanket. "You're right," she said.

"The thing is," she continued, but she didn't know what the thing was. The thing was indefinable—it was stuck in the back of her mind and existed as a feeling instead of an idea she might be able to verbalize. Still, she knew she owed something to Slip An' Slide, now more than before.

So she tried again. "The thing is, I didn't mean to brush you off and I didn't avoid your questions on purpose. I just don't know what I'm doing out here. I didn't put much thought into this trip when I left home, and I certainly didn't plan on my car going up in flames and staying in Stacklen for the summer. Maybe I kept pushing you on why *you* stayed because I hoped it would give me some idea about why *I* stayed." She tucked a stray piece of her dark red hair behind her ear.

"I don't know," she said quietly. "I got a good education, one that I liked, one that had potential. For the first time I was off track and it scared me. Dane, Stacklen, this entire summer just…" she struggled to explain, "it made me second-guess everything I'd done up to now." Vika paused again, and Slip An' Slide listened, head half-cocked, unmoving, except for the occasional expansion of his chest. "I've never second-guessed my future before."

After what seemed like eternity, he sat down on the bed next to her.

"I'm not exactly sure what I'm doing here," she whispered.

"Well, that's what we're here for," Slip An' Slide responded with a smile, "for 'not exactly sure.'"

Vika laughed. She scooched back on the bed and leaned against the wall. Slip An' Slide followed suit.

"I thought," Vika speculated, "that the hike would help clarify things for me, but it made everything a little more confusing."

Slip An' Slide sighed, "Life becomes difficult when you have too many things you like to do."

"That's for sure," she said, letting the back of her head hit against the wall softly and closed her eyes for a second. The katydids continued their chirping and an owl sounded from one of the trees in the yard.

"But I think," she continued, "that we're missing the same thing. I know I haven't been out there as long as you have –"

"I shouldn't have said that."

"It's true, though, but I think you underestimate how much I get it."

He sat quietly for a second next to her, both of them looking out into the coop in front of them. "I miss the mountains, Slip An' Slide. Everything made a little more sense there."

She heard him let out a soft chuckle. "I guess you do get it."

"Can I ask you another question?" she asked after a moment.

"Hmm," he pretended to think hard about the proposition. "I don't know…" Slip An' Slide smiled at her.

"How did you get your trail name?"

"Oh," he answered. He took a breath and Vika thought he wouldn't answer but at last, he started, "Some Trail Angels in Big Bear, the McKennas, have you heard of them?"

She shook her head.

"Awesome people," he continued. "Anyway, they had a Slip An' Slide at their house down a little hill. Me and a few guys extended it with some tarps and, well, there you go. I dislocated my finger, actually."

"Eww!" She managed to laugh despite wanting to shudder. "Tell me about the McKennas," Vika said, changing the subject.

"Well," he said, clamping his mouth, thinking. "Married couple. One kid doing research on a boat somewhere, I forget. Super, super nice. They had this garage, or barn, or something in their yard they stocked with a ton of bunk beds. It was pretty sweet. They set up the normal hiker necessities like a microwave, refrigerator, computer. A lot like this one. They let us use their shower and laundry and Isabel cooked for us."

"Did they ever hike the PCT?" Vika asked.

"Nah," Slip An' Slide answered, "They picked up some hikers about eight years ago, Mike said, and they got to talking. They started just going out to the trailhead, driving people around. "Post office runs," he called them. Then the next year they let them sleep in their yard. I guess it just evolved from there."

Vika smiled.

"What?" Slip An' Slide asked.

"It's just," she started, "I don't know. It kind of restores your view of humanity, the PCT. Doesn't it? These people don't know who you are, where you're from, and they just let you in. Then there are the people who pick you guys up on the side of the road, too."

"Hikers need a lot of help."

"I bet a bunch of people you get rides from or meet at stores and things don't understand why you choose to do this hike." She laughed again and teased, "So why do people pick up hiker trash like you?"

"You tell me. You did."

She looked over at him. "Yeah, I guess I did," she said.

VIKA WOKE UP IN THE MORNING next to Slip An' Slide feeling lighter than she had in a long time, but that didn't fix her morning caffeine addiction. Vika rolled away from him in search of that medium-roasted cup of motivation. The sky was blue with pink hues fading into the horizon as Vika walked across the dewy lawn.

Grandma Peach was packing up her music scores for her piano lesson as Vika opened the screen door and climbed the steps of the camper.

"Do you have a piano lesson this early?" Vika asked as she went to the cupboard and pulled out the coffee grounds. Cassie stirred in her bunk only feet away.

"Oh, no, dear," Grandma Peach answered, shrugging into a light jacket, Quasi sniffing around her feet, anticipating her departure and hoping he was lucky enough to be able to accompany her, "I'm going to breakfast with Milly first."

Vika separated a filter from the stack and shoved it into the holder. "That'll be nice," she said. "What are you going to play at your lesson?"

Grandma Peach patted her bag. "I'm in the mood for some Billy Joel," she said and smiled.

"A little 'Piano Man'?"

"You got it, kid," Grandma Peach remarked and walked down the steps. She turned and patted the dog when she reached the ground. "You stay here. I'll be back in a little bit," and she carefully latched the screen door in front of his nose. As he did every time Grandma Peach left, he whined and pawed at the door. After a couple minutes, he climbed the steps and lay down, only to turn around and stare at it.

Even though Vika slid the divider over the little hallway separating the kitchen area from the sleeping area, Cassie was awake before the coffee finished brewing. The ponytail Cassie had worn the night before had done its best to try and break free. Loose, dark brown strands fell along the side of her face, and she swiped at them with hands that were covered still with her long-sleeved shirt. She wore short boxer shorts and nothing on her feet, where Vika could see the stem of a purple freesia start near her painted black toes, sweep across the top of her foot and creep up the side of her calf where it bloomed.

"Where were *you* last night?" she asked sleepily, a half smile that she could muster pulling at one corner of her mouth.

Vika shrugged innocently. "We made up," she said happily as she poured a mug.

"The best kind," Cassie responded, reaching for the pot as Vika went to put it back on the burner.

"We didn't make up that much," Vika said, "Forrest and Medusa were around somewhere. Speaking of which, I didn't see Medusa this morning. She must have already hitched back."

"Those hikers are crazy."

BY THE TIME THEY MADE IT into the house, Dane and Forrest were on the roof, and Dark Horse and The Brit had finished insulating the first floor and were progressing up the stairs with the strips of recycled denim.

"How's Detour doing?" Cassie asked them as she and Vika stepped into the foyer.

Dark Horse shrugged. "She's OK. She's at the clinic now. Hopefully, it all goes well."

"Yeah, I hope she's OK," Vika said. "Of course, you're more than welcome to stay as long as you'd like."

"Thanks," the guys said in unison as Cassie and Vika gathered their tools for rock lath installation.

CHAPTER 24

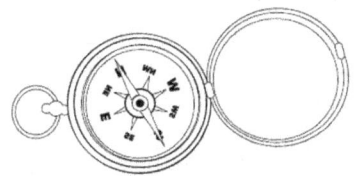

MARMOT AND MR GOODBAR were at the far edge of the yard as Vika and Cassie descended the porch steps for a lunch break, hanging up gear on the clotheslines.

"Need anything?" Vika asked from the short distance away.

"No, thank you," Marmot answered, "Dane showed us the coop. We'll go over to Stevie's to eat."

"Oh, perfect," Vika said.

Vika and Slip An' Slide were sitting on the porch swing later that evening when Marmot and Mr Goodbar steered their bikes into the driveway.

"I can't believe they caught up," Marmot was saying, pushing out the kickstand at the corner of the porch and unstrapped some snacks from the back of the bike.

"I know," Mr Goodbar said, pulling up next to her. "I mean, I guess it was only a matter of time." He looked up at Vika. "You have two more hikers coming in tonight. They hitched into town from the trail and we ran into them at Stevie's. They're going to try to get picked up, or walk here."

"Great!" she responded. "You guys have hiked with them?"

"We did the first, I don't know, four hundred miles with them, until we left for Tucson. Then we caught up and hiked with them a little around Donner Pass to Burney Falls. We haven't seen them since then."

"Tucson?" Vika asked. "Is that where you guys are from?"

"No," Marmot answered, her quiet voice clear. "Mr Goodbar had to go to his sister's wedding. I went along as his plus one."

"That must have been nice," Vika said, tucking her feet up on the porch swing and leaning in to Slip An' Slide. "To see your whole family for a day. Did you fly? Those tickets must have been atrocious."

Marmot slid a sideways look to Mr Goodbar. "Well," Marmot said, biting her lip wondering how to continue, "on that trip, we hopped freight cars."

"Oh," Vika responded, eyebrows raised. "How exactly do you hop freight cars?"

"Illegally," Mr Goodbar said as the pair climbed the stairs to the porch and took a seat on the bench.

"We hiked into Big Bear and we had both done a lot of hitchhiking," Marmot started to explain, "so we wanted to switch it up a little. Neither of us had done it before, but we heard stories from people who did." Marmot poured herself a cup of tea.

She turned to look at Mr Goodbar, who at the moment was content sipping his coffee and listening. "Who was it in the Cascades?"

He thought a moment, and then offered, "Morning Glory. He said he almost died of hypothermia going through the mountains."

"Right," she said, "and then there was Gladiator. He broke his hand and had some story about rolling out right next to an alligator nest in the Everglades."

Mr Goodbar shook his head, "That guy, I swear, he plans these things just so he can tell people about them later."

"Or just makes them up," Marmot said, dismissing the account easily. She turned back to Vika. "Well, we were told that if you can count all the bolts on the side of a boxcar, then it's going slow enough for you to jump on."

Vika shook her head slowly.

"And that we would probably get thrown in jail," Mr Goodbar interjected.

"Thrown in jail? You guys did it anyway?" Vika said through an astonished grin. Slip An' Slide chuckled next to her.

"Right," Marmot said, "they both said we might get thrown in jail, but that sounded a little extreme. I don't know, maybe we didn't believe it?" She looked at Mr Goodbar for an excuse but neither had one. They shrugged together. "Anyway, so we hung out in the bushes but the trains that went by were too fast." Marmot paused and said slowly, "It seemed really dangerous so we changed our plan to get a boxcar in the yard. We found one, no problem and when it started to go, the car rattled around, wind blew through every crack you could see and every crack you couldn't see. It was loud, that's what I remember."

"We were that much closer to Tucson, though," Mr Goodbar said. "That was about when we realized that we heard how to get *on* the train, and we didn't really know how to get *off*."

"That sounds so risky!" Vika said, trying to digest the new level of insanity.

Marmot laughed and clapped her hands on her knees. "We were texting Morning Glory all night, like, 'Where do we get off?' 'How do we get off?'"

"'Is there a special roll?'" Mr Goodbar put in. He watched Marmot telling the story with amusement.

Marmot grinned again, "But, of course, he was in the mountains hiking—well, probably sleeping by that point—and had his phone off and we were going to have to wing it. We figured it was a bad idea to jump out in the middle of the desert, but getting out in a yard would be just as bad, considering we were warned multiple times about getting caught. So we thought, 'OK, we have to do this like a mile, maybe two, outside of town.'"

"And," Mr Goodbar said, leaning forward onto his knees, "you can see town lights from at least twenty miles away, and it's really hard to tell how close they are getting, especially when it's four in the morning and you've been awake for about twenty-two hours."

"I can't even imagine," Vika said, shaking her head yet again.

"Then all of a sudden," Marmot continued, "the train just powered down. We were trying to get all of our stuff together and we were about to jump out—literally, crouched in the doorway—and this massive spotlight landed on us. Then another guy, had to be the engineer, comes out with a shotgun!"

Vika groaned, "You're kidding."

"I wish," he answered. "He pointed a 12-gauge right in our faces, yelling all kinds of things. He knew we were there all along—he had to have. He must have called ahead to plan an ambush in the yard." A smile pulled on the corner of his mouth. "Nearly pissed myself. We had rolled right into the yard—it was outside of town a little—without seeing it coming. So then the cops came and we were tossed in the drunk tank for the night."

"I bet that was fun," Slip An' Slide took a sip of his beer.

Mr Goodbar paused to take a sip of his tea, and Marmot looked at Slip An' Slide before continuing, "Ugh, it was nasty. The dirtiest I've been on the trail, and I've gone ten days in the desert without showering before. The judge moseyed in at about eleven the next day, called us up. He started firing off questions and we answered, head down, looking guilty, you know, 'What were you doing?' 'Riding in a boxcar.' 'Why?' 'He has to get to his sister's wedding in Tucson.' 'Why didn't you just take a bus?' 'We should have, sir. We're sorry.' Then he asked, 'How much cash do you have on you?' I told him, '$48.52,' and he goes, 'Good! Your fine is $48.51! Save that last penny for luck. You'll need it. Now get out of my town!'"

"Still," Mr Goodbar said chuckling, "we thought we had made it out with basically a slap on the wrist. Of course, we had yet to step outside in the daylight and *see* the town. By then, it was high noon in the desert, and he took all of our cash. There were maybe seven buildings total, and none had an ATM. We weren't about to start hitching in front of the courthouse, so we started walking. Since we couldn't buy anything at the store, we had to fill up on water at a horse trough half a mile down the road."

Marmot shuddered at the memory, "I half expected them to drive out and arrest us again for trespassing."

"They were probably watching you through binoculars from the air-conditioned courthouse laughing," Slip An' Slide said.

"Probably," Marmot agreed. "We were sure we'd get sick, but somehow neither of us did. We had to walk another two miles until we saw the sign marking the town line, made it immediately on the other side and threw our rain flies over some bushes for some shade and took a nap. When it was cool again, a couple hours later, we started walking again, through the night. Thirty miles to the next town that had bus station. We made it to Tucson five hours before the wedding bells chimed. My hair looked like a ball of tumbleweed and Mr Goodbar had dried blood down his leg from catching it on a bolt on the boxcar. We were a mess."

"My sister almost killed me."

Slip An' Slide laughed and Vika silently sided with the sister.

The unmistakable *click, click, click* of hiking poles on pavement chipped its way louder and louder into the conversation and the hikers on the porch fell quiet. They watched together as two figures with the slim silhouettes of lightweight packs turned from the road onto the driveway. Their lengthy shadows stretched and slithered as they crossed the grass and approached the porch. It was early evening, and the sun still floated in the sky, though it became heavier and heavier as minutes passed, and prepared to sink below the horizon.

"Hello again!" Marmot called and one of the men gave a little wave as they made their way smiling across the lawn. They looked to be in their mid-forties, no gray, but more seasoned bodies than much of the crew Vika had seen. Their skin was thicker, their eyes deeper, their midsection holding on to just a tiny layer of extra skin. They were good looking, and they both gave a charming smile to Vika as Marmot introduced them as Bloodhound and Spinner.

"I still can't believe it," Spinner said as they approached. "We've been so close the last couple months, reading about each other in the registries."

"We thought for sure you'd catch up to us in Sisters with the fire, but you leapfrogged right on by," Bloodhound said.

Marmot nodded, "We called about a room, but all the hotels were booked, so we just hitched around."

Mr Goodbar added, "It worked out. We took a zero in Cascade Locks and actually, we thought you'd catch up to us there. We had moved for a nice long stretch. Etna to Cascade Locks. We got a little restless around Tahoe because we stopped in a couple towns right in a row, so we decided to keep moving in Oregon."

"I hear you," Spinner said, looking pointedly at Bloodhound. "We went into Sisters, and then took a half day at Timberline and by the time we got to Cascade Locks and Bloodhound suggested the same thing, I told him no sir. I don't know about you, but I'd like to be done by Christmas."

"Yeah, and he's said no to every zero since then," Bloodhound complained.

"Look who we met up with, though! Now we can party together in Stehekin!"

"You'll have such a good time there," Slip An' Slide said.

"Really cute," Vika added.

"You guys have been there?" Spinner said.

Slip An' Slide nodded, "Vika and I hiked from Highway 2 up and took the ferry back on Lake Chelan."

"No shit."

"I'm going for the food," Mr Goodbar said. "Do they have good food?"

"The best," Slip An' Slide said.

"Lemon meringue pie," Spinner said, "that's what I want."

"How's the hiking?" Marmot asked.

Vika answered, "I thought I died and went to paradise. It was unbelievable, you'll love it."

"Did you see any wildlife?" Bloodhound asked her.

"There was a bear," she responded.

"A bear? A big bear?"

"Well, I didn't actually see it," Vika said. Though she thought about her painting and how she could imagine the black bear plodding through the acrylic paint.

"No?"

"No, it came in the middle of the night, tried to eat our food," Vika explained.

"Yeah," Slip An' Slide interjected, "there was a little warning scratched in the path, but we camped there anyway." A statement to which Bloodhound shook his head, even though he had a look that suggested he would have done the same thing.

"It just poked around a little but we scared it away," he finished.

"It didn't get your food, did it?" Spinner asked.

"Nah."

"Speaking of wildlife," Spinner turned to Mr Goodbar, "glad to see you haven't been eaten by a cougar. Yet."

"You, too, man. You, too. Have you seen one?"

"No! I mean, we're down to crunchtime now. We met a guy who saw one, though."

"Yeah," Bloodhound added, "it wanted to eat his dog."

"You're kidding!" Marmot exclaimed. "What happened?"

"It was right out of Trout Lake," Spinner began to tell them, dropping his pack to the ground. Bloodhound left his on and took a seat on the edge of the porch, his feet rested in the grass.

"We're walking along and this guy comes around the bend, his dog—big dog, too, like a German shepherd or something—trotting along in front of him and he's yelling, 'I just got attacked by a cougar! I just got attacked by a cougar! Don't go that way!' To me, he looked fine, I didn't see blood on him or his dog, so I kind of just waited for him to get to us and explain what the hell he was talking about. So anyway, he's freaking out. He said that he didn't hear or see anything and, all of a sudden, his dog looked back and his fur stood up. I guess he growled or whatever so the guy turned and the cougar was *right there*. About three feet away. He said his dog just looked at him as if to say, 'This is the end right here. I'm gonna miss you man.' The guy's just like, 'Fuck no! Not my dog, you bitch!' all Mrs. Weasley style and he chucked a rock at it.

"He said the cougar just looked at him. So he threw another rock and it ran off behind a bluff."

"Of course by then, he's got us all freaked out," Bloodhound continued, "and the poor guy is shaking, practically begging us to turn around and walk the other way." He pulled up a shoulder and let it drop. "But we weren't backtracking for anything. Even for a psycho cougar. Plus Spinner wanted to catch a glimpse."

"From a safe distance, of course," Spinner added.

"Of course," Marmot agreed, as though anything else was absurd. Because it would be, Vika thought.

"So we all picked up a rock, and bid each other adieu."

"Well, you picked up one," Spinner corrected, "I picked up two. A small one for a warning shot and a big one to do some damage."

"Oh, yeah," Bloodhound laughed. "Your long-range and short-range rocks."

"You'd be destroyed without me, but dammit, I didn't see it. I was walking backwards for at least a mile and a half. Not even one little swish of a tail."

"Why were you walking backwards? Is that some sort of superstition or—"

"They attack from behind," Bloodhound said.

"Sneaky bastards," Spinner put in.

Marmot shook her head, "How long did you walk around with the rocks?"

"Six miles, give or take."

"Spinner did," Bloodhound said, "I tossed mine after about a half mile. I wasn't about to make rock collecting one of my hobbies of the PCT."

"I kept telling him the cougar might have been stalking us! For miles and miles!"

"They do that?" Vika asked aghast.

"Sure," Spinner nodded, "they'll go after little kids. Dogs, too, normally not as big as a German shepherd, but well, never say never."

"Kids?" Vika said in disbelief.

"Like I said, sneaky bastards."

Bloodhound gestured in Spinner's direction. "He held on to his ammo. I wasn't worried," he said to Marmot and Vika.

"I would be holding on to the rocks," said Vika, her eyes wide, "probably for the rest of the trip. I'd sleep with them."

Marmot must have noticed the tension in Vika and gently touched her arm. "You don't have them around here."

"How do you know?" Vika asked, thinking about Quasi and how devastated Grandma Peach would be if anything happened to him.

"*Most* cougars are really skittish. Wary of humans. They get a bad rap because of stories like this, but they're really beautiful animals. Powerful, and yes, they're clever, and—"

"Stealthy as hell," Spinner interrupted.

"If they're desperate, they'll go after adults or big dogs, but people rarely see them in the wild; that was an oddity. Trust me." Vika nodded slightly to Marmot's reassurance, who glared at Spinner.

"You have chickens running around," Bloodhound offered. "If you had a cougar around, they'd be more . . . dead."

"Smooth," Spinner jested, "that was almost poetic."

"Shut up," he responded, "I'm too tired." That sentence was the last for some time, until Marmot mentioned a thirty-mile stretch with a pebble hidden in her shoe and that evolved into nearly an hour-long discussion about gear flaws, which rolled into discussion about a potential Continental Divide Trail thru for the next year.

"I think I'm going to turn in for the night," Mr Goodbar said at last, getting to his feet.

"Already? It's nine thirty!" Spinner said.

"Yep, hiker midnight, man," and Mr Goodbar disappeared into the dark towards his tent.

One by one, they stood and stretched, placing their mugs on the tray.

Vika remained on the porch, watching the hikers disappear into the dark yard, just a light from their headlamps bouncing along through the darkness. She finished the last sip of her tea and reached over to turn off the coffee pot.

But instead of heading to the camper, she leaned back into the swing and tried to stretch the muscles in her neck. The light of the headlamps bounced across the lawn and disappeared into the coop. She had become so accustomed to hikers that a person walking 2,600 miles seemed almost normal. Or at least, not surprising.

Footfalls soon sounded behind her and Forrest emerged from the dark house. He nodded to Vika as he passed and set out to the coop.

"Good night, Forrest," she said.

"G'night, Vika," he answered.

"Wait! Forrest?" Vika started, "Why, um, did you decide...um?" Her question faded into awkwardness as she realized the impulsivity of the question, not to mention the tactlessness of it. Vika already knew his wife had died; she didn't need to hear it from him. She tried to think of a substitute question, but Forrest stopped walking and turned to look at her. He had a grasp on the unspoken words.

"People start the hike for a lot of reasons," he started, not waiting for her to continue. "And they keep hiking for a lot more. Why did *I* decide to hike? Because when I'm hungry, I think about food, when I'm thirsty, I think about water, when I'm tired, I think about sleeping." He shrugged. "That's why I didn't stop. Couldn't. Wouldn't. With every fiber of my being. I *wanted* to be hungry and thirsty and tired. Thinking about a cheeseburger is a hell of a lot easier than thinking about your dead wife."

She nodded. "I'm sorry," she whispered.

"Maybe if you figure out what it is you're trying *not* to think about, you can figure out what you *want* to think about." He turned towards the yard, slowly, and descended the stairs.

Vika watched him go. As he disappeared into the coop, her gaze dropped to the deck of the porch.

A firefly blinked into her line of vision. She slid out her phone.

"Vika?" her brother's tired voice came through cyberspace.

"Hey, Alex."

"What's up?" his voice seemed slightly more alert.

"I'm just calling to say hi."

"Oh, V, I'm...man," Vika could practically hear him rub his eyes. "I'm sorry, can you call back tomorrow? I've gotta go to work pretty early."

"Oh! Alex, I wasn't even thinking—" about the time? About the day of the week? If it wasn't a Sunday, there was little distinction. "I'm sorry. Go back to sleep."

"Wait," Alex said, "V? You there?"

Vika brought the phone back to her ear. "Yeah, Alex, I'm here."

"Good. What did you want to tell me?"

Vika smiled to herself, "Just that, you know, I mean, that I'm happy here. I wanted to tell you that I like it here, and that I miss you."

She could hear him sigh. "That's good, V. I miss you, too."

"I didn't run away from you guys."

"I know."

"You know? You made it sound like—"

"I know what I said," Alex paused. "I was jealous of you. I said it to piss you off."

"*Jealous?*" Vika mentally backtracked through that conversation. "Of what?"

Alex let out another still-tired sigh. "I was here and you left. It was like you just set out to go to the ends of the Earth to find what you were supposed to be doing. That takes a lot of courage, Vika. I was jealous."

Vika almost laughed, but held it in. "Well, it didn't feel like anything even remotely close to courage."

"And I was here. Living at home, working at that damn store that I'll never leave. It made me feel like I was lazy."

"It felt more like I was playing Russian roulette with my future."

Alex grunted. "Better than waiting for a 'get out of jail free' card."

Vika laughed, "You have something in your back pocket. I'm your twin sister, I know these things, spill it."

There was silence on the other end. "I'm looking into government opportunities."

"You're joining the FBI."

"…or something similar."

Vika shook her head and pride pulled a half smile on her lips. She knew he had a card and it was big. "You nark," she teased.

"Yeah, but for real, don't get involved with any shady people out there. They interview everyone."

"So we should stop running guns over the Canadian border?"

"Not funny."

"Have you told Mom?"

"Hell, no."

"Gee, I wonder why. Dad?"

"I think he suspects."

"He won't be the first to say it, though."

"Nope."

Vika took a deep breath in through her nose. "Well, good for you, Alex."

She could hear a little smile in his voice as he answered, "You too, V, you too."

CHAPTER 25

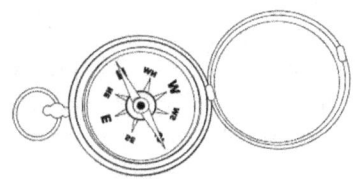

"PREPARE TO SHORTEN SAIL, FOLKS!" boomed Dane's voice from the door where he stood, feet planted as the wind exploded into the coop around him. He wore yellow waders, with a grin wide enough to cross Lake Chelan, and his thin hair was blowing around his face. The sky was nearly black, though not a single raindrop had fallen. Dane looked excited, caught in the vivacity of the impending storm. Vika looked past him to see gusts rip through the fragile bonds that connected leaves to trees, sending them in a tailspin around the yard.

Soon enough, Dane got everyone scurrying around the yard, picking up any camping gear left out on the lawn to dry. Vika fumbled with the coffee maker on the porch, as it was certain to blow away and break—she had her priorities.

Three hikers replaced the plastic tarp over the hole where the front door should be. Grandma Peach tried valiantly to herd the chickens into the coop, while Quasi tried equally as valiantly to herd them out of the coop and around the yard, and for a while the chase ensued—Grandma Peach chasing them one way, Quasi chasing them everywhere else. Not until the first boom of thunder shook the earth and Quasi ran scared into the house was Grandma Peach able to regain control of the wild brood.

Then the first drop dropped, and it echoed through the house. Up the stairs, through the kitchen, around the basement. Silence followed. Hikers peeked around the gear they were hanging to look out the window with bated breath. Card games ceased midround, sandwiches paused halfway to the mouths of hungry hikers, and even Quasi ran to the window, rested his front paws on the sill and waited, perfectly still. Then another drop dropped. And another and another. They splatted on the window, they pinged off the copper gutters, they smacked off the plastic tarp, assaulting the house. Threatening to breach the barriers, the drops dropped.

The first night, as the rain pounded down, the house creaked, and the temperature fell enough for a fire to roar. Shadows tore across the windows, and wind whistled through every crack and crevice. Some hikers slept through the night, some read, and all of them thought about the other hikers in the mountains.

It rained for a week straight and Dane, Grandma Peach, Cassie, Slip An' Slide, and Vika worked hard to clean up the first floor of the house to make room for soggy hikers from the overflow of the coop. Dane installed a new stovepipe for the wood stove, Grandma Peach swept up nails, and Vika stacked the dry firewood on the porch. They only had a couple cords, but Dane had insisted it was covered by a tarp even during the driest days. His foresight was well appreciated.

Hikers were coming in tides. The coop was impassable and the house was hardly navigable, between the packs, the sleeping bags, and the tents hanging from nails in the ceiling in the front living room, dubbed the "gear drying room." Hiker boxes were retrieved from the barn constantly and hikers sat around in groups sorting through their food, some trading, some giving tips on how to cook, some looking at the four thousandth packet of instant oatmeal with a look of dread on their faces.

Vika saw a lot of mac and cheese, energy bars, trail mix, oatmeal, instant rice, and peanut butter come out of the resupply boxes, though a few hikers went for organic concoctions or homemade foods.

Some of the hikers stayed just one night, some stayed until the rain stopped, though most stayed about two days. They were too close to the border to stop for too long in one spot. Restless spirits moved on, even in the rain.

Vika and Cassie made numerous runs each day into town with a full bus to the laundromat, where hikers commandeered the entire line of dryers for their clothes and sleeping bags. Some were there for hours, watching their down bag go around and around, only to pull it out, pull on the feathers, and throw it back in with a couple tennis balls. They made several trips to the Goodwill to stock up on replacement clothes, and within the week, they had filled an entire drawer with sweaters worthy of a "Bad Sweater" Christmas party.

Dane took full advantage of the free labor, and he gave a demonstration of installing rock lath to anyone who looked at the drill. They easily finished the second floor, and the master bedroom began to take shape. With Forrest getting two or three volunteers in the bathrooms installing cement board and laying tile on a daily basis, the house almost looked habitable.

At last, on the morning of the fifth day, the clouds receded. There was still a steady drizzle and the sun was yet to be unveiled, but there was a feeling that they had made their way through the worst of it.

Along with the break in the rain, Forrest emerged from the coop on the fifth day, pack packed. There was no warning, there was no ceremony, no tearful goodbyes. Just like that. He had reconstructed as much as he needed to reconstruct, and it was time to move on.

He was going home. Back to California to turn on the heat before his pipes started to freeze, he said. But he'd be back the next summer to help landscape. He hadn't offered, actually, Dane told him to return, and since he hadn't said no, it was implied he'd be back in Stacklen before the next group of long-distance masochists came through.

After saying a simple, polite goodbye and thank you, he walked toward the road to catch a ride, jeans and trucker hat on, shirt tucked in and goatee freshly trimmed. He walked more upright, and with a couple more pounds, Vika noticed, than he had when he first arrived.

Working with Dane that day was as close to boot camp as Vika had ever been, and she learned quickly to not talk back.

"Hold the drill like this!" he snapped at Vika.

"Flush, people! Flush! It's not flush if I can fit a chicken through that crack!" he yelled at Cassie.

"Careful with the rock lath! We already finished deconstructing!"

"Dad, c'mon," Cassie said with a sigh at one point.

"What? Quality work isn't important to you?" he fired back.

She rolled her eyes.

"Oh," he continued, "right. I forgot. Quality is too much effort. Cheap and shoddy, that's what you want?"

Cassie let the drill swing to her side. "You didn't invite me out here to insult me, did you?"

"I bet that boy—"

"Oh, my god," Cassie shot back. "What boy?!"

"That boy you brought to Easter."

"Jackson?"

"Figures he'd have a last name for a first name. Everything was backwards about that kid—"

"DAD! Once! Just once! Please speak plainly, or...just," Cassie let out a groan. "Whatever, I don't want to hear it anyway, it didn't work out, so you don't have to say anything." Cassie sighed. "Is this about med school?"

Med school? Vika thought. Well, that put earlier conversations with Dane into perspective a bit.

Dane spread out his hands. "I just don't know if you're ready for that, Cass. I—"

"NOT READY?" Vika fidgeted with the pace of the conversation and shuffled a step back.

"I'm not ready?" Cassie continued to yell. "At least I'm committed to *something*. What exactly have you been committed to? Your career? What is it, by the way?"

"Oh, please," Dane scoffed.

"When do you think I *would* be ready, Dad?" Cassie charged on with such force that Vika scooted back another couple steps. "You know, when Mom was my age, she was married and pregnant with me! And you're worried about me being in *school* for a few more years?"

Dane's hands flew out. "You and your mother are two different people!"

"I know." Cassie said flatly. "You like to remind me of that."

Dane turned pink. "Cut it out, Cass."

"You know what," Cassie shot back, "never mind. I suppose you'll just treat me like a child incapable of making my own decisions for...forever, is it?" She put the drill down forcefully, but without causing damage, and stomped out through the foyer. Dane watched her with practically glowing eyes, and then let them drop to slide under Vika's gaze and started towards the back room.

Vika knew there wasn't an exit that way, and didn't want to be in the way when he eventually passed through again, so she carefully put the rock lath down and moved slowly towards the front doorway.

"HEY," VIKA SAID later that evening as she walked out onto the porch where Cassie was already curled up on the swing, pushing it back and forth gently with her toe.

Dane had exhausted himself and left the house earlier, stomping away to the canvases in his barn. Vika could feel the bass of the music in her chest when she walked by through the grass, and imagined the tubes of paint lying around, Dane's brows furrowed with concentration as he swept his brush across a massive canvas.

"Hey," Cassie answered, lifting her chin high and pushing her hair out of her face. She managed a smile.

"You OK?" Vika asked, taking a seat and occupying her hands by pouring a cup of tea.

Cassie lifted a shoulder nonchalantly and let it drop. "Nothing I haven't heard before," she said, without emotion. She smiled halfheartedly again.

"You're dad is..." Vika stopped as she let the words fall.

"Opinionated?" Cassie offered. "Blunt? Crass? Hostile?" She paused. "Impossible?"

Vika laughed, "Pretty much."

Cassie snorted.

"Do you guys, uh, get along?" Vika asked awkwardly.

Cassie looked up, an eyebrow raised slightly.

Vika backtracked. "Sorry," she said, "I didn't mean to pry, I—"

"It's fine," Cassie reassured her. "We are both…stubborn. We have different variations of the same ideals, I would say, and when they don't quite match up, we're like Zeus and Thor battling to be the only god of thunder, you know?

"Sometimes he gets carried away," Cassie said, looking down at her cup and swirling the contents. "He thinks about things for too long and comes up with these elaborate connections, or schemes, or," she shrugged. "I don't know. I can't even keep up with him half the time. Sometimes…" She leaned back and scrubbed a hand over her face. "Sometimes he makes me so mad.

"He can't stand people who limit themselves, and he thinks that the amount of time spent in med school will limit me. He loves learning skills and most everything he considers a skill. At the same time, he would be in heaven if he were locked in a library. He just…just…" Cassie's eyes searched the yard in front of her for the rest of her thought process.

"Won't learn anything because someone else tells him to learn it."

"Yes." Cassie leaned back and chuckled. "He's such a pain in the ass. I don't know how Grandma Peach still puts up with him." She heaved a sigh, "But he's my dad. I gotta love him, pain in the ass or not."

Vika shrugged, "It's kind of refreshing, though, to find someone who does something about what he stands for. Even if it's completely bizarre to most people. You don't get that in Jessup very much."

Cassie raised a shoulder in a neutral gesture. "Maybe," she said.

The two girls let a moment sit between them. "Have you always done the Sunday dinner?" Vika asked.

Cassie said as she rolled her eyes. "Come hell or high water, we sat together at the table. I thought he would have fallen out of the habit by now," she said, "but apparently not. He says the greatest minds argued over dinner and that arguments were a stepping stone to ideas and ideas led to plans and plans led to action and the only way things ever change is if people argued over dinner."

VIKA AND SLIP AN' SLIDE SAT next to each other in the room at the top of the stairs later that evening, reveling in the quiet they hadn't experienced in days. Their sides touched, their thighs touched, Slip An' Slide had an arm around her shoulder and Vika leaned into him. They sat like that for ten minutes, twenty minutes, Vika didn't know, and didn't care. Somewhere, Quasi was tormenting a chicken, and the annoyed squawking drifted through the hole where the door should be, and up the stairs. Other than that, the house was empty of noise.

"Do you think Dane's right?" Vika asked.

"About what?"

"About anything. About everything. About experience and diplomas. About this house, about the hikers…about artists and scientists."

"Yes," he said quickly, and then Vika felt him stiffen and his second answer was quiet, but firm, and slightly disheartened. "No."

When he didn't continue, Vika asked, "Why?"

He sighed and leaned his head back against the wall, not to separate from her, though he did, but in an effort to more clearly consider his response. "I want to. I want to believe that everyone is as invested in the pursuit of new ideas as he is, but it's not realistic. The people who have the potential or desire to care that much are already doing it. He's preaching to the believers."

Vika stared out the window, into the clouds on the other side. They shifted over a blue backdrop, forming shapes, dissipating, forming more shapes.

"I get that," she said at last. Slip An' Slide absentmindedly played with a few stray strands of her hair and she saw a single nod out of the corner of her eye. "To an extent, I guess. But I wouldn't have come up with Trail Angeling or hiking 2,600 miles unless I saw someone do it, I think. And now it's hard to imagine not caring about that."

"Yeah," he said. There was a long pause, broken only by a single bark from Quasi. Vika felt Slip An' Slide shrug in admission. "We had to learn it from somewhere."

Vika rested her head against the wall. "So, Cassie's leaving soon."

"I know," he answered.

"I'm not ready to go home yet," she said after a moment.

She felt him turn his head slightly towards her. "Me neither," he whispered into her hair.

"But I can't stay in this house without any hikers," she continued.

"Maybe we could go somewhere together. Postpone the real world as much as possible."

She nodded as she slipped back under his arm.

VIKA WENT IN SEARCH OF CASSIE and Dane and heard the drill echo through the house. She imagined them yelling at each other while attempting to install something or other.

Two cups of coffee, a quick shower and change later, she headed towards the house, but instead of hearing the drill, she heard a couple elevated voices.

"Dad! I've told you a million times, I want to be a doctor," Cassie was saying. She stayed in the foyer and appreciated the rock lath in the kitchen to block their view of her. She felt bad eavesdropping for about a second and a half and was over it. She listened intently.

"I just don't think you've explored all your options."

"Yes," she said, clearly tired of explaining, though with slightly more patience than the afternoon before. "I have. I have wanted nothing else since you bought me that puzzle of all the body parts when I was seven. That and mom's stories of the ER."

"Oh, yes," Dane said, "I remember that puzzle. They made the liver the wrong color—maybe they gave you a model of an alcoholic." Dane's indistinguishable muttering that followed was hard for Vika to hear.

"So, why didn't it work out between you and...that boy?" Dane asked the question slowly, shamelessly failing to cover his happiness.

"It just didn't," her answer was curt.

"That's too bad, I really liked him."

Vika rolled her eyes and heard Cassie say, "You are unbelievable." There was a beat of silence, and then she added a little more quietly, "He talked in a lot of circles. All talk, no walk."

"Huh," Dane said, "I didn't notice."

This time, Vika heard Cassie laugh and she had to stifle her own.

"Didn't notice, my ass," Cassie said.

Instead of feeding her another bullshit line, Dane asked, "So you really want to be a doctor?"

"Yes."

"Why?"

She heard Cassie exhale. "Because. I want to help people and I love that type of environment. Thinking fast, you know?"

"Oh," Dane said, "so...trauma."

"Yep." Vika heard Cassie pause. "I love medicine. I love learning how the human body works. It's something that I don't get bored with and at the rate it changes it will always be exciting, you know? And I've had enough random jobs to know that I would never last doing something that doesn't help someone else. I really want to make someone's life...better. Easier."

"Interesting," he mused.

"Why?" Cassie asked this time.

Dane took his time responding, and then his voice carried through the house, "In high school, my father's best friend, a surgeon, offered to pay for my college if I chose to go into the medical field. I always thought it would have been ER stuff."

"You told me that when you gave me the puzzle. I think that's when I decided trauma." Vika recognized the sound of sandpaper on the wall. "Why didn't you do it?"

"Too much ass kissing," Dane said. "Too many people out to find an excuse to take away licenses. I didn't love it enough to put up with that."

Cassie laughed. "You weren't worried someone would take away your artistic license?"

"Oh, man," Dane said, teasing. "That was worse than one of *my* jokes."

Silence trickled in after the laughter and Vika stepped forward. But before she was in sight, she heard Dane's voice continue and she froze.

"Cass, will you do me a favor?"

"Hmm...depends what it is." Vika could hear the smile in her voice.

"Will you remember this?"

Cassie hesitated with her response. "Remember what?"

"This conversation. Remember why you want to be a doctor. Don't ever give up on discovery. On that thrill of having everything at your fingertips."

Again, Cassie took her time responding. "That's why you divorced mom, isn't it?"

"I never said that." Dane's voice was firm.

"But it's the truth. You two always said you grew apart, but you think she gave up."

"Cassie—"

"You think she gave up on life. You think she gave up on learning."

"It's not her fault. That feeling fades for a lot of people—"

She didn't interrupt with words, but sighed impatiently, "She's stronger than you give her credit for." There was an awkward break in the conversation. "Did you know she started her own business?"

Vika could practically see Dane's surprised expression through the walls. "No," he said.

"Being a nurse in the ER is wearing her out. She wants a backup plan so she's making teas, growing a bunch of herbs in her garden."

"Is it successful?"

Cassie paused. "It's only online right now, and a little corner shelf in her friend's store, but everyone loves them. I think it will be."

"Oh. Good for her," Dane's voice sounded genuinely happy. "Is she...uh...you know—"

"Dating?" Cassie finished. "She's been seeing this guy. A physical therapist at the hospital."

"Is he good for her?"

"Meh."

There was another pause. "Then you know what you have to do."

"What?" Cassie asked amused, "You want me to sabotage the relationship?"

"You wouldn't have come up with that word if you weren't already thinking it."

"Dad—"

"Hey, Cass?"

"Hey what?"

"Don't end up in an old house all by yourself."

CHAPTER 26

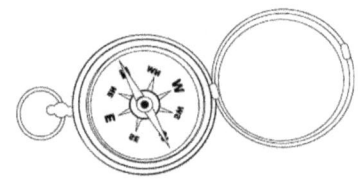

"SO THEN," BEAR CLAW CONTINUED his story to the hikers leaning in around the woodstove of the coop, while Vika brought over cookies that Grandma Peach made, and stocked the dressers with new replacement clothes. "The LAPD comes up over the mountain, *fwump fwump, fwump* and they found me with their spotlight. Two other choppers come over and I hear a voice yell, 'You OK?' I tell him, 'yeah, yeah,'—I give 'em a wave—and a guy dressed in black lowers out of the helicopter *zoooop*. He has me put on a helmet and harness. Then we were lifted right back up." Bear Claw leaned back and sipped a beer.

"I bet that's an expensive taxi," someone said from one of the armchairs behind Vika's back.

She heard Bear Claw respond, "Nope. Not a penny. Don't know how, don't know why, but I wasn't about to ask."

A pause followed, and as Vika turned to as a third hiker spoke up to the other hiker in the armchair. "What about you, Celestial Sojourner? You ever get lost?"

The man frowned, "I've been confused a couple times, but never...lost." Bear Claw laughed. "I've never had to be rescued by a chopper," he finished.

"Never say never," the third hiker warned, "you might have a cloudy night to suffer through."

Vika interrupted the story swap. "Dinner will be in the dining room in about an hour. Grandma Peach made a lasagna."

A chorus of thank-you's and sounds that suggested most of the hikers would be in attendance sounded throughout the coop.

It wasn't just a lasagna dinner, though; it was Cassie's last dinner in Stacklen. Fall classes were creeping up faster than anyone wanted to admit.

Vika's feet carried her across the grass and into the camper, where Grandma Peach and Cassie worked side-by-side making a salad.

"Can I help?" she asked.

"Well, dear," Grandma Peach said, "we're almost done—"

But Vika had already squeezed her way into the tiny space left at the counter with the two women and picked up a knife to cut some peppers. She focused intently on the pepper, but her purpose of preparing a salad was secondary.

"Yes, dear, of course you can help," Grandma Peach said quietly and continued to slice up a pile of garden fresh radishes.

They chopped slowly, and when one pile of vegetables ran out, Grandma Peach plopped some more in front of them, until the chopped vegetables in the bowl far outweighed the amount of lettuce.

The three of them stared at the bowl, knowing the moment someone took it, it meant time charged on and they would be that much closer to Cassie's leaving. As is usually the case, the wayfarer finally took hold of the bowl. Grandma Peach followed Cassie with the rolls, and Vika with the dish of lasagna.

They brought out lasagna to the house for the hikers, and while they were talkative, Grandma Peach, Dane, Cassie, and Vika picked at the food, took dainty bites, and said something meaningless about the weather, or laundry that needed to be done, or how the lawn needed to be mowed.

VIKA AND SLIP AN' SLIDE FOUND CASSIE under her Jeep the next morning, the hood popped open and Dane standing nearby, scowling at Cassie's feet, which were currently kicking the dirt to find traction.

"I can't get it!" Came her voice from the undercarriage.

"Try once more, and then I guess I'll have to do it," Dane continued scowling. "I don't know why you wait until the last minute to do these things, Cass."

Cassie's feet stilled. "I told you three times!" She kicked once, fast, and said, "Got it." After a second, as Vika approached the car, she added, "It's barely three thousand miles. Perfect timing. This will get me until Christmas."

Cassie's feet shuffled to the side and a hand reached out to grab a metal tray next to the front bumper. Cardboard scraped against the stones in the driveway with the movement.

"What are you guys doing?" Vika asked, looking under the hood as though she knew what she was looking for.

"Cassie's changing her oil," Dane explained, still scowling, though now at the engine. He sighed, "Last minute, as usual."

Cassie's face emerged from underneath the car as she slid out on the piece of cardboard. "Perfect timing," she corrected, "as usual."

"You tightened it up?" Dane asked.

Cassie feigned shock. "I was supposed to put that screw thingy back on?"

Dane glared at her. "Yeah, yeah," he said, "then I don't have to ask if you wiped it clean?"

"Nope."

"Take off the old filter," Dane said, after Cassie's hand had already disappeared into the mess of tubes and contraptions under the hood.

"What do you do with the oil?" Vika asked.

Dane offered her a brief glance. "I know a guy in town."

"You always know a guy."

Cassie laughed. "No kidding."

"He owns a garage," Dane continued. "He'll recycle it for me."

Cassie pulled out a small cylinder, dripping with black oil down the sides and over her hands. She walked it quickly to a five-gallon metal bucket.

"Fast," Dane urged her. "We don't need Quasi out here licking up the drops."

"I know, I know, I'm going," Cassie answered.

Dane held out a much cleaner cylinder and Cassie took it. She slid her oiled finger quickly over the threads and put her hand back in the bowels of the vehicle. When she took it out a minute later, it was empty.

"Now, there's nothing else you need on this car before it goes back to Seattle, is there?" Dane asked, handing her a quart of oil. She took it and poured it into the engine. "Hey, don't pour it all over the manifold," he said, annoyed.

"No," Cassie answered without blinking, as she traded an empty bottle for another quart with Dane. "She should be good as new."

"All right then."

Cassie and Dane traded bottles a few more times as Vika watched, in silence. Saying goodbye was getting old. She felt as though she had been saying goodbye—and not just any goodbye, a goodbye forever goodbye—all summer. In a word, it was awful. Each time it left her gut in a knot and her mind spinning.

But this time, admittedly, it was of a different flavor than Vika was used to.

It was sad, a thousand spices of sad, but there was a hint of sweet and comfort evenly blended in. Vika thought it was because Cassie was going directly to a fixed location, accessible by a swipe of the thumb, whereas the hikers left into the unknown.

Grandma Peach had tears in her eyes when Cassie hugged her and promised to be back for Christmas. Dane had told her to not date any more morons and Cassie rolled her eyes, but Vika had no doubt she appreciated the caring advice. If it could be classified as advice.

She drove away after breakfast and no less than three cups of various hot beverages that Grandma Peach insisted she have, which she graciously took, as though looking for an excuse to stay just five minutes longer.

Dane stood in the driveway waving as she left, a shadow of a hand waved back from inside the car as it pulled out onto the pavement and drove away. He remained standing there for ten minutes after she left, watching down the road, wondering if he would have to work as hard next time to get her to visit, hoping she wouldn't be corrupted by society—it was everywhere in a city—and that her ex had big goddamn holes in his ears. The only comfort he had in watching her leave was knowing that she wasn't going back to that fool.

Otherwise, he might just have to move permanently to Seattle. Maybe he'd even have to stop by to see Steph and ask about her tea. Dane planted his hands on his hips and huffed out a sigh.

Vika looked over at his hulking frame every once in a while as she spread plaster across the foyer walls. When he finally turned to come back to the house, Vika turned back to her trowel and went back to work. Slip An' Slide worked methodically next to her.

HIKERS DWINDLED IN NUMBERS. More often than not, new arrivals had stories of leaving the trail for days, if not weeks, in the middle of their trek. They pushed on with caution, having been warned of casual winter previews—flurries in the mountains. Old snow was much different from new.

Grandma Peach sent them off with hot chocolate packets and a phone number, telling them to call once they were back in civilization. And those piano lessons were paying off because she remembered every hiker she had told, and the day they should make it to the border.

When three hikers left one afternoon—tired, dirty, and holding on to every belief in the trail they had—Vika left the house, too. She walked as she did months before, but with much less haste, and called her mother to tell her she'd be home by Thanksgiving...maybe. Her mother answered in her usual explosive way, though Vika's heart rate remained normal. She even smiled as she said goodbye over the screeches in her ear and hung up. It was dawning on Vika that she and her mother would never be on the same page. Vika liked the world she was creating with Slip An' Slide, the hikers, and the mountains much more than the suburban world in which her mother existed in North Dakota, and vice versa.

Maybe one day they would be able to have reasonable conversations instead of yelling matches. This was not the day, though Vika believed it would happen eventually.

VIKA TURNED TO WANDER UP THE WALK, past the Italian "welcome" sign. Smith answered the door, the radio playing in the background. He didn't say hi, he didn't tease her about pouting, he just stepped aside. She walked through the entry way, looked briefly at the paintings of the red velvet cupcake above the dining room table and stopped short in kitchen doorway. The baking appliances were still there, but dirty and in the sink.

"Smith," she started as he came up behind her.

"I figured you couldn't leave without some cupcakes," he said. She walked to where they sat on the counter, beautiful, exquisite pieces of art, mountains and lakes on the circular frosting canvas of each one.

"They're beautiful," she breathed.

"I hope they taste all right," he answered.

She smiled, "There's only one way to find out." They toasted before they took a bite of their own cupcake. Rich, chocolaty, gooey—Vika's favorite.

"Perfect," she said through a mouthful.

They ate quietly for a couple minutes, until Smith put down his half-eaten cupcake and said, "Hang on, I have something else for you."

He walked out of the room, and Vika watched him. When he returned, it looked like he was carrying a flat piece of poster board. He pulled a piece of tissue paper off the top, and Vika saw it was a print of the *Alba Madonna*. She sucked in two lungfuls of air and held them, so full of emotion she feared she would lose some if she exhaled.

"It's not an original," he said.

Vika breathed out and smiled at the absurdity of the statement, as she grazed her fingertips slide over the image. "It's gorgeous," she whispered.

"Dane said it was your favorite." Vika nodded, biting the inside of her cheek. "I got it in Florence," he continued, smoothing it on the table. He adjusted his reading glasses, and brought his chin up to look down through the lenses. "We were going to hang it in the den, but it didn't fit, really. Sophie likes her rooms balanced. I thought you could find a better home for it."

She nodded again and offered him a shaky smile.

"Oh," Smith said, "you're not going to cry about this, are you? Here, have another cupcake."

She laughed and wiped her eyes. "Thanks, Smith," she said.

TWO WEEKS LATER

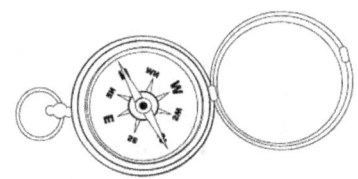

SHE STOOD IN THE DOORWAY, looking at her room. Hers. She smiled. The house was Victorian, but the room had a cottage feel to it. She had painted the room a straw color, with faint tones of rose, with the exception of the wall the headboard rested against. It was a rich red color, with purple undertones. The furniture was black cherry and looked antique, with decorative brass handles on the dresser drawers, and little holes for a skeleton key. The dresser and the mirror rested on the same wall as the door, across from the two windows with long, sheer, cream-colored drapes, the bed ran parallel, between the two walls.

Above the bed, glued to a thin wooden board and nestled between the four sides of a wonderfully gaudy golden lacquered frame she had found at a thrift shop, rested the *Alba Madonna*. Mary, Baby Jesus, and John the Baptist owned the wall. The painting was religion for whoever wanted it to be religion. It was science for whoever wanted it to be science. It was a demonstration of bewildering talent for those who believed in talent, or training for those who believed in training, or a combination of any of the above. Most of all, it was an exhibition of love and dedication. Maybe a tiny bit of money. But mostly love. Vika was sure of it.

She snapped a picture of the room and sent it to her brother. She had written, "Hike your own hike. Live your own life."

There was a black cherry chest at the foot of the bed, with extra linens. A red, cream, and deep purple quilt with slight chocolate brown accents covered the mattress, and she had a narrow map of the PCT tacked between the two windows.

Vika passed the small nightstand—the one she had picked up the day Someday and Time Warp went back to the trail—and looked around the room again. This was just one stop, one room, but she hoped it would be the comfort for the last push north for the hikers. She wanted them to make it.

Heavy, Dane-sized footsteps came up the stairs behind her.

"You did well with the space," he said, and took a sip of coffee. "I like the bench under the window with the books. Not intrusive."

"Thank you," Vika said, trying to keep her voice steady and unaffected by the rare praise.

He took another glug of coffee. "So what're you up to now?" he asked, still looking at the room. Fiddling with a handle of the dresser. He bent down to feel the fabric of the rug.

"Slip An' Slide and I...we're going to fly to Florence. Rome, too. Maybe we'll get up to Venice, but mostly Florence."

"For what?"

Vika answered plainly. They both knew he asked as a final exam of sorts. Her answer would be a summation of the battle she had been having with herself the entire summer: Where was she going? What was she doing? And how was she going to go about it?

"Florence is the birthplace of the Italian Renaissance," she said, "and I want to experience it firsthand. I want to look at those paintings and wonder what motivated them to paint. I want to observe them as an art historian, and I want to observe them as a scientist. I want to experience art, nature, and math as a single, complete creation.

"You know," she said with a smirk, "see if I can discover if the artists were in it for love, money, or revenge. I mean, nepotism."

Dane remained feet planted shoulder width apart, hands in his pockets, chin up, eyes observing—always observing—and a grin peeked through his beard. "You're not suggesting the Ninja Turtles were only in it for the money, are you?"

Vika looked back towards her room and shrugged, "No, some guy I met in a run-down house in the mountains said they were. I'd like to prove him wrong."

"Huh," Dane answered, "he sounds like a lot of hot air. You know, Vika, you shouldn't believe everything you hear."

This time, Vika laughed out loud.

"What are you going to do after Florence?"

Vika paused. "I don't know," she answered quietly, "I'd like to read more," she said eventually. "I'd like to discover more. I'd like to learn more, I'd like to try more, help more, travel more, believe in more, absorb more. I'd like nothing more than to believe in something so fiercely that I can't return to the life I've had before."

Dane smiled and raised his coffee mug. "Maybe you should try the PCT," he said, and took a sip.

Vika stared into her room. Maybe. "What are you up to?"

Dane shrugged and sighed, "I don't know. It's a rare day when I do." Vika saw him work through an onslaught of ideas and she let him sort through them. Eventually he continued, "I'd like to do this. You know, the usual."

"Right. The usual." Vika bit her lip. "Dane," she started, "why do you paint those...um...landscapes? Your retirement fund?"

Dane snorted, "You don't think I like painting those?"

She shrugged.

"Vika, I believe in persistence and survival. Every single one of those paintings is dominated by nature in some way, or represents longevity of something nature-made. Look closely. I've never painted something I didn't believe in. Speaking of," he said, as bent around the corner into the hallway, "you forgot something."

He straightened and held out his hand, and Vika reached out to grab what at first Vika thought was a tube of wrapping paper. She rolled out the canvas on the bed, the reds and purples of the fiery landscape she had painted blended into the quilt. She again traced her fingertips through the trees, feeling the faint ridges where the brushes had applied the acrylics, following the lines of the trail, and the borders of the mountains.

"It was taking up space in my barn," Dane said, "I think it might do better here."

Dane stayed a few moments longer to inspect the room and turned to leave, giving her a single but firm pat on the shoulder. Vika looked back to the painting. The edges were shredded from where Dane had cut it from the frame, and strings of the fabric hung loose around the perimeter of the landscape. Vika liked it that way. She hadn't created the painting with precision, and she thought the edges should be able to reflect a certain abandonment of structure as well. It was a mountain painting after all, and if she learned anything about the mountains, it was that they could never really be contained. They spilled over the edges, bled through the strands of the canvas, up to the clouds and down to the deepest roots. The landscape should be able to fall along the wall, weave through the wood grain of the floor, and root itself in the foundation of the house.

Vika picked up some thumbtacks from a plastic container on the dresser and pressed them through the corners of the canvas into the wall opposite the *Alba Madonna*. Perfect.

She stepped back to look at the room again, knowing she would return to visit someday, but knowing it wouldn't be the same. So her eyes swept the room slowly, locking every detail firmly into her memory.

Her phone buzzed and she opened the message from Alex. "First interview: t-minus 22 days."

EVENTUALLY, AFTER SHE WAS SURE was ages, she retreated out the doorway. The bedroom across the hall was simpler, the walls more mellow in color, but similar PCT-themed decorations adorned the walls. Instead of a double bed, this boys' dorm had three bunk beds. She walked across the new hardwood floors through a small common area towards the back of the house to the master bedroom, which had completely transformed from a bat cave to a gorgeous space, new dormers and all. It would turn into a co-ed dorm during the hiking season and though only three bunk beds occupied the room, though there was room for at least three more.

Vika descended the back stairwell into the pantry area and into the expanded kitchen with ceramic tile floor and refinished black cherry cabinets, major appliances straight ahead from the doorway and a large table towards the addition, which Dane had kept on because "the hikers will need a gear drying room, and this piece of shit will be perfect for that if for nothing else."

She glanced into the bathroom briefly, admiring the authentic feel of the room, porcelain from top to bottom and small black and white hexagonal tiles adorning the floor.

The girl's dorm behind the stairs mimicked the boys' with subtle colors and functionality. The living room and dining room in the front of the house commanded the most attention, boasting bold colors, ornate lamps and seating for at least twenty.

A large piano occupied space in the living room, and it hadn't been there five minutes before Grandma Peach started pounding out Carmina Burana on the keys. Of course, Dane had gotten it from some guy in town, and it hadn't been tuned in twenty-five years or so. The off-key notes forced themselves throughout the house, out the windows into the yard, around the chickens, through the cool, autumn air to bang on the door of the hiker coop, Quasi howling along from his spot near the pedals. The piano sang of travelers and adventure as it glided over and into any embodiment of curious intellect that would let it. In fact, when Grandma Peach stopped, the song remained in the air about the house. It stayed as a beacon, tingling, humming, calling out to the roaming souls in the mountains.

Board games, new and old, were fitted under the window seat. Over the mantle in the dining room, Dane had attached a glass board to the wall, under which he had slipped pictures of hikers at the northern terminus. Their tanned and thin faces smiled out at Vika, the thumbs up many of them displayed were possibly the biggest understatements Vika had ever seen.

There was one photo in the center and slightly to the left behind the glass. In it, Dane, Grandma Peach, Cassie, Vika, Forrest, Slip An' Slide, Someday, and Time Warp all wore the same genuine smile of pride and happiness. They stood together, some touching, some tilted their heads, but somehow the eight of them stood in such an integrated and intimate way that as Vika looked at the image, she had to catch her breath.

Her eyes moved down from the photos, onto the painted white mantle beneath. She lifted her hand to let her fingertips trace the words Dane had etched into the wood: "Veni, vidi, vici."

Vika walked to the foyer at the end of which was a door. Dane hemmed and hawed the entire time he was installing it three days before and as he shut it for the first time, silence filled the house. Only seconds old, the silence became stale in a house created for company. It was uncomfortable to Vika, and she knew it must be unbearable for Dane. Vika heard his response a moment later, unaware Vika was within earshot, "I'm taking this down the minute the first hiker comes by."

The registry was open at the bottom of the stairs, propped on a stand, opened to the last page, inviting a visitor to read or write. She flipped through the entries she had read countless times, some dog-eared weeks before, pausing here and there to read ones she had memorized.

The first entry was written in an aggressive hand, slanted and large.

"This house is for you," it started. "You walk through the wilderness that reminds you that you have everything to gain and in any way you choose. For these miles, you report to no one. You walk as you choose, rest as you choose, eat as you choose, you struggle as you choose, you observe as you choose, you contemplate as you choose, you *exist as you choose*. You've blasted through pessimists and bad press, narrated by that poor bastard on the other side of the sneeze guard who has never slept in a tent in his life. 'Watch out for the bears!' he says. 'The only thing they love more than blackberries is some human meat in a down sleeping bag!' You slam through the lengths others will go to warn you of your own demise and in doing so, you have sunk every excuse—hunger, pain, and fatigue to start with.

"*You* are what I believe in. Your *attitude* is what I believe in. This house was built by you and for you, out of grit, will, or spite, which are the only reasons for things to be built if you ask me."

Vika read it and read it again. Eventually, she shifted her gaze from Dane's entry to Grandma Peach's.

"'God bless you all. I've watched you come and go this summer, and nothing has impressed me more in my 82 years than your dedication to this endeavor. I truly hope you have gotten what you need from this trail and you can return safely to your homes with lovely stories. On behalf of all the mothers, please give them a call when you reach the border.

"The tea will always be hot, the door will always be open, the sheets will always be clean, and we will always be here. Visit us again, we already miss you."

Vika read through Cassie's, Someday's, Time Warp's, and Slip An' Slide's, congratulating the hikers and expressing excitement about the end.

The lump in her throat flared up again and she let the goose bumps run up her spine as she thought about all of the memories she held in her hand. She took a deep breath and wrote the last entry of the year in the notebook.

"It was the summer of couch surfing and hitching, mooching and stitching, and miles, miles, miles. The summer of car fires, bon fires, forest fires, blazing suns, new identities, and bad puns. Of Renaissance and revolution, of 'not exactly sure' and absolution, with houses and hikers built out of 'why not?' The summer of strangers. The summer of family. The summer of strangers who became family, strange family, and familiar strangers.

"It was a summer on the PCT."

Acknowledgements

IN THE PRODUCTION OF *Hold For Hiker Trash,* a great many people helped bring this book to the public, and I'd like to acknowledge their contribution here:

Thank you to the entire team at Creators, including: Rick Newcombe, Jack Newcombe, and David Yontz, who have been nothing but courteous and hugely collaborative from the very beginning. Simone Slykhous, my editor, who first championed my manuscript, and whose patience, advice, and faith has been invaluable throughout the entire process. And Evelyn Yau, who, despite my lack of dedication to social media, found avenues upon avenues to beautifully introduce my book to the world.

My family has always been a solid launch pad for all of the projects I have undertaken over the years, and though this barely grazes the surface, my thanks go to: My parents, who have always supported my adventures across the globe, even though I may have given them a number of grey hairs in the process; my brother, Ben, who introduced me to long-distance hiking and taught me how to question limits; and Allie, my sister and confidant, who put up with my insecurities, read drafts of everything along the way, and served as an all-around brilliant sounding board. Hope you're ready for more, kid, 'cause I got lots.

I'd also like to thank the family I don't share DNA with: My "hetero lifemates," Hannah and Jessi, who have been with me for decades now, and were some of my first readers on this book. The Pacific Crest Trail Association, trail associations across the country, and the volunteers who make it possible for people like me to wander in the mountains for days, weeks, or months at a time. I owe my sanity in a large part to you. And, of course, the Trail Angels scattered throughout trails and life, after whom this book is written.

Last, but certainly not least, thank you to you, the reader, for picking up this book and bringing it in out of the cold for a few nights. I will forever be grateful for the opportunity to share this story with you.

About the Author

K.A. HRYCIK GREW UP in a small town in Western New York, where she could be found outside in the midst of one adventure or another, like catching frogs with her sister or snowboarding with her friends. The adventures progressed, and, at 18, she got in a plane for the first time … then jumped out. That evolved into a summer in Alaska, another summer on a tall ship in the Pacific, and time abroad.

It's hiking trails that keep calling her to come back to America though. It could be a two-mile loop in her backyard or crossing the High Sierra in California. Her brother first introduced her to the idea of long-distance backpacking when he thru-hiked the Appalachian Trail. The idea turned into reality in 2012, when they hiked 1,600 miles of the Pacific Crest Trail together. In 2014, Hrycik returned to California to start the PCT at the Mexican border at dawn on a cool May morning. Three and a half months later, in true hiker fashion, she reached the Canadian border dirty, smelly, tired, hungry, and with awe, pride, and phenomenal calves. She was hooked—to put it lightly—and, including the PCT, she's logged over 4,500 miles.

In addition to her travels, Hrycik received a degree in biology and a minor in art history from Vassar College, and enjoys including the intersection of science and art in her writing. Western New York is her home base, where she tutors and teaches swimming. Sometimes she even helps her brother renovate his Victorian house, after which Dane's house in *Hold For Hiker Trash* is modeled—though she refuses to scrape paint.

She's not exactly sure where she'll be next, but she has people for "not exactly sure," so she's OK with that.

HOLD FOR HIKER TRASH
is also available as an e-book
for Kindle, Amazon Fire, iPad, Nook and
Android e-readers. Visit
creatorspublishing.com to learn more.

o o o

CREATORS PUBLISHING

We publish books.
We find compelling storytellers and
help them craft their narrative,
distributing their novels and collections
worldwide.

o o o

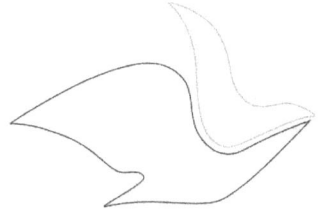

www.ingramcontent.com/pod-product-compliance
Lightning Source LLC
Chambersburg PA
CBHW070656180626
46817CB00006B/2402